STOP THIS MAN!

When Catell gets out of prison, Schumacher has a job lined up for him—a bar of gold in a lab, ripe for stealing. What neither of them know is that this bar of gold has accidentally been rendered radioactive. So as Catell makes his way around Detroit, he gradually begins to poison everyone he comes in contact with. And now the FBI is on to him, and Schumacher is dead. With no one to buy the gold, Catell follows a lead to California, to a man named Smith... and a woman named Lily. But right behind him is Selma, the crazy alcoholic who won't let him go. Selma is going to follow Catell to Hell and back before she lets him get away.

TOBRUK

The time, September 1942. The place, northern Africa. The mission, to cross 800 miles of desert and blow up the German fuel supply at Tobruk. The instigators, a motley crew of British soldiers under the command of by-the-books Colonel Harker and a handful of German Jews set on revenge—disguised as German POWs, they are led by the reluctant Major Craig and the hard-headed Captain Bergman on a mission none of them have a lot of faith in. The distraction, Cheryl, the nymphomaniac daughter of a British spy on a secret mission to Cairo. The bigger problem, a traitor in their midst. The outcome... one chance in a million.

D1292987

PETER RABE BIBLIOGRAPHY

From Here to Maternity
  (1955; non-fiction)
Stop This Man! (1955)
Benny Muscles In (1955)
A Shroud for Jesso (1955)
A House in Naples (1956)
Kill the Boss Goodbye (1956)
Agreement to Kill (1957)
Journey Into Terror (1957)
Mission for Vengeance (1958)
Blood on the Desert (1958)
Anatomy of a Killer (1960)
My Lovely Executioner (1960)
Murder Me for Nickels (1960)
The Box (1962)
His Neighbor's Wife (1962)
Tobruk (1967)
War of the Dons (1972)
Black Mafia (1974)
The Silent Wall (2011)
The Return of Marvin Palaver
  (2011)

Daniel Port series:
Dig My Grave Deep (1956)
The Out is Death (1957)
It's My Funeral (1957)
The Cut of the Whip (1958)
Bring Me Another Corpse
  (1959)
Time Enough to Die (1959)

Manny deWitt series:
Girl in a Big Brass Bed (1965)
The Spy Who Was Three Feet
  Tall (1966)
Code Name Gadget (1967)

As by Marco Malaponte
New Man in the House (1963)
Her High-School Lover (1963)

As by J. T. MacCargo
Mannix #2: A Fine Day for
  Dying (1975)
Mannix #4: Round Trip to
  Nowhere (1975)

Short Stories
"Hard Case Redhead"
  (*Mystery Tales*, 1959)
"A Matter of Balance"
  (*Story*, 1961)

STOP THIS MAN!
TOBRUK

Two Novels by
PETER RABE

Introduction by
Cullen Gallagher

Stark House Press • Eureka California

STOP THIS MAN! / TOBRUK

Published by Stark House Press
1315 H Street
Eureka, CA 95501
griffinskye3@sbcglobal.net
www.starkhousepress.com

STOP THIS MAN!
Copyright © 1955 by Fawcett Publications
and published by Gold Medal Books, New York.

TOBRUK
Copyright © 1967 by Universal Pictures
and published by Bantam Books, New York.

Reprinted by permission of The Estate of Peter Rabe. All rights reserved
under International and Pan-American Copyright Conventions.

"Peter Rabe's Bookends: *Stop This Man!* and *Tobruk*"
copyright © 2021 by Cullen Gallagher

ISBN-13: 978-1-951473-45-7

Book design by Mark Shepard, shepgraphics.com
Proofreading by Bill Kelly

PUBLISHER'S NOTE
This is a work of fiction. Names, characters, places and incidents are
either the products of the author's imagination or used fictionally, and
any resemblance to actual persons, living or dead, events or locales, is
entirely coincidental. Without limiting the rights under copyright
reserved above, no part of this publication may be reproduced, stored, or
introduced into a retrieval system or transmitted in any form or by any
means (electronic, mechanical, photocopying, recording or otherwise)
without the prior written permission of both the copyright owner and the
above publisher of the book.

First Stark House Press Edition: October 2021

Peter Rabe's Bookends: *Stop This Man!* and *Tobruk*

by Cullen Gallagher

If you are familiar with the work of Peter Rabe (1921–1990), then you don't need me to tell you what makes this collection so special. But if you're new to Rabe, let me welcome you to one of the most unique and captivating mid-century crime authors, a writer who inspired no less a legend than Donald Westlake (a.k.a. Richard Stark) to remark, "When he was on track, with his own distinctive style, his own cold clear eye unblinking, there wasn't another writer in the world of the paperback who could touch him."[i] And Ed Gorman called him "Probably the most original of the GM [Gold Medal] authors . . . . Someday he will be recognized as being at least as important a crime writer as Jim Thompson or David Goodis."[ii]

The two novels collected here in Stark House Press's thirteenth volume of Rabe's work, *Stop This Man!* (1955) and *Tobruk* (1967), are not among the author's best known or most celebrated novels. They are, however, among the most fascinating and most overlooked. While on the surface they seem worlds apart—a taut thriller about a manhunt for radioactive gold and a World War II adventure epic— the unlikely pairing reveals that the novels share more in common than not and also provides a unique lens through which to study Rabe. Like bookends, they represent two poles of Rabe's career: a writer in ascent and (at least in terms of commercial success) in descent. Unappreciated in their own time, this collection not only gives readers the opportunity to enjoy two out-of-print should-be-classics, but also to reevaluate their artistic merits and place them within Rabe's artistic body of work.

Stop This Man! was Rabe's first crime novel, and second novel overall (released the same year as *From Here to Maternity*, a comedic account of his wife's pregnancy, which he also illustrated). The story is about

Tony Catell, recently released from prison, who singlehandedly pulls off a daring gold heist. The problem? Unbeknownst to him, the gold is radioactive. More than just hot, it's practically glowing, leaving a trail of radiation-sick victims as he criss-crosses the country to Los Angeles to try and unload the stuff by himself and score big. It's a book of promise, uncertainty, and transition—characteristics that describe not only the protagonist's circumstance, but also that of the author.

Born in Halle, Germany in 1921 as Peter Rabinowitsch, Rabe fled the Nazis in 1938 and was fortunate to make it to the United States, where he eventually obtained a Ph.D. in psychology from Western Reserve University. Unsatisfied with his work in the science field, Rabe dreamed of becoming an author. "I was living in Maine at the time," Rabe recalled to George Tuttle, "and was doing a lot of winter reading of paperbacks. I felt that some were more boring than need be, and having the time and inclination, I started to write for publication in this market. ... I had a former friend from college who had become an agent. So I sent the manuscript, and he sent it to Gold Medal, and Gold Medal bought it." [iii]

Rabe was certainly starting out at the top: at the time, Fawcett's Gold Medal line of original paperback novels was the apex of the softcover market. They would publish the vast majority of Rabe's novels, a total of 22 between 1955 and 1974.

At the time, critics mostly ignored the book (as was typical for paperback originals); those that did review it were not enthusiastic. "The gambit is bright and timely but Mr. Rabe seems distracted by his hero's sexual as well as his criminal history and most of it is pretty dull," wrote James Sandoe in the *New York Herald Tribune*.[iv] Even Anthony Boucher, who would become one of Rabe's staunchest supporters, was unimpressed. "Hopelessly crude, confused and amateurish," wrote Boucher in the *New York Times*. "The editors who have published such authentic Hammett-Chandler successors as John D. MacDonald, Howard Rigsby and Charles Williams, have the memory of a mayfly." [v]

This isn't the first time that reviewers missed the mark. And they missed a lot. From the opening scene, Rabe's unique perspective, informed by his Ph.D. in psychology, is apparent in his acute attention to behavioral patterns, which offer insights into the mental states of his characters. As Brian Ritt explains in his reference guide *Paperback Confidential*, "[Rabe's] work in psychology undoubtedly helped him delve into the minds of his brutal, warped characters." [vi] As you read the novel, pay close attention to how Rabe introduces characters through their actions, and the emphasis he places on their gestures and movement.

Over the next five years, Rabe would publish an astounding total of 19 novels. And then, in 1960, things came to a halt. "The reason I stopped was because of a combination of things," Rabe explained to George Tuttle. "One thing was that I became very ill at the time with no prospect of recovery, which turned out to be wrong, but what that set up was some very deep disturbances. Out of those disturbances emerged a man who no longer felt like writing that sort of thing. Not to mention, at that particular time, the market changed radically, that was the end of the fifties and the beginning of the sixties, and from my point of view, it changed in such an arbitrary way that I simply couldn't adjust myself to the change." [vii]

By 1962, Rabe had recovered physically and was back to writing, but his career would never be the same. His output had slowed considerably. He continued to write for Gold Medal, producing *The Box* (1962), and a trilogy of spy novels about Manny DeWitt, *Girl in a Big Brass Bed* (1965), *The Spy Who Was Three Feet Tall* (1966), and *Code Name Gadget* (1967). In between he also did several sleaze novels, *His Neighbor's Wife* (1962), and two under the pseudonym Marco Malaponte, *Her High-School Lover* (1963) and *New Man in the House* (1963).

The same year as *Code Name Gadget*, Rabe tried turning to Hollywood, penning a pair of teleplays for *Batman* about Two-Face that went un-produced as written (though Lorenzo Semple, Jr. adapted them into episodes about the Joker), and his first novelization. [viii] Based on a script by Leo Gordon and directed by Arthur Hiller, *Tobruk* would be the antepenultimate novel that would bear Rabe's own name (at least during his lifetime—thanks to Stark House Press, *The Silent Wall* and *The Return of Marvin Palaver* found their way into print in 2011).

The plot of *Tobruk* centers around Major Craig of the Long Range Desert Group, who is rescued from Vichy forces by Jewish members of the SIG, working with the British. They deliver him to Kufra where he reunites with the LRDG to attack Rommel's fuel depot and supply chain at Tobruk. In order to infiltrate enemy territory, the SIGs masquerade as Nazis and the British troops as prisoners. Along the way, they receive two prisoners from the Tuareg, Henry Portman and his daughter, Cheryl, who are on a mission to deliver a Nazi message to Cairo that would unite the Egyptian army against the Allies.

"I got the *Tobruk* job because my agent found that they needed somebody to do a novelization," Rabe told Tuttle. "At that point, my writing career was already on the skids or you wouldn't have found me doing novelizations of movie scripts. On the other hand, I found it a challenging piece of work to put the script into the form of a novel, an unexpected trial. The way the story jumps from one thing to another in the visual medium would leave enormous holes once it's put in print. The job took a great deal of writing that wasn't in the script. The script barely provided the skeleton of what you ended up with, which was a total surprise to me. So on that basis, as an exercise in the craft, I liked doing it, even though it wasn't my own story." [ix]

Novelizations, in general, are still an under-appreciated form of literature, a foolish, outmoded, and unfair prejudice stemming from the fact that they are based on pre-existing scripts. Theatrical plays and screenplays are based on books, so why should the same respect not be accorded novelizations? If one needs proof of the legitimacy and integrity of the novelization, look no further than Rabe's *Tobruk*. As he intimated to Tuttle, his novel is greatly expanded from the movie, whose script was bare-bones and action-oriented. Rabe's book is deeply cynical and far more existentialist and nihilistic than the movie. A noir-inspired spy thriller with greater emphasis on character psychology and emotional isolation than on the mission, Rabe's book seems more in line with espionage classics by Graham Greene and, perhaps, John le Carré, whose *The Spy Who Came In from the Cold* (1963) had been published just a few years earlier.

Many of the scenes in Rabe's book do not appear in the movie, and they provide clarity to the plot and depth to the characters. Among the characters most improved by Rabe's novel is Cheryl Portman, the young socialite accompanying her father on a mission to deliver a message from the Nazis to Cairo. In the movie, she's little more than a side-character. In the book, however, she is devastated by the death of her lover (a Nazi spy murdered by his own side after his mission was over), and whose deep feeling of loss sends her on a crash-course for oblivion as she seeks sensation and connection wherever she can find it. Her character adds an unexpected emotional core that was absent from the movie, and Rabe uses her to address philosophical questions related to identity, purpose, and human connection that are the underpinnings of his novel.

Rabe clearly knew that his career was in a tailspin when he wrote *Tobruk*, and one can interpret the sense of failure, uncertainty, and anxiety that runs throughout the novel as an extension of himself and the feelings he was experiencing in his own life. Much like Major Craig, Rabe continued on with the mission as professionally as he could even if he had lost conviction. After *Tobruk*, Rabe published only four more novels: *War of the Dons* (1972) and *Black Mafia* (1974) for Gold Medal, followed by two Mannix novelizations, *A Fine Day for Dying* (1975) and *Round Trip to Nowhere* (1975) (both as by J.T. MacCargo).

Though they're separated by twelve years and represent two distinct periods in Rabe's life and career, *Stop This Man!* and *Tobruk* speak to each other in many ways. They're both cross-country chase narratives. They're both about disguise, deception, and decoy. They're also both about failure—without giving away too much, one can't expect a happy ending to *Stop This Man!* when the main character is running around with a suitcase full of radioactive gold, and in *Tobruk* the objective hardly seems worth it by the novel's end, and the survivors have lost so much it's hard for them to fathom if they've gained anything at all. This brings to mind one of Westlake's astute observations that connects Rabe's disparate careers in the arts and the sciences: "[Rabe] did research at Jackson Laboratory, where he wrote several papers on frustration. (No surprise.)" [x]

And the biggest connection between both novels is Rabe himself. His style. His insight. His professionalism. His artistry.

Without further ado, here's Peter Rabe, at the dawn of, and at the twilight of, his career.

[i] Donald Westlake, "Peter Rabe," in *Murder Off the Rack: Critical Studies of Ten Paperback Masters*, edited by Jon L. Breen and Martin Harry Greenberg, Pulp Hero Press, 2018, p. 97.

[ii] Ed Gorman, "The Golden Harvest: Twenty-Five-Cent Paperbacks," in *The Big Book of Noir*, edited by Ed Gorman, Lee Server, and Martin H. Greenberg, New York: Carroll & Graf Publishers, Inc., 1998, p. 184.

[iii] George Tuttle, "A Too Brief Conversation with Peter Rabe," in *The Big Book of Noir*, p. 256.

[iv] James Sandoe, *New York Herald Tribune*, October 16, 1955, pg. E14.

[v] Anthony Boucher, "Criminals at Large," *New York Times,* October 16, 1955, p. BR39.

[vi] Brian Ritt, *Paperback Confidential*, Eureka, CA: Stark House Press, 2013, p. 257.

[vii] Tuttle, p. 258.

[viii] Bat-rss, post to "Scripts: Peter Rabe's 'Two-Face' and Semple's 'The Joker's Last Laugh,'" The 1966 Batman Message Board, April 10, 2021, 12:33 am, http://www.66batman.com/forums/viewtopic.php?t=7813&p=74632.

[ix] Tuttle, p. 261.

[x] Westlake, 100.

....

Cullen Gallagher lives in Brooklyn, NY. His writing has appeared in the *Los Angeles Review of Books*, *Paris Review*, and *Not Coming to a Theater Near You,* as well as in the anthologies *Cult Cinema: An Arrow Video Companion* (2016) edited by Anthony Nield, and *Screen Slate: New York City Cinema 2011-2015* (2017) edited by Jon Dieringer. His western fiction appears in the anthologies *Bourbon & a Good Cigar* (2018) and *Time to Myself* (2018), both edited by Scott Harris. He blogs about noir and western fiction at *Pulp Serenade* (www.pulp-serenade.com).

STOP THIS MAN!
BY PETER RABE

Chapter One

Twenty-four Chester Street was a rooming house. Every morning at eight, weather permitting, the old woman from Room 4 stepped out on the porch, dragged a wicker chair to the railing, and sat.

This one morning she didn't show until eight-thirty. She stood for a moment wheezing the fine spring air into her lungs and patting her frizzy hair. Then she patted her cheek, doing it gently, as if the bright color of her face gave her pain. She dragged the wicker chair to the railing and sat.

The old woman had a trick she did with her upper lip, curling it back and giving a frightful view of her false teeth. That happened every few minutes, like clockwork, except this time. She suddenly got up from her chair, not quite fast enough, and vomited.

At a quarter to nine the two girls from Room 11 found her there on the porch. The old woman started to twitch a little when they dragged her back into the house, and by the time they had her under the light that hung by the staircase she was struggling to get free.

"Lemme go, for heaven's sake, lemme—"

"Mrs. Tucker, you fainted. Lie still now, Mrs. Tucker."

"Get your hands offen me, you! I never been sick a day in my life. Get your hands offen me," and she started to screech the way she always did.

They left her sitting on the stairs, under the twenty-five watt bulb, because they had to be at work ten minutes later.

Mrs. Tucker tried to get up but another retch tightened her insides and she doubled over. When the spasm had passed, she looked up. The landlady stood there, a big shape wrapped in a pink housecoat that was meant for a much more beautiful woman.

"You sick or something?" said the landlady. "You trying to mess up my front hall?"

"I never been sick a day in my life," and the old woman tried to get up. That's when she fainted the second time.

With a fat man's grunt Dr. Junta hauled himself up the porch steps. He eyed the woman in the pink wrapper who was sloshing water over the planks of the porch and said, "I'm the doctor. Did somebody—"

"Number Four. End of the corridor on the left. And if she got something catchy," the landlady yelled after him, "get her out of here."

Number 4 was right next to Number 5; in fact, the two rooms had been one. There was a dividing wall, beaver-board on one side and the bare studding showing on the other, where the old woman had her bed.

"I don't want no doctor," she said when Junta came in. "I never been sick a day in my life and I didn't call for you."

"I understand you fainted." Dr. Junta put his satchel down.

"You got no call comin' in here like that. I didn't ask for you and I don't want you."

"If you're worried about the money, I'm from the Relief Board. Now, what happened? You threw up?"

The old woman did the trick with her teeth and gave Dr. Junta a cold stare.

"Indigestion is all. I know how to take care of myself."

"When did it start?"

"Just this morning. I'm all right now, so there's no need to hang around."

Dr. Junta sighed and opened his satchel. He wasn't a very enthusiastic man, but there were certain routine things that he always did. He shook down the thermometer and walked up to the bed. That's when he noticed the color of the woman's face.

"Where'd you get that sunburn this time of year?"

"I ain't got no sunburn. Where would I get a sunburn, anyways, holed up in this rat trap?"

"If you don't like the place," the landlady said from the door, "you can git any time, Mrs. Tucker. Any time!"

"All right, both of you," said Dr. Junta. "Now, once more, Mrs. Tucker, try to remember how you've felt the last few days. Any complaints, any discomforts."

"Nothing. I been fine."

"She been fine like a sick dog," said the landlady. "Sickish for days, borrowing my aspirin and lying in that bed of hers."

"She's wrong. Listen, Doctor—"

"How long has this been going on?" asked Dr. Junta.

"Lemme see now." The landlady rewrapped herself and looked up at the ceiling. "Right after that one-nighter was here. Smith, he said his name was. Middle-aged guy, real pale face, wore a blue overcoat. Right next door, he stayed, in Number Five."

"Was his bed behind this wall here?" Dr. Junta tapped on the thin partition.

"No. That's where the closet is."

"Was Smith sick, as far as you could tell?"

Smith, the pale man in the blue overcoat, hadn't been sick as far as any of them knew, but the hot, sore color of Mrs. Tucker's face wasn't a simple rash, as the old woman was trying to say, and Dr. Junta couldn't decide just what it might mean. That night, playing it safe, he committed

Mrs. Tucker to the Hamilton City Hospital.

Jack Herron threw his cigarette on the floor and stepped on it. Then he picked it up and put it in the ashtray on his desk. He looked at his watch, then at the phone next to his elbow. He had been doing this all day, but nothing had happened. No news.

Stiff from sitting, Herron walked up to the dark window and looked at his reflection in the glass. He looked properly nondescript. An FBI man looks like anybody else and makes an effort to stay that way. He patted his thin hair into place self-consciously, wishing the early balding didn't show so much.

Herron smoked another cigarette and then he couldn't stand the waiting any longer. He grabbed his hat off the hook, clicked the safety lock, and slammed the door behind him. Lettering on the door said, "Federal Bureau of Investigation, District Office, St. Louis, Mo."

A few blocks from the office Herron turned up a broad flight of stairs and walked into the Central Police Station. Maybe something had come through since he left the office.

There was a little room right off Communications smelling of varnish and sweeping compound. Herron walked in and said hello to the two men at the table. They were sitting in shirtsleeves and the older of the two was pouring black coffee into paper cups. The young one was wearing a shoulder holster.

"Hello, yourself," said the one with the holster. "If you want coffee, we got. If you want news, we ain't got."

The old one who worked in the next room put a cup before Herron and poured from a tin percolator. "I know what he wants," said the old one, "but he's going to get coffee."

Herron sat down, sipped from his cup, and said, "That's too bad, Starkey."

"He don't like your coffee," said the young cop who was wearing the shoulder holster. "He thinks it's just too bad for words. Myself, I drink Starkey's coffee because I like the flavor of the paper cups. Eh, Starkey?"

"Shuddup," said Starkey.

Herron knew there was no point in asking whether anything had come through. Starkey would have told him.

"Listen, Herron," Starkey said. "Why all this mummery with a message? If it's got to be coded, why don't you guys receive it yourselves? Why have us receive it?"

"That's because the FBI is federal," said the young cop. "They do things different. They have the local police receive their messages so the police can phone it in and waste a little time getting it through. It's more complicated that way."

Starkey laughed, but Jack Herron didn't think it was so funny.

"First of all, the message isn't coded. Secondly, we got no night operator. And why aren't you watching your ticker?"

"I got Jones watching," Starkey said. "And Jones knows as much about it as I do: 'Upon receipt of the following convey immediately to local office Federal Bureau of Investigation, viz. Diagnosis probable. Admitted time such and such, place such and such, patient's residence such and such.' And after me watching those crazy tickers for ten years, the bright Mr. Herron from the FBI tells me that this ain't no code!"

"Have you tried reading it backward?" said the cop with the holster.

"I have," said Starkey. "By God, I have."

At that moment the buzzing and ticking from the next room stopped dead. Communications was quiet as a library. The three men in the little room held their breaths. Herron slopped some coffee. Suddenly the clatter exploded again. They looked at each other and the cop with the holster made a noise in his throat.

"As I was saying…" he said.

That's when the door from Communications flew open and Jones looked in.

"Your message, Starkey. It's on the ticker."

Herron and Starkey ran to the teletype. It was still hammering with a nervous beat and the message read: "Diagnosis probable. Admitted 10:15 p.m., Hamilton City Hospital, Hamilton City. Patient's residence, 24 Chester Street, Hamilton City." When Starkey tore off the sheet, Herron was already halfway out of the door. He'd got his message. A hundred miles away they'd found the first victim. Finally the trail was hot. Real hot. The patient had radiation sickness.

Cal and Tom hadn't known each other for more than a few hours but they had been stepping fast. They'd been stepping so fast that by midnight it seemed they'd been buddies all their lives. That's why Cal had been buying the drinks for Tom and then Tom had been buying the drinks for Cal. So it was a sad moment when the two buddies sat down at the curb and discovered that their friendship was wearing thin.

"Stop rubbing them stubbles," said Cal. "You trying to drive me crazy with them stubble noises?"

Tom kept rubbing his stubbles and said, "Bah."

They sat for a while staring at the dark street and then they looked at the empty pint in the gutter. That brought up the next point.

"Cheapskate," said Cal. "Just lookit this empty pint."

"Cheapskate!" Tom jumped up from the curb. He stood straight and steady after a while and yelled, "Cheapskate! You're talking to the man what bought that pint, ya bum!"

"It's empty, ain't it?"

"So it's your turn, ya bum! It's your turn for the next one."

Cal got up from the curb and held himself by Tom's sleeve. "Listen, cheapskate," he said. He stuck his face close to Tom's. Tom tried to lean back and out of the way. "I got the pint afore this one and I barely recall buying that pint and it's empty. Then I barely recall this pint coming along and it's empty. Unnerstand?"

Tom didn't. He tried to lean his face out of the way and they both started to sway.

"So it's your turn," Cal said, and it sounded like a conclusion.

They swayed for a while, staring at each other from close range, but Tom didn't know what to say next.

"I knew it," said Cal. "You're a cheapskate. You stink!"

Tom jerked his head back and wiped his eye. "Don't say 'stink' like that. A bum what can't talk polite never gets nowheres."

He took a few steps and leaned against a dark store window. It made a dangerous sound. Then Cal came over and leaned against the glass. They looked inside as best they could.

"More cheapskates," said Cal. "The whole store full of bulbs and wires and no light anywhere."

"That's because he sells 'em," Tom said.

They looked at the display of fixtures, bulbs, and fluorescent tubes. There was a display of fluorescent tubes like sun rays coming out from a face in the middle. The cardboard face was smiling.

"What's he got to smile about I can't figure," said Cal.

"He's thinking of that drink he's gonna have. He believes in miracles and he's just smiling away there, thinking—"

Tom didn't get any further because Cal had burst out crying, loud and hard, sobbing that he'd always believed in miracles, but not anymore.

"Cal boy! Cal buddy! You're busting my heart, honest, Cal boy." Then he patted his buddy on the back and gradually his face got stern. "Cal!"

"Yes, Tommy?"

"We got to have a miracle."

"There ain't—"

"First guy comes along we ask for a miracle, Cal buddy."

Cal had stopped crying. He felt like himself again. "Maybe an angel's gonna come down the street? Carrying a pint?"

"Shut up. Here he comes!" and they both listened to the footsteps that came down the dark street. They were coming at a fast clip.

"Or maybe Jesus Christ Himself."

"Shut up already and get over here!" Tom dragged his buddy to the entrance to the house next to the electrical store. "Here comes the miracle. Watch me make a touch."

"Oh, surely. Maybe Jesus Christ—" He stopped when they saw the figure come through the dark.

Tom stepped into the street, all energy and smiles. "How do you do, sir? I do believe—" He got no further. The man was at the window now when a sudden glow of eerie white suffused the dark. The display of fluorescent bulbs glowed brilliantly, and against the sudden brightness the dark figure of the man appeared surrounded by a halo.

"Jesus Christ!" Cal said, and fell down on his face.

Tom hadn't moved a muscle. By the time he managed to breathe again, the lights were off and the middle-aged man in the blue overcoat had gripped his yellow leather case and run into the night.

Tony Catell hurried up the stairs of the railroad station and pushed his way through the crowd without looking right or left. Once inside, he went to the far end of the large hall, where the ornamental columns made shadowed recesses along the wall. He stood there watching the ticket windows. When one of them was empty, Catell walked over and bought a ticket to Detroit.

Twenty minutes to traintime.

Catell went to the short-order counter and sat down, but the seat faced the wrong way. He got up again, walked to the other side of the U-shaped counter, and found a seat that faced the entrance of the station. With a slight turn he could also see the gateways that led to the trains. He put his yellow leather case on the floor under the counter and ordered a glass of milk. After he had finished the milk he smoked a cigarette, ordered another glass of milk, and watched the waitress behind the counter. She was young, but nothing special. Catell watched her for the same reason he drank a lot of milk. He hadn't had much of either for the past eight years.

Without moving his head, Catell glanced at the waitress, the entrance, the crowds, and then at the waitress again, but there was no particular expression on his face. He looked tired and lined. His long jaw had a bluish cast that made the rest of his face look like the color of wet chalk. A small muscle jumped in his cheek, but otherwise Catell sat quite still.

Ten minutes to traintime.

Catell picked specks of dust from the sleeve of his blue overcoat and wondered whether to order another glass of milk. But suddenly the thought made him sick. His forehead glistened with sudden sweat and he swallowed hard. Then the nausea passed.

Perhaps he was overdoing the milk. Catell rubbed his pale forehead. His whole face was pale, very pale. Catell hadn't been out of prison very long.

Five minutes before traintime he paid the waitress and got up. Carrying his yellow leather case, he started for one of the train gates.

A redcap walked up behind him. "Carry that for you?" The redcap put his hand on the case.

Catell jumped. "Let go."

But the redcap didn't catch the tone of Catell's voice, and he reached for the leather case again. That's when Catell spun on the balls of his feet, his fist thudding into the porter's stomach. Before anybody had seen a thing, Catell was walking toward the train gate, his thin face a mask, his movements controlled. The redcap lay on the floor, doubled over in groaning pain. For all of his fifty years, Tony Catell was very fast and very strong.

One minute before traintime he entered his compartment and locked the door. When the train started to move, he put the leather case on the seat, took off his hat and coat, and sat down. It was hours before the train would hit Detroit, but Catell did not make himself comfortable. He sat without leaning against the cushions, his narrow hands folded between his knees, only his eyes showing how tired he was. He hadn't slept much during the past few days, because he had been nervous and unsure of himself. When Schumacher had explained the heist to him, Catell had felt unsure. The feeling had stayed with him when he had cased the job, when he had pulled it, and when he had holed up in that burg Hamilton City for a few hours of fitful sleep.

The job had been too easy. Catell pulled out a cigarette and then forgot to light it. He wondered if prison could have made him feel this way, broken down to the size of a gutless punk, a nervous rat. But that didn't make sense, because he had been in prison before. He was a three-time loser, out for the last time, out for good until he died—one way or the other.

Catell jumped in his seat and made an automatic move for the leather case next to him. He had fallen asleep there, sitting there with the doubt and the fear scrambling his brain.

He cursed through his teeth, trying to shake the weariness out of his bones. He was getting too old, maybe, a crazy has-been who was trying to wrench himself back up by dreams of an old reputation; a reputation so old it didn't even fit the picture any more. He had slipped badly; he'd slipped so hard that they'd sent him up for that third time.

But that was going to be the end of that. They didn't know it yet but they had given him his other chance. Nobody was going to call Catell a has-been, an old broken-down three-time loser with a lot of fancy memories and a long list of dead friends.

He was going to pull that big one once more, the one that only Tony

Catell could handle, the job that meant big time. And he wanted to walk away from it with a bundle. Perhaps this heist had looked so easy because he still had that old touch. And he certainly had walked away with a solid piece of swag. He patted the briefcase beside him. There was nothing small time about its contents, a thirty-six-pound ingot of solid gold.

Chapter Two

Otto Schumacher chewed his gray mustache and pushed his glass back and forth on the table. He looked across the crowded room of the roadhouse, but he didn't focus on anything in particular.

"What time is it, Selma?"

"Eleven. Five minutes later than the last time you asked me."

Schumacher hardly heard the woman. He was nervous; he disliked public places.

"Otto, lemme have another drink." Selma waited a moment for an answer and then waved for a waiter.

She got her drink and rolled a little bit of the liquid on her tongue. She liked the fine sharp sting in her mouth.

"Otto, how about another one for you?"

Schumacher looked at his glass, half full with a tepid brown liquid. "No, thanks. You have one."

"I just got one."

"Good. Good. Anything you want, Selma."

"I want a hot-water bottle."

"Fine. Fine, Selma."

"I want two hot-water bottles, you bum!"

"You want—Selma, what are you talking about?"

Selma looked at Schumacher as if he were a sick dog and made an ugly sound in her throat. Then she swallowed her drink.

"Selma, what was that for?"

"For you, lovin' cup. I want another drink."

"You're the one that wanted to come. I told you this was strictly business, but you had to tag along."

"That's right, lovin' cup. I had to tag along to this converted hash joint. I had to tag along. That's how much fun I get hanging around you, lovin' cup."

"Selma, I have spoken to you before and I will speak again. I give you anything, the best—"

"With you, the best ain't much, lovin' cup."

"You're no spring chicken yourself, dear Selma." There was a short silence. They didn't look at each other.

"I want another drink."

Schumacher went to the bar to buy Selma another drink. He was disgusted with himself for losing his temper. Besides, Selma was all right, a fine woman to have around. Just right, now that she was slowing down a little.

He brought the drink back to the booth and noticed that Selma was getting tight. The little wrinkles around her eyes showed up more clearly and one of her curls was hanging down the side of her ear.

"Selma, I got business tonight and I must ask you to go easy. You know what it means to us."

"Yeah. I bet he won't show."

Schumacher narrowed his eyes for a moment. "He'll show. I've known Tony for twenty years and he'll show."

"And what if he shows and the deal didn't come off?"

"The deal came off all right, Selma."

"So what are you worried about? Why do you have to sit there like a fireplug the dog passed by?"

"It's not that simple. There's some trouble."

"Oh, sure. Schumacher, the brains from way back, he gets himself the best jug heavy in the field, his old buddy Tony Catell, who, just fresh from college, is eager to please his old buddy Otto, and he sets him up with a setup like happens once in a lifetime, he sets him up. And when Tony delivers the goods, all of a sudden there is some trouble. With you, Schumacher, there is always some trouble!"

Schumacher didn't answer. If she didn't stop shouting and making scenes, he'd tell her to beat it for good. He'd tell her she was through and she could pick her stuff up in the morning. Off the sidewalk, where he'd throw it. Schumacher turned toward Selma but she wasn't saying a thing now. Her lidded eyes were wide open, her thin mouth was smiling vaguely, and her chin was tilted up as if she were looking over somebody's head. Selma was patting her tight curls and then Schumacher saw Tony Catell in the crowd.

He was slowly worming his way past the bar, around the crowded tables, and up to the booth. Catell walked past the booth without a sign of recognition. He went to the men's room, came back to the booth, and sat down.

"What's she here for?"

"Otto and I are always together," Selma said, and she put her hand through Schumacher's arm. She leaned forward on the table and smiled at Catell. He looked at the V of her dress. Selma was small there. What

Catell remembered about Selma was her fine skin and her wide hips. He saw she still had a fine smooth skin.

"My boy, I congratulate you," Schumacher said. "That was a fine job you did there."

"Thanks. You figured a neat setup. No troubles."

"That's what I wanted to speak to you about, Tony. We're not quite through yet. The fact is—"

Tony wasn't listening. His white face looked worn with sleeplessness and his hands were nervous.

"Lemme have a drink first, Otto. I'm beat."

"That's right, lovin' cup. Let him have a drink first, for chrissakes. You and your business all hours of the day and night. I'll have one with you, Tony." Selma smiled at him again.

Schumacher didn't say anything. Above all, he wanted to keep peace. It was difficult enough to explain things to Tony without Selma acting up.

When the drinks had come, Schumacher cleared his throat and said, "Tony, pay attention. Something slipped up."

Catell only shifted his eyes. "Nothing slipped. Nobody saw me, nobody followed me, nobody knows I'm here in Detroit. And we got the gold, didn't we? Selma, want another drink?"

She smiled at him and pushed her glass toward him. Before she leaned back in her seat she touched his sleeve and ran one finger along the back of his hand.

"How about you, Otto? Another drink?" Catell said.

Schumacher shook his head and swirled the brown liquid in his glass. He didn't like the way things were going.

"Listen, Tony," he said. "This trouble we got is the kind you wouldn't know anything about."

"What trouble? We got the gold and nobody knows it. What more do you want?"

Schumacher leaned forward in his seat and stared at Catell with an exasperated look on his face. "What do I want? I want to sell the stuff, that's what I want. And the trouble is, I can't sell it now!"

"What?"

"I said we can't sell it. That gold is radioactive."

"What in hell are you talking about?"

"I'm trying to explain. When I staked out the job, I didn't get the full story. I didn't know that gold would be radioactive. I just found out."

Catell understood two things: He understood that Schumacher said he couldn't sell the gold, and he understood that Schumacher was serious. He could tell by the old man's face, by his sick-looking eyes, and by the way Schumacher sat hunched forward in his overcoat. Why didn't the old bastard ever take his overcoat off? What was he trying to pull with his double talk? Catell's brain was too tired to think straight. All he could do was sit there and hate Schumacher, hate his reasonable ways, his messy-looking mustache, his slut Selma, who kept grinning at him with her big face.

"Catell, are you listening to me?"

"Yeah." He took his eyes off Selma's naked arm and forced himself to concentrate. "All right, Schumacher, what's this crap about radioactive? The stuff is gold, isn't it?"

"Jesus, Catell, don't you know what radioactive is? That metal is pure poison!"

Catell held the whisky glass up to his mouth and licked the rim with a slow motion of his tongue. When he looked at Schumacher, his eyes glittered with fatigue. "Otto, are you giving me the runaround?"

Schumacher caught the tone of Catell's voice and he had a bad moment. Then he talked with a voice that was harsh and hurried.

"I don't think you understand, Catell. That ingot of metal you got is dangerous. It gives off radiations that can make a man sick, and for all I know, it can kill a man. Now shut up for a minute. When this deal came up, all I knew was that the government was shipping one ingot of gold to the Atomic Research Center of Kelvin University. The gold was going to be there about a week and they were going to do some kind of fancy radiation work on the thing. When, how, why, and so forth—that I didn't know, except that I had a good idea it wasn't going to be during the first two days. That's why I planned the heist for the second day after the gold got there. Well, the setup was good and you came through as expected. The setup was real good. They got their security rules and so on, but the work at that research place isn't really so secret. They only do limited work and nothing very new. So it doesn't call for full-dress security. Besides, it's a university and no Fort Knox. So the whole deal worked out easy as pie except now we are stuck with a worthless chunk of gold."

Catell took a deep breath, with an effort. When he spoke his voice sounded squeezed. "Otto, how come you know so much? How come it's on again, off again, and nobody knows but you?"

Schumacher started to toss his hands in exasperation. Then he stopped as if the gesture had exhausted him.

"Tony, for God's sake, I'm telling you straight. Something slipped and the bar you got was already hot. You're worried how come I know so much? From the horse's mouth I know, straight from the FBI bulletins on the radio, ads in the papers, and all of them screaming that the loot you got is radioactive. They send out warnings. Haven't you read it or heard it?"

"I haven't had time to read the papers."

"All right, so I'm telling you. When radioactive stuff disappears, maybe stolen, they right away put out a total alarm. To you, to the guy that's toting that dangerous stuff around and doesn't know it." Schumacher leaned back in his seat and unbuttoned his overcoat. He was sweating. "So listen to me, Tony, and listen to reason. We don't know how hot that gold is, perhaps just a little, but it's poison just the same. We've got to stay clear of it and we can't move it right now. Not for a while. That radioactivity wears off in time, so it'll be safe again after a while, but right now—" Schumacher made a helpless gesture.

Suddenly Catell felt so weary he could have lain down in the booth and slept. He felt that if he couldn't sleep right now he might cry.

"The deal's got to be canceled," Schumacher was saying. "It came off good but it ended up bad. Later, maybe. Right now it's a flop."

The words came to Catell like a curse. They stung him with a fine, deep pain that gripped his body and shook him awake. He gritted his teeth and leaned toward Schumacher.

"And now I'll say my piece. I don't know about this radioactive crap, Otto, and it's not going to scare me. It may be true what you say, and then again it may not. I've been toting this stuff around and nothing's happened to me. If it's rotten or if it's hot, that stuff won't stop me, because I'm not stopping. Get that, Otto. Nothing's going to stop me and I wouldn't want you to be the one to try it."

He took a deep breath. He felt all right again.

"Selma," he said, "how's it been for excitement?"

He was glad Selma was there. Right then he felt she was the sexiest female he had ever seen. He didn't notice the wrinkles around her heavy eyes or the loose skin under her chin. He just saw her big face, which had been very handsome, and he noticed her white arms, which still had beautiful skin.

"How about a dance, kid?" he said.

"Tony," Schumacher said, "where's the gold?"

"Oh, leave him alone now, Otto. Can't you ever stop talking business?"

"She's right, Otto. We'll talk tomorrow. We don't need to push that stuff in this town. So we get rid of it someplace else. We'll figure some other way. We won't let this thing die on the vine, eh, Otto?"

This was the first time Catell had smiled in a long time. But he wasn't looking at Otto. Selma smiled back at him and started to push her way out of the booth.

"Tony," said Schumacher, "where's that rotten gold?"

"Lemme out, Otto. Tony wants to dance with me." Selma pushed against Schumacher's side.

"Let the lady out, Otto," Tony said. He got up, taking Schumacher by the arm.

"All right, Tony, all right. Go dance. But where'd you stash that gold? You got to tell me."

Tony had pulled Schumacher to his feet and Selma got out of the booth. She stood close to Catell and didn't move when he put his arm around her and dug his fingers into the flesh of her waist.

"The loot is safe, Otto. I left it at your place."

"At my place? How'd you get in?"

"How'd I get in!" He laughed at Schumacher's worried face.

"Tony, get it out of there, man. I'm telling you it's dangerous stuff." He clutched at Catell's arm.

"Let go," Catell said, and he gave Schumacher a vicious push.

The older man sat down in his seat with a thump and looked up at the couple. "Selma, you reason with him," he said. "You and I aren't safe with that thing around. He's got to get it out."

"What makes you think I won't be safe?" Selma said, and her smile was hazy with alcohol.

Catell made an impatient gesture. "I'll move it. Don't worry. Otto. I'll move it in a day or so, once I get my bearings." He gave Selma a sharp squeeze and pushed her ahead of him toward the dance floor.

"Tony!" Schumacher called after the couple. "Tony, tonight. Please do it tonight!" But nobody heard him. He sat hunched in the booth and followed the couple with his eyes. They did not dance. They skirted the dance floor and went out the front door.

After a while, Schumacher thought of ordering a fresh drink for himself, but decided against it. He hated drinking in public places, and he hated this place in particular. He sat and waited only because he was afraid to go home. He waited, hoping Catell would come back and agree to move that ingot out of the apartment tonight.

When the band packed up, Schumacher got up and left. There was no point in waiting any longer. Catell must have taken Selma to town.

Outside, Schumacher shivered in his overcoat and smoothed a finger over his gray mustache. He felt cold and alone. With an old man's awkwardness he hunted in his pockets for the car key. When he had found it, he walked into the parking lot.

Before he put his hand on the door, Schumacher felt the car move. In the back seat he saw them. He saw Catell's back and he saw one of Selma's legs.

Schumacher left quietly, thinking with dread of the dreary bus ride home, and of the thing that waited for him there.

Chapter Three

Jack Herron didn't much like to go on a case with his chief. It made him uncomfortable and awkward. Jones never said much and always wore a bland face. Without talking they walked down the main corridor of the Research Center of Kelvin University until they came to a door marked "C. A. Tiffin, Director." At the Research Center, Tiffin was top dog. He was bald, thin, and ugly, but he was top dog and he always let you know it.

"Well, gentlemen, what have you done about this outrage besides handicapping our work at the Center? I suppose you have come back for another one of your double checks?"

"Outrage, Dr. Tiffin?"

"The theft, Mr. Jones. The almost unbelievable—"

"We're handling that matter. For the moment we are concerned with another aspect of the—uh—outrage; the aspect that was your responsibility."

"I beg your pardon?"

"The drained shielding wall around your atomic pile. The radiation leak that made the stored gold radioactive in the first place. Have you determined just how radioactive the ingot may have been at the time of the theft?"

Tiffin shuffled his papers around. He pushed his chair back abruptly and stood.

"The difficulties are such—" he started.

"Have you figured it out?"

"My assistants are still working on it, Mr. Jones."

Jones shrugged. "Before we leave, please show us the scene of the theft once again, Dr. Tiffin." He held the door open.

They walked through the central hall of the building and turned into a corridor. It was long and bare.

"There is not much to see," said Tiffin. "Our atomic pile is small, extending from about here to here." He paced off close to forty feet in the corridor and pointed to one blank wall. "The room housing the device is completely shielded. Follow me, please."

They turned the corner of the corridor and Tiffin opened a door. A wooden sign stood next to it, face to the wall. Herron turned it around and read, "Danger. Radioactivity."

"It's quite safe now. The sign was only put there after the leak was discovered. Ordinarily this room is not exposed. Follow me, please."

The small room held racks and a trapdoor in one wall. There was moisture on the floor.

"This wall," Tiffin said, "shields the business end of the pile from the storage room in which we stand. The wall is actually a series of large canisters filled with water. Sometime during the day previous to the theft, this drainpipe—you can see it near the floor—seems to have leaked water out of the lower series of tanks."

"And there was nothing in this room except the gold ingot?"

"Nothing else. That's why we cannot say for how much time, if any, the gold was subject to bombardment."

"So it may not be radioactive at all."

"Possibly. Or it may be only partially radioactive."

"How do you mean, partially?" Herron wanted to know.

"Only a part of its mass, let's say a fraction of an inch on the surface, may have become radioactive. Which would be a blessing," Tiffin added. "That is, if you can find it at all."

"We'll find what's left of it," Jones said.

"Left of it? What are you talking about, Chief?" Herron asked.

"Irradiated gold," Tiffin said, and he sounded indulgent, "has a half-life of one day. That means that after a day has passed, its radioactivity has reduced itself by half; the following day there is again a reduction to half of what was left, and so on. What remains, young man, is not gold. What remains is pure stable mercury."

"You mean nothing may be left to that stuff except quicksilver?"

"Hardly, Mr. Herron. That kind of total deterioration of a large ingot would require more energy than our pile can muster. And besides, the thief wouldn't have left here alive."

"That's good to know," said Herron. "So we're still looking for gold."

"Considering our source of radiation and the possible length of time the ingot may have been exposed, the affected part of the gold would be quite small, but nonetheless dangerous. Of course, once the radiation has dissipated itself, the body of the ingot is again quite harmless. Pure gold, with traces of mercury."

They left the storage room and went back to Tiffin's office.

"Will there be anything else?" Tiffin stopped by the door.

"Just your report, Dr. Tiffin. We must know how sick the thief may be, and how dangerous the ingot may be to the population."

"Mr. Jones, our guess as to how long the gold was exposed may not help you as much as you think. Nonlethal doses of radiation may cause a variety of symptoms, and they may appear to be harmless things."

"What are they?" Jones asked.

"In general, the first signs are weariness, headache, digestive upset.

The mucosa of the digestive tract seems particularly sensitive to radiation. Sometimes skin irritations occur, like a sunburn. In severe cases skin ulcerations develop or simple sores that refuse to heal. The most specific effect, of course, is the destruction of bone marrow with consequent blood deterioration. After that, any infection becomes a serious matter. But I'm sure you knew all this."

"That much we knew, Dr. Tiffin. In the meantime, please hurry with your report."

"I don't see how a mere guess—"

"An intelligent guess, Dr. Tiffin. Good day, sir."

Herron thought Jones had done that very well. He followed his chief down the long corridor and out into the open. The sun was shining and some new flowerbeds made a good smell in the air. Herron was glad to be out of the building. There hadn't been any windows in the place.

They walked across the campus to the parking lot while Herron kept thinking about the things Tiffin had said.

"Has anybody answered our alarm yet, Chief?"

"Hundreds of hypochondriacs."

"At least we'll have our man worried."

"Not necessarily, Herron. If he's got half a brain, he'll keep from exposing himself after hearing our alarm, and any mild symptoms he might get he'd be apt to overlook at first."

"Till it gets worse."

"It might, Herron. A few repeated exposures, each one of them small, and the effect will grow. At any rate, what have you found out in the meantime?"

Herron pulled a notebook out of his breast pocket and began to recite.

"Besides the Hamilton City case of radiation, no further reports, and they're not sure it is radiation burn. Three of our sources report heavy spending by two of the suspects, Ham Lippin and Jerald Jenner. Ham is in Miami Beach and Jerry is in San Diego. I also got that list of parolees you asked for. It narrows down to seven: the two Corvetti brothers, Sam Nutchin, Gus Eisenberg, Tony Catell, Carl Lamotte, and Mug McFarlane. Three of them aren't very likely, considering everything. Sam Nutchin is very sick, Tony Catell is a has-been without connections, and one of the Corvettis is drunk most of the time. So that leaves us with the younger Corvetti, Eisenberg, Lamotte, and McFarlane."

"That leaves us with a lot of nothing."

"Sorry, Chief, that's as far as I could get, so far."

They walked in silence till they came to the parking lot behind the library.

"Have the two watchmen come up with anything else?" Jones asked.

"Same story. Somebody slugged them from behind. They don't know whether there was one or more assailants."

"How are they getting along?"

"No change. Bad concussions."

"Any new evidence that the lab boys dug up?"

"They find evidence of one person only."

Jones and Herron got into the car. Jones took the wheel.

"Seems like quite an order for one man," Herron said. "Two watchmen slugged, three doors jimmied, two electric-eye circuits ruined, one vault door blown, not to speak of the missing gold."

"What might help us is the fact that the loot could be radioactive. I hate to think of it, Jack, but that might make it more convenient for us to track it down."

"It hasn't so far, Chief."

"I know. But a thirty-six-pound block of radioactive gold is going to make somebody sick."

"Yeah. Especially since the thief probably didn't know the stuff could be radioactive. If he'd known, he wouldn't have kept the stuff in the same room with him when he holed up in that crummy rooming house in Hamilton City."

"That may not mean a thing. Don't forget, we still haven't a trace of the thief or the gold, which probably means he hasn't slowed down any himself."

The drive from Kelvin University back to St. Louis took them one hour, but at the end of that time, neither Jones nor Herron had come up with any new ideas. When the trip was over and they pulled into the underground garage of headquarters, they were glad to get out of the car. Herron looked rumpled and tired, but Jones appeared as bland and neat as ever.

"Who knows, perhaps we'll have a break when we get to the office, eh, Chief?"

Jones smiled back for a moment, but didn't answer. They took the elevator to their floor and entered the bureau.

"Come to my office, will you, Jack? I want you to look at the follow-ups I got on some of the possible brains behind this job. Right now we're going on the assumption that this was not a syndicate job."

"Why?"

"Lots of reasons. For instance, they would have used more than one man at the scene. I'll show you the analysis later. Now, as I was saying, that narrows the field quite a bit. There aren't too many independents left."

Herron opened the door for Jones and they walked into the Chief's office.

"All right, Jack. Here's a dossier on Charles Letterman, alias Chauncey Lettre, alias Professor Letters. Sixty-five years old, convicted twice for complicity in bank robberies. Light sentence each time. One conviction for illegal possession of stolen goods. He's suspected of planning a long list of crimes. Take a look at it. Present address, Two-o-seven Desbrosses Street, New York City. Next, there's one Otto Schumacher, sixty-eight, no aliases. A very careful planner. When you look at the list, you'll find he's supposedly been behind a lot of inside jobs, but don't let that prejudice you. Otherwise, little is known about him except that he was probably behind some of the biggest heists during the twenties. And he's never been convicted of anything. Take the file along, Jack, and hold it, because we haven't found him yet."

The phone rang. Jones picked it up and said, "Jones." He listened for a while, then said, "Good. Thanks." He put the receiver down and told Herron not to bother with the other dossiers. "Just read the one on Otto Schumacher. They found him. It seems he spent last month in Kelvin, presumably to use the university library. He roomed at the same house as one of the night watchmen of the Research Center, and they often played checkers together. At present he lives in Detroit, where the local office has him staked out. They're going to pull him in tomorrow, and I want you to be there. We have little to go on with Schumacher except that his cleaning woman showed up at the county clinic today. Complaint, headache and diarrhea, plus a possible radiation burn of the sole of one foot. Could be a coincidence, though. He's your case, Jack, but remember, he's never been convicted. Good luck."

"Good luck, Otto. I think I found a contact out West who'll take the stuff."

"Tony, for God's sake, where have you been." Schumacher yelled into the phone. His hands were shaking. "Do you realize that damn thing is still in this apartment? Have you any idea what a time I had trying to keep from going nuts waiting for you? Either you come at once or I'll get somebody else to take it out of here. Tony, are you listening?!"

There was a short silence at the other end of the wire and then Catell's voice, very quiet: "Don't do it, Otto. I'm warning you."

"All right, all right. Are you coming?"

"I'll be there, Otto. Have you moved it any?"

"Are you insane? I haven't—"

"Don't blubber, Otto. You could have done something to shield it. I heard lead—"

"For God's sake, Tony, get over here and don't lecture me. I haven't been able to think straight with that thing under the floor!"

"I'll be over, Otto. I got a lead apron from a guy, like they wear when they take X rays. We'll wrap it in that. I'll be there this afternoon."

Schumacher sighed with relief and wiped his forehead. "Thank God. Make it soon, Tony. I'll be waiting. Ah, Tony… are you in town, Tony?"

"Yeah. Why?"

"Nothing. Just make it soon. And Tony—"

"Yeah, what is it?"

"Ah, everything O.K. with you?"

"Sure, sure. See you later, Otto."

"Tony, is Selma all right? Tony?"

But the line was dead. Schumacher put down the receiver and walked to the window. Four stories down he saw three kids playing with a ball. Two of them were tossing the ball back and forth and the third kid was trying to catch it away from them. Then a man walked up and caught the ball out of the air. He put it in his pocket and turned down the street, the three kids running after him.

Schumacher left the window and wiped his forehead again. He went to the kitchen to get a drink of water, then changed his mind. Schumacher felt sickish and sticky.

There were three rooms in the apartment and Schumacher kept pacing back and forth from the living room to the bedroom, from the bedroom to the living room. The third room was closed and Schumacher didn't go near it. Nobody had been in the room since Catell had come back, except for the cleaning woman. Schumacher had found her standing near the bookshelf, dusting and humming a tune. He argued with her from the doorway to come out and leave his books alone. He screamed at her and she screamed back, but she didn't move from her spot till she finished dusting the books. Right under her feet, under the flooring, lay the radioactive gold.

Schumacher remembered the incident and looked at the closed door. The thought of that silent yellow thing, radiating death with no noise, no odor, no natural signs at all, made him feel clammy. "I'm cracking," he mumbled. "I've got to hold on, for God's sake."

He went to the bathroom and turned on the cold water. When he leaned over to wash his face, his vision blurred and he lost his balance. Schumacher grabbed the washbowl with both hands, but his head slammed into the cabinet over the basin. The sudden pain cleared his head and he felt better. Straightening he inhaled deeply, but his eyes refused to focus. He doubled over, a sharp cramp twisting his insides, and retched. He retched till he thought his head would split with the pressure. When it was over, Schumacher staggered from the bathroom, found the front window, and pulled it open. He leaned over the windowsill and took greedy breaths of the fresh, cool air. After a while his strength came back, and with it the horror of the knowledge that he was sick. Not just sick like anyone else, but sick with the hard live rays from the radioactive gold. His mouth shook.

When his head cleared, Schumacher looked up and down the street. He saw nobody. What happened to the kids with the ball? What happened to those people who usually stood on house steps, walked down streets, loitered at corners? But there were people loitering at the corner. There were two men at each corner.

Seized with a sudden hunger, Schumacher went to the kitchen and ate a plate of cold stew, some dry bread, and a few spoons of peanut butter. Then he went back to the living room and lit himself a cigar. The window was still open. Now there were three men at one corner and none at the other. A closed truck had pulled up to the curb near the fireplug next to the corner. And there were two men walking toward the house where Schumacher had his apartment. One was smoking a cigarette, the other was carrying a small, square satchel.

"What time is it?" The one with the cigarette sounded nervous.

"Five to three."

"They should be at the back now, you think?"

"Give them another few minutes."

They started down the street slowly. The one with the satchel opened the top of the leather case and flicked the switch for a dial that showed through the opening. Immediately the box began a faint and intermittent crackling.

"Turn that damn thing down, man. You wanna arouse the whole block?"

"Take it easy. You can hardly hear it. What's the matter with your nerves, anyway?"

"Nothing. There's nothing wrong with my nerves."

"You scared of this Schumacher, maybe? He's over sixty, you know. Here, have another cigarette."

"Thanks "

"Well? Go ahead and smoke it."

"For chrissakes, stop picking on me. In case you and that damn box there haven't heard, Schumacher's got a reputation that goes back to when you were tripping over your diapers. And turn that crazy ticker off, or whatever it is."

"Can't do that, Harry. It's science. And science never—"

"Aw, shut up!"

They walked without talking for a while. Only the traffic at the ends of the street made a noise, and the box they had along. Every so often it ticked and crackled.

"Why's that damn thing ticking all the time? Is everything radioactive, for chrissakes?"

"This is nothing. You should hear it tick when there's hot stuff around. But I guess you won't hear it perform today. Schumacher would be crazy to keep that gold around. What time now?"

"Three sharp."

"O.K., let's go."

"Wait!"

At the end of the street where the closed truck was parked a man had appeared and seemed about to enter the short street. The driver of the truck climbed out of his cab and started toward the man. The stranger stopped, bent toward the wall of a building, and lit a cigarette. Then he continued past the street and disappeared.

"Thank God," said the man with the Geiger counter. "For a minute I thought that guy in the blue coat was coming this way. All right, let's go. We stay in the hall for ten minutes while the guys from the back go upstairs and check the corridors. Then Herron joins us and we go up."

"I just hope that guy in the blue coat doesn't decide to come back."

Tony Catell had spent his life trying to avoid trouble, and he had developed a sharp nose for it. When he turned into Schumacher's street something brought him up short. There weren't enough people. It was too quiet. Two guys down the block were walking too slowly.

Cops.

Catell controlled a panicky urge to run and took a step toward the wall of the nearest building. He lit a cigarette. Looking over his cupped hands, he saw a man climb out of a truck, turn toward him, and stop. The guy wasn't sure, but he was watching. Who did they want? Schumacher? Himself? Suddenly a strong hot hate boiled up inside him, killing his doubt, his fear, his short moment of hesitation. Nothing was going to get in his way, nothing! Catell didn't wonder how they had found Schumacher, whether they knew the gold was there, or whether they knew about him. He didn't even stop to figure what to do, or how, or when. Catell turned into a thing possessed with one thought only: Get that gold!

He had lit a cigarette to make his stop at the corner seem natural. He walked on so they wouldn't bother to look at him. And then he saw the delivery car. It was parked in the driveway a few yards ahead, and on the side of the car was lettered "TV Repair." The driver was opening the door in the rear.

It took Catell a few quick steps to get behind the man at the truck and less than a second to jab his hand, stiff fingered, into the driver's right kidney. The man didn't scream. He exhaled with a rattle in his throat and started to sag. Catell jerked the rear door open, tossed the man in, and jumped after him. Without bothering to close the door, he smashed his fist into the groaning face and the man went limp. Catell took off his hat and coat, ripped the jacket and cap off the unconscious driver, and put them on. Then he jumped out the back. Whistling a tune, he slammed the back door shut, jumped in the driver's seat, and drove back to the corner that he had just left.

Catell pulled around the corner fast, skimming the parked truck by inches. The unconscious man in the back rolled heavily against a television set. Glass broke and picture tubes without their housings crashed around the floor. Catell came to a sharp stop in front of Schumacher's house and, still whistling, jumped out of the truck and opened the door in the back. With one hand he pulled the television set toward him; with the other he reached for a wrench. A few sharp blows and the tube in the set was broken, leaving a large, empty space. Carrying the set in both arms, Catell slammed the rear door with his foot and went up the stairs of the apartment house. Catell kept on whistling loudly, even when he saw faces looking at him through the glass of the door.

Cops.

Again he didn't have to think, to decide.

"Is one of you jerks going to open that door?"

For a moment they didn't move, just stared at the man with the television set. Through the glass Catell saw the lips of one of them move, and he seemed to be saying, "Of all the rotten luck—"

The one with the cigarette opened the door and Catell went through. He gave the man with the cigarette a push with the back of the television set.

"Pardon me, buster. Step aside." He went to the stairs and up, whistling as before.

He didn't see an agent on every floor, but he knew they were there. They didn't worry him. The one on the fourth floor—he'd have to get rid of him.

When Catell came to Schumacher's door, he looked down the corridor and saw a man busying himself with the hallway window. The guy was concentrating very hard on the window.

"Hey, buddy," Catell said.

"You calling me?"

"Yeah. Gimme a hand, willya?"

That's the guy he had to get rid of. When the agent came closer, Catell pushed the television set at him.

"Hold this for a second, buddy?"

The man put his arms around the bulky cabinet and looked at Catell with a question, but just as he was going to say something, Catell's arm whipped out and the ridge of his hand slashed across the man's Adam's apple. That was all there was to it. Catell caught the set and let the man drop. Then he kicked his foot against Schumacher's door.

"Open up. It's Tony."

Schumacher pulled the door open a crack.

"Open up quick. Drag that cop in here." Catell pushed past Schumacher into the apartment. "Don't stand there, goddamn it, get that guy on the floor there!"

Schumacher dragged the unconscious man from the hall and kicked the door shut.

"Tony, what goes here? Did you say 'cop'?"

"Quick, where's the stuff? Same place?"

"Of course. You didn't think I was going to go near—"

"Shut up and listen. The place is lousy with cops. Feds, I think. The whole street is staked out. Now I'm going to take this stuff and walk right out of here. You stay put. They got nothing on you, they don't find nothing, and you don't say nothing. Understand? I'll contact you."

Catell went to his knees before the bookcase and pulled up the rug. Then he lifted three boards, stuck his hand inside the hole, and dragged out the battered yellow cartridge case he had hidden there. When he lifted it, something thumped inside the locked case.

"Wanna take a quick look, Otto?" Catell started to undo the latch.

"For God's sake, Tony, leave it closed. That gold is poison, Tony. It's poison of the worst kind."

Catell had shoved the box inside the television set and started toward the door.

"Tony, I beg you, I beg you to listen—"

"Out of my way!"

Catell had his hands full with the cabinet. He kicked at Schumacher with his foot and caught him on the shin. Schumacher doubled up with pain.

"Out of my way, damn you. Now open this door."

Schumacher moved awkwardly, limping. He opened the door.

"Tony, please—"

"You heard what I said. I'll get in touch with you. When I'm downstairs, throw this guy back out in the hall." Catell was at the stairs already.

"Tony! Tony, I'm sick!"

Catell was running down the stairs. He was whistling again. For a moment Schumacher staggered with a new rush of nausea that choked his throat and blurred his vision. Then, sweating with the effort, he dragged the limp agent back out into the hall. Panting and weak, Schumacher closed his eyes. When he looked at the man on the floor again, their eyes met. With a horrible effort the hurt agent strained his injured throat and let out a weird, loud scream.

As Schumacher staggered back into the room he could hear them clambering up the stairs. He was fumbling for his gun in the desk drawer. When they clattered up to the door, guns drawn, a rushing nausea curled Schumacher's insides. He lost sight of them, and with a head-splitting effort he retched helplessly. He heard noise, he heard the crash of the guns, and when he retched the second time, there was blood in the vomit.

They stepped up to him, dead in a mess on the floor, and they saw that he wasn't even holding the gun right.

At the corner of the street two men sat inside the closed truck among equipment and instruments. One sat at the short-wave radio; the other was fingering a Geiger counter. Suddenly the instrument crackled and ticked with a wild rush of discharges. Another ticker, standing nearby, did the same thing. The two men jumped.

"Christ Almighty, what in hell was that?"

Outside, a television repair truck turned the corner fast and lost itself in the traffic.

Chapter Four

The taxi wound slowly through the late-evening traffic. A thin spring rain had been drizzling all afternoon, almost like a fog, and the lights of downtown Detroit looked hazy. Catell and Selma sat in the cab, far apart on the back seat, not smiling.

"Hear the latest?" asked the cabby.

He didn't get an answer. Catell looked at Selma, who had wrapped a fox stole high around her neck, as if to protect herself from the thick dampness in the air.

"Did you hear the latest about the killing?" said the cabby, a little louder this time. He was a determined man.

"Answer the guy," Catell hissed. "Act natural."

"Uh, no, I haven't. What is the latest?" asked Selma.

"Remember reading about that killing in Highland Park a few days ago, where the cops shot a guy called Shoemaker? Well, they found out who the other guy was. The other guy who was in with old Shoemaker."

Catell tensed and leaned forward a little, his hands curled on the back of the driver's seat.

"Yeah?"

"Well, it turns out the other guy was a dame—beg pardon, a woman." The cabby let that sink in, waiting for some sound from the back.

"Oh, really?" Selma said at last.

"That's right. She was in the building all the time, disguised as a cleaning woman." The cabby paused significantly and then said in a triumphant voice, "And here is the pay-off: After the cops had went out, what does she do?"

"What?"

"She goes up to that Shoemaker's apartment, and she goes ahead and cleans up the mess there."

"She did? What mess?" Selma asked.

"The mess, you know. A guy gets shot up, there's a mess on the floor. Blood and so forth."

"That's terrible," Selma said.

"I'll say. Them molls are cold as ice when it comes to that kind of thing. Of course, she only did this to cover."

"Cover what?"

"To cover up her real purpose, that being the hidden goods."

"Oh, I see," Selma said. "What were those goods?"

"Well, they didn't say in the papers, but my wife knows the super's wife in that building. In other words, I have what might be called inside dope."

"And?"

"This friend of my wife's, the super's old lady, she figured Shoemaker for a suspicious character from way back. No visitors, no visible means of support, hardly ever went out—you know what I mean. Well, she'd go up to his place now and then, just to check. She'd look at the plumbing or the wallpaper, anything like that to check up on what was going on there. And what do you think she found?"

The cabby paused, but nobody said anything.

"She found stacks and stacks of road maps!"

"I don't understand," Selma said.

"Don't you get it? Road maps! Where do you get road maps, I ask you, except you walk in a filling station and ask for one? That's how he'd been collecting those road maps!"

The traffic got lighter on upper Woodward and the taxi speeded up. Selma didn't say any more. She sat huddled in her corner of the seat, weary and withdrawn.

"So what was this moll picking up?" Catell asked.

"I'll tell you what she was picking up! Remember I was telling you about all them road maps? Do you also remember that slew of gas stations that got stuck up around Detroit and vicinity the last coupla months? Well, the guy what done it, he'd walk in the gas station, ask for a road map, and then stick the place up. Now, do you still want me to tell you what was stashed away in that apartment there?"

"Never mind," Catell said. "I can figure it. Schumach—I mean, Shoemaker had all the money from those gas station holdups stashed up there, and his girl friend came to collect after he'd been shot, right?"

"You certainly are right," said the cabby with a sense of achievement.

Catell sat back in his seat. He pulled out a pack of cigarettes, lit one for himself, and then offered one to Selma. She shook her head and turned away.

How she remembered those road maps! Otto and she would sit on the couch nights and study the maps, talking about trips they'd take someday. Schumacher never took her on any of those trips, but he'd talk about them often, and Selma was sure he meant to take her away someday, to drive along the highways through different states, and to see all the points of interest that were marked on the maps. And Selma had liked the planning ahead; she had felt comfortable sitting on the couch there with old Otto.

"What's eating you?" Catell said.

"Nothing."

Selma bent her head so Catell couldn't see her eyes. She felt terribly alone and wished she could cry out, weep.

"Do something with your hair, kid. Those curls are coming down," Catell said.

"It's the damp, honey. I'm sorry."

"Well, fix it. We're almost there."

The taxi had swung off Woodward, out toward the country. A garish neon sign came closer, off to the right of the highway. It said, "Paar Excellence," first in red, then in pink, then in blue, and finally all together—red, pink, blue.

"Get happy, kid. Here we are." Catell straightened his tie.

The Paar Excellence had two sections. One was a roadhouse with name band, fried chicken, dancing, and drinks. The other was a private club. Freddie Paar ran both of them, and he probably even owned the place, though nobody knew for sure. In the roadhouse section he had a friendly nod for the patrons; in the club he knew everybody by name. He had to.

When Selma and Catell walked into the club entrance, a bruiser in a tuxedo asked for their cards.

"No cards," Catell said. "Just blew into town and haven't joined yet."

"No card, no enter," said the tuxedo.

"I been here before," Catell said.

"No card, no enter."

"Call Paar. Tell him Catell is here."

The tuxedo picked up a phone in the wall and talked into it. Then he hung up and said, "Wait here. He'll be right out."

They waited while the bruiser looked Catell up and down. He didn't give Selma a second look.

Then Paar came through the door that led to the club proper. He was short and his tuxedo was built around him like a piece of architecture. Above the upholstery in the shoulders his head looked small, even though his thinning black hair left him with a monstrous forehead.

"My dear Selma," he said, and kissed her hand. "And Tony, of course. Come in, come in."

They followed Paar through the door and into a dim, low room with a fireplace, a long bar, and scattered couches. A girl in black stockings and very little else took Selma's fur and Catell's overcoat. Then they took one of the couches while Paar sat opposite on a low coffee table.

"Well, Tony, what have you decided?"

"No business, Paar. We came on a social visit."

"Of course, Tony, and forgive me, Selma, but answer me just this, Tony. Am I your man, or do you do it directly?"

"Directly."

"Fine, Tony, fine. No hard feelings, you understand, but do call on me for any help, eh? And now I want you to have a drink on the house. I may join you later."

He smiled at both of them, patted Selma on the knee, and was gone. He did it all so smoothly that Catell felt like a clod. He saw that Selma was smiling at Paar's back, but he was in no mood for an argument.

A blonde waitress brought them their drinks. She was wearing a little apron that was attached to her body in some mysterious way. "On the house," she said. Catell didn't know whether he should smile back at her or not.

"What did he mean by that remark, is he your man or not?" Selma caught Catell in the middle of a thought.

"Huh?"

"Paar. What was he talking about?"

"Oh, nothing. About the heist. I talked with him about unloading something."

"So?"

"He was interested but I wasn't. He's too high."

"He knows what we got?"

"What *we* got?"

"Yeah, what *we* got! You weren't thinking of leaving me out of this, were you? You weren't thinking you could pay me off with rent money and an occasional date in a nightclub, were ya?"

Selma leaned her large face close to Catell and he could see the make-up and the pores of her skin. One of her curls was still hanging down and bobbed up and down like a spring when she talked.

"Calm down, damnit. We came here for a good time."

"So I'm asking again. Does he know what we got?"

"No, he doesn't know what *we* got. All he knows is there's a lot of it."

"So you said no to Paar. And how, big shot, are you gonna move the stuff we got, seeing you ain't too pleased with Paar?"

"Selma, for chrissakes, let's have a good time, huh?"

"How ya gonna move it?"

"All right. Stop yelling. I'm going to take it where Paar would take it. He let slip with something. Out on the West Coast."

"Where?"

"I don't know yet. I gotta make connections there first. L.A., probably."

Selma let herself sink back on the cushions of the couch. Catell could see where her corset pinched her and looked away.

"I love the sunshine. Gee, Tony, won't it be fun on the beach there and everything?"

"You want another drink?"

Selma didn't answer. She was looking up in the air, smiling and saying "*Gee*" every so often. When the fresh drinks came, Catell took her hand.

"Honey, listen. Let's get one thing straight. This deal isn't through yet, and until it is, we gotta go easy. When Schumacher was around he staked me to some dough, but now there isn't any. Not till the deal comes through. So till then, we gotta go easy, not to speak of the risks. The way I figure it, you stay here and I do the scouting alone. Then I send for you. And then we can go anywhere you want. Whaddaya say?"

"But Tony!" Selma sounded hurt. "You mean that?"

"Just till I finish this business, honey. You know I can't be seen with you now. They know you been a friend of Schumacher's, and I don't want to get connected to him in any way. It's too risky. Besides, I haven't got any dough right now."

"Tony, I got some. I got two thousand at home. I been saving it the longest time. And honest, Tony, I don't mind."

"It's no good, Selma. It's too risky for both of us. As long as I'm not connected with Schumacher in any way, everything is jake."

"Now you listen to me, Tony Catell. You better take care of me or else. Otto never would have acted that way. I'm going with you or else."

"Or else what?" Catell said it slowly and quietly, but Selma caught the tone.

"You don't scare me one bit, Tony Catell. If you think you can trample all over me and then walk out you got another guess coming. First you make me leave Otto, then you go get him shot to death so he's out of the way, and then you think you can just give me the boot and light out. Not on your life!"

"Selma, you're talking crazy. You got everything wrong. I never intended for Otto to end up that way."

"Oh, yes, you did, lovin' cup. I know your kind, but it ain't gonna happen to me." Selma gave Catell an ugly look and drained her glass. "I want another drink, right now. And don't tell me you're broke, lovin' cup."

Catell controlled his temper and waved for another drink.

"And from now on, any plans you got you discuss with me, lovin' cup, understand? I been around long enough to know how to handle your kind."

"That's for sure."

"What's that? And another thing. I want you to know I despise you from the bottom of my heart, lovin' cup, for what you did to my Otto. That was the lowest, swiniest—"

"Stop calling me loving cup."

Selma stopped in the middle of her sentence and looked vacantly at Catell. Then suddenly she buried her face in the palms of her hands and started to cry. She bawled with a wet and cowlike sound, crying, "Lovin' cup!" between hiccups.

"My dear, my dear, my dear!"

Paar had reappeared from somewhere and he was patting Selma on the back and stroking her bare arm.

"Beat it, Paar. She'll be all right." Catell felt uncomfortable.

"My good Tony, you don't seem to know how a lady likes to be treated at a time like this. One moment, Tony. You are my guests here, so allow me to help you with this little matter. Why don't you go and buy some cigarettes, and when you come back, everything will be all right. Won't it, Selma dear?" He put his hand on Selma's shoulder.

Catell got up and looked around the room. Let that bald monkey handle that mess and her sloppy curls. Live and let live, he thought. How that lousy bag got him to make a pitch for her he didn't know. Catell walked to the bar and ordered a shot. Back on the couch he saw Paar sitting next to Selma, who was patting her eyes and nodding her head. If Paar thought he was getting a deal there, he had a big, mushy surprise coming. And welcome to it.

Catell let his eyes wander over the dim room. Couples were sitting or standing together, there were groups of young punks in tuxedos, and everybody looked prosperous. Catell recognized one or two faces; the rest were strangers to him. Everybody was young, slick-looking, and everybody seemed very sure of himself. Then Catell thought of California. Pretty soon now he would be back on top. In a very short time all these punks were going to hear about Tony Catell.

"Where do I get smokes in this place?" he asked the bartender.

The guy nodded to the left and kept on wiping a glass. Catell was going to say something else, but his eyes had followed the direction of the nod. He saw a young blonde with long wavy hair who was carrying a cigarette tray in front of her. She was dressed in a brief thing like a corset, all black, and the rest of her was the most satiny, fair thing he had ever seen. The girl had the improbable figure of a calendar nude, and most of it showed. She turned around and came his way. She walked with a high-heeled bounce that made her breasts move. They were full, and Catell noticed that the black corset just made it in front.

He asked for cigarettes and she took a pack from her tray. Then she tore the pack open, shook out a cigarette, and offered it to him. He stuck the cigarette in his mouth and she gave him a light from a small gold lighter she carried. Over the cigarette Catell caught the girl's eye. She looked at him in an unconcerned way, smiling with the corners of her mouth. Then his eyes wandered down again.

"Don't you want them, sir?"

"What's that?"

"Your cigarettes, sir. Don't you want them?"

He grabbed the pack out of her hand and gave her a bill. She smiled her thanks and slowly moved down the aisle in front of the bar. Catell could have sworn that she didn't know he was staring at her.

He walked back to the couch where Paar was sitting next to Selma. She was smiling again, looking pretty good in the dim light. Paar's hand was lying on her thigh. When Catell walked up Paar moved his hand away slowly, as if he didn't care one way or the other.

"I see you got some cigarettes," he said.

"Yeah."

"I think I fixed your little quarrel very nicely, Tony, my boy. Selma is in a very good mood again and I don't want you to spoil it for her."

"Yeah?"

"He won't," Selma said, smiling at Paar. "He's really a nice boy, aren't you, lovin' cup?" She had a brassy smile on her big face. " 'Scuse me, gents, while I do a little fixing." She got out of the couch with an effort.

"Sit down, Catell, sit down. Selma and I have become great friends while you were gone. She tells me you're leaving us. You have other interests, maybe?"

Ignoring Paar's question, Catell jerked his head toward the blonde cigarette girl. "Who is she?"

"Selma is a little upset about your plans. Or at least she was before she and I had our little talk. We both feel you should stick around, Tony."

"What's in it for me?"

"She's only eighteen, Tony. Besides, she's been spoken for. However, as I was saying—"

"We got no business, Paar. I told you I'll only deal direct."

"As you wish, Tony. But let me remind you, Selma is a very emotional woman. Ah, did you know that our little Lily is leaving us?"

"Who?"

"Lily. The young thing you've been admiring so. And as I've said, she's been spoken for, Tony. She's leaving for Los Angeles."

"So what?"

"I think Selma mentioned something about your going to Los Angeles, or am I mistaken? Of course, Selma doesn't know that Lily is going to Los Angeles, Tony."

"And what if she does? What exactly are you trying to pull?"

"Just this, Catell: I think you might do better staying here. And, I repeat, if there is any way in which I can be of help to you—"

"Can it. Here's Selma."

When she sat down on the couch, Paar rose and turned to go.

"Don't leave now, Paar honey," said Selma, grabbing his sleeve. "Sit down for a minute and we'll talk some more. With Tony here," and she gave Catell a cocky smile.

"Later, dear Selma. We'll all have a nice chat, I promise you." Paar wasn't smiling this time.

"Paar." Catell's voice was matter of fact. "Who are the two guys just came in the door?"

"Who?"

"Don't jerk your head. By the door."

Paar turned and glanced toward the entrance. Then he gave Catell a patronizing smile.

"You are jumpy, Tony. They come quite often. Local detectives looking in on a private club."

Catell rose slowly. He put his hands in his pockets, turned his back to the cops, and looked casual.

"I'm blowing. Where's the back door?"

"My dear Tony, this means absolutely nothing. Please sit down."

"Shut up. I can't be seen with Selma right now. Where's the back?"

"Now, really, Tony boy." Paar put his soft hand on Catell's arm.

Catell stepped close. "Hear this, Paar. See to it I don't tangle with your copper friends there. Keep them and anybody else you know out of my way. If you don't, I'll get you."

Then he walked away, slowly, without turning. Paar's big forehead was sticky with sweat.

Once through the swinging doors in the back, Catell turned quickly and glanced through the glass into the room he had just left. Paar was standing with the two cops, patting one of them on the back. Then they started to walk his way, chatting.

Catell turned away. He found himself in an empty kitchen with one light over the huge refrigerator. There was a door to the left. Catell went to the door, opened it, and stepped into a long hall. More doors. He picked one, opened it, and found himself in a small cubicle without windows. Pipes ran along the ceiling. There was a mop and bucket in one corner, and a clothes rack in the other. A naked light bulb made a hard light, and under it stood Lily.

She had taken her shoes and stockings off and her hands were at her back, trying to undo the black corset. Catell closed the door behind him and she looked up, without recognition.

"Hi," Catell said.

"Hi."

"Fancy meeting you here, Lily."

She didn't answer. Only her eyes moved.

"If you were going to scream, don't," Catell said. He turned the catch of the door. "I'm just staying a minute."

She looked at him, frowning, and put a hand to her breasts. "Please," she said. "Please leave."

Catell heard footsteps in the hall and leaned lightly against the door, both hands on the knob.

"Not a word, kid."

"Please, mister, I—"

Catell moved across the small room fast and clapped one hand over her mouth, holding her up against him with his other arm. He didn't have to say any more. She saw his face grow stiff, mean, and she stayed very still.

After the footsteps had passed, Catell didn't move right away. He felt her soft mouth under his hand and the curve of her thighs against him. Then he let her go. She stepped back, red marks showing on her face where his hand had been.

"Please go now."

"Not yet."

"Please, I have to change. I'm late."

"Go ahead."

"But I have to change, mister."

"The name's Tony."

She bit her lip but didn't say anything. One of the pipes along the ceiling started to hiss. Lily looked up and back at Catell, who was still leaning against the door. Neither of them moved.

"Come on, go ahead and change. Don't tell me you never been looked at."

She stood in the middle of the bare room, under the hard light, her mouth trembling.

"Answer me," Catell said.

"I—I don't know what you mean."

"I said get undressed. It can't be the first time."

"I never—"

"You're lying."

"Never like this, I mean."

"Fine. I like to be the first. Now get it off."

She hesitated. He took a step toward her, looking at the girl with cold eyes. A muscle jumped in the side of his face. Lily shrank back, real fear in her eyes.

"Stay where you are. Under the light."

Catell leaned against the door again and watched.

Lily arched her back, her hands fumbling for the zipper. Her eyes shone wet. When the zipper opened she let the corset drop. It rolled on the floor without losing its shape. Then Catell raised his eyes slowly. He saw her narrow ankles, her calves. She had full thighs that curved with a satiny sheen, wide round hips, and a sharp curve where her waist drew in. Catell chewed his lip but otherwise made no movement. He noticed that she had the same shape as she'd had in the corset, the skin of her body smooth and unmarked from the stays, and her breasts high. They were ripe, coming to impudent points, and they threw sharp shadows, which moved with her breathing. He looked at her face. She was very young.

"Turn around."

She turned slowly, looking at him over her shoulder. "Now lie down." She lay down on the cold cement floor, legs drawn up. "Stretch out." She did. She pointed her toes, legs together, and put her arms over her head. All the while she looked at him with large eyes. Catell never moved from his place by the door. After a while he told her to get up. He walked over to her and brushed the lint from her naked back. Then he went back to the door.

"You can get dressed now, Lily."

While she put her clothes on, Catell lit another cigarette and smoked without looking at her.

"May I go now?" Lily had stepped close to the door.

"Sure."

He opened the door for her and let her pass. Just as she went by he grasped her arm and said, "I'm the first? Right, Lily?"

"Yes, mister."

"Tony."

"Yes, Tony."

Their eyes held for a moment. Catell frowned.

"You're a hard one."

She started to smile, gave it up. "No," she said.

Catell closed the door again. Lily waited.

"So why'd you do it, just like that?"

"I didn't, just like that."

"Why'd you do it?"

This time her small smile didn't make it at all. "It didn't hurt," she said.

"What does?"

She smiled a moment. "Not much," she said, and looked down at her feet.

"Lily."

"Yes?"

"Your folks in L.A.?"

"I don't think so," she said. She said it in no special way, and that's what gave it the meaning.

Catell didn't ask any more. He opened the door, stepped back. When he put his hand on her arm again it surprised both of them.

"Lily."

"Yes, Tony?"

"See you?"

"I'd like to," she said.

She finished saying it and then went out. He closed the door behind her.

When he had smoked his cigarette he crushed it under his foot and walked back the way he had come. He didn't see the two detectives, but Paar was standing by the swinging doors.

"You may come out now, Tony." Paar smiled.

"They gone?"

"Yes. In fact, quite a while ago. And furthermore, I'm afraid you will have to go home alone. Selma has left, too. They took her."

"What are you talking about?"

"The detectives. They took her along for routine questioning about old Schumacher, it seems."

Catell didn't answer right away.

"Lily gone too?" He didn't look at Paar.

"Why, yes. Tony. She had to make an early plane. L.A., you know. I think I mentioned it."

"You did."

"I didn't mention, though, who she's going to join. I don't know if you've ever heard of him, but his name is Topper. And if I were you, Tony, I'd stay away from Topper."

Catell left Paar standing there. He got his coat and took a taxi back to town. He left Detroit that same night, but first he stopped at Selma's apartment and took the two thousand bucks that was there.

Chapter Five

Paar didn't like Catell very much. He didn't understand him, and he didn't have any patience with his kind. But Paar didn't want Catell to come to any harm. Not yet, anyway.

After Catell had left the club, Paar walked slowly toward the bar, then changed his mind and went to his office. He closed the heavy door, took off his dinner jacket, and sat down behind his desk. Without his padding Paar looked narrow and stoop-shouldered. He put his hands on the large desktop and frowned. It would be very nice to let the cops pump Selma dry. The drunken slut would implicate herself and get locked out of the way. She would spill what it was Catell had hidden and Paar had enough pull to find out whatever the cops might get out of her. And finally they'd find out for sure whether she knew where Catell was going from here. If she didn't know, then Paar would be happy to know that he didn't have to bother with her. If she did know, the cops would get to him first, and Paar wouldn't have a chance. The thought pained him, but he'd have to take Selma on himself.

Paar sighed, picked up the phone, and dialed a city number. A butler answered at the other end.

"Let me talk to him," said Paar.

The butler knew Paar's voice and said, "One moment, sir."

Then a voice said, "What is it, Paar?"

"Two dicks hauled in a friend of mine, a woman. She'll be at the Fifth Precinct house for questioning. Get her out…I know it's two o'clock in the morning, but I want her out…No, just questioning. No warrant…I'll be over there in half an hour to pick her up, so do what you have to do. She was picked up at my club. The men's names are Porter and Levy. So long."

Paar put down the phone, took his jacket and overcoat, and left the club. Twenty minutes later his chauffeur-driven limousine stopped in front of the Fifth Precinct police station. Paar entered the building with an affable smile for everyone; two drunks, one plainclothesman, and the desk sergeant. Paar leaned his elbow on the high desk and offered the policeman a cigarette.

"No, thank you, Mr. Paar. We haven't seen you in a long time."

"That's true, Sergeant Stone." Paar smiled at him. "Is the young lady ready?"

"I'm very sorry, Mr., Paar, they're still questioning her."

Paar's neck got red and his voice didn't sound polite. "Didn't you get a call to release her?"

"Sure, Mr. Paar, but—"

"Well?"

The Sergeant leaned on his desk and lowered his voice. "Don't try and throw your weight around, Paar. The Feds are in on this. They're with her now."

For a moment Paar was stunned. He recovered himself with an effort and asked, "What room?"

"Two-o-five."

He went to the second floor and walked through the door of 205 without knocking. What he saw made him blanch. Four men were sitting around the figure by the table. It was Selma, head back, mouth open, eyes closed. One arm hung down limp.

"Who are you?" They turned around and looked at him.

"Come here," said another one.

Paar stepped closer, staring at Selma. One of the four men leaned over from his chair and grabbed Paar.

"Under the light, Bud. Let's take a look at you."

Paar's big forehead glistened and his berry eyes blinked. "Gentlemen, please. What—what have you done?"

"This is Freddie Paar, friends," said one of the men. He was a detective out of the Fifth Precinct. The others were FBI.

"Freddie Paar is our local glamour boy of the dark, dark underworld. Name any smutty business, Paar is in it. Right, boy?" The man laughed.

With an effort Paar straightened his back. "I came to fetch this young lady and they sent me to this room. However, this shocking scene—"

"This shocking scene!" the detective said, and laughed.

Paar turned to him with a face like poison. "I'm not without influence in this town. This outrage—"

"This outrage!" aped the man, and he doubled over with laughter.

"There are laws," Paar said, his voice getting shrill. "Clubbing women into unconsciousness—"

At that point Selma began to snore. "Unconsciousness!" the man roared.

This made Selma start. She woke with a sick face, licking her dry lips.

"Selma," Parr said. "What have they done to you?"

"Lovin' cup." Her voice was raspy.

The detective stopped laughing and got serious. "Lovin' cup," he said to Paar, "your friend here was drunk when she came in. She fell asleep."

"You mean she hasn't been questioned yet?"

A quiet voice from the end of the room said, "No." Herron stepped forward and looked at Paar. "And what is your interest in this matter, may I ask?"

"The young lady is a personal acquaintance, sir. She spent the evening at my club, and when I saw her leave with two detectives, naturally I got concerned and made inquiries."

"With whom did she spend the evening?" Herron asked.

"I don't know. Some young man or other."

"Where is he?"

"I couldn't tell you that, sir."

"I think we'll throw you out now, lovin' cup," said the detective. "Shall I throw him out, Herron?"

"No. Mr. Paar may stay. As soon as his lady friend has recovered, he'll want to take her home, I'm sure."

Paar was very anxious to take Selma home. He didn't like Herron. Polite cops made him uncomfortable and Herron smelled like FBI.

"Selma, are you ready to leave?"

"Oh, Jaysis," she said, holding her head.

"Did they annoy you, Selma? Question you?"

"Jaysis."

Paar couldn't make anything of that remark and it upset him. He straightened himself and looked at Herron. "I demand an explanation. What is this lady doing here?"

"She is suffering from a hangover," the detective said.

"And we wanted some information from her about an acquaintance of hers," Herron added.

"Well, you must realize by now that you're wasting your time," Paar said. "If I can be of any assistance—"

"No, thank you, Mr. Paar. Our information is complete, for the moment."

"If you're wondering about her escort, Mr. Catell has left town New York, I think."

Herron shifted his head slightly and the man next to him made notes on a stenographer's pad in front of him.

"You didn't know this?" said Paar, who had noticed the movement.

"No. We were actually interested in one Otto Schumacher."

Paar cursed himself under his breath. Now they had Catell tagged and Paar himself had done the damage. He smiled nervously.

"Well, it's of no consequence. And as I was saying, Mr. Catell was here only briefly. He mentioned to me how anxious he was to get back to New York. In fact, I believe he took the one-o'clock train."

Herron made no comment. The stenographer was sharpening his pencil, the detective stood near the wall picking his teeth, and the fourth man was holding a paper cup of water to Selma's lips.

"Oh, Jaysis!" she said.

The silence made Paar uncomfortable. He still didn't know whether they had got anything out of Selma.

"If you gentlemen are through, I believe I'll accompany the lady home now." Paar took Selma by the arm.

"Of course, Mr. Paar. We'll be in touch with her. And you," Herron added.

Paar helped Selma out of the chair. One shoulder of her deep-cut dress was slipping down her arm and her left stocking sagged. She looked terrible. Outside, even the cold night air didn't seem to help her. Selma sat in one corner of Paar's big limousine, never saying a word. Nor did Paar. It could wait till morning, he figured. He and Selma were going to stick together for a while, seeing they were both after the same man. Meanwhile, there'd be some compensations, and he looked at Selma's inert figure leaning in the corner of the seat.

"End of the line," Paar said in a cheery voice. It didn't cheer Selma.

"Jaysis," she said.

He helped her out of the car and into the apartment building. They went up in the elevator. Once in the apartment, Paar locked the door.

"Selma, dear, sit down and be comfortable. Your wrap, oops, thank you. And now, sweet, the hair of the dog for you."

Selma straightened up and patted her hair. She looked more animated now and struck a saucy pose. The dress had slipped off one shoulder again.

Paar sat down next to Selma and handed her a glass of straight whisky. She drank it fast, wrinkling her eyes at him over the rim of the glass.

"Paar, baby, you're a lover." She put a whisky-wet kiss on his big forehead.

"How would you know?" Paar said. He patted her shoulder. "But it's good to see you cheered up again, Selma. Your ordeal at the station—"

"One more, Paar baby." She handed him her empty glass.

"Did they question you long, dear?" Paar refilled Selma's glass and held it just out of reach.

"Come on, baby, come on." He gave her the glass quickly, noticing how easily she could lose her temper. After two swallows Selma put the glass down and leaned back, sighing. "Paar, you're so good to me."

"Don't mention it, my dear. And stay as long as you like. In fact, Selma, what do you say you move in with me? The place is large, I'm alone, I could use an attractive hostess when I entertain."

Selma wasn't answering. Her face was flushed now and she was staring at the ceiling with a vague smile.

"Selma, my dear, are you all right?"

"Jaysis."

Paar saw it was no use. She didn't resist when he pulled her up and steered her toward the bedroom. He hadn't expected she would. Sitting on the large bed, Selma smiled pleasantly when Paar started to unbutton her dress.

"You'll be comfortable soon now." His hands were sweating. "We'll talk about Catell in the morning, sweetness. And you'll tell me all about your bad, bad time with the police."

He took her dress off, Selma lifting her rear so he could pull it up. Sitting down again, she swayed a little, eyes closed. Paar steadied her and started to fumble with her brassiere.

"Soon now, my dearest, soon you'll be all right, eh, Selma?" He got the brassiere unhooked and pulled the straps off her shoulders. His voice was shaky when he said, "Darling."

Selma sank back on the bed, sighing. With nervous movements Paar fumbled with his dinner jacket while he ran to the light switch. He was pulling his tie off when he clicked the light switch.

Out of the darkness Selma said, "Jaysis."

Chapter Six

"Why'd you let 'em go?" The detective was still picking his teeth.

"I got all the information I need at the moment," Herron said. He was shuffling through the stenographer's notes,

"Coffee, anyone?" The fourth man stuck his head in the door.

"Not for me." Herron lit himself a cigarette and shuffled through the notes again.

"Bring me one, Charlie, black," the detective said.

The detective walked from the door to the window, looked down into the dark street, and walked back again. "I got all night yet," he said.

"Yeah?"

He walked again. The stenographer had put his overcoat on and gone out.

"What you learn, Jack?" the detective asked. He spat out a little piece of toothpick and sat down opposite Herron.

"Well, for one thing, that Catell didn't go to New York."

"Yeah, that Paar sure was anxious for you to think so."

"Where's the phone?"

"Next room. Wish Charlie'd hurry up with that coffee."

Herron went next door and dialed a number. "Hello? Herron here. Who's on duty?...O.K., give me Agent Polnik." Herron waited, scribbling in his notebook. "Polnik? Listen. Have somebody check if there was a train for New York at one A.M. Get the New York office to have a man wait for the train, if there was one...What? Not till five A.M.? O.K., then skip that angle. Now, listen. We're looking for Anthony Catell. Look him up in the file I left in the office... Yes, one of the files I got there. Next, cover the station, airport, bus terminals for the next twenty-four hours... Yes, same man. Pay special attention to anything leaving for Los Angeles... No, I'm not sure. We have one informant to go by, but she was drunk. But Catell might fit into the picture because of other information... Uh-huh, he knew Schumacher. One more thing, and this is important. Have the men carry Geiger counters. And check baggage rooms... Yeah. O.K., 'bye."

Herron hung up and went back to the other room. The detective was drinking black coffee and chewing a fresh toothpick. Charlie was spooning a milk shake out of a paper carton.

"How you can eat that stuff is beyond me," the detective was saying.

"Makes more sense than eating toothpicks."

"Well, Jack, what next?" The detective looked up when Herron came in.

"We're covering the usual. Probably useless. Catell is no greenhorn. Lemme have a sip." Herron took the coffee cup and drank.

"Whyn't you buy one? Charlie asked you if you wanted one."

"I don't want a whole cup, just a sip. Coffee keeps me awake."

"So let's have my cup back."

Herron stacked his notes together and got up to leave. "Does Paar have any connections in L.A.?"

"Yeah," Charlie said. "Some syndicate tie-up. You can find out downstairs."

"O.K., I will. Anybody here to take the teletype?"

"Try three doors down the hall, you can't miss the racket."

"Thanks. Night, all."

"Night."

"Lucky bastard."

Three doors down Herron dictated his message. In St. Louis, Chief Jones watched the teletype as it hammered out: "Herron to Jones. Circumstantial evidence of association with deceased O. Schumacher and former girlfriend of same make T. Catell definite suspect. Screening of Detroit exits ordered. No present trace of stolen object. Presumably in suspect's possession. Am proceeding Los Angeles via plane to cover suspect's connections and possible arrival there. Details follow. Communicate L.A. district office."

At ten-thirty-five A.M. the next day, Herron boarded a through plane to Los Angeles. He arrived late that evening, checked into the district office, then got himself a hotel room. He slept for nine hours and then went back to work. He checked leads, covered angles, made reports, waited. He did this for days without finding a trace of Tony Catell.

On a hot stretch of road in Arizona, Catell stopped the car and wiped the sweat off his neck. He listened to the gurgling of the radiator, watching the steam hiss out from under the hood. He pulled out a cigarette. Before he got it lit the thought of the smoke made him feel sick and he threw the thing away. He got out of the car. For a moment he fought nausea that rose in his throat like wet cotton. The feeling passed.

It had started a few days after he'd left Detroit, and now it came every day, at odd times, first a vague dizziness, later sick waves of nausea and knots of pain, till the car would swerve and he'd pull himself together again. Then it would pass away. Sometimes he wondered whether Schumacher had been right about the gold. He'd called it rotten. But there was a better reason. Catell looked at his watch and pulled a sticky candy bar out of his pocket. Two o'clock. Time.

Every two hours Catell ate a candy bar, whether he was hungry or not. By the time he reached Los Angeles he would have gained ten, fifteen pounds, maybe. Already he looked like a different man, with more bulk, the lines of his face less deep. He had a tan, and his hair, black and straight, was getting longer.

When the car had stopped sizzling, Catell walked around to the front and lifted the hood.

"Troubles, Buddy?"

Catell jumped around and saw the police car. A lean man in uniform and cowboy hat looked at him.

"Jumpy, ain't ya?"

"I didn't hear you come up."

"Stranger here, ain't ya?" The man climbed out of his car and stretched his long legs. There was a sheriff's badge on his blue shirt. "I said, you must be a stranger here, huh?"

Catell didn't like the man. Not just because he was a cop, but because there was that grinning curiosity on his face, that eager prying of a lean dog scurrying around to find something, anything. The man stuck his neck out, red and wrinkled like a turkey's, and spat.

"Speak up, stranger."

"Yeah. I'm a stranger here."

"Where from?"

"Look at the license."

The sheriff looked without wanting to. It said Louisiana.

"I'm asking you."

"New Orleans."

"City fella, huh?" He stalked around the car and kicked at the loose fender in the rear. "You drive this junker all the way up from the Gulf?"

"Sure. And don't kick it again."

The man just laughed. "You know, city feller, we got an ordinance about junkers. We like people comin' through here to drive a safe car. Don't want folks around here to get endangered."

"So stop kicking at it, hear?" Catell's voice shook with rage and he suddenly felt cold under his wet shirt. That bastard was getting to him.

"How about pullin' that heap off the pavement some more, city feller? We got an ordinance about highway parking."

Catell got behind the wheel and kicked at the starter. The gears crashed and the car jumped ahead a few feet, off the paved strip of highway. That bastard, that lousy hick bastard. Catell took a deep breath. What he could do to that raw-necked, rat-faced— Better not think like this. Better think of the big things at stake here, better look like you're taking it. Got to take it.

"One more thing, city feller. Don't park where you're parkin' there. We got an ordinance." He laughed, his Adam's apple bobbing. He jumped back in his car and pulled it up even with Catell's.

"I'll be by after a spell. Better not be here no more." He shot away, the wheels spitting gravel at Catell's windshield.

After a few minutes Catell got out of the car again and slammed the hood shut. It made a nasty sound and something came loose, leaving the hood jammed at an angle. The damn car was coming apart at the seams. First he'd had a pretty good one, but it had Michigan license plates and the car had to be ditched. He hid it in a ravine somewhere in Indiana and buried the license plates. Then he hitchhiked for a hundred miles. Next he bought a prewar job in southern Indiana and drove it as far as Kentucky. That's where he drove it into an abandoned mine after throwing away the plates. At night he walked to the nearest town, took a train for two hundred miles, and then bought the third car. He drove it to Terryville, Louisiana, left it in a vacant lot, and bought his last car. This was a real junker, but there wasn't much choice. Selma's two thousand was almost gone.

Catell started the car and headed it back on the hot pavement. There better be a town close by. The radiator was almost empty and there probably wasn't much oil left. The old car gathered speed, whining down the white road and shooting thick black clouds out the tailpipe.

A sign flipped by, saying: "You are entering—" and it was gone. After a bend in the road a tree appeared, two trees; then Catell saw the houses. They were gray clapboard and looked old. Some were adobe. The only new-looking place was the filling station, rigged up like a fort, and Catell breathed easier.

When he pulled up to the pumps he heard the gravel crunch on the right. A car stopped sharply and the voice said, "City feller, don't they got not ordinance about speeding where you come from?"

The sheriff got out of his car and grinned, crackly lips drawn back over his gums.

"Get out," he said.

"What in hell do you want now?"

"Don't get porky, stranger. I'm the law around here and you just broke one of our ordinances."

"What goddamn ordinance?"

"The one about speedin'. You gonna pay up or you gonna spend some time in our jail?"

"How much will you take, *officer?*"

"Seeing it's you, city feller, that'll be seventy dollars."

"Why, you stinking sonofabitch!" Catell jumped out of his car. His door hit the gas pump and slammed back into his chest. Before he could get free, the sheriff had come around the car, swinging a sap that came down hard and caught Catell on the shoulder. But the sheriff was slow; too slow for Catell, anyway. Twisting his injured shoulder back, Catell lashed out with one foot and caught the tall man in the groin. Before he had time to double over and groan, Catell's hand caught the back of his neck and jerked it down, and a knee smashed up into the sheriff's face. Then a sharp kick into the chest and the half-conscious man flew back, crashing hard into a pump. There wasn't any time for Catell to enjoy the sight because a sharp blow from behind made him buckle and pitch, and then all turned black.

"I guess they both ain't gonna be much for a while," said the thickset man who was holding a two-by-four in his hand.

"Reckon," said the short one next to him. "What'll we do now?"

"To the jailhouse. The stranger here has some explainin' to do, and Harry—well, Harry just natcherly belongs in the jailhouse, seein' he's our sheriff." They both laughed.

"Sure makes me feel good, seein' our Harry get his for a change. Had it comin' for a long time," said the short one. "I just feel kinda sorry for that stranger here, once Harry starts feelin' like himself again."

They laughed again and then started to drag the two limp figures over the gravel.

Chapter Seven

A bottle fly kept buzzing around the cell. It hit the walls with a small flat sound. Every time it hit, fine yellow dust sifted down from the adobe. A few times it made for the light that came through the barred window, but even though there was no glass, the fly didn't find its way out. Then it angled down into the shadow, hit the wall again, and landed on Catell's face. It sat there for a long tune without Catell's knowing it. When he came to, he did so with a start, slapping his hand over his forehead with a wide awkward swing. He jumped up, but weaved and doubled over. There was a blue ache in his left shoulder, and the pain in his head made red fire flash before his eyes.

After a moment he straightened up. His eyes ran over the adobe walls, the barred hole of a window, and the bars that made one wall of his cell. There was a room beyond, but Catell didn't take it in because closer by, near the iron door, the sheriff sat hunched on a three-legged stool. His eyes and nose were puffed with a purple shimmer, and his lips were curled back, showing his long yellow teeth. Three teeth in front were missing, and his tongue was probing back and forth over the reddened hole.

"Sleep good, city feller?" He talked with a hiss. Catell walked up to the bars but didn't answer.

"I'm askin' because for a spell now that's goin' to be your last good sleep."

The sheriff got up slowly and walked to a desk near the door beyond. He came back with a pencil and pad. After sitting down again he said,

"What's your name, stranger?"

"Jesse Weiss."

"Age?"

"Forty-eight."

"Where from?"

"New Orleans."

The questions went on and Catell gave answers. He kept his voice even and his eyes down. There were going to be no more mistakes. In the time of a minute he had made all the bad ones: attracting attention, resisting arrest, assaulting an officer of the law, landing in jail. No more mistakes now. Don't offend the man; do what he says; act small and a little scared. And wait for the breaks. This wasn't the end. This was bad, but not the end. For God's sake, this was not the end!

"Now listen close, city feller, because I want you to know what I got in mind. Like I tried to tell you once before, I'm the law around here, and you went ahead and broke that law more'n a couple of times. Now we can't have that around here, city feller. You gotta learn how to stay on the right side of the law."

Catell had his hands around the bars, listening with eyes down, when the sheriff stopped talking. Catell looked up and caught the blurred movement too late. The sap smacked down sharply, cracking across the back of his right hand.

"You listening to me, New Orleans? You paying attention to what I say?"

Catell didn't hear him. He had jerked back, gasping with the pain that exploded in his hand. His knees buckled and he groaned hoarsely, his good hand tightening around the wrist of the other arm. The sheriff had got off his chair, watching. His tongue was working the hole in his gums like a lazy snake.

"That's just so you know who to pay attention to around here, New Orleans. Now, like I was saying, you gotta learn to respect the law, and I'm just the man what can teach you how."

Catell sat on the floor, his breath making a harsh labored sound. The hand was puffing up fast.

"So I figure the best way of doing that, city feller, is for you to stay around here a little while. Then, when I see some real improvement, why, then we'll start figuring on some kind of trial for you. The judge at the county seat is a friend of mine, so we'll see what can be done in the case of the Law versus City Feller. Any questions? No? I didn't figure so."

The sheriff stood a while looking at Catell on the floor. Then he started to laugh. He laughed with a slow babbling sound that could have meant anything.

"I'm going to leave you for a spell now, seeing you'd rather be alone with your little aches and pains. And in case you crave company, there's a deputy right beyond that door, sittin' on the porch."

The sheriff turned away and left, still shaking with his slow gobble of a laugh.

Catell stayed on the floor for a while, watching his hand. The swelling was dark red now, but the pain wasn't so unbearable any more. Except when he moved his fingers.

Alone in the jailhouse, Catell started to look around. Standing at the bars, he could glimpse a cell on either side of him. There was a door to the left, half open, with a toilet visible. Beyond the corridor was the long room that served as an office. Through the two windows Catell could see a porch and a country street.

The bars of the window in his cell were solid. So were the ones that formed one wall of his cell. But the lock of the cell was nothing. A strong nail, bent, or perhaps a spoon, he thought, any simple thing like that would do it. Tonight? Tomorrow. Sitting down carefully on the cot, Catell thought about it. Why rush? That bastard hick of a sheriff wasn't in any hurry to move to court. So wait. Wait for the breaks. And the longer the sheriff waited, the more he would get in the wrong. And the more he got in the wrong, the less of a leg he'd have to stand on. Catell felt better.

Suddenly he jumped up, fright in his eyes. The gold! Where was his car? In panicky confusion he ran to the bars, shaking them, rattling the door. He curled the fingers of his injured hand, not feeling the pain, with only one thought in his mind. The gold! Then he ran to the window, to shake the bars, to reach his arm far out of the yellow hole that faced nothing but hot dust and weeds. Then he saw it. His car was standing in back of the jail. One door was half open and nothing looked any different about the car than when he had bought it. He could see the back seat, undisturbed. Draped over the seat was the lead apron.

With a deep breath Catell stepped back from the window and sank down on his cot. He was tired. He stretched out carefully, with one arm over his eyes, the injured hand resting on his stomach. The dull heat of the cell lay like lead around him, but Catell hardly noticed it. He slept.

"Just look at him sweat," said the deputy to the three ranchers. They stood outside the cell, watching Catell asleep on his cot.

"You think he's sweating now, boys, just wait till I get through with him," said the sheriff. "Ben, get me a bucket of water."

The deputy went outside and came back with the bucket. "Whatcha gonna do, Harry?"

"Just step back and watch."

Heaving the bucket in a wide arc, the sheriff tossed the water at Catell. It caught him full on the neck and face. The sleeping man jerked up with a wild gasp, dumb bewilderment in his face. There was a roar of laughter from the men who were peering through the bars, with stamping of feet and back-slapping.

"What's his name?" one of them asked.

"Call him New Orleans," said the sheriff. "He likes to be called New Orleans. It makes him think of the big city. Right, New Orleans?"

Catell stood up slowly but didn't answer.

"He don't answer," said another rancher, and they all looked at the sheriff. "Harry, he don't answer."

"He will." The sheriff pushed the men aside and stepped up to the door. He pulled out a large key and swung the door open. In the silence there was only the creak of the old floor and a soft swish as the sheriff unholstered his gun. Leveling the long revolver at Catell, he stood back with feet wide apart.

"Come out."

They all stood still, waiting.

"Come out, city feller."

Catell stepped forward slowly. His head was down and water dripped from his hair.

"Walk to that door."

Catell walked. He walked out of his cell, past the staring men, past the sheriff with his gun. Suddenly the sheriff kicked out his foot and Catell was flung to the floor. Shaking his wet head, he heard the guffaws of the men behind him.

"It don't pay being hasty, New Orleans." The sheriff roared again. "Lemme give you a hand."

Catell obeyed.

"The other hand, city feller."

He reached up his swollen hand automatically but jerked it back, afraid of the pain.

"Your hand, city feller."

Catell shrank back when the sheriff's foot caught him under the chin. His head snapped back and hit the floor with a sharp thump. He lay limp and unconscious.

The sheriff doubled over with loud, dry laughter, slapping his thigh.

"Hey, New Orleans!" Then he noticed that he laughed alone. The young deputy stood by, snickering; the ranchers looked embarrassed.

"We'll be goin' now, Harry. We got things to do."

"Sure, Harry. We'll be seeing you. So long, Harry."

They looked away and hurried out. They didn't look at Harry, or at the limp wet man on the floor, and they closed the door softly behind them.

The sheriff holstered his gun and gave the young deputy a mean look.

"Throw him in the cell. And mind, you stay around an' keep an eye on him. He bears watching." Then he walked out, hitting the floor hard with his heels.

When it was getting dark outside, Catell woke up. He breathed carefully, feeling the aches in his body. He heard dim voices from the porch. The door opened and the sheriff came in, followed by a few other men. Catell stiffened. This time, he swore, this time he'd kill the bastard, no matter what the consequences. But they didn't come his way. They stood talking in the front room and only the sheriff gave him a glance. He didn't smile or make a crack, he just gave Catell a cold stare.

They shuffled around the room, moving chairs and hanging up their hats.

"One of you gimme a hand," the sheriff said, and left the room with one of the men. Catell stood in his cell, suspicious, waiting for the next trick. That's when he heard the noise.

Outside his window in the deserted space behind the jail there was a rustling and the sound of low voices. Catell moved to the window slowly and leaned his arm on the sill. The darkness outside was almost complete and a cold breeze made him shiver in his moist shirt.

There they were, beside his car. The rear door was open, one figure had crawled into the back, and the other was leaning in, straining, as if lifting a great weight. When they hauled out the rear seat, Catell grasped the bars of the window. A stiff, sharp fear tensed his body and he trembled violently. The taut skin on his swollen hand cracked, but he didn't notice. He only saw the two figures carrying the rear seat of his car and then disappearing. In a few moments the door in the front of the jail opened and the two men came in, carrying the seat between them. They had removed the lead apron and presumably left it in the car. They put the seat on the floor. The sheriff said something about the damn weight of the thing and somebody answered with a joke, but Catell hardly heard. He sank down on the cot, feeble and numb with lost hope. How did they know? How had they found the place so fast?

Head down, hands limp between his knees, he sat not caring, not hearing the voices. Only a while later did he start to wonder what they were waiting for. In the other room the men were sitting around a flat box, talking in low voices, playing cards. Some sat on chairs, others on a bench, and the sheriff on Catell's car seat.

"Put up or shut up," said one of the players.

The sheriff was chewing on a cigar. He threw his cards down and said,

"Damn you, Shivers, I'm out."

Catell threw his head back and started to laugh. He laughed loud, hard, and with a shrill fury. When he looked again the sheriff was standing by the iron door, fumbling with the lock.

"Come out, you bastard." He flung the door open.

"Tell 'im, Harry. Tell 'im you don't always lose." The men laughed. They were looking toward the cell.

Catell got off his cot and walked to the open door with an arrogant swing, grinning. When the two men were face to face, the sheriff took one step backward. He crouched.

"All right, city feller, smile good. There won't be nothin' to smile at when I get through with you."

His voice was low and hoarse, but Catell kept grinning. He stood easily, never taking his eyes off the sheriff's face. Then he took one step closer to the sheriff. The sheriff hesitated a moment, shot a quick glance at the card players behind him, but he saw they weren't looking. The sheriff straightened up, his voice loud now.

"Try something, hog face. Go ahead!"

Catell just stood still, fixing the raging man with his eyes.

"Go ahead, you bastard. Hit me!" The sheriff's voice was cracking. His head was thrust out, the cords of his neck twitching, and slobber came through the hole in his teeth. Catell could feel the man's breath.

"Hit me!"

One of the players turned around.

"Harry, for chrissakes, pipe down."

"Come on, you yellow, no-good sonofabitch, hit me!"

"Harry, boy, stop that yelling." They kept on with the cards.

Catell didn't move a muscle. He stood still, a slight smile on his face, and his voice was even.

"Did you want something, Sheriff?"

"*Hit me!*" The sheriff's voice was a screech.

"Do we deal you in this time, Harry?" One man was shuffling the cards; another was lighting his cigar; some were arguing about the game. Catell stepped back into his cell and pulled the door shut. Then he sat down on his cot and looked at the ceiling.

"You're yellow, you bastard. You lousy, stinking sonofabitch of a bastard!" The sheriff was shaking the bars of the cell, his face red, his voice a harsh, rasping scream. "You no-good, chicken-livered bastard, you're yellow!" he screamed.

One of the men came up and took the sheriff by the arm. "Stop that yellin', Harry. We're trying to get a game started."

"Lemme at that bastard! I'll kill 'im, I tell ya, I'll kill 'im!"

"Now shut your mouth, damnit. Sit down over here and shut up. Else we take the game to Charlie's."

"Take your lousy game to hell for all I care. Leggo my arm. You're interfering with the law."

"Harry, for chrissakes—"

The men had stopped their playing and were standing around, undecided.

"Nobody interferes with the law around here, unnerstand? Nobody! I'm gonna teach that filthy jailbird a lesson he ain't gonna forget any too soon. And you guys, stick around if you wanna have some fun. Stick around and I'll show ya how to enforce the law around here."

But they weren't listening to his raving. One by one they took their hats and walked out of the door.

"We'll be at Charlie's if you want in," said the last one. "See ya, Harry."

The sheriff stood in the empty room. Panting, cursing under his breath, he kicked the door shut and walked around the empty chairs and boxes a few times. Then he sat down on the car seat. The sheriff's hunched figure moved only with his breathing, and there was an expectant glint in Catell's eyes as he watched him.

For a while nothing happened. In the silence the thudding of a moth against the bare light bulb made a noise like a wet rag. With an irritated motion the sheriff tore his hat off and flung it at the light. He missed. Catell snickered in his dark cell. The sheriff jumped around as if stung. He got up from the seat slowly and walked to a part of the room that Catell couldn't see. When he came back, he carried a six-shooter and a long stick.

Standing by the cell, he peered into the darkness. "City feller, did you say something?"

Catell snickered again. When the sheriff came toward him, kicking the cell door aside with his foot, Catell knew this was the pay-off. He also knew that the man at the door was a coward, dangerous because he was afraid, but weak because he was unsure.

"You want something, Sheriff?"

"Come over here with your hands up!"

Catell did.

"Now walk thataway, down the hall. Stop."

This suited Catell fine. They were alone and they could not be seen from the outside.

"And now, jailbird, turn around."

Catell turned, watching the sheriff, who stood in a crouch. Catell noticed that the gun hung loosely, but the hand that held the stick was tense, with knuckles white. The sheriff wasn't thinking of doing any killing; he was going to have some sport. Then later, maybe, if he could make it look like an escape…

"Just so we understand each other, jailbird, I'm about to make you over."

"Don't call me jailbird."

"What!" The sheriff leaned forward, startled by Catell's matter-of-fact tone. His face reddened and he sucked in his breath. "Are you telling me what to do? You talking back to me, jailbird?"

Catell didn't answer. He just watched the man, who was starting to tremble with rage.

"Say something, jailbird! Open that filthy mouth once more!" The sheriff prodded his stick at Catell.

At that instant Catell whipped out his hand and yanked at the stick. The sheriff, stiff with hate and fear, stumbled forward and caught Catell's foot under his jaw. The gun clattered against the wall. Catell reached for the man's ears and jerked hard, and both men spun to the floor. Before the sheriff could start to struggle, Catell's weight jammed the wind out of his chest and two thumbs dug painfully into his Adam's apple.

"Now I'm going to do the talking, Harry, and listen close. You called me a jailbird. Well, you're right. I can bust out of better jails than yours, but you aren't getting a thing on me that you can prove. So I'm sticking around a short while longer, but you better learn how to behave yourself. I want you to lay off, hear? I want you to lay off or else you're going to be the one that gets hurt. Because one day after I'm out of here, you're going to get a visit the likes of which you've never seen, except maybe in the movies. I got connections, Harry boy. I won't even come back here myself to make a cripple out of you for life. I know plenty of eager young boys who'd break your legs on my say-so, or dig your eyes out for a sawbuck. So lay off me, Harry boy, or haven't I made myself clear?"

Catell gave a sudden sharp squeeze to the sheriff's neck. Then he jumped up.

"Did I make myself clear?"

The sheriff, face blue, gasping for air, got up on one arm.

"Did I make myself clear?"

Catell kicked his foot at the man's arm, digging his toe painfully into a muscle.

"What's your answer, Harry?"

With an effort that made the tears shoot into his eyes, the sheriff gagged out a word: "Yes."

"That's fine, Harry. Now, I'm going back to my cell. I'm expecting a good night's sleep, so keep your voice down and step lightly. But lightly, Harry boy."

Then Catell walked to the toilet. He washed his hands, dried them, and threw the towel on the floor. The nail on which the towel had been hanging was big and loose. Catell pulled it out and stuck it in his pocket. Then he went to his cell, clanked the door shut, and stretched out on his cot.

After a little while the sheriff came by. There still was a heavy wheezing in his throat and he didn't look right or left. He sat down heavily on Catell's car seat, arms folded, looking like a man in deep thought. When the front door opened, he hardly turned his head.

"Say, Harry, you comin' over to the game? We're movin' to Rodney's place."

"Beat it."

The man hesitated, then put his hand on the doorknob.

"Just thought I'd let you know. Rodney's place, case you change your mind." He went out.

In the middle of the night Catell woke from the throbbing in his hand. Sitting up, he saw that the light in the room up front was still burning. The sheriff, head sunk on his chest, sat asleep on the car seat. Catell saw it and laughed to himself.

The next morning Catell woke early, uncomfortable and stiff. The sheriff was still asleep on the seat, and Catell laughed again.

During the next week nobody moved the car seat. It stood in the middle of the room, and ranchers dropped around and sat in the seat, and the sheriff sat there. The sheriff used the seat every day, sitting around brooding or looking out the door.

Catell was left alone. He busied himself with the nail he had taken from the toilet, bending it and flattening one end as best he could. Nobody paid much attention to the prisoner, least of all the sheriff, who acted dull and sickish. The day he threw up the first time, Catell finished with his nail. That same evening the sheriff had a sharp headache and bad cramps in his stomach. Catell laughed.

The next morning when the sheriff came to the jailhouse feeling weak and nervous he found Catell's cell empty and a crooked nail on the floor by the door. He saw that the car seat had been moved. Some stuffing was strewn around the floor and there was a big, empty hole in the seat.

Chapter Eight

By the time Catell hit Los Angeles he was broke. He got out of the Greyhound at the Sixth Street station, wearing a wrinkled suit, a dirty shirt, and a two-day growth of beard. He had lost his tan and a lot of weight. Catell didn't look so good.

The station was full of bums and drifters trying to keep out of the cold night air. Catell got lost in the crowd easily. Once he was sure that nobody was looking for him, he went outside and turned toward Main. With his hands in his pocket he jingled some coins, counting them for the thousandth time. Ninety-eight cents. About eighty miles out of Los Angeles he had buried his gold where nobody would look for it. Catell thought about his gold, $20,160 worth. He jingled his coins again. He was broke.

Main Street was twice as windy as Sixth and Catell turned up the collar of his suit. When he came to a bar he went in. The narrow room was full of smoke, sour and thick. But it was warm. At the far end of the counter where they sold hamburgers and coffee, Catell sat down. The grill made a greasy warmth. Catell ordered coffee.

On one side of him a shrill-looking whore was eating a doughnut that left sugar grains sticking to her lipstick. On the other side two bums were making a coffee royal with gin. Behind him people were pushing by to go to the john or to get out of the draft from the door. Catell felt a slight pressure at his pocket. His hand reached back fast; his fingers closed around a wrist. An embarrassed face peered at him when Catell turned.

"Pardon me, mister. A natural mistake."

"Your last, dippy." Catell grabbed for the small man's shirt front.

"Tony!"

"For chrissakes, if it isn't the Turtle!"

"Well, Tony!"

"Not so loud, not so loud."

They looked at each other, grinning, not knowing exactly what to do next.

"How about my wrist, Anthony feller? How about letting me recuperate my wrist?"

Catell let go and grinned. "You're losing your touch, Turtle. You're not doing so good."

"You may have a message there, Anthony. Indeed, indeed." And then in a serious tone: "Just rusty, Anthony. I'm in semi-retirement, you know."

Catell grinned at the Turtle and looked him up and down. The small man had a tight suit on, pepper and salt, but it was a good one. His pointed shoes looked scuffed, but they were expensive. As always, the Turtle's shirt was too large at the neck. Catell didn't remember the time when the Turtle's skinny neck had had a collar to fit it. But that wasn't the only reason for his name. He had a face like a turtle's: a nose and forehead shaped in a humpy curve, a thin long mouth with a chin that made a flat angle, and round eyes without lashes. The Turtle had a way of looking dreamy or astonished or dumb, and any one of these expressions was an asset in his trade.

"Semi-retirement, huh? That why you're picking on a bum like me?"

"Now, Anthony. I was just practicing. Just practicing, you understand. Coming out of winter retirement, so to speak."

"How about retiring your hand out of my pocket?"

The Turtle gave him his dumb expression, then the astonished one. He pulled his hand out of Catell's pocket and looked at it. There was ninety-eight cents in it.

"You ain't retiring, I notice."

"Just a little short this minute."

"Don't kid your old friend, Tony. You look strapped."

"Nothing to worry about. I got a deal on."

"Like eight years ago?"

"No, not like eight years ago. Never again."

"O.K., O.K., friend. I was just making merry."

"So sit down, Turtle, talk to me."

But the Turtle didn't sit.

"What time is it?"

"Eleven."

"Eleven. Recline here for a minute, Anthony. Don't move I'll be back in a shiver, so don't move. Promise."

"O.K., I'll be here."

The Turtle squeezed through the crowd and went out.

"I couldn't help hearin' you, friend," said the whore one seat down. "You sure all you got is ninety-eight cents?" She smiled, licking the sugar from her lips.

"What's it to you?"

"Just warmhearted interest. If you're broke, I thought you may be needing a flop. If you're not," and she cocked a hip, "I got another idea."

"Save it."

Catell turned his back to the woman. He could feel her looking at him and he got uncomfortable. When he turned around she caught his eye and winked.

"Cut out the kid stuff. I'm not interested."

"I wasn't trying to give you any kid stuff."

"Save it!"

"I've been!"

"Well, I don't want it."

Catell started to look for a cigarette, but before he could shake one from the pack the whore pulled one out of her purse and handed it to him. When she leaned over the V of her blouse opened up and Catell got a good look.

"Thanks."

"Don't thank me for that, baby. I got something better to offer."

"I ain't buying."

But the woman didn't give up. She swiveled on the stool and swung her leg slowly against Catell.

"Who's talkin' of buying, baby?"

Catell got impatient, but before he had opened his mouth a voice said: "Is this lady annoying you?"

They both turned and saw the Turtle. He was wearing the dumb expression. Then he said, "Blow, lady."

"Now, listen here, runt—"

"Lady, blow. No lovers' quarrels, puleeze."

"Tell this creep to go away," she said to Catell.

The Turtle put a hand on her shoulder and spoke in a confidential tone. "Sweet, you're making too many mistakes. My friend and me are a couple of fairies, and very much in love. We're gettin' wedded tonight and no bridesmaids. So, puleeze, lady, drag outa here."

The whore gasped at the Turtle and then looked at Catell. She made an offensive sound, got up, and strutted away.

The Turtle sat down next to Catell and waved to the short-order man. "Vegetable soup, two scrambled with ham, side of fries, apple pie a la mode, glass of milk, coffee. For my friend here. For me, a spot of tea."

"Now, listen, Turtle—"

"Shut up. You're broke, I ain't."

"Turtle, not the milk."

"Shut it, Anthony. Milk's good, and you look like hell."

"You don't kid me, Turtle. You don't look so hot yourself."

The Turtle didn't answer. He pulled bills out of various pockets and folded them together. Then he stuck the money away.

"You were speaking to me, Anthony?"

"Where'd that come from, all of a sudden?"

"Where else?"

"You were only gone about fifteen minutes."

"A master does not need time, only opportunity."

"Opportunity on Main Street, L.A. Don't tell me!"

"I did the movie crowd on Broadway. Deceived by the balmy breezes of our daytime weather, few citizens were wearing coats tonight. A true blessing to the likes of me and the likes of your empty stomach. Now stop crapping and eat."

Catell ate and they didn't talk for a while. The Turtle sipped his tea, trying to look elegant with one finger sticking out. He was very proud of his delicate hands, but when he sipped the tea, he made a loud, slurpy sound with his mouth. When Catell was on his coffee, he lit a cigarette and leaned his elbows on the counter.

"Well, Turtle, say something."

"I can tell you feel better. You say something."

"What?"

"What's the big deal you got on?"

"The big deal. I need a little help, Turtle. You want in?"

"If it's within my interests, count me in."

"Is money?"

"Anthony, count me in."

"Like I said, Turtle, I need some assist. The deal is all done with, except I got to unload the swag here in town and I don't know my way around."

"Nothing's easier, Tony. Just name the name and I find. By the way, anybody looking for you?"

"Yeah, the Feds."

"Oi! They know you're here?"

"That's one of the things you gotta find out for me."

"Will do. What are they after?"

"Big-time stuff, Turtle."

"A lot of cash in it, huh?"

"Not really. Not that much, but it's big-time, Turtle, and I pulled it off neat. No hitch so far."

"Dope?"

"Naw. Gold."

"You mean—you mean a solid, pure block of it? Nothing but gold?

"Uh-huh."

Turtle closed his eyes and hummed through his lips, low and long. "Now, that kind of merchandise, Anthony, you can sell *anywhere*."

"No, that's just it. It turns out the stuff is radioactive or something. Some kind of rays that get to you, because it was accidentally exposed to one of those atom piles. It makes you sick."

"That sick I'd like to be."

"Anyway, I don't know the details. All I know is there may be a contact for the stuff in this town."

"Who?"

"Smith. S. S. Smith, I think."

"Oi! Contact, he says. Smith ain't no contact, Tony boy. Smith is it!"

"All right, fine. Where is he?"

"Where is he? Where is he, he says." Turtle clapped his hands around his throat. "Now listen, Tony. I want you to understand something. Nobody goes and sees Smith. Smith sends for the people he wants to see, and that ain't many."

"All right, stop with the courtesies. You sound like the Chamber of Commerce. Where is Smith?"

"Tony, to tell the truth, I ain't sure. Who told ya, anyway?"

"Some guy back in Detroit. He was bragging about his big-shot contacts and out slipped the name. So from then on I didn't need the guy back in Detroit, see?"

"Yeah, I see. You ever deal with the syndicate before, Tony?"

"No. Why?"

"I'm trying to tell ya. They are big, complicated, like a corporation. Like a government. You don't just walk in, you see. They got red tape to go through."

"Just how big is this Smith?"

"Locally, very big."

"The biggest?"

"No—not for sure, anyway."

"All right, Turtle, when do I find this big shot?"

"Lemme find out for sure, Tony, willya? Lemme listen around, get everything set up, and then we make our pitch."

"Nuts to that. I gotta get this thing over with. Ninety-eight cents isn't even life-size these days."

"I'll stake ya, Tony. You gotta play the angles a little in this town before you get anyplace. Like for instance, your suit looks like hell. You need new shoes."

"You said you'd stake me."

"Sure, sure, but give it time."

"I'm going to find that guy tomorrow, Turtle, with you or without you."

"All right, I give up. There's a machine shop on Victory Boulevard in Burbank. The Quentin Machine Company. Try there. Smith's got an office in the back there. Maybe you're in luck. Does he know you're coming?"

"Might be. I don't know."

"Whaddaya mean ya don't know?"

"That guy in Detroit. He might or he might not have passed the word. I don't know."

"Anthony, you're looking more stupid to me by the minute. Either—"

"Can it. I'm going tomorrow. What I need from you is a few bucks to get a shirt and a press job. Also, keep your ears open about those Feds. Also, I want to know everything you can get ahold of about my deal with Smith. If I can make a deal with Smith tomorrow, I want to know how they feel about it, who's in on it, et cetera. The works, hear?"

"I hear."

"Can you do it?"

"Anthony, you are looking at the original underground kid. I get to know everything."

"You sound better already. From here on in, Turtle, you and me hit the big time. With this job out of the way, I got a career ahead of me. Shake?"

"Shake. And now, mine Anthony, how about the last cup of mud and we blow?"

"Let's just blow. I gotta find a flop yet."

"Flop? Anthony! Cart that thought outen your vocabulary. It so happens I got an extra corner in my room, and you're staying with me. On second thought, you look too tacky for the likes of my accommodations. First I take you to a Turkish bath. Whilst you melt your tackiness with steam and soap, I get your suit done over and fetch a new shirt. And underwear?"

"Yeah. Underwear. And socks."

"And socks. Only then, Anthony, will we be off to my chamber and a good night's rest. Ready?"

"Let's go."

They left the bar and walked a few blocks to the Turkish bath. As they went up the stairs, the flashy whore from the bar was coming down. She stopped swinging her hips and leaned against the wall to let them pass. The Turtle stopped next to her and chucked the woman under the chin.

"You work here too, honey?"

She made that nasty sound with her lips again.

"Whyn't you go blow?" she said.

"Precisely," and with a busy look on his face the Turtle ran up the stairs after Catell.

In the small lobby Catell took the Turtle aside. "What the hell is this place, coeducational?"

"Whassa matter, Anthony, you prejudiced or something?"

"I want a steam bath and a wash is all."

"If that's what you pay for, that's all you get. Now stop worrying about the opposition sex and let's have those raggedy garnishments you're wearing."

A little later the Turtle left with Catell's suit and shoes. Catell took a steam bath, showered and shaved, and after his massage he went to the locker room. An attendant brought him his pressed suit, clean socks, underwear, and a new shirt. His shoes were polished.

"Your friend left 'em, with a note."

Catell read the note: "Dear Anthony. Got tired of waiting. When done come to my place," and then there was an address. It was signed, "T."

Catell got dressed and combed his hair. He was feeling good. In the mirror he noticed that his shirt collar was a little big. Either he had lost more weight than he'd realized or the Turtle was constitutionally incapable of buying a shirt that would fit anyone.

Outside, Catell walked fast to keep from shivering. After a few blocks he came to the address on the Turtle's note and walked in. It was a narrow apartment house converted into a hotel, gloomy and crowded-looking. But it was warm inside. Catell went past the clerk, past a pimply bellhop who was sleeping in a swivel chair, and walked up to the second floor. He stopped before the door with the number 206. Then he heard the movement inside. There was a slight rustle and a low voice. Two voices. The mumbling stopped. Catell stood frozen in the still corridor, a curse twisting his face. What had gone wrong?

He turned carefully and started to walk back to the stairwell when a door at the end of the dim corridor creaked. He flattened himself against the wall, his blood throbbing under his skull. The door clicked shut and a figure came toward the stairwell. It was a man. He looked like a bum, but so what? Then the man turned down the stairs, never looking in Catell's direction. Licking his dry lips, Catell started to move when the voice behind 206 started to mumble again. Then there was a cackling laugh—the Turtle's laugh. Catell pushed open the door and looked in. There was no light in the room, just the red reflection from a gas heater that stood near one wall. The light showed the bare legs of a woman who was shaking a skirt down over her head, and it showed the droopy pajamas of a short man. When Catell clicked the door shut, the Turtle turned around, looking surprised.

"Why, Tony, we thought you'd never come. Didn't we, sweetness?"

The woman had the skirt down now and pulled the zipper over her hip. She was still naked from the waist up, her big breasts making a billowing shadow on the wall. She turned and Catell recognized the whore from the bar.

"For chrissakes, you again?"

"It's destiny," said the Turtle. "I always say, don't try to buck destiny. What do you say, Millie?"

"I say, speaking of a buck—" and she planted her hands on her hips and looked hard at the Turtle.

After the Turtle had given her a bill she picked up her brassiere and slipped the straps over her shoulders. She did it slowly, looking at Catell with a mean look on her face. Catell didn't think she looked so bad at all, and he leaned back in his chair. He fumbled for a cigarette, looking at the woman in the red light from the heater. She pulled the cups of the brassiere around her breasts and arched her back to hook the clasp. Catell noticed how the big shadow on the wall had changed shape. Then he looked back at her.

"One more look and you pay," she said to Catell.

He grinned.

"Throw me my blouse, Daisy," she said.

Catell threw her the thin blouse. She put it on and Catell watched how it buttoned tight across the front.

"Now the shoes. Under your chair, Mary."

"You don't need 'em," Catell said.

"The shoes, Mary. I'm a respectable woman. I wear shoes."

"The hell with the shoes. You look more sexy with your feet naked."

"Come on, faggot, the shoes," and she stamped her foot.

"Do that again, baby. It makes you wiggle so nice." Catell grinned at her. She came at him with mouth curled back over her teeth and her loose hair flying. When she reached out to claw at him, Catell caught her wrists and pinned her arms to her sides. Trying to wrench free, she popped a button and the blouse fell open.

"I get more cooperation from that button than I get from you," he said.

"I told ya I'm a respectable woman," she hissed, kicking at him.

The Turtle had picked up his bathrobe and was just opening the door to go out.

"Leave some dough on the table. Millie's going to earn it." Catell leaned over to reach her mouth and she bit him. He jerked back and laughed. "Millie's gonna make whoopee with a fruitcake, ha, Millie?"

The door shut behind the Turtle and Catell reached for the woman's straps. She stepped back fast, knocking his hands out of the way and lashing at his face. Her nails cut a fine line of blood down his cheek and her other hand caught him flat on the nose. Catell stumbled back, cursing, and fell over the chair. When he looked up she was standing near the rim of the red reflection. Her skirt was a heap on the floor, and the light made dim patterns on her bare legs and belly. Then the blouse fell off, and the brassiere. When the woman was naked she came at him again, but she didn't try to scratch this time.

Chapter Nine

Catell left for Burbank at nine in the morning. For the next five hours he shuffled back and forth in one bus after another, missing stops, rooting around for a connection, letting a bus go by to catch a bite at a street stand. By the middle of the day the hot sun had brewed up a smog that burned in Catell's eyes and made the inside of his nose feel like shoe leather. When he got out on Victory and found the Quentin Machine Company, he was grimy with sweat and sore.

Inside the shop it felt hotter than outside. A couple of big fans swished the oily air around so that the draft made you feel prickly with dirt.

"Yes, sir, you lookin' for somethin'?"

A thin man in clean, starched suntans came up to Catell and stopped in front of him.

"I'm looking for Smith," Catell said.

The thin guy took his rimless glasses off, put them back on again, and patted himself on his bald head. Catell noticed how the man looked dry all over. Why didn't that bastard sweat like everybody else?

"We got two Smiths here. Kind of a common name, I guess. Which Smith you innerested in?"

"S. Smith."

"Sherman!" the man yelled. "Come here once."

A man who had been working on a drill press came down the aisle between the machines and looked at Catell.

"Yeah?"

"You S. Smith?" Catell asked.

"Yeah. Who are you? Do I know you?"

"I just came in from Detroit. Friend of Paar's."

"Paar? You got the wrong guy, feller. I don't know no Paar."

"Sorry, my mistake," Catell said. "Perhaps the other Smith is the one I want." He turned back to the man in suntans.

"Might be, except that he ain't here today. Hurt his hand on the shaper. Hot chips, ya know, burned a hole right in his arm. You go back, Sherman. Guess you're the wrong guy."

Catell watched the machinist walk back to his drill press. That wasn't the Smith he wanted, and his Smith hadn't got hurt working on a shaper, either.

"There's another Smith here," Catell said. "He doesn't work on a machine. He's got an office here and I want to see him."

"Well, now, I'm the foreman here and there's no other Smith works here. Who're you, anyway?"

"Where's the office?"

"I guess you didn't hear me, mister. What's your name and business?"

Catell gave the foreman a bland look. "I guess you didn't hear me, either. Where's the office?"

"Mister, I don't need to tell you anything, but just to get rid of you, I got my desk right over yonder." He pointed to a windowless corner with a desk and files separated from the rest of the shop by some badly tacked beaverboard.

"There's another office. Where is it?" Catell took a step.

The thin guy in suntans stuck his arm out and held Catell by the lapels. "No further, mister." He pulled Catell close.

The two men stared at each other, almost nose to nose.

"Tell me, foreman, how come you don't sweat?"

The man didn't answer.

"I said, how come you don't sweat?" Catell jabbed two fingers into the man's stomach.

The foreman let go of Catell's lapels. "You lookin' for trouble, mister, you got it." Wheezing in his throat, he swung at Catell with a flabby roundhouse. Catell just stepped back, right into the arms of two machinists. They twisted Catell's arms in opposite directions and, with his feet hardly touching the ground, walked him to the rear of the shop.

There was another door there. Through the tool crib and past a noisy pump motor there was another office. The foreman opened the door, the two machinists gave a light push, and Catell stumbled into the room. The foreman kicked the door shut and Catell couldn't hear the pump motor any more. He suddenly felt pleasantly cool.

Aside from the soundproofing and the air conditioning, there was nothing special about the room. White composition walls, a leatherette couch, a small desk with three phones, no windows. The light came from fluorescent fixtures in the ceiling.

"Don't try anything, mister. You and I ain't alone here."

"I figured we weren't," Catell said. He got off the floor and watched the foreman go through another door. Catell sat down on the couch. He couldn't hear a sound except for the faint humming of the air conditioning. Then the foreman came back. Without bothering to look at Catell he walked past and out through the soundproofed door. A while later the inner door opened again.

The man was well built and well tailored. He had glossy hair and his mouth was very red. If this was a syndicate man, Catell figured him for one of those smart young kids who came up fast because he knew how to take orders without questions, and how to follow through without scruples.

Tailor-made stopped opposite Catell and gave him a dead look.

"What's your name?"

"What's yours?"

For a second the dead look came alive and Catell thought the guy was going to jump him, but then he relaxed and sat on the edge of the desk.

"You got this wrong, Blue Lips," he said. "I don't answer, I ask. And you, Blue Lips, you answer what I ask. Now, what's your name?"

"If you're Smith, I'll talk. If not, I don't talk."

"I'm Smith, Blue Lips. Mr. Smith, that is."

"O.K. My name's Catell. Tony Catell. I got your name from a friend of mine in Detroit. Paar's his name. If you got the time, I'd like to talk to you about something."

"I got the time, Blue Lips. Talk."

Catell didn't like the way things were going, and the tailor-made punk was getting under his skin. What made Catell really hot was the fact that he'd been had. This punk wasn't S. S. Smith any more than the foreman had been a big shot. No big shot talked tough like a punk.

"Call me that name once more and the next time you look in the shaving mirror you won't recognize the face you see. Now where's Smith?"

Catell noticed that the guy didn't move after the speech. He saw him go stiff and his chin started to quiver, as if he wanted to cry. He didn't cry, though. The next thing Catell saw was the business end of a banker's special, and Tailor-made was holding it. He was holding it very steady.

"What name you talking about, Blue Lips?" His voice sounded very gentle.

Catell looked at the steady gun and then there was the sound of shoes creaking. The gun came closer. It was very still in the room, just the slow creak of the new shoes. Catell's shirt felt wet and clammy on his back, and he started to rise.

"Go ahead, Blue Lips. You can get up if you want." That voice was as smooth as silk.

Then it was very quiet again. The shoes had stopped creaking, the gun was very close. Suddenly there was a sharp, nasty sound, loud like a splintering tree. The gun was cocked now. Cold with sweat, Catell looked up at the man's face. The lidded eyes looked soft, the mouth was lax and very red, and nothing moved but the chin, still quivering. Then Catell saw the man's neck. It was a smooth neck, and with a weird fascination Catell could see how the neck was swelling. Slowly it started to bulge over the starched collar and a thick vein grew under the skin, like a glistening worm.

Then the mouth moved and the soft voice said, "Now, Blue Lips?"

"Now what, gentlemen?"

They both jumped. A portly man stood by the inner door, his short arms folded across his front, and he was smiling around a cigar.

There was no emotion in the way the gunman moved. He stepped back slowly, turned his head toward the open door, and slipped the gun very smoothly under his tailor-made jacket.

"Mr. Smith," he said. "I didn't know you were there."

"I know," Mr. Smith said. "I was just watching."

Catell wasn't taking the whole thing so lightly. When the gun had disappeared he had suddenly felt very weak. He sank back on the couch, wiping the sweat from his face. He noticed that his hands were shaking when he dropped them back to his lap. There was a fine sharp pain running up his arm from his left hand. There, on the back of it, he saw the reddish skin of the healed wound where the sheriff had sapped him. Only the skin wasn't all healed. It had cracked again and a little dark blood was running out.

"Did you hurt Mr.—ah, Mr.—?" Smith looked concerned.

"I didn't touch him. His name's Catell."

"Is this true, Mr. Catell?"

"You Smith?" Catell was back on his feet, but his voice had a sudden crack in it.

"*Mr.* Smith," said the punk. He stepped up to Catell and grabbed him by the lapels. "The name to you is *Mr.* Smith," and he jerked the lapels hard. Catell didn't try to resist. His head had started to spin and he felt like a rag. Then his strength came back as suddenly as it had gone, but now Smith had come up close.

"You may stop that," he said to the gunman, and there was a hint of coldness in his voice. "And you, sir, I'm sure you will overlook our hot-blooded friend. Would you care to introduce yourself properly now?"

Catell shook his jacket back into shape and ran his fingers through his hair.

"Sure. As your friend said, my name's Catell. Tony Catell. A friend of mine in Detroit—"

"Paar," said Smith. "Yes, I've heard of you. And you wanted to speak to me?"

"If you got the time."

"Come in, come in. There's been too much ceremony already, so let's sit down and get to it." He laughed with a short, hiccuppy gurgle.

The inner office was larger than the anteroom, but it looked much smaller, full with a large desk, couch, chairs, files, and telephones.

Smith sat down behind the desk and Catell settled himself into an easy chair. Tailor-made put his hand on the back of the chair, the knuckles touching Catell's shoulder.

Smith looked at Catell with a winning smile on his round face, and Catell looked back at Smith, trying to get his bearings. For a while nobody said anything.

"Well, Catell, let me help you along. I understand from your good friend Paar that you have something to sell. Now you, of course, know nothing about me, except that I'm a friend of Paar's, that I do business on the West Coast, and that I might be able to help you. Now then, what's your story?"

"How about Monkey Boy here? How about him getting the hell outa here?"

"Oh, well now," said Smith, and he made benign sounds.

Catell turned around in his seat, looking up at the gunman. They stared at each other without moving.

Smith said, "You were saying, Catell?"

"I wasn't saying anything. And I'm not saying anything, Smith, unless Monkey Boy gets out."

A knuckle dug into Catell's shoulder from behind and the gentle voice said, "It's *Mr.* Smith, Blue Lips."

Catell jumped up, kicking the chair backward. It didn't move much, but the gunman stumbled. Half crouched, he was reaching into his jacket when Catell gave the chair another kick. The back of the chair slapped the gunman's knees, making him buckle again. With the edge of his hand Catell knifed down on the man's neck, jamming his face down against the top of the chair. But when the man rolled over, half on the floor now, the gun was in his hand and coming up fast.

"Enough!" Smith's voice was sharp.

Catell saw that the gun stopped moving instantly and then disappeared again under the jacket.

"In fact, I think you'd better leave. I won't need you now. I feel Mr. Catell and I will get along quite nicely. I can reach you at the club?"

"Sure, Mr. Smith." The gunman got off the floor. His face was soft and calm. Without looking at Catell he turned and went out. Catell noticed he was carrying his head at a slight angle.

"I'm sorry you had this little brush," Smith said. "Topper is a very fine young man. A little too exacting sometimes, but perhaps for that reason particularly valuable to me."

There was a noticeable undertone in Smith's words, the kind of tone that Catell would ordinarily resent. But he hadn't caught it. He'd caught only the name Topper, and there was a thin twitch in Catell's left cheek. He ran a hand over his face and sat down again.

"Do you know what I'm selling, Smith?"

"No, I have no idea. I am interested, though, because of Paar's—ah—recommendation. He doesn't phone me too often, but he did feel obliged to tell me about you. What are you selling, Catell?"

"Gold."

Smith didn't answer right away. He just sat with his hands folded, smiling at Catell.

"Did you say gold? Plain gold?"

"Yeah, plain gold."

There was another silence while Smith pulled his lower lip and looked at Catell with that smile.

"Let's understand each other, Catell," he said finally. "What you have isn't plain gold. It's radioactive gold."

Catell didn't back down under the voice. He leaned forward in his chair and looked at Smith with a plain, hostile stare. "All I know for sure is I got gold. Maybe it's radioactive, maybe it isn't. When it's radioactive, the stuff makes you sick, doesn't it? Well, I'm not sick. I've had it with me for a while now and I'm O.K."

"You still have the gold then?"

"I've got it."

"Have you seen it lately?"

"I've got it and I want to sell it."

Smith swiveled his chair to face in the opposite direction. With head back, he sat like that for several minutes, thinking. There were a lot of things that Smith knew about. He knew about business, about organizing men, about demand and supply, he even knew about scientific things. When he'd organized his territory for prostitution, he'd got together information on incidence of venereal disease, on percentages of income groups patronizing whorehouses. When he'd heard about Catell's heist, he'd studied the properties of radioactive substances, gold in particular. What he was not sure about was whether the gold had actually been made radioactive. Scientists and FBI men were the worst sources of information.

"So you say you have this gold, eh, Catell?"

"Look, Smith, like you said, let's understand each other. Either you want it or you don't. Say no, and I leave. Say yes, and we talk terms."

For just a moment Smith didn't move at all. Then he leaned forward on the desk and chuckled with a wet sound. "Catell, I like that. Of course I believe you. Not only because you are that kind of man, but also because, after all, there's no percentage in your lying to me. In fact—But let it go. So you want to sell your gold. I want to buy it. How much have you and how much do you want?"

"I got thirty-six pounds—regular pounds like in weighing machines, not troy pounds. At thirty-five dollars a troy ounce, that comes to twenty thousand, one hundred and sixty dollars. On the market, I understand, it's worth more. About twenty-eight thousand. I'll give it to you for twenty even. Well?"

"Mr. Catell, I'd like to help you, but that's more than I can pay."

"Whaddaya mean, more than you can pay? You broke or something?"

Smith hiccupped and gurgled his laugh for a while and then stopped abruptly.

"No, Catell, it's not that I'm broke. I'm experienced, though, and while I've never handled this large a piece of gold, I predict it's not going to be easy to move. Please don't interrupt. You want to tell me that lump gold is one of the easiest things to move. Perhaps. But are you forgetting that this stuff may have radioactive properties? And even if it doesn't, it still has that reputation. All in all, Catell, the circumstances of the entire deal you pulled tend to limit the number of potential customers quite radically. And that, you know, means more work for me, more risk, and therefore less money for you."

"How much less?"

"Twelve thousand dollars."

Catell jumped out of his chair and leaned over Smith's desk. "Smith," he said, "why don't you go drop dead?" Then he straightened up and started to turn.

"Wait a minute. Sit down, Catell. Now, look. The least you should get out of this is some good advice. How long have you been out of stir?"

"Two months."

"And you act like it. I can see your point of view. Here you get out, pull a brilliant piece of work, and naturally expect your recognition. Well, times have been changing. First of all, your lone-wolf type of operation doesn't mean so much anymore. We work by organization these days. Secondly, things have got tight. In money and everything else. Did you know Slater, biggest fence operation in the Frisco area? Well, he's locked away. Or Jensen in New Orleans, imports and exports, if you know what I mean? He got life. And so it goes. Let me advise you, Catell, count your friends, take your pay, and learn to play ball."

"I know one thing, Smith: You're offering me less than that crook Paar. How do you account for that?"

"Catell, please." Smith sounded pained. "Personally, I like you. In fact, knowing your quality of work, I respect you. Well, look, Catell. What do you say to fifteen thousand? I'm honestly trying to help you. What do you say?"

"No."

"No? Catell, you've got to wake up. There's nothing else that anybody can do for you. You're lucky you came to me, because even though you may not know it, I'm taking a personal interest in you. And do you want to know why? Because, like I said, I admire your work. I have good men in my organization, believe me, but they aren't artists. In fact, artists are getting few and far between. So, call it sentimental if you want, I'd like to do you a good turn. However, you're asking too much, Catell, way too much."

Catell had been sucking on a cigarette, only half listening to Smith buttering him up. What did the bastard want from him?

"Listen, Catell, I just had an idea. Ah, have you ever considered working for us?"

"I've had bad moments like that, Smith, but I'm not having one now. Right now, I'm trying to talk a deal with you, nothing else."

"So am I, Catell, so am I. By the way, you're broke, aren't you?"

"I'm getting by."

"Sure. Just about. Are you getting by enough to say no to five hundred down?"

"Down for what?"

"Here's what I have in mind, Catell. You want to move your swag? Fine. You want to move it at your price? Fine again. I'll give you what you ask, twenty thousand. But as I've been trying to explain, Catell, I'll be overpaying you. So it's no more than a square deal for you to trade me something else. I'm talking about your experience, Catell. Now, shut up a minute. I don't want you to underestimate yourself, because you have something we can use. I'm not asking you to come in with us. Just hiding out, I'd call it. So here's the deal: I give you twenty thousand for the gold, and you come in on one deal we've got coming up. What's more, we'll pay you for your services, and as a friend, here's five hundred down."

Smith leaned back in his chair and looked at Catell, putting a hopeful smile on his face.

"It's no good, Smith. All I want to do is sell my swag."

Smith's smile dropped, but he didn't look disappointed. He just said, "Take it or leave it, Catell."

There was a cold silence. Catell knew that aside from a slight blow to his pride, nobody was getting hurt in this deal. If Smith was on the level. Smith just had to be on the level. Guys like him paid for services rendered and that was that. And then there was five hundred cash, more cash to come, and all this on top of finally moving the gold.

"When do I get the cash for my gold?"

"After the other deal."

The bastard!

"And what's my cut for the other deal?"

"A flat fifteen hundred. No cut out of the swag. Just a flat fifteen hundred. After all, Catell—"

"Plus five hundred now?"

"Minus, Catell. Five hundred now, a thousand after the heist, and the gold deal after that. I'm trying to be generous with you, Catell, really I am." Smith took a stack of bills out of his desk. He flapped them back and forth against one hand, smiling again.

"All right, Smith, it's a deal."

They both got to their feet. They shook hands, exchanged a silent look, and then Smith gave the bundle of notes to Catell. The wrapper was still on them, and it said "$500."

"I'm sure you won't regret this, Catell, and I'm glad to have you working for me."

"I'll do my job, Smith."

"Of course you will. Call me in two days and we'll get together for the briefing. The whole job should be duck soup for you."

"And now," said Catell, "I'll have me a go at this town. And a few clothes would be in order. By the way, what's that club you mentioned before?"

"The Pink Shell. Topper runs it for me."

"That figures."

"Now, there are some other places you probably haven't seen yet. The Hideaway, or the—"

"Pink Shell sounds fine, Smith. Where is it?"

"You go out to Malibu. Do you know the way to Santa Barbara? It's on that highway, just the other side of Malibu. A very nice place, Catell, you can have a lot of fun there—that is, if you stay friends with Topper. And I might mention, Catell, I don't like quarrels in my organization."

"Listen, Smith, I only—"

"Of course, you're just here to help me out with one little job, so all this talk is really unnecessary. But while you're here, Catell, try to keep clear of Topper, eh?"

"Sure, Smith, sure. I'm not going out there to see Topper."

For the rest of the day Catell kept thinking of the Pink Shell and what he thought he might find there.

Chapter Ten

Chief Jones watched the teletype ticking out the end of Herron's sentence: "…therefore requesting your decision for possible change in present plan."

Jones tore the sheet off the machine, looked at it again, and then stepped over to the window. The St. Louis traffic was crawling along four stories down, and Jones wondered what he would do if he had to find the person with the brown hat who was just crossing against the light, and if he could ever get anywhere with his strategies, scientific methods, trained agents, and what have you, unless of course he had an informer to steer him the right way. Perhaps that man in the brown hat who was now turning the corner by the newsstand was Catell. Or perhaps Jack Herron in Los Angeles wasn't having any success, not even a false steer, because Catell was dead someplace, dead from radiation, or starvation, or too much liquor, or too many women.

If only they knew a little more about the man. He'd been operating for years and years, he'd been caught three times, but he'd never been so successful or so menacing or so crazy that the name Anthony Catell had meant a whole lot. Catell worked fast, like an expert, and then he'd disappear. He had probably pulled twice as many jobs as he'd ever been suspected of having pulled. Not a very encouraging train of thought. Or let's say Catell is dead; then what?

The teletype started chattering again and Jones walked over. "…dead man in ravine next to abandoned car. No license plates. Initial check indicates car driven from Detroit. Age of deceased estimated 85. Cause of death, heart failure."

The thing was sent by the Indiana State Police and there was a brief reference to the FBI's request that all unusual or unexplained deaths and hospital admittances be reported.

No need to jump at that one. Jones had been getting the lowdown on the death of every bum from here to Hudson Bay and he was beginning to wonder how soon they would all die out.

The machine started to clank again but Jones barely gave it a look. "Diagnosis probable," it said, and then Jones was back at the teletype, watching the letters creep out. "Admitted 6 A.M., Winslow General Hospital, Winslow, Arizona." Then it gave the name of the patient, a sheriff in a small desert town.

He was alive. Catell was alive and Herron's first guess might still be right. Jones looked at both messages again. Michigan car abandoned in

Indiana. No plates. That would be like Catell. Then he appeared to have shown up in Arizona, making the southerly swing through all the rural stretches he could find. Maybe Mexico next? They would take care of that, and Herron… Leave Herron in Los Angeles.

Chief Jones sent a message to Herron and stepped back to the window. He ran one hand over his face. For a minute there he had felt good, but it was still a wild-goose chase. He stood by the window and down at the street corner. The man in the brown hat was back. Or was it the same man? It could be one of his own agents, coming back from lunch. Didn't Malotti wear a brown hat like that?

Jones left the communications room and went back to his office. He picked up the phone and asked for Agent Kantovitz. He wasn't in. "Tell him to make another local check with his contacts on that Schumacher matter. He'll know what I mean. And Betty, do you happen to know if Malotti wears a brown hat? He does?… No, it's nothing. Forget it."

The phone jangled on Herron's desk and he looked at it for a second before answering it. Another lead, no doubt. In the movies, they always got leads coming in at the last minute. He picked up the phone.

"Hello, Herron here."

"Where else? I figured you'd be there, seeing you're answering the phone."

"Larry? What in hell you want now?"

"I got a lead for you."

"I knew it. So you got a lead for me, huh? Where's it leading to—your newspaper column?"

"Naw, listen. This may be something."

"I bet. When the FBI needs local copy boys to crack a case for 'em, then that long month of Sundays has really come."

"So this is a long month of Sundays. Oh, well, seeing you ain't interested, I think I'll talk to somebody worth while. I got a dictaphone here, for instance—"

"All right, tell me. What's this lead you got?"

"Well, you've been telling me you came here to pick up some old-time hood, and so far no luck, right?"

"Yes, I'm sorry to say."

"Well, this may or may not be anything. I was in Santa Monica last night, down in the Mexican section and had a beer with a hood friend of mine. He's pretty harmless mostly, but he's in with some of the lower-rung syndicate punks. So we were talking about this and that, me trying to get a certain thing out of him—nothing special, just something I needed for a cross check—when he ups and says, 'Larry,' he says, 'I don't know if I ought to be talkin' to you like this here,' and he clams up."

"Larry, that was very nice of you. Real nice of you to call me up and explain about this lead you got. This real hot lead! Any time you feel the urge to—"

"Will you shut up and listen? That is by no means all, you flatfoot."

"Pardon me, Larry, pardon me. So go on."

"All right, then. So I say to him, 'Hood, why the silent treatment? Why this unfriendly relationship?' So he tells me there are things brewing. 'What, what?' I say. I must have sounded eager or something, because he answers, 'Even if I knew I wouldn't tell ya.' So I switch to acting coy and disbelieving. 'You don't know nothing and this is just your way of acting big. Show-off, if you know what I mean.' This gets him. 'I know plenty,' he says. 'Just for instance,' he says, 'I know they got an import to handle a deal for them.' I say, 'An import? A torpedo? And who's gonna be pushin' daisies?' 'Naw,' he says, 'nothing like that. A jug heavy or something. All the way from out East. But I mean, all the way.' Then he goes on to brag about a dozen other things he had predicted for me, all of which was a lie, so I bought him a few more beers, but no further info.

"So that's it, Jackie. Maybe the guy you want is the same guy my hood friend was discussing. His description sort of jibes with the one you've used. Now, did I tell you something?"

Herron didn't talk for a moment, just patted his hair where it was getting thin.

"Larry," he said finally, "perhaps you do have something there. I certainly appreciate your calling. I'm going to follow this up. What's the name of this hood friend of yours?"

"Nix, Jack. Professional ethics, you know."

"Ethics? Why, you crumb, you wouldn't have a column, a single sentence of your column, if you had any ethics."

"I don't publish ethics, but I get it ethically, Jackie. However, I can't expect you to follow that. As with all flatfoots—"

"Shut up a minute. Is there anything else, anything, that you could add to what you've said?"

"Surely: 'You're welcome.'"

"For chrissakes, be serious. Listen, when you say the syndicate, you mean the S. S. Smith operation here on the Coast?"

"The same."

"From what you know about him, would you say he'd be likely to import independent talent?"

"Why, Jackie, you asking me?"

"Yes, I'm asking you! I'm after popular opinion, so to speak. I got my own data on Smith, but I'm just asking in general. So what do you say?"

"I say, 'Jackie,' I say, 'you're shouting at me again.' Your nerves, twittering from long inactivity and suppressed rage at failure, are beginning to show their frazzled little heads. No, I wouldn't say about S. S. Smith. In general, he might do anything. He's big enough to seem inconsistent in his doings."

"What kind of double talk you giving me? I got the distinct feeling you're getting tired of talking to me. What else do you know?"

"Honest, Jackie, nothing else."

"Come on, come on!"

"Honest! I got an idea, though. I got an idea you need a little relaxation. How about covering some night spots with me tonight?"

"Can't make it, Larry. I've got to hang around here. There're a few interviews and so on, then this lead you gave me I've got to check, and—well, I just can't."

"Jack Herron. This will be on me. My expense account. Come on, now, you just suffer from lead in your pants. What do you say?"

"I'm not a drinking man."

"Sure, Jackie. Uh—I bet you never did see a movie star in real life."

"The hell with movie stars."

"O.K., forget they're movie stars. They still got the most beautiful rear ends, the most monumental chests. I'm talking about the female ones, of course."

"No, I don't think so, Larry. Ah, when are you going, anyway?"

"Meet me at nine. At the paper. You know my office. And then we'll talk some more. Who knows, something might turn up during the night. I pick up the cu-rayziest items, you know."

"Don't I. O.K, Larry, at nine."

"So long, Investigator."

Before Herron left the office for the day he went to the communications room again.

"Nothing for me?" he asked the girl who was sorting message sheets at a long table.

"Nothing here," she said. "But let me check in the back."

She smiled at Herron and got up. He watched her walk the length of the room, paying close attention to the way her hips moved. But then he looked away, worrying about Chief Jones's answer to his teletype. Was he going to be pulled off the assignment? Better let Jones know about Larry's lead right away. Perhaps it did mean something.

Then he saw the girl come back. This time he watched her front move.

"Nothing yet, Mr. Herron... Mr. Herron, I said—"

"Ah, yes, fine. Will you take something down for me, for teletype?"

"Of course, Mr. Herron."

She sat down and picked up pencil and message form. Herron watched her bare arm as she made date, hour, and name entries. She had a nice brown arm.

"The message, Mr. Herron?"

"Of course. Uh—where'd you get that nice tan so early in the year?"

"Santa Monica, the beach. It's not really so early in the year for us."

"Oh, I see. Very nice tan. You must tan beautifully. I mean, on the beach there."

She looked up at him with a light laugh, but didn't say anything.

"Ah, tell me. I have an assignment tonight, ah, involving nightclubs. Would you like to—can you perhaps come along? What I mean is, less conspicuous, you know, being a couple. Besides, I would very much like—"

"I'm sorry, Mr. Herron. It's real nice of you to ask me, but I'm married."

"You're married?"

"Why, yes. Surprises you?"

"Ah, oh, no, I didn't mean that. No surprise, actually. But a disappointment. Ha-ha."

She laughed too and looked down at her message pad again.

"Well, the message, then," he said. Herron dictated, not looking at her arm.

That evening he went out with Larry.

Chapter Eleven

"So I see you made a contact," said the Turtle. Then his eyes bugged out more than usual when he got a closer look at Catell. "Behold the Duke," he said. "Just get a load of the Duke in them fancy duds. Tonio, you musta made goodio. What happened?"

Catell dropped the cartons he was carrying on the bed and took off his new sports jacket.

"Put it back on," the Turtle said. "That neon shirt is kicking my eyeballs."

"Whaddaya talking about? It's California style, isn't it?"

"No, it ain't. You see anybody walkin' around like that who ain't a tourist or an actor or somethin'?"

"Well, anyway, I just got this one."

Catell sat down and lit a cigarette. The Turtle stood opposite, waiting.

"So give. What's the glad news?"

"No glad news, Turtle. I think I'm going to get someplace, but so far I've been roped."

"Roped? How?"

"I'm doing a job for that fat Smith guy. First the job, then the gold deal."

"So whaddaya kicking about? So you pick up some extra change plying your trade and also make a most evaluate contact and this you call roped!"

"Yeah, roped. Because I don't want no part of that syndicate and the way they run things. I need a free hand. I'm no soldier, you know, or a college kid getting a bang out of playing fraternity. That's what I'm talking about."

"Did you sign up for twenty years, maybe?"

"Maybe I did! I don't know who's gonna plan this heist or if it's any good, and maybe some ass I don't even know screws the works and I get it in the neck. So don't talk to me about that goddamn syndicate or I might even change my mind. Well, forget it, Turtle, I'm just jumpy is all. Here's your cut."

"My cut?"

"Yeah. Your share. I got paid five hundred on account. There's over four hundred left. Take it already."

The Turtle took the money and stuffed the bills in his pocket without counting them.

"Thanks, feller. You an' me—"

"Cut the mush, Turtle. And now for some fun. Tonight you and me are going to hit the Pink Shell. Whaddaya say?"

"Man, you're stepping. You know what that place costs? I been in this town five years, off and on, and I only been hearing about the joint."

"Tonight we'll see it."

They went to the Pink Shell by taxi. After paying a fortune for the fare, they walked around the wide stucco building fronting on the ocean. There was a big moon up and a long pier reached far out over the black, rolling water.

"I hear they got parties down here sometimes. Private parties on the beach," the Turtle said.

"Too damn cold. Let's get inside outa this wind." Like Paar's place, the Pink Shell was both a regular nightclub and a private club. But in this case the public part was no crummy roadhouse. White baroque columns supported the arch of a rose-colored ceiling. The walls were covered with pink satin, draped in fancy patterns, and stucco statues of naked mermaids flanked the shell-shaped booths along the walls. The mermaids all had pink nipples and red painted mouths.

"Like a dream," said the Turtle. "Just like a dream. Pinch me, Tonio. No, let Mabel do it." He watched the hostess come forward.

If a snake had legs, that's the way a snake would have walked. The hostess slunk up to them, carrying a little pink book in which reservations were marked.

"It may be difficult to find you a table," she said when Catell told her they had nothing reserved.

"Don't bother with this room," said Catell. "Too crowded. Something a little more private."

"I'm sorry, sir. Without—"

"Call Topper. Tell him Catell wants a space off to the side there, that low room over there."

The girl went to the wall phone and made a call. Then they watched her come back. She had a high, complicated coiffure, but the dress she wore was simplicity itself. High neck, long skirt, and sleeves coming to points over her hands. What recommended the outfit was the way it clung to the girl's body. She waved them to follow her and led the way to a side room.

"Tony, that dress!" The Turtle clutched Catell's sleeve. "That dress is better than skin."

"The Pearl Room, gentlemen. Miss Rosemary will take care of you."

Miss Rosemary could have been the other one's twin. Same hairdo, same body, same dress. Her face was a little different, but that wasn't the main attraction, anyway. Miss Rosemary led the way to a small table. There was a pink tablecloth and just enough room for elbows and perhaps a glass or two.

"Two bourbons on the rocks," Catell said, and Miss Rosemary drifted off, smiling.

"Tony, I think I'm too impressed to have a good time." The Turtle spoke in a whisper.

When the drinks came, a waiter was carrying them.

"I'm sobering up already. Here's to you, Anthony."

"Mud."

They drank.

When they ordered their second round, a piano started to crash out some chords and a rose light hit a curtain at the end of the room.

"A floor show yet! They must have one of them stages in every room here."

"Must be. Christ, look at that!"

The curtain whipped open with a fast swish and five chorus girls, dressed like the belles of the nineties, came tearing out on the small stage. Brass trumpets and drums joined the piano, but that didn't drown out the girls. In high-pitched voices they screeched a kind of ragtime ballad about an evil baron and five poor sisters, all innocent and beautiful till the baron came along. All the while they kept bumping and grinding fast. When the refrain came, they tore off their hats. A midget dressed like a Turk rushed around to pick up the hats. Next refrain, off came the gloves. Next refrain, the dresses. The midget kept picking things up. Then the chemises came off. The song got louder, the rhythm jacked up to a terrific pace. Off with the corset. Practically naked, they shivered themselves back and forth. Then the last refrain. With crashing of trumpet, drum, piano, and high voices, they ducked behind a skimpy screen that left their legs and shoulders exposed. The music jumped once and stopped. In the silence only some rustling could be heard, legs and arms moving behind the screen. Then the loud tune started up again, frantic and harsh, and bras and panties came flying over the screen. With a last scream of the music each girl ducked from behind the screen into the wings of the stage. There was just a glimpse possible as they ran across the short open space.

"My, my, my," said the Turtle. "Oh, my, oh, my! Why wasn't I born a midget? My, oh, my."

Then the music changed to strings and sax. To a slow rhythm the girls came out again holding fans in front of them. The song was a tired thing now, something about five virgins no more, but another one already catching the black baron's fancy, another one pure and young, not knowing of the fate that lay ahead. At that point the rose light got dimmer and a white spot grew against the back curtain. It opened slowly and out walked Lily, Paar's cigarette girl. She half sang, half talked, moving up to the ramp with a slow swing of her hips.

Catell picked up the Turtle's half-full glass and poured it down.

"Christ," said the Turtle. "She can't sing, Tony."

"Shut up!"

"All I said—"

"Shut up!" Catell's voice sounded raspy.

Lily was standing still now, doing her lines, and her only movements were those made by her breathing. She was wearing a long, plain dress, all white, and like the things on the hostesses, the cloth held her body like a second skin. But Lily looked like no snake; Lily looked like a woman.

When her song was over the lights went dead. After a minute they went on again, showing the stage empty.

Catell got to his feet. Then a smooth voice said:

"Leaving so soon?"

Topper was standing beside the table.

"I said, are you leaving already?"

"How are you, Topper? Nice club you got here," Catell said.

"And who's the runt with you?" Topper asked.

Catell sat down again and kneaded the fingers of one hand. "Topper," he said, "I want you to try to watch that tone of voice. You're talking about a friend of mine, and when it comes to crappers like you I don't mind getting my hands dirty messing you up."

"Now, now, Catell, that nasty, nasty temper of yours. I don't think Mr. Smith would approve of any of this. We should try and be friends. Don't you think so, Bugeye?" He turned to the Turtle.

Catell jumped up, but Topper had already stepped back and around the table. He stumbled against the Turtle, who hadn't said a word, but then regained his balance. With a bored expression he turned and left.

"Turtle, listen. I'm sorry about this and I promise you the sonofabitch will pay for it. Right now I'm trying not to make a commotion, but believe me, he's going to pay for this, Turtle. So—"

"Stop jabbering, Antonio. He's paid already, so let the poor sap go." The Turtle leaned back, looking disinterested.

"Turtle, listen, I mean it."

"Can that sentimentation, friend. And let poor Topper go. Like I say, he paid already." Turtle reached into his jacket pocket and showed the edge of a thick sheath of bills.

"Christ! Turtle—"

"Anthony, you are sentimentating again. Now let me finish."

From his breast pocket the Turtle pulled another handful of folded bills, letting just the edge of them show from under his hand.

"What did you do with the wallet? Are you trying to get us killed right here, you jerk?"

"Anthony, of what you speak, I know all about it. Now slosh another drink for yourself while I return the recriminating evidence."

"Why, you nut! How—"

"Quiet. I am an artist." The Turtle left the table.

Topper was standing near the archway of the room, greeting two men who had just walked in.

"Did we miss the show, Topper?" one of the men asked.

"You did, Larry, but why don't you catch the one in the Boudoir, or in the Shell Room?"

"Second best, Topper. I wanted my friend Jackie Herron to see Lily. Jackie, you oughta see Lily sometime, if only out of scientific curiosity. She doesn't do a damn thing, and you should see how it goes over. Topper, meet my friend Jackie."

Topper shook hands with the one called Jackie, but they didn't pay much attention to each other. Jackie seemed to be watching one of the hostesses, and Topper was watching Larry.

"There's nothing going on today, Larry. No celebrities."

"Topper wants to get rid of us, Jackie," Larry said, but Herron wasn't paying attention. He had been watching the backside of Miss Rosemary, and now he was watching her front.

"You want to be introduced?" Topper said.

"Oh, ah, why not?" Herron tried to look unconcerned.

"I'll tell you why not." Larry took Herron by the arm. "Because neither your expense account nor mine could take care of that situation. So, if you don't mind, Topper, we'll just walk around for a look-see and then breeze, eh?"

As they started to move, Topper bumped into the Turtle for the second time. The Turtle, looking apologetic, tried to fade back, but Larry spotted the maneuver.

"Hey, if it isn't the Turtle! Now, don't run, Turtle. Since when have you been admitted to the likes of this here pleasure dome?" He turned confidential. "Or is it strictly business, ha?" The Turtle looked as uncomfortable as a hung-up dog.

"So say something, Turtle. Listen, Jackie, this guy Turtle has a very interesting background."

"Larry—uh, Mr. Metcalf, I mean—I don't think—"

"Oh, shush yourself, Turtle. I wouldn't wash your old socks right here in public. I'm just chatting, you know, trying to make everybody feel at ease. So tell me, how are pickin's these days, Turtle?"

"I don't know what you mean, Mr. Metcalf. What you mean by pickin's, I mean."

"Just talking, Turtle, just talking. So come here and meet Jackie. Jackie, the Turtle; Turtle, the Jackie. Ah, you know the Turtle, Topper?"

"No. How do."

"Sure. And now, if you'll—"

"Don't go, Turtle." Larry grabbed him by the arm. "Why don't we chat a little longer? Like how's business and so forth?"

"What is your business?" Topper wanted to know.

"Then you *don't* know the Turtle!" Larry sounded full of happy surprise. "Well, now, the Turtle used to go by another name. And this is confidential, of course. Shut up, Turtle, I'm telling a story. He used to be a magician, Dippo the Short or something like that. How that guy could make things disappear!"

"Dippo? What kind of a crazy name is that?" Topper frowned.

"Yeah, Topper. Dippo the Short, wasn't it, Turtle?"

"So help me, Mr. Metcalf, you promised to lay off'n me."

"Never you mind, now, there's no harm done."

"If you'll excuse me, gentlemen," Topper said, and he stepped past them in order to greet another party.

They let him pass, looking after him. Larry said, "Watch him, Jackie, watch what he does now. Hey, you too, Turtle. Don't run off. Haven't you got any pride in your work?" Larry held the Turtle by one sleeve.

"What's he supposed to be doing?" Herron wanted to know. "I don't see a thing."

"You see it, don't you, Turtle, ha? Look, he's doing it now."

Topper had stopped at the entrance to the main room, and he was patting himself, as if he were hunting for a cigarette. Then he slipped his hand inside his jacket, looked in, and straightened up again. That was all.

"You mean he's looking for a smoke?" Herron said.

"Smoke! With your training, Jackie? I'm dumfounded."

"Was he looking for his wallet?" Herron looked at the Turtle with a little more interest.

"As the Turtle will tell you, Jackie, yes. He was looking for his wallet."

Herron started to grin. He looked down at the Turtle and said, "You little weasel, so you were—"

"Turtle, Jackie. Not weasel."

"So you were trying to lift his wallet, right here in front of everybody?"

"Now listen, you guys, all you're trying to do is get me in complications. If I told ya what's what you wouldn't believe it noways."

"You mean you did lift it? But—"

"Jackie. He didn't lift it. Didn't you see Topper pat himself? He found it."

"Well," Herron said, "I guess you can't always win, can you, Turtle?"

Larry noticed the look on the Turtle's face.

"Now you hurt his feelings, Jackie. You hurt his feelings and cast aspersions and disparagement—get those words, Turtle—on his professional standing. Tell him, Turtle."

"He won't believe me." The Turtle looked stony.

"So I'll tell him."

"Never mind, I'll tell him," said the Turtle. "I was returning the wallet, I was."

"You dumfound me, Turtle," Herron said.

"Well, if you don't mind—"

"No, you don't." Larry grabbed for the arm again. "First you buy us a drink, ha?"

"No, I'd rather not. In fact—"

"Perhaps you're broke, Turtle?"

"Larry! Are you disparaging my finances?"

"God forbid, Turtle. I wouldn't do such a thing. So come along, one and all. The Turtle is going to quench us."

"Naw, I don't think your friend here—"

"Turtle," said Larry, "let's not try stalling men like me and Jackie. You owe us a drink, don't you? Listen to me, Turtle, I'm now speaking with a significant voice: You owe us a drink, don't you? Because you owe your success to us, don't you?"

"What in hell you talking about, Mr. Met—ah, Larry?"

"Come on, Turtle. Don't tell me you gave Topper back a full wallet?"

"All right, dumfound you, I'll buy you guys a drink, and I hope you get aspersions from it."

Topper watched the three men from afar. When they sat down at the bar, he patted his breast pocket again. The wallet was there, plump as ever. If that little runt was a dip, even if he was a friend of Catell's— Topper didn't like any of the three men at the bar. Larry was a snooping nut, and with enough stuff behind him to be a real danger. That Herron character somehow didn't sit right, either. One of those characters you couldn't place. And the Turtle, a friend of that slime Catell—

Topper put his hand in his pocket and pulled out his alligator billfold. It was so stuffed that the flaps opened up in his hand.

Suddenly Topper's eyes got droopy, the way they had done when he had tangled with Catell in the machine shop. His color got darker, and his neck swelled out. Topper opened the billfold all the way. Folded inside there was a pink napkin.

When Topper got to the bar, only Herron and Larry were sitting together.

"Where's your friend, Larry?" Topper sounded smooth and unruffled.

"My who? Topper, you hit a sensitive spot there. I have no friends."

"That other guy, the runt. Where is he?"

"What I mean is, no *real* friends, Topper. You were saying?"

But Topper had turned and gone. He went around a corner to get to Catell's table. It was empty.

Back at the bar, Topper used the house phone, giving instructions.

"Oh, Topper, you looking for the Turtle?" Larry was leaning over the bar, waving an arm.

"Yeah. Your friend."

"He left, Topper. He left after buying us two of your most expensive drinks. Tell me, Topper, why do you charge—" but Topper had turned and gone again.

"Not very friendly," Herron said.

"This is nothing. Sometime you should introduce yourself as the cop you are, Jackie, if you want to study the ultimate extent of true unfriendliness."

Meanwhile Topper was walking down a service corridor. He was licking his lips and there was a mean wrinkle down the middle of his forehead. Footsteps sounded and one of his boys came around a bend.

"Well, where is he?" Topper said.

"Not a trace, Topper. I swear we looked everywhere. I think he musta—"

"Don't think, damn it. Find that dip. Find him, I don't care where, and bring him back. Alive. Just so he's still alive. Now beat it."

"Yes, sir. Another thing, the car's ready out back. That is, if you still want it,"

"Yeah, yeah, I want it. I'm getting Lily now. Have Rudy drive her home."

"O.K., Boss."

Topper walked up to a door that had a paper star glued to it and started to open it when he heard voices.

"Of course I remember you." It was Lily's voice.

Topper stopped, stiff.

"I'm glad," Catell's voice said.

Silence. Then: "And I remember you, it goes without saying."

"Is that why you came back?"

"You might say that. I came back for more."

"Of the same?" Lily's voice sounded amused.

"Don't kid yourself. I mean that you and me—"

"It's no good, Tony. This'll only mean trouble."

"Listen, kid. Maybe you're too young to know, though I doubt it, but it's worth the trouble."

"I don't know. I think you'd better go, anyway."

Catell couldn't make her out. Was she interested, was she just playing, or was she afraid? It could also be, with her wide-eyed face always looking a little vague, that Lily didn't have any feelings about this thing, one way or the other. Catell wondered how she'd look when she was excited. She must get that way sometimes.

"Leave the worrying to me, Lily. I got plans in this town, and one of the biggest of them is you. Lily, I'm not just playing around. I'm not just…" Catell's voice halted, getting nowhere. In the silence, he heard the door open. He spun around.

Topper walked in. "Go on, *Tony*. I might as well hear the rest. For that matter, you might as well finish what you had to say while you can." Topper had an easy smile on his face.

Lily blinked her eyes but there was no clear emotion on her face. Catell stood wide-legged, his face turning to sharp stone.

"Let's have it out right here and now," Catell said. "I didn't come here to get in your way. I came here after Lily, and no matter what gets in my way, I mean to have her. And I'd just as soon kill you, Topper, you and anybody else who gets in my way. I'm not trying to beat your time, either with Lily or with your boss. I just want what I want, and I'm going to get it, and I don't go for the kind of gaff that punks like you hand out."

Catell's voice had stayed on an even pitch, but he felt a harsh excitement and a powerful certainty surge through him as he stood tensed, hands curled at his sides, his sharp face very still.

Topper gave the only answer he knew how to give. He reached for his gun. Before he had it out, Catell grabbed Lily's arm and swung her in front of him.

"Catell," Topper said, "how yellow can you get?"

Catell didn't answer.

"Catell, I'd just as soon shoot right through this dame to get you."

"Baby!" Lily's voice made a sound of surprise.

"Shut up! You think you're special? You think I wouldn't just as soon kick you over?"

Lily started to moan, but it wasn't so much because of Topper's words. Catell's hands, holding the girl in front of him, had dug into her arms like claws.

"Make him move, Lily." Topper stepped closer. "Make him move. Kick back."

But she didn't. She stood still, facing Topper and his gun. Then her head sank down and her knees bent.

"Drop her, Catell. Drop her or I shoot the both of you." Topper took another step forward.

But Catell didn't move. He knew that Lily hadn't fainted. He could feel the muscles in her arms tense under his hands. Then she kicked her foot, hard and swift.

It caught Topper square in the groin. He buckled slowly, his eyes rolling blindly in their sockets and his red mouth puckered. When Topper hit the floor, Catell let go of Lily's arms and reached down for the gun. Then he straightened up and took Lily around the waist.

"Thanks, baby," he said.

When he leaned over to kiss her cheek, she drew back and hit him in the face. She didn't slap him; she hit him hard with a closed fist.

"For chrissakes! What in hell was that for?"

But Lily wasn't listening. She stood by the wall, her hands over her face, crying in a concentrated way. Catell shrugged and turned back to Topper.

"Can you hear me, punk?"

Topper opened his eyes and his face relaxed a little.

"Listen close, Topper. You touch Lily for this and I'll get you for it. I'll get you for it so you die in the end, but way in the end. And it's going to take time, Topper. You listening?" Catell grabbed the man's lapels and jerked.

"Stop it, stop it, you!" Lily, hands over her cheeks, stood by the wall, screaming.

"Lily!" Catell got to his feet. "What is it with you?"

"Stop it now, for God's sake stop it, you two!"

"You in love with this crud? What's—"

"I want you to stop this. I don't care what you do, but please, no more, please," and she ended with a sobbing mumble behind her hands.

Topper got to his feet slowly. He looked at Catell with a poisonous hate in his eyes, and there was slobber on his wet lips.

"Catell—"

"Shut up. You heard what I said?"

Topper didn't say anything, just looked.

"And another thing, Topper. Remember you and me are on the same team. I don't think *Mr.* Smith is going to like you very much if anything happens to me now. So keep your distance, Topper. Just another few days and I'll be blowing town. After that, anything you want to throw my way, throw it. And when it comes back at you, don't say I didn't warn you."

Catell put Topper's gun in his pocket and walked to the door.

"I'll be seeing you, Lily," he said. She didn't look up. He shut the door behind him.

He stopped for a moment to light a cigarette. There was movement in the room, feet shuffling. Catell could hear a dull smacking on flesh and Lily moaning. Then Catell walked on down the corridor and left.

"Jackie, this dullness dulls me. Let's you and me climb off these stools and go someplace else." Larry pushed his glass back and made ready to go.

"Why not hang around here, Larry? I might get to like it here." Herron kept watching Miss Rosemary move around.

"Come on, Jackie, up. I got to make the rounds yet. It's my bread and butter, and this place is a dud."

They got up and left because there was nothing going on at the Pink Shell.

Chapter Twelve

The tension was greater in Catell than he had ever felt it before. He stood at the open window of the Turtle's room, staring through the yellow smog where the sun was coming up. He didn't remember sleeping last night, just jumping up several times, fully awake. The Turtle hadn't come yet.

Catell didn't worry about the way he felt. He didn't think about the why, the how, or any of those things when it came to the state he was in. He didn't worry about the way Lily might feel, either. For all he knew, she hated his guts. For all he knew, she'd been doing daisy chains since she was ten. He didn't give a damn. He wanted Lily now, without question and without thought of consequence.

He put on his jacket. When his right hand came through the armhole he winced at the strange feeling in his hand. The sharp pain of yesterday had gone, but there was an unpleasant dull pressure around the old cut. Catell looked at it and wondered at the pulpy, dry hole in his skin.

According to the old janitor at the Pink Shell, Lily lived in an apartment in Westwood. Catell took the bus down Wilshire, got out at the Village, and walked the rest of the way. He didn't remember ever feeling like this before, except perhaps that first time he ever did anything big. He had been fifteen and Joe Lenkovitch had promised him fifty bucks. Just jump in the car, drive it to the garage under the store where Lenkovitch had a paint shop, and collect the fifty bucks. When he'd first started the motor of the stolen car, he'd felt excited, crazy. The feeling stayed with him all the time he drove through town, wound around dark streets, and then pulled down the drive into the basement garage. He was so hopped up when he delivered it that he walked out without even asking Lenny for the fifty bucks.

There was a short hill up to the apartment house where Lily lived, and Catell felt winded when he reached the building. He was still breathing hard when she opened the door.

"I came to see you, Lily," he said.

She stood by the door with that open look on her face, showing nothing one way or the other. But Catell wasn't studying her face. She was standing in front of the light that came through the large glass doors of the sun porch, and there was nothing vague about the rest of her. Her shorts just reached the curve of her thighs. She was wearing a man's white shirt, the tails tied in a knot at her midriff, the folds of the material stretching up and over her breasts. When she finally moved, Catell saw she was naked under the shirt.

"I don't think you should come in, Tony," she said.

"Try and stop me."

"Tony, it isn't safe. I don't think—" Catell put his hand on the doorknob and slammed the door open. Then he stepped inside and pushed the door closed behind him. The spring lock clicked.

"Tony, he has a key. Topper has a key."

Catell ran his hands up and down Lily's arms, stroking gently.

"I hurt you last night?"

"A little."

"I'll make it up to you, Lily."

She didn't answer him, standing still under his moving hands. There was a short distance between them, just enough so he could not feel the touch of her breath. She stood quietly, only moving her tongue once, to moisten her parted lips. She breathed more deeply, never moving. Then Catell stepped back; his voice sounded squeezed when he said, "Like the first time, Lily. Go ahead."

She unbuttoned the front of the shirt, untied the knot. The thing fell to the floor. When she reached around to pull the zipper on the side of her shorts, Catell watched how her arm pushed the breasts together.

Then Lily was naked.

Catell curled his fingernails into his palms, trying to kill the tingling. One more second, he thought, one more second. Just reach out there, and then… Now there was a smile on Lily's face. Clearly, no question about Lily any more.

Her eyes widened, staring, and she moved as if to hide herself. Catell reached forward, lunging, and the world jarred with a screeching, searing flame of red that weaved, burst, and then sank sharply into itself, leaving nothing but a total dead black.

"I don't like this, Topper. I think you're making a mistake."

"I'm not asking you to think. Just drive this car and shut up."

"Boss, listen, I ain't never butted into your business before, but—"

"So don't start now, Nick. I'm warning you to shut up."

Nick didn't say any more. He concentrated on driving the car through the Santa Monica traffic, but he didn't feel right about the whole thing. With a slight twist he could see Topper's face in the rear-view mirror and the sight made his skin crawl. The face was pale, showing the red lips like raw flesh, and two ugly lines curved around the corners of the mouth. Nick couldn't make out Topper's eyes. They were closed, mostly, with only a wet glitter showing through the lashes.

When the car reached the end of Wilshire, Nick turned right on Ocean Drive. The sharp turn threw Topper to the left so that his head moved out of line with the mirror. Then Nick saw Catell lurch into his line of vision. Only the top of his head showed, sticky with blood.

The car straightened out and shot north. Topper pushed Catell back into the other corner of the seat by jabbing his knuckles painfully into Catell's ribs. Catell didn't seem to notice. He was still out.

"Reach me a light, Nick."

Topper took the car lighter and put it to his cigarette. When he was through the thing was still red, and slowly Topper pushed it into the limp man's neck. At first there was no reaction from Catell, but suddenly he started to twitch and a dry snore rattled out of his slack mouth. He didn't wake up, though.

"Take the light, Nick."

They drove in silence for a while.

"Lend me one of your fags, Topper?"

"When you gonna start carrying your own? Here."

"Thanks." After a deep drag Nick said, "Still going through with it?"

"Sure. Why?"

"Just asking."

"Let's have that pack." Nick handed it back. "And the light."

Topper lit his cigarette and gave the lighter back to Nick. A hot sun beat down on the highway, making the inside of the car like a steam bath. The windows stayed closed. Nick pulled his tie open by yanking the shirt collar away from his wet neck, but he didn't open the window. Topper didn't like to smoke with the wind blowing in his face.

After a while, Topper asked for the lighter again. He didn't like to light one cigarette from another.

"Boss."

"What?"

"Boss, listen. You nervous?"

"What's eating you, damnit? Spill it and shut up."

"Topper, now don't blow your top, but this is all wrong. You can't afford it, Topper, I know."

"Nick, what do I have to do to shut you up, damn it? Stop riding me or I'll—"

"Yeah, I know, Topper. You can do all kinds of things. But there's one thing you can't do, and I'm going to say it anyway. You can't buck Smith. If you rub out Catell, you're bucking Smith."

"Shut your crazy mouth and drive."

"Smith is counting on Catell for the job. If he finds out—and he will, you know—"

"To hell with Smith. To hell with your crazy talk, you stinking sonofabitch. Just do what I tell you."

Catell woke up with a sharp painful start, the light of the sun and the thick cigarette smoke stinging his eyes, his head a big bursting throb that jangled his senses at the slightest move. Topper sat next to him, a gun in his hand.

When the car turned into a dirt road Catell was just starting to think clearly. When the car bumped to a halt, hidden by the walls of a quarry, Catell knew for sure.

This was it.

"When you step out, Catell, don't stumble or anything. I'm right behind you." Topper jabbed the gun into Catell's ribs.

All three of them stood in the empty quarry, in the hot dust, looking at each other. The bright light made the shadows on their faces black and sharp, giving all of them the same expression. They stood without talking. The man who had driven the car started to push a stone around with his foot, not looking at anybody. Catell licked his dry lips, his brain a useless mess of pain, fear, and hate.

Then Topper started to smile. He held it so long that Catell thought time had stood still, or perhaps he was going out of his mind.

"Walk to the wall, Catell."

Catell walked. If Topper had told him to stumble, to hop on one leg, anything, he would have done it. He wasn't in a trance any more. His pain-sharpened senses raced for a clue, a sign, a hope, scanning the scene for that inevitable last chance.

"Stop."

Catell stopped.

"Turn around."

With his back to the baked wall of the quarry, Catell looked the way he had come. It wasn't very far. Topper stood with his gun in his hand. Then he raised the gun and took a careful stance and a slow aim.

"Hey, Catell, here it comes!"

Catell wished he had never come out of that trance. Even the harsh pain in his head no longer distracted him from the clear, real thing before him.

"Here it comes, Catell!" and the shot whipped out.

Spraying sand stung the back of Catell's neck before the true panic of the situation hit him. He wanted to scream, but there was no air in his lungs. He wanted to move, but his muscles were like glass, hard, near breaking.

"Guess I missed that time, eh, Catell?"

Never having finished—or even started—the scream of fear that choked him, that pushed his eyeballs from behind, he stiffened again when the gun moved up.

Again Topper shot.

"Seems I'm not doing so good, Catell, ha?"

The gun went down and Catell saw Topper change his stance. Time. Time to scream, to unwind, to melt like jelly in the heat. But nothing like that happened. The grip on Catell's control was frozen like ice. And then he began to tremble. The trembling hurt his head, his muscles, above all his head, but there was nothing to be done about it.

Topper laughed and shot again. The bullet hit close before Catell's feet. The trembling turned into a jagged, spastic horror of uncontrolled jerks, more intense each time a shot rang out.

Then there were no more shots.

"Catell, you can stop dancing. Hey, Nick, look at him. Christ! Hey, Catell, you can stop now. Take a rest while I load this gun. Catell, hey, look. Catell, I'm ready!

But Catell didn't respond. As his trembling died down his eyes became dull, and he stood, mouth open, breathing hard and deep.

"Come here, Catell. Come here!"

When Topper came up, cursing, Catell had gained a strange sense of detachment. He saw everything, he felt everything, but it didn't matter. The only thing that mattered was that Topper was still around, and that the time would come when Topper would be at the other end. Topper was just playing. There wasn't going to be any end yet. There was going to be time for Topper at the other end, because right now Topper was just playing.

The fist crashed into Catell's neck, making him fall to the ground. He could hear Nick's voice: "Don't muss him up, Topper. Remember about Smith." Catell knew he was getting a beating, but it didn't matter to him any more.

Later he woke on the beach, cold and sore, and the moon was up. He remembered everything, but it didn't really get to him. When he got back to the Turtle's room, he still felt the same about it: Topper had shot his bolt. Next it was going to be Catell's turn.

Chapter Thirteen

At four in the afternoon Catell was back in shape and ready to leave for Smith's place. First he had slept, then he'd gone to the Turkish bath, and then, after a hot meal, he hadn't felt so bad. His muscles were sore, but there was hardly a mark on him. Topper must have been using a newspaper. The cut on his head was tender, and a round burn on his neck looked an angry red, chafing under his collar. Only his hand worried him. The pulpy hole in the skin had puffed up, dripping a little, and the edges had turned dark. There was no real pain to it, just that strange ache.

The Turtle hadn't come home yet.

Catell picked up the gun he had taken from Topper in Lily's dressing room and checked it. There were six short bullets in the cylinder. The gun looked clean, had an easy action, and it fitted the hand well. There was no extra ammunition around, but Catell didn't figure he'd need it. He rarely carried a gun. If he had to use this one, six bullets were going to be plenty.

Catell went out, flagged a taxi, and gave an address in the Valley. Then he sat back and went over the whole thing again.

Meet at Smith's for last briefing. That would be at five. Drive to San Pedro with the team of three. Cruise Ruttger Road, where the Maxim Loan Company office was. Do that twice, and then stop two blocks down. That would be at eight P.M. Drop off Smiley, the guy who was going to help him. Drive another block and at eight-oh-five drop off the lookout. At eight-ten Catell would get out, carrying his suitcase, and walk the four blocks to the loan office. The driver was going to blow. At eight-twenty-five the lookout would stand in a doorway opposite Maxim's. Catell would enter the side door of the large office, and at eight-twenty-seven Smiley would join him. Besides having left the side door open, the inside man would have wedged the alarm bell, marked the position of two electric eyes, and cut the wires to all overhead fixtures. If something should go wrong, at least nobody could flood the place with light. Then Smiley and Catell would knock over the safe. It was an old-time job, with an alarm that cut in when the door cleared a contact. Catell was going to try to burn the hinges, tape the contact before it could cut in, and then pry the door back just enough so Smiley could squeeze through. Smiley was five feet tall and weighed eighty-one pounds. It shouldn't take too long. After Smiley handed out the bills, they'd leave the joint with the bills in the suitcase and let the loan office keep the tools. That would be at nine-ten. At that time the getaway car would pull up, having been parked two blocks down for the past twenty minutes. Now south, toward Laguna Beach. Halfway there, they'd gas up at a station in Corona del Mar. That's where they'd switch the suitcase to another sedan. The two men in that car would leave for Burbank, to deliver the stuff. Simple.

If they were interrupted anywhere along the line, it was every man for himself.

When the taxi made ready to turn off Van Nuys, Catell told the cabbie to stop. He got out, paid his fare, and walked five blocks to an address he hadn't given the cabbie.

The house sat far back from the street, behind a wall, a stretch of trees, and an open lawn. The big place looked empty, but the door opened as soon as Catell came up the broad steps.

"To the rear, last door on the left," said the maid who had opened the door. She was a maid only because that's what the uniform said. For a regular maid her legs were too good, her face was too much like a doll's, and her hair was too blonde.

Catell walked back. The room was a big, dark thing with leather chairs, carved tables, and a fireplace like a cave. A plaster stack of electric logs was plugged in there, giving off a steady red glow.

"You're prompt, Catell. Sit down." S. S. Smith waved his hand at Catell but stayed near the window, rocking on his heels.

When Catell sat down, the door opened again and two more men came in. One was a sullen kid with yellow hair and high cheekbones. The other was Topper. They sat down opposite Catell.

"Where's Smiley?" Smith wanted to know.

"Haven't seen him," said the kid with the cheekbones.

Topper looked across at Catell and grinned. Catell nodded. There was no expression in his face.

Then Smiley came in. He opened the door and held it for the girl in the maid's uniform. She carried a tray with five highballs, gave one to each of the men, and turned to go.

"But you just came, Rose," Smiley said. He held her arm.

"Let her go. This is business." Smith's voice was cold.

"Aw, come on, S. S. Just to look at. You know, an ornament. I ain't seen Rosie—"

"That's enough, Smiley. And you may leave, Rose."

They all held their highballs, not looking very comfortable, waiting for Smith to talk.

"You've gone over this deal enough times to do it in your sleep. If there are any questions, ask them now."

Nobody asked anything.

"All right. You know your places, you know your schedule. Catell and Smiley to knock the place over; Swensen, you're the lookout; Topper drives. I repeat this to make you understand one thing: Each has a job, one job and only one job. Do it, and the deal works. Muff it, and every other man is no better than a body minus a head. From now on, Catell takes over. His word goes for the rest of the operation. All right, Catell, it's all yours."

"There's just a few things. Once we hit that car, I don't want a lot of chatter. You know your jobs; there's no need to talk. Until you get on your stations, keep clammed up. Swensen, don't read a newspaper on your job. Looks too much like you got time to kill or just hanging around. And don't smoke. Same reason. Topper, any cruising you do, drive normal speed. Don't creep along, attracting attention, making it easy to remember you. Also don't ever gun the car. No two-wheel turns or any crap like that. Smiley, I'll talk to you once we're inside. That's all. Questions?"

No questions.

"All right, drink up and let's go. You got fifteen minutes."

Then they sat back and relaxed a little, but there wasn't much to talk about. Swensen offered Catell a cigarette and they said a few words. Topper went to the garage, turned on the motor of the limousine, and left it running. Smiley excused himself and disappeared down the hall. Smith smoked a cigar.

"How's it look to you, Catell?" Smith had walked over.

"O.K. Shouldn't be bad."

"Good. Think you can keep on schedule?"

"Should. If the dope on the safe is right."

"Good. All right, everybody. Time. Where's Smiley?"

Smith walked to the door when Smiley stepped in.

"Where the hell you been?"

"Time, S. S., I been making time."

When the four men passed through the front hall, Rose came the other way. Her apron was on crooked and her dress looked as if it didn't fit any more.

The kid who was going to be the lookout said, "They call him Smiley just to be polite. His real name is Mink. You get it, Catell? Mink." He laughed with a short, dry cackle.

Nobody talked on the way to San Pedro. Topper smoked one cigarette after another, drove the car well, and paid no attention to Catell, who was sitting beside him. Catell's suitcase was between his legs. When they cased Ruttger the first time, they didn't see anybody except a few pedestrians. When they drove past Maxim's the second time, there were a few pedestrians again. One of them had been there the first time.

"Slow down," Catell said.

"The time schedule—"

"Shut up, you sonofabitch, and slow down."

The short guy near Maxim's was the Turtle.

"Pull over."

"If you say so, Catell, but—"

Catell's left hand snapped across Topper's Adam's apple, making the man gasp with pain.

"Do only what you're told, Topper. Now pull up." The gun was in Catell's hand.

Catell opened the window and leaned out. When the Turtle came up, Catell said, "Wait for me two blocks down, fifteen minutes. All right, Topper, get going."

The rest of the drive went on schedule. Topper drove well, kept to himself. He looked bland.

When Catell came to the corner, the Turtle fell in with him. They walked, nodding and smiling at each other, and sometimes waving an arm.

"What's up, Turtle?"

"I don't know, Tony. I'm not sure. Christ, I'm sorry if I muffed something for you, but I couldn't get to you sooner. I knew you'd get here today, but I couldn't—"

"Whaddaya mean, couldn't get to me sooner?"

"Since that time at the Pink Shell I had a time shaking a couple of guys who was after me. Christ, did I have a time! Coupla Topper's men, on accounta that snatch I pulled on him, I think."

"That all?"

"Something else. I picked up a word something was cooking with you and Topper, so I tried to follow it up. Christ, did I have a time, with those torpedoes on my tail!"

"Hurry up, Turtle, what else?"

"I don't know for sure, Tony. Something about Topper getting to you. I couldn't get the details."

"Never mind. He got to me. That was yesterday. Now blow. I'm turning off here."

"No, Tony, that wasn't it. Yesterday wasn't it. I know he took you for a ride, but the word is there's a cross on."

"Frame?"

"Could be, Tony. Listen, this heist—"

"It's coming off as planned. Don't argue. When I cross over now, keep walking to the end of the block. Stay there. After ten minutes, take the other end of the alley next to Maxim's loans. After twenty minutes, the other end of Ruttger. Watch for Topper and the sedan two blocks down at nine. That's nine sharp, Turtle. He'll pull up here ten minutes later. Got it?"

"Check."

"See the kid in the doorway, reading the billboard? He's our lookout. Now blow."

The Turtle kept walking down the block and Catell crossed to the alley. He turned once and looked at Swensen. Catell pointed with his finger at the Turtle, then made a circle with thumb and forefinger. Swensen nodded. Then Catell was at the side door and turning the handle. No hitch. The door opened and Catell stepped inside. For two minutes he stood in the dimness without moving. Then Smiley came in. They stood another five minutes, close to the door. Half a foot away, on a wooden railing that ran from the side of the door to the middle of the large room, there was a chalk cross. The two men dropped to the floor and lay flat on their backs. Pushing with hands and heels, they snaked their way along the railing, away from the door. Once past the chalk cross, they got up and walked.

"That eye was close to the door." Smiley was whispering. "Did you see it?"

"No. Just the cross. Good job. I guess we beat it through. Nothing happened."

Just before they reached the large safe door, built flush into the wall, they saw the second electric eye. This one didn't need a marker. The post with the light and lens stood two feet from the wall to the left of the safe; the post with the photoelectric cell was opposite, on the right of the safe.

"Man, that's close." Smiley wiped his forehead.

Catell was sweating too. He had been dragging the heavy suitcase and the hand with the sore was throbbing. He didn't know whether he was nervous about the job, but he didn't feel so good. Almost feverish.

"That eye's too close, Smiley."

"You're telling me! The diagram said eight feet."

"That's what comes from not doing your own casing. That jerk who mapped this layout is going to be one sorry-looking bastard."

"Whatcha gonna do?"

"I gotta figure this. It's risky, but I could work inside two feet. No good, though. Once that door falls, the beam's cut."

"Jee-sus!"

"Open that bag, Smiley."

"O K. Now what?"

"There's a pencil flashlight in the pocket. Take it out. Now turn it on. Got it? The button, stupid, the little button. Now step close to the eye, point the light at it, and slip the flashlight up in line with the beam. But be ready to run, Smiley. I'm going to cut my hand through the beam back here, and if you hear a click in that thing, bolt! Understand? Fast now, go!"

Smiley slipped the flashlight in line with the eye fast, but steady. Nothing happened.

"Hold it now, Smiley. Here I go," and Catell swung his hand through the beam from the post.

They listened tensely, Catell feeling the cold sweat run down his back. He shivered. No click.

"Once more, Smiley. Here goes."

Catell stepped into the beam. No click.

"It works. Now listen, Smiley. You'll have to hold that thing from here on. I don't care if your hand drops off, but keep that light steady."

"Got you, Catell. Get to work, and good luck."

Catell pulled his tools closer and laid them out in a small half circle. After a swift study of the door, he changed his mind about the hinges and went to work on the tumblers. He stuck chisels, hammer, and probes in his pocket. Then, standing close to the door, he went to work on the lock with a drill.

"Keep looking out the window now and then, Smiley."

Catell worked without pause.

"How's your arm?"

"Dead. You getting anywhere?"

"Little more. Just keep that light steady."

After a while Catell put the drill down and used the chisels. The lock cover and a few disks came off. Then he went to work on the tumblers. Catell's movements were deft, sure, but he kept shaking his head.

"How's the arm?"

"Let's not talk about it. What I wanna know is are we gettin' anywhere?"

"I'm fixing the tumblers. It's going O.K."

"Whyn't ya use the soup?"

"And trip the alarm? This job wasn't laid out that way."

"Well, they tell me you know your stuff. But when you're through, don't pat me on the shoulder. My arm might drop off."

"Not much longer, Smiley. Keep it up."

There was silence for a while. Catell, working mostly by touch, started to swear under his breath.

"What's eatin' ya?"

"This whole goddamn job was laid out wrong. That's what comes from not doing your own casing. Whose cockeyed idea was it to burn this door through, anyway? This job should have been done by rewiring the alarms, cutting in on the timing circuit, and then knocking the safe over any way at all. But this horsing around with a live alarm contact— How's your arm?"

"What arm?"

"Anyway, looking at this place now, I would've knocked it over in the daytime, somehow."

"And shoot the place up? That's old-time stuff, Catell."

"Not the way I do it. Uh, I think— Here she comes, Smiley!"

There was a last click inside the tumbler chamber and then Catell spun the wheel. The large bolts slid back into the door with an oily swish, making the door swing free on its hinges. Catell jumped fast, catching the door before it swung out of its frame.

"That goddamn live contact. That sonofabitchin' live—"

He leaned against the door, sweating. "And this lousy door couldn't have been hung straight. No, they had to hang it so it swings open."

"Whatcha gonna do now, Catell?"

"I'll yank that desk over, to hold the door. Then I'll try burning part of the flange so I can slip through the crack and get that contact. And it better be where they said it was. Else we could be burning around here all night."

"How in hell you gonna get a desk without that door swinging open on you?"

"Yeah, how? I'll stay close up to the door. You move out of the beam and get the desk. That'll spell you, too. How's that?"

"Fine. Aren't ya gonna ask can I move my arm?" Cautiously Smiley got out of the way of the beam.

"One more thing, Smiley. If it clicks, jump and we open the safe as is. We'll grab some lettuce and the hell with that door alarm. I figure we're safe for about four minutes. O.K.?"

"O.K."

No click.

Smiley got up, groaning, rubbing his arm.

"What time is it?" Catell asked.

"Eight-forty-five. Can you make it in time?"

"Don't worry about it."

A few minutes later Smiley had edged a desk up to the beam, and Catell, still leaning against the safe door, was getting down to the floor to pull the desk up close. Smiley was starting to maneuver the flashlight into line with the photoelectric cell.

"Tell me when," Catell said.

"There's a guy by the front windows," Smiley said.

"Stay put. May be nothing."

The shadow against the window moved away while the two men lay on the floor, immobile.

Then the side door opened. It opened fast and shut fast.

"Relax, Tony. Turtle speaking."

"Stay where you are."

It was dark enough in the large office so that distant objects were hard to make out.

"How much change in my pocket, that first day in the bar?"

"Ninety-eight cents."

"O.K., Turtle, but don't move. They got electric eyes up."

"Tony, something's up."

Smiley's hand with the flashlight made a short jitter.

"Topper didn't show up, Tony. I waited four minutes, no car, no Topper."

"What is this?" Smiley's voice was shaky.

"You sure, Turtle?"

"Positive. Two blocks down, no car, four minutes late."

"A frame! Smiley, move out of the beam and beat it. I'll hold the safe till you get to the door. Go!"

In the silence of the dark room there was only the harsh breathing of Catell, leaning against the safe, and the sound of Smiley scraping across the floor where the other electric eye was.

They came in from all sides. Four of them burst through the front door, scattering behind desks and balustrades; four others swarmed through the side door, knocking the Turtle into the beam of the eye, stumbling over Smiley, who was still on the floor.

The alarm went off. The big bell over the front entrance started a dull rattle, getting sharper all the time. The wedge in the bell wasn't holding. The men at the side door had grabbed Turtle and Smiley, and a voice from the front yelled, "Hands up and walk out slow. The whole place is sealed."

Somebody flipped a switch, but the lights didn't go on.

Catell rolled away from the safe into the shadows of the back, and the safe door swung open slowly. There was a moment's complete silence as the light from inside the safe grew with the movement of the door. Then shots. Twice, four times.

"Cut it out, up front! We got two of them here."

"Parker, that you?"

"Yessir. We got two here. Wait'll we get the light."

"They don't work."

"Down, everybody. Here comes the flashlight."

One beam cut through the darkness, then two, three.

"Parker?"

"Yessir."

"You and Litvinoff take the prisoners outside. Lobos, bring a flood through the side. Chester, you get one from the front. The rest stay down."

They flooded the place with light, finding tools, Smiley's cigarette stub, an empty suitcase, a desk moved out of place, and the safe open. Then they gathered outside to look at the prisoners.

"We got these two, and one from across the street."

"Find anyone else inside?"

"Well, there were only supposed to be three."

"Guess this is them."

"What's your name?"

"I wanna see my lawyer!"

"What's yours?"

"Florence Nightingale."

"Yours?"

"Catell."

"Tessman, what was that name in the report?"

"Catell."

"Guess that wraps it up. Take 'em downtown. Parker, Lobos, you stay here. All right, boys, move it."

At eleven o'clock that night, Catell moved slowly out of the storage room and back into the main office. Lobos sat up front, smoking in the dark. Parker sat by the desk at the side door, his head on his arms, snoring. The cold draft from the door woke Parker with a start, but by then Catell was half a block away. He got to Burbank three hours later.

Catell paid the taxi and walked up to the dark machine shop. At the back a hair of light was visible through a scratch in one of the painted windows. There were two cars at the side. One was a fish-tail convertible; the other was the getaway car.

The guy that stopped Catell inside the shop recognized him and let him pass. Catell walked past the machines, through the windowless room, and opened the door to the inner office without knocking.

"—is a funny sort of timing, Topper," Smith was saying.

"But I saw them, Mr. Smith. I saw them—" And then Catell stepped inside the room.

Smith, leaning back in his chair, rolled the cigar around in his mouth. He looked at Catell, never changing his expression. It was calm, level, and just slightly interested. But Topper jumped.

"Why, you—how—" Controlling himself, he took a deep breath and said, "I see you made it, Catell."

"Yeah."

"How—what I mean is, did they follow you? Did you come alone?"

"Alone. Except for you, Topper."

"You trying to be funny, Blue Lips?" Topper got up slowly, his eyes slits and his neck swelling over the white collar.

"Not funny, Topper. Serious."

And while Smith sat in his chair, hands folded over his paunch, Catell's hand whipped out, grazing Topper's drawn lips. Topper had caught the jab with a fast block, and that was his mistake. With his full weight behind the punch, Catell, pivoting a half turn, rammed his other fist into Topper's stomach. The man doubled over, gasping, when Catell fired a roundhouse at the contorted face. Something cracked, and through split lips three front teeth jagged out.

Topper crashed sideways across the desk, pushing phones and papers to the floor. Smith got up and stepped back. He was holding the cigar between his teeth.

When Topper kicked his leg out, catching Catell on the chest, he tried to follow the kick with a fast turn that would bring him back to his feet. But Catell stepped back and pulled. Holding on to Topper's foot, he twisted and pushed. Topper slammed to the floor, screaming, one leg doubled over at a crazy angle. Then Catell knelt down over his chest.

Two minutes later he got up, leaving the ruined man curled on the floor.

"Do you carry a gun, Catell?" Smith came out from behind the desk, flicking some ashes on the floor.

"It belongs to Topper."

"Give it to me." Smith put out his hand.

Catell handed over the gun. Smith took it by the grip, and without seeming to aim he pulled the trigger. Three close shots crashed out and Topper twitched once, twice. Then he lay still.

"Too bad about Topper," Smith said. "Valuable man."

Then he walked around the puddle of blood on the floor. He pulled open a desk drawer and handed Catell two bills.

"Here's your thousand. Got a way home?"

"No."

"Take the limousine. And call me in a day or two."

"So long."

"See you, Catell."

That night Catell didn't go back to the Turtle's room. He drove to Westwood and parked the car a few blocks from Lily's apartment.

She opened the door for him, smiling a little. He could feel her warm body through the thin robe she was wearing. Walking to the bedroom with her, he could hear the fever pounding in his ears. A hysterical tension trembled through his body, making objects change shape before his eyes, plucking at his muscles.

They sat on the bed, and then his head sank into her lap. She hummed to him while he moaned into the cloth of her robe.

Chapter Fourteen

"I see nothing but gloom," Smiley said. "I see gloom turning the corner, bearing poisonous grub."

The police guard came up to the cell. Balancing a tray in one hand, he started to fumble with his keys with the other.

"Lemme give you a helping hand, Inspector. You hold the tray and I'll just—"

"Keep your hands off, Short Stuff! Maybe you think I'm stupid or something?"

"You're gettin' warm, Pop. You're gettin' real warm."

The guard stepped back and put the tray on the floor. When he raised himself, the exertion had turned his bald head a shiny purple, and he puffed air through his white mustache.

"Nature is cruel," Swensen said from the back of the cell. "Look at all that gorgeous hair under his nose, and nothing but bare rocks on top."

"You guys don't shut up I'll take the food back," said the guard.

"And eat it yourself?" Smiley asked.

"He's bluffing," Swensen said. "He come to poison us good and proper this tune. All this threatening is just a bluff."

"Let's see ya eat the stuff, Pop. I dare ya."

Mumbling through his mustache, the guard unlocked the cell door. Then he stepped back to pick up the tray, but stopped halfway down, grunting when he straightened up again.

"One of you guys come out here and pick that tray up."

"So's you won't be blamed for the consequences? Swensen, whaddaya think of old Pop now? Pretty sharp, this switch, eh?"

"Pretty sharp. Experience, I'd say."

"Whaddaya say, Tur—uh, Catell? Ya think we should do this thing for Poison Pop?"

"Give 'im a thrill, Smiley. Go out there and make a break for it."

"Come on, you nuts." The guard sounded querulous. "One of you come out here and pick up that tray."

"All right, men. When I give the signal, we rush him. One, two—"

The old man started to look confused. He stepped back.

Smiley said, "Good thing I can't count to three, Pop. It saved your life."

Then he stepped out of the cell and brought the tray back in.

"Knock on the bars when you're done." The guard was locking the door. "Knock on the bars and I pick up the tray."

"Get that," Smiley said "How's he expect us to knock on the bars, us dead from poisoning and layin' here stiff?"

"Buncha nuts," said the guard, shuffling off.

"Poisoner!"

They started to eat, laughing about the old man and making small talk. But they didn't feel right. They didn't feel right about being caught in a double cross.

"That Catell sure got a friend in you, Turtle. You realize what this means?"

"That's O.K. I been in stir but twice. Builds character, I always say."

"Yeah? I rather be without character," Smiley said. "Got a smoke?"

"Won't be much for the Turtle," Swensen put in. "What are they going to charge him with, lying to an officer of the law?"

"Associating with bad company. It's us they got over a barrel, Swensen. I get faint just thinking about it."

"Smith'll come through. I've seen him come through before. So you get a few years, rest up. You know."

"Swensen, for chrissakes, don't talk like that. Me, I'm a vital boy. I can't stand being locked up someplace."

"Whaddaya yammering about? You had Rosie yesterday. Look at us with nothin' to give us strength."

"Ah, Rosie. Such a friendly, friendly girl."

"Listen to that mush," Swensen said. "And I bet he don't even remember her face or the color of her hair."

"I ain't in the habit of remembering broads by unimportant details, Swensen."

"Oh, Christ. A jump artist. Wait'll they get you up to—"

"Catell. Up front." The police guard opened the door.

"But we didn't rattle the bars yet, Pop. Look," and Smiley held his plate up. "We ain't finished yet."

The Turtle got up and, stepping over Swensen, went to the open door.

"Fare thee well, men. And whilst I'm off to the torture chambers, fear not, for Pop here will be with youse."

"Come on, Catell, get a move on."

They walked down the corridor that led to the door and the precinct desk.

"Keep in touch," Smiley called. "You're O.K."

They put handcuffs on the Turtle and put him in a police car. Then they drove him downtown, to the office of the FBI. The Turtle didn't say anything during the long ride. He didn't think that funny talk would make any difference any more.

Herron closed the folder, left his desk, and walked across the hall to the room they used for interrogations. There was a table in it, a water cooler, and a few chairs. On the wall was a two-year-old calendar with a big picture on top. It showed some kids jumping around in the water of an old swimming hole. A sign said, "No bathing."

Herron sat down on the table and lit a cigarette. His palms were wet and he sucked on his cigarette with nervous puffs. Then the door opened. Two officers and the Turtle came in.

"Here he is, Herron. Friendly as all get-out."

They unlocked the handcuffs and one of the men sat down at the table with a pad and pencil.

"This is supposed to be Catell?" Herron swallowed hard a few times and stared at the Turtle. "You mean this guy is Catell and just a few days ago I shook hands with him in a nightclub not knowing he's the guy I've been chasing all over the country?"

The Turtle looked down modestly.

"Sure it's Catell. And like the tip said, we caught him red-handed, knocking over that safe."

"Have his prints been taken?"

"Sure. Last night yet."

"Did you run them through?"

"No, but we will, if you want. Shall I get them started on it?"

"I wish you would, Parker. And let me know right away."

When Parker closed the door behind him, Herron got off the table and walked around the Turtle, looking him over.

"I must say—uh—Catell, you don't look much the way I figured. You don't look much like your pictures, either."

"Couldn't have been a very flattering likelihood," said the Turtle "You know how them mug shots distract a guy's personality."

"Yeah. I guess. Tell me, Catell, how's your health been lately?"

"Lately? Fine, till yesterday."

"Yeah? Then what?"

"Well, it's like this: There was this guy they call Poison Pop; old geezer runs the clink at the Twenty-ninth Precinct in San Pedro. Now, soon as me and the boys—"

"Never mind. All right, Catell, let's cut out the bull and get down to cases. I guess you know we got you dead to rights this time and anything you do to stall the investigation can only make things worse. You understand that?"

"You mean worse than life? What, I ask, can be worse than life?"

"Where's the gold, Catell?"

"What gold?"

"When did you see it last?"

"See who?"

"Dick, you got that down? Catell, every attempt to stall this investigation will be held against you. And just to get things straight, it might interest you to know that we are preparing a charge of assault with intent to kill. One of the guards at the university isn't doing so hot."

"Listen, Herron, you I can do without."

"Now you listen, Catell—"

"Catell? You talking to me, Herron? Because if you are, Buster, you got the wrong man."

Herron didn't say anything for a moment. He watched the stenographer finish his entry.

"That's the name you gave when arrested."

"That's the name *they* give *me* when I was arrested. For what, I know not. And now, if you please, who is Catell?"

"What's your name?"

"Who's Catell?"

"Listen, you. What I said before about co-operation still goes, no matter who you are. What's your name?"

"I wanna lawyer."

"All I want is your name, for chrissakes. You can give me your name without fear of self-incrimination, can't you?"

"You wouldn't say that if you knew what my handle was."

"What is it?"

"Egbert."

"Egbert? Egbert what?"

"Egbert the Terrible."

"Oh, for chrissakes!"

"I useta be a wrestler. They gimme the handle on account—"

"What you got, Parker?" The door had opened and Parker came in with papers in his hand.

"They don't match up, Herron. This guy ain't Catell."

"Didn't I tell ya, Mr. Herron? Didn't I just—"

"Aw, shut up. So who's this guy, Parker?"

"Local dip. Two minor convictions."

"And his name?"

"Turtforth. Egbert Turtforth. And get this: Used to be a specialty wrestler called Egbert the Terrible. Then for a while he was a magician with—"

"For the lovamike, get out of here. Hold him under your own charges, drop him in a well, I don't care what. Dick, let's go. Wait till Jones hears about this. Christ, I can just see him now."

They walked across the hall to the large room where Herron's desk was.

"One blind alley after another. One funk after another. So help me, Dick, I don't think there is such a guy as Catell. I think this whole thing is nothing but a sly way of testing a man's sanity. Did you ever hear such a name as Egforth?"

"Egbert. Egbert Turtforth."

"All right, all right. And I bet you can read that name backward and get a valuable clue on how to win a box top free. I have a good mind right now—"

"You're wanted on line three, Herron." An agent at one of the desks was holding the phone, waving at Herron to take the call at his own desk.

Herron picked up the receiver. "Agent Herron speaking, may I help you?"

It was a woman's voice. It was a slurry voice that nevertheless made no attempt to disguise itself. "Hi, you Herron? Listen, I bet you haven't found my boyfriend Catell yet, have you? Well, it's time you got a little help around here. Wanna meet me?"

"Who's this calling? Your name, please."

"I'm in the Lifeboat, Beverly and La Cienaga, you know. You come on over, Mr. Herron. Ask for Selma."

Chapter Fifteen

When Catell woke in the morning, he remembered the way the night had started. He turned, leaning on his elbow. Lily was asleep there, her naked back a breathing curve. Catell remembered the rest of the night and felt better.

For the next five days they lived together, seeing no one, needing no one.

"I've never had it like this," he said. "Never in my life."

"Me neither," she said.

"That's because you're so young," he answered.

They ate out of cans, and Catell boiled coffee. Lily didn't know how to cook.

After two days they left the apartment and drove to Santa Barbara. During the day they lay on the beach; at night they stayed in a motel near the pier. It had two tiny rooms, fixed up like a home. Lying in bed at night, they could hear the surf; if they sat up they could see the slow roll of the breakers on the long, empty beach. The little ruffled curtains would move in the breeze.

"Let's play house," Lily said.

"We can't. You don't know how to cook."

"You hungry?"

"Nope."

"Then why're you talking about cooking?"

"Because you said that about playing house."

"I may not know how to cook, but I know how to play house." Lily smiled and let herself fall back on the bed.

There was nobody in Santa Barbara that they knew or that bothered to know them. Either way, they wouldn't have paid any attention. On the beach they lay in the hot sun, watching the play around them, not caring to join in.

"See those kids with the ball, Lily? High-school kids."

"They are?"

"Yeah. They're your age."

"Maybe. But not really," and Lily stretched in the sand, like a cat rubbing her back, smiling at Catell with a slow sideways look.

Catell suffered only in the evenings, or early in the mornings. None of his wounds had healed, and sometimes he felt weak, shivery, his body like a rag doll soaked in water.

"How long have you been like this, Tony?"

"I don't know. A long time, it seems."

Lily bandaged his hand; the gauze became stained quickly. And once, in the waves, his body froze with a sick terror, a steel vise cramping his chest, and the breath stuck in his throat like a solid thing. This he never told Lily, but the rest of the day he kept still, lying flat, sweat breaking from his pores with each movement.

Sometimes he thought of his gold; each time the hard will that dominated all his acts flashed up like a blinding flame, forging his doubts, his pains, even his pleasures into a sharp steely point, like a weapon. The new start, the new life, the big time. Lily. Did any of this exist without Lily? The gold had been there before Lily, and all his sudden strength that came on him suddenly like a cramp, that too had been with him before Lily. But all this, no different now than it had been before, existed now because of the girl—the woman he had found.

Lily had never spoken of such things. Her face was open and seemed to say nothing, and she gave her body without gesture. Lily had happy days with Catell.

When they left Santa Barbara they moved into an apartment in Santa Monica. Then Catell called Smith.

"I have an office downtown," Smith said. "The Western Development Company. Look it up in the book. I'll expect you tonight at eight."

Lily went to the club to do her job, and Catell went downtown.

The place looked like any other office that used more than one desk. There was a railing with a swinging gate, there were several desks and filing cabinets and a switchboard. In the back an office was set apart by frosted glass. The place looked empty.

When Catell started through the swinging gate, the office door in the back opened and a goon with a face like a tomato came out.

"He's waiting for ya. Step right in," and the goon came past Catell and sat down at the switchboard.

Smith looked as he always did, rotund, a little jovial, his mouth busy on a cigar.

"Nice tan you got. Sit down, Catell, sit down."

Catell sat.

"And how's the little Lily?"

"She's— Why do you ask?"

"Just polite, Catell, just a polite inquiry."

"She's fine. You know why I'm here, Smith, so let's—"

"Of course. The gold. What do you think we ought to do, Catell?"

"What's there to think? We made a deal, we set the price, and this is it. Where do you want it and when? That's all there is to do, Smith."

Catell had started to raise his voice, but he controlled himself. He saw a speck of dust on his pants and brushed it off with a short movement. "Our agreement stands, Smith. You're not dealing with a punk."

Smith exhaled noisily, letting the sound die down. Then he leaned back and looked at the ceiling.

"You say we have a deal on, Catell, and you are right. You did a job and I paid you. I paid you even though I didn't make a cent on that heist. In fact, it's costing me. Would you like to know how much it's costing me? However, that's neither here nor there. And the fact that you couldn't deliver is certainly not your fault. Nevertheless, the fact remains that the job did not come off."

"Just a minute, Smith. Before—"

"Please let me finish. You and I have a deal. That stands. I'm not trying to pull out, Catell, because that's not the way I work. But I'm asking you to stand by the terms of our agreement, just as I do. You've got to deliver."

"You blaming me for that fluky setup?"

"Certainly not. And those to blame have been dealt with. You were present on one of the occasions yourself. I am suggesting, in all fairness to both of us, that you go along with me once more. I have—"

"I don't operate that way, Smith. When—"

"I realize that, Catell. I realize the last operation cramped your style, there were holes in the planning, and I certainly didn't get the benefit of your talent. The next time, all that will be corrected. I want you to be in on the planning, you can do your own research, and I'll give you a percentage of the take."

"You have it all worked out, haven't you, Smith?"

"I have."

And Catell knew there wasn't anything he could do about it.

For a moment the thought made him see red. A thousand acrid hates rose in his throat. He closed his eyes, trying to control the fine trembling that crept through his body. He took a harsh breath. Watch it, Catell. You're getting like a hophead taking the cold turkey. Hold on, for the sake of—for the sake of everything. Why am I cracking now? The knowledge of his strange new weakness drove fear into him.

"Is anything wrong, Catell?"

He opened his eyes, face still. "Nothing, Smith. Too much sun, I figure.

Nothing's the matter," and then his strength came back. There were small beads of sweat on his forehead, but he was himself again.

"I was just thinking, Smith. I was thinking you're right."

"Good. We'll talk about the details some other time. In general, it's the same operation as the last. There's a little resort up in the Sierras, small but expensive, where they run a sizable gaming room on weekends. You'll go up and have a look yourself. I'll give you a flat three thousand plus a percentage. We'll go over that the next time. This will definitely be your last commitment—if you wish—and we'll complete the rest of our affairs as soon as this is over."

Smith opened his wallet and took out three bills. "Fifteen hundred on account. Take it."

Catell picked up the money and stuck it in his pocket. Then they shook hands, Smith making a brief smile. When Catell was at the door, Smith said:

"Before I forget it. There was a call for you. A woman by the name of Selma."

"What!"

"The past, apparently, rearing its head, eh?"

"What did she want?"

"Nothing. I took the message, because she came well recommended. Our friend Paar gave her my number."

Catell walked back into the room "Why did she call?"

"She said to tell you she had arrived in town. And you should give her a ring at the Empress Arms."

"That all?"

"Yes. I'm not sure whether she was asking you or telling you. Why, Catell, you look almost human!" Smith gurgled a laugh and watched Catell's face turn glum. "Ah, I don't often do this, Catell, but would you care to talk about it?"

"There's nothing to talk about. I was just surprised for a minute."

"I noticed that. Sit down, Catell. Here, have one of my cigars."

"Thanks, I don't smoke cigars. Anyway—"

"Sit down, Catell."

They sat for a moment while Smith unwrapped a cigar for himself.

"I'm not concerned with anything in your life, Catell, except insofar as it affects your work in my organization. Please understand that. Now, just as I cannot tolerate a squealer in my work, I cannot tolerate the kind of problems that some men seem to have with women. I don't like messes, Catell."

"You're going a little far, aren't you, Smith?"

"I don't mean to. It's true, though, isn't it, that this Selma is a lush?"

"Would you believe it, Smith, I don't know. Selma was a dame I knew about ten years ago."

"How about Detroit?"

"Nothing. I'd just been out of stir a short while."

"Ah, I don't mean to sound superstitious, Catell, but the man who lived with Selma—Schumacher, I think—and the man who was with Lily, they are both dead now."

"I don't follow that. If you're not superstitious—"

"I'm not. Only some men, for vague reasons, unknown reasons, some men have a way of concentrating disaster around themselves, and it might be that you—and you'll admit there is nothing average about you—that you could easily—"

"I don't get any of that crap, Smith. I'm a guy like any other guy who knows what he wants and does all he can to get it. I've had my share of kicks, sure, but I'm as careful as the next guy." Catell sucked on his cigarette, hard. "Especially now," he added, and tossed the butt to the floor.

"Uh, now?"

"Yeah, now. I'm no spring chicken, Smith. It's time I made good and found something solid. I haven't got time to horse around. One, two solid jobs and I'm off this racket. I got some playtime coming to me and I mean to have it."

"Speaking of playtime, are you including Lily in all this?"

"I'll tell you this much, Smith: She isn't playtime. Let's just leave it at that."

"I'm sorry if this riles you, but, as I have said before, my only intent is—"

"Yeah, I know. Commercial."

"And that's why I cover all angles, Catell. Of course, I'm glad to see that you are serious-minded, and that your attitude is sober. But that's why I'm wondering. Don't you think Lily is a little young, uh, for you?"

Catell got up and went to the door without answering. Then he turned and said, "I'm forgetting you asked that, Smith. And remember, don't pump me again. You and me, Smith, we don't discuss Lily. Understand?"

Smith shrugged his heavy shoulders and turned the swivel chair the other way.

"Don't forget your message," he said to the opposite wall. "You're supposed to call this Selma."

Catell stepped through the door and slammed it behind him.

He took the Freeway to Hollywood and then cut over to Sunset. He turned on Vine, parked the car, and walked back to the corner.

The corner of Sunset and Vine was crowded with characters. Professional characters, unintentional characters, and the plain crazy variety. There was the guy who once had the bad luck of writing one hit song, and nothing since. There was the slob who had another deal on and he was bending somebody's ear about how the deal was hot. A high-stacked blonde was waiting for the light to change, looking busy and detached in dark glasses. Tourists hustled around in pairs, all atwitter with free passes to a TV broadcast. Catell saw them line up like sheep in front of CBS, all looking very much alike with cameras, Hawaiian shirts, and health shoes.

With nothing else to do, Catell walked into an ice cream parlor and sat down. He ordered Pistachio Delight, which came in a clifflike arrangement and smelled like perfume. He hated ice cream, but the glass dish felt cold in his hands, and he held on to the bowl as if it could draw the waves of fever out of his bones. Catell felt sick.

From where he sat, the night didn't look like night. An unnatural glare covered the street, making harsh black shadows. Catell lit a cigarette. After a few drags he pushed the butt into the wet mess in his ice cream dish, where the cliffs had turned into a soggy bog, and went outside.

Catell wasn't the only one just standing around in the street, but he was the only one who wasn't rushing. Another hour before he could see Lily.

He would have liked to see the Turtle. For a moment Catell forgot he was a hunted man and started to figure what to take to the Turtle during visiting hours tomorrow. That's probably what they were waiting for. There were probably men watching the Turtle the way an angler concentrates on his hook, after a long day without a nibble.

Catell leaned against a wall and closed his eyes. Everything started to spin. He walked up and down the street like a very busy man, late for an appointment, or perhaps anxious to get there ahead of time, this being a really hot deal. It didn't work. He couldn't have cared less. He watched a young dish walk by, her high-heeled strut making highlights dance all over her. Just for the hell of it, he pushed himself away from the wall, turned toward the girl, and gave her the eye. She looked back so coldly that the whole vision of her turned ugly. But it wouldn't have taken that much to make Catell lose interest. A minute or so later he couldn't remember what she looked like.

Catell looked at his watch and started for his car. Pulling out in a sharp U turn, he drove up to Sunset and joined the traffic toward Beverly Hills. But he didn't start to make any time until he passed the Beverly-Wilshire, where the traffic thinned out a little. Catell had started to smoke the way Topper used to: one cigarette after another and the windows closed. When he got to the Pink Shell, his pack was empty.

Lily still used the same dressing room where Catell had found her that first time. He went in and waited for her, folding and refolding the empty cigarette pack.

When she came in, Catell got up and smiled. "You're looking good, baby. How was it?"

"O.K., I guess. You been waiting long, Tony?"

She went behind the screen to take off the red corset and net stockings she was wearing.

"Why're you going behind that thing?"

"Just because."

"Because what?"

"I don't know. Just because, you know."

"Come on out."

"Aw, Tony, please. That's not right."

He didn't answer her. He sat with his elbows on his knees, cracking his knuckles.

"How was it, Lily?"

"Reach me that bra, hon. How was what?"

"Where you came from, just now. That party."

"O.K., I guess. We just danced. I sang a song."

"What else?"

"Nothing, Tony, honest. Just a private party and we entertained. You know."

"I bet you entertained. Anybody make a pass at you?"

"Tony!"

"Listen, I know those parties. Did anybody—"

"Nobody did nothing, hon, really. To me, anyway."

"What?"

"Well, some of the girls stayed, you know. They're still there. But nobody tried anything with me. They all know I'm your girl, Tony."

She came out from behind the screen, wearing the white dress, high and smooth around her ripe body, the dress she had worn the first time he'd heard her sing.

Catell got up and took her waist. "They knew you were my girl, huh?"

"They did, hon. That makes me special," and she smiled up at him. "You feeling better now, Tony?"

"Sure. And all this is going to change. One more week, Lily, two weeks at the most, and you and I beat it out of here. No more of this life, Lily." He kissed her hard and she gave the kiss back, slowly, earnestly.

"My number's up, Tony. You sit out front?"

"Don't say your number's up. Bad luck." He chucked her under the chin. "Say, 'I'm going on stage,' or something."

"O.K., Tony. You'll be out front?"

"I'll be right there with you."

They did the number about the evil baron again, and Lily did her song. Catell sat and waited. His throat felt hot and raw from smoking, so he drank a glass of milk. When Lily was through she came to the table and sat down.

"Why don't we go home?" Catell said. He had one hand on Lily's arm, working his palm against her wrist.

"One more number, Tony. The short one. Can I have a drink?"

"Sure. What?"

"Just bar whisky. And a glass of water."

"Bar whisky! How can you stand that stuff? We can afford better, you know. Besides, it's on the house."

"Just bar whisky. I like a little shot. It makes me warm inside. You know, Tony, I don't care for the flavors, I just like the heat inside."

"Of course you know how fattening it is."

"It is?"

"Oh, yes, very, and you are getting fat. Here."

"Tony! The people!"

"And here."

"To-nee!"

"True. At your age, getting fat is a bad thing."

"Tony Catell, you do that once more and I'll leave."

"You'll leave! Where to?"

"I don't know yet, and besides, I wouldn't tell you, anyway. So there!"

They looked at each other and laughed, not really knowing why. And in the middle of their being together, a cold anger suddenly pulled Catell's face into an ugly mask. He got up.

"What in hell do you want?"

"Why, lovin' cup, you old boozer, where have you been keeping yourself?"

Selma came up to the table with a rush, gesturing, looking back and forth between Catell and the seated girl.

"You gonna ask me to sit down, lovin' cup?" She sat down next to Lily.

"This is my friend Lily. And this is Selma."

Selma's wide mouth was spread in a stiff grin and she kept crinkling her eyes as if she was suppressing a real killer of a joke.

"If you knew just how happy this makes me, to see good old Tony again. I've been asking around and around, ever since I got here, Tony, and finding out all kinds of things about you. I hadn't heard about you, though," Selma said, looking Lily up and down.

"I bet," Catell said. He waved to the bartender.

"Me too, lovin' cup. Scotch." Selma looked at Catell as if he and she were the only people at the table. She put her chin in her hands and moved one shoulder. The strap of her evening dress slid down.

"Your thing slid down, Miss—Mrs.—"

"Just Selma, dear. Just call me Selma."

There was an ugly scratch in Selma's voice when she talked to Lily. Lily looked as she always did.

While they were waiting for the drinks, there was a moment of silence, the kind of silence that everybody hopes no one will break, but somebody has to.

Then Selma laughed. "Well, Tony, tell me about yourself. You been doing any good? Uh, pardon me, dear, I don't mean you." Selma gave Lily an indulgent smile.

"Selma." Catell's voice pressed out with a hiss. "Selma, I want you to get one thing straight. Leave the kid alone. In fact, leave her out completely. She's done nothing to you, and you, sister, mean nothing to me. So get off my back, Selma. Just stay off my back."

Before there was an answer the drinks came and Selma lifted her glass. Then she put the glass down without putting it to her lips.

"Don't get me wrong, Tony dear." She kept her eyes down. "I don't mind what you did with the chippie. Now that you and me are back together again." Then she tossed down the drink.

Lily was watching Catell with a puzzled look. His hands were shaking. She stretched her hand out, slowly, trying to touch Catell. Selma turned on her with hate in her eyes.

"Don't you try and wheedle him, you slut. And don't you forget for a minute that your kind—"

That's when Catell hit her.

He did it so fast that nobody saw it clearly, and there was nothing to show for it but a slow red welt on Selma's cheek.

She stared at him open-mouthed. Lily, eyes wide, had started to get up when Selma's expression changed. With a soft, tired voice she said, "Don't be upset, dear. He's like that. Perhaps you haven't found that out. You would if you stayed with him, Lily. He has crazy ways of getting his kicks. Why, I remember once he woke me up at four in the morning and asked me—"

"Selma, either you stop or you'll regret it for the rest of your life."

There was something in Catell's voice that reached the woman. She swallowed and patted her hair. "Buy me another drink, Tony?"

"No. And now you listen to me. All you and I ever were to each other was a dance and a drink and a jump. That's all. I've asked you once to stay off my back. This time I'm telling you. Keep out of our way and nothing will happen to you. Cross me and you'll regret it. So remember what I say and act your age. That's all I've got to say to you, Selma, and I'm not going to say it again." Catell took a deep breath and sat back in his chair. "Now if you still want that drink, I'll get you one."

"Yes, Tony, thanks."

With the unpredictability of a lush, Selma's attitude had turned helpless and soft. When the drink came, she sipped at it, throwing shy glances at Lily and Catell, never raising her head.

"Tony," Lily said, "I'm on. My number's up."

"Don't say that!" His voice was a shout.

"I'm sorry, darling. I mean—"

"I know what you mean. I'm the one that's sorry. Selma, finish your drink. You're leaving too."

"Yes, Tony." Selma got up, trying to move with a contrite grace. She stepped close to Catell and looked at him through her lashes. "Lovin' cup," she said with a voice suddenly hard, "I'm not through with you yet."

She turned and left.

While Lily did her number, Catell sat hunched at the table, stirring the ashes in the ashtray with a dead match. He knew for sure that Selma was not through with him.

Chapter Sixteen

When the sun came up, Catell was still in the mountains. He had pushed the powerful car all night, trying to get to Pasadena early. It was five in the morning, still time to get to Smith's before noon.

Catell opened the thermos on the seat beside him and drank some of the hot black coffee. He put the stopper back in the bottle and lit a cigarette. He was satisfied with the week he'd spent at the resort.

The place was isolated, with only one telephone line coming in through the long stretch of woods. There were two roads out of the place, one road going downhill to join the main highway, the other going uphill to join the same highway farther away. Then there was one more way of getting out: across the lake, two miles through the woods, and then a different highway that never actually got near the resort. Catell liked the layout.

Inside the main building of the resort there were three major safes, it seemed. There was one for guest deposits, behind the registration desk. Another one, for the hotel intake, was in the manager's office, right off the main lobby. The third safe was a movable, compact job, probably a new model, and it stood in the basement of the lodge. That was the building where the big dance was held on Saturdays, and where the gaming tables operated. The lodge stood close by the lake, and the basement of the lodge was right next to the boathouse.

Catell had the plans in his pocket.

He had stayed at the resort long enough to cover two weekends. He had gambled freely, always dropping a game after a short time, going from one table to another. He had a fair idea what the house took in. On Monday mornings, he figured, there was close to a hundred thousand in that safe in the basement.

Catell had the figures in his pocket.

There was a routine about the way each employee worked. Some were important to Catell, others weren't. He had clocked the ones that were important for over a week.

Catell had the schedules in his pocket.

Nine o'clock. The highway was dipping steadily, twisting through the last hills before the valley of the big city. Catell stopped for gas once and then pushed on. The traffic got thicker, and dusty olive trees lined the long highway that cut through flat vineyards and hot stucco towns.

Ten o'clock. Catell entered Pasadena and found his cutoff. He wound through still little streets that looked alternately like futuristic movie sets and old Spanish settlements. Catell was glad to be almost there. The job he had set up looked good, but best of all, this thing would be over soon. First the cash for his job, then the cash for the gold—waiting in the dust near a desert town—and then he and Lily. They were going away. Mexico? Uruguay? He had a friend in Uruguay. A friend with a business that was legit, as far as anyone could tell.

Catell found the address. He stopped the car under a long port and walked to the front of the house. There were no other cars in sight.

A houseboy opened the door and let him in. It was cool inside. The modern sweep of the building had been deceptive, because there didn't seem to be more than five or six rooms. Catell was led to the rear terrace, where he saw that the house was all glass on one side.

"Mr. Smith will be with you shortly," the servant said.

Catell sat and waited.

When he heard footsteps again, it was a woman. She was a stately figure, gray-haired, and with the graciousness of those who can afford to concentrate on nothing but the pursuit of a well-mannered life.

"I am Mrs. Smith," she said, smiling. "My husband told me he was expecting one of his associates. Please sit down."

"Catell is my name." He sat down again, awkwardly.

"I think I'll ask Kimoto to bring us something cool. Gin and tonic?"

"Fine, that would be fine."

When the drinks were brought, Catell waited for Mrs. Smith to take her glass before picking up his own. The stuff was good. The whole setup was good, he thought. A respectable address, the best little house a man could want, a real lady for a wife. Everything neat, comfortable, and right. The life. How would Lily look when she was older? She wasn't so tall, like Mrs. Smith. Lily was different, too, in the way she acted. Not so polite. But Lily was friendlier; she was quiet most of the time, but really friendly.

"Have you been with my husband long, Mr. Catell?"

"Ah, no, not very long. Just a little while."

"I don't suppose that's unusual, though. In my husband's business, old employees of long standing, so to speak, aren't so essential as they are in some types of enterprise."

What in hell was she talking about?

"But then, of course, my husband has so many business interests. Which one are you associated with, Mr. Catell?"

"Uh, that's hard to say. What I mean is, we're just discussing things. You know, to see what can be done."

"I think I understand." She laughed. "In the investment field you can't always put a precise name to the nature of any given business at hand."

Didn't she know a damn thing?

"Mr. Catell, would you like a fresh drink?"

He accepted another one and they talked about the heat and the lawn.

Eleven o'clock. When she rose, Catell got up too, and she offered her hand.

"I'm sorry my husband is keeping you so long, and now I must run too. I'm taking a little trip and my packing isn't half done. You will excuse me?"

Probably a little trip to Hawaii or someplace. Catell finished his drink. He was getting annoyed with the rising heat and the long wait. He tilted his glass and sucked on the small piece of ice that was left. Then he heard a car crunch on the gravel, and a few minutes later Smith came through one of the glass doors.

"Sorry to keep you waiting, Catell. Didn't really expect you till later. Christ, the heat!" Smith sat down, mopping his big face. "I see you've tried to cool off. Join me in another one?"

"Sure."

"Who's been drinking with you? My wife?"

"We chatted a while. She's packing."

"Still packing? What did you talk about?"

"Investment business."

"Oh."

Kimoto brought two more drinks and Smith leaned back with a sigh. "How'd it go at the resort?"

"Fine. I got everything here in my pocket."

"Not now, Catell. Let me catch my breath."

"Should be a cinch, that place."

They drank quietly for a while.

"Get your expenses down?" Smith asked.

"Yeah, right here."

"Never mind. How much?"

"Twelve hundred. The gambling—"

"Never mind. Here."

Smith counted out some bills and pushed them across the glass-topped table.

"Not a bad business, this, huh, Catell?"

"Thanks, it's O.K."

"What do you think the take will be?"

"Perhaps close to a hundred grand."

Smith took a cigar out, unwrapped it, lit it.

"Not a bad business, huh?"

"Looks that way."

"Catell, listen. You still going through with your plans?"

"What do you mean?"

"Look. This heist is worth three, four times as much as that gold of yours. Did you ever think of sticking around? Right now, I'm giving you peanuts for your work, sure. But—"

"You trying to pull out from under?"

"I've told you once before, Catell, I don't operate that way. What I'm offering you is a chance to come into my organization."

"No deal."

"What's the matter with you, you crazy nut? Just what's so much more important about heisting a stick of gold for a guy like Schumacher than to do the same work for more dough in this outfit?"

"A hell of a difference, Smith. Forget it. Besides, I got other plans."

"Well, my offer stands. For a while longer. Think about it. Now let's finish up and get going. I asked you to come here so you could give me a lift to Burbank. It's on your way."

They got up and walked to the carport. Catell was gritting his teeth at the delay, but he didn't say anything.

"You drive." Smith sat in the back.

When they pulled up to the side of the machine shop, the heat had become like a simmering liquid.

One o'clock.

There were four other men in the office, none of whom Catell knew. They were waiting in their shirt sleeves, collars open, hair sticky. The air-conditioning had broken down.

"Fellows, I want you to meet Tony Catell, head man on this job. Catell, this is Penny, Gus, Plotke, and Corvean. All good men. They'll go with you."

"I only need three."

"Why?"

"I only need three, Smith. You'll see why."

"Never mind. Gus, you beat it."

"Wait a minute," Catell said. "Why Gus? Maybe I want Gus and not one of the others."

"I said Gus goes." Smith sat down. "All right, gather around. Any time you're ready, Catell."

Three o'clock.

They went over the job for the hundredth time. Every detail, every eventuality, every movement and step.

Five o'clock.

"Plotke, go out there and tell that slob foreman to get some more fans in here. And sandwiches."

"How about some beer, boss?"

"No beer. You drink water till we're through."

Seven o'clock.

"All right, we'll go over it once more. We leave both cars…"

Eight o'clock.

"Everybody here same time tomorrow. And don't write anything down in the meantime. Memorize, memorize."

When Catell drove to Santa Monica he was exhausted. The heat, the tension before the job, his strange faintness, all made him wish for a cool, still darkness and peace.

He stopped at a drive-in on the other side of Hollywood and dialed the apartment. Lily didn't answer. He dialed the number again and let the phone ring a long time. Lily must have gone to the store. She didn't work tonight. Buying some more cans at the store, probably.

Ten o'clock.

When Catell put the key into the door, it opened. Lily came at him in a rush, throwing her arms around his neck, kissing him.

"Hold me, Tony. You've been so long. Tony, Tony!"

Then Catell saw Selma.

She was sitting in an easy chair by the empty fireplace. The bottle on the small table next to her was more than half empty, and she had crossed her legs, swinging one foot against the andiron on the left of the fireplace. Her foot went tap, tap against the sharp spike of the black metal.

"Where'n hell you been, lovin' cup?"

Catell swung the door shut and stepped into the room.

"Tony, make her go. She's sat there for hours, Tony, saying things, drinking, and the phone rang and she wouldn't let me answer, drinking there, talking— Tony, please!"

Catell held the girl close, stroking her back, his head deep in her hair. When Lily stopped sobbing she stepped back and looked up at Catell. He smiled at her, then turned his eyes to Selma.

"What have you been doing to her, Selma?" Catell sounded like ice.

"The facts of life, lovin' cup. I just been tellin' her the facts of life. Right, dearie?"

Lily retreated to the back of the room, pulling her dressing gown around her tightly.

"Anything you got to say, say to me." Catell stepped close to Selma's chair.

"But I got nothin' to say to you, lovin' cup. I was talkin' to the chippie there. She's the one needed talkin' to. You, lovin' cup, got all the answers, so I don't need to say nothin' to you."

"What answers?"

"About us. You sendin' for me and us takin' up again. You shoulda told her sooner, lovin' cup."

Catell looked over at Lily and their eyes met. Catell knew he didn't have to explain. Then he turned back to Selma.

"You aren't making a ripple around here, so why don't you give up and beat it? Why don't you take your booze and your filthy tongue and that vicious mind of yours and beat it, Selma?"

Catell hardly expected her to move, but he had the wild hope that she might. His insides were crawling with a shivering sickness and there was a pounding in his ears.

Selma didn't move. "Don't try to bluff the poor kid," she said. "I explained everything." Selma picked up the bottle and poured herself another drink.

"Out, Selma."

He stood, staring down at her. She looked up at him over the raised glass, understanding nothing.

"Out!"

"Out," Selma said, flinging her arms back and forth. "Out, out, out, out." Then she burst into a shrill giggling.

"Selma!"

She didn't hear him.

"Selma, shut up!" He reached for her arms, yanking her out of her seat so that her head flopped back.

"Out, out, out," she giggled.

"Shut up, shut up!" He shook her back and forth as if he were possessed.

Suddenly she stopped giggling. Her eyes opened wide, and long folds grew down the sides of her mouth. Before she could start to cry Catell slapped her hard on the cheek.

"Do you hear me, Selma?" His face, sharp and drawn, was close to hers.

With a sudden softening of her face she leaned up against Catell and tried to kiss him.

"You crazy lush!" he yelled, and pushed her back into the chair. There was hate in his motions. "You goddamn crazy lush, don't you know when you're through? You make me crawl, you hear? You make me crawl!"

He stood over her, panting, a wild fevered glitter in his eyes, shaking all over.

"Tony, please!" Lily came forward. "Let her go."

"Tony, please." Selma was mimicking the girl's voice. "Let her go, Tony."

Catell had started to shake from head to foot. He sat down, panting, doubled over.

Selma looked puzzled only for a short moment; then she jumped up and ran to him. Lily was there already. She was stroking his head, murmuring to him.

When Catell straightened up his face was quiet, except for the muscle that jumped in his cheek. Then he got up and turned to Selma. What she saw in his eyes wasn't good.

"Tony," she said, "I'm sorry about everything. Really I am, Tony. Look at me. All I want is to have you back, like before, and me taking good care of you. You need a woman, Tony, not a kid like that."

"Selma, there's nothing to talk about."

"Not a kid, Tony. I'm not saying she's no good, I can tell by looking. But she's a kid, Tony, and you're a man old enough—"

"Selma!"

"Tony, look at us." Selma's voice was getting faster, more urgent. "I'm your kind. Anything you want, I can give you. I can—"

"Selma, I'm sick of your voice."

"Listen to me, Tony. She's no good for you. Look what she's done to you, and look at her. Just a brat. A brat decked out like a woman. Christ, Tony, don't you see. She's nothing but a free lay. I know her kind.

She's—"

"Enough, now!"

"—flashy, dolled up, no good. Look at her, Tony. That dumb face, and—and—why, she's got breasts twice the size of mine! It's indecent, Tony. She oughta be—"

That's when he hit her the second time.

She fell. When she jumped up from the floor, her big teeth were bared as if she were going to bite.

"Now you've done it, big shot." She was hoarse. "I told you I wasn't through and you can bet your last dime this is the straight stuff. You think you can get away with just about anything, huh? Well, I've got a surprise for you. And you know who that surprise is? The name wouldn't mean a thing to you, but it's Herron."

Selma was panting now, the words stumbling out, making a mean, clattering sound.

"No, lovin' cup, I'm not talking about a boyfriend. This is bigger than you, big shot. This guy is the FBI. You hear me? The FBI!"

Nobody moved when Selma stopped for breath, and before Catell had got the full punch of her words, she started again.

"And he's a friend of mine, lovin' cup, a real good friend of mine. So you better listen to what I say and do what I say, because one little word, lovin' cup, one little word outa my sweet lips, and you can kiss the world goodbye!"

The hate that shook him was bigger than the world. It tore at his muscles, pushed through his veins with a roar, and he felt as if his skin were too small for him. Without a sound, like a snake striking, he was at Selma's throat, shaking her, crashing her head against the mantel of the fireplace, tasting the blood where his teeth sank into his lip. At first, through the brilliant curtain of his rage, he heard nothing, saw nothing but the ugly face that blurred in front of him. Then he heard Lily's voice, crying with a desperate pleading, "Don't do it, don't, Tony, please! We can leave her, Tony! Darling, I'm here, here!"

And he stopped.

The strength of his feeling was still with him, but it no longer had anything to do with Selma.

"Get dressed, Lily. Fast." He turned the girl around and pushed her toward the door of their bedroom. Trying to follow her, he felt hands clawing at his leg.

"Let go. Damn you, let go!" He was trying to pick himself loose when Selma suddenly released his leg. She rolled back, staggered to her feet. With grotesque movements she lurched toward Catell. Her hair straggled over the contorted face, lipstick a wild smear. One shoe had come off and she limped.

"Let go?" she screeched. "Let go? Let go?"

"Not again, please!" Lily threw herself between Catell and Selma, who was reaching out with crooked nails.

"Let go?" she screeched again. "Let go?" And her nails dug into the soft shoulders of the girl. Before Catell could leap at the crazed woman, she had spun Lily around and tossed her to one side. Lily staggered back, over the shoe, and then there was a curious sound.

Gathering all his rage into the whip of his arm, Catell swung out, but the coiled thing inside him never landed, never exploded.

Lily was on the floor, face up, and yet she was not on the floor. As if suspended in space, her body angled up, gently, toward the side of the dark fireplace. Beneath her neck, where her head tilted, stood the black andiron with the spike.

There was only a slight short twisting, then the soft slump of final surrender to death.

In the first instant of seeing, of knowing, Catell heard the terrible sounds of everything that breaks, bursts, and rips apart beyond repair, and the mad turning of all that moves, speeds, dashes about for a while, turning like a giant wheel, around, around. Then the wheel stopped.

At his side was Lily, still strangely suspended, lax now, and as always her eyes looked out in their quiet, wide way. Catell reached for her hand, then let it drop. The wheel had stopped.

Selma crept forward, staring at the two things there on the floor. "Tony," she said.

There was no answer.

She noticed how the curtains moved in the wind, never quite making it before they collapsed again. It was hot in the apartment.

Eleven o'clock.

When she could not stand the silence any longer, she looked for her bottle. It stood where it had always stood, on a small table beside Catell. She took it, brushing up against his back.

There was some ice in the kitchen, and Selma suddenly decided she needed ice in her drink. When she came back into the room with the fireplace, Catell was still in the same place. And the other one.

"Tony," she said.

When there was no answer, she tilted the glass and drained it.

"You need a drink, Tony."

She splashed whisky into her glass and held it down. She moved it closer, touching the rim to his mouth.

That was the first time Catell moved. He moved sideways, avoiding the glass. That was all.

"Tony, for chrissakes. You know I'm sorry, Tony. You know that, don't you? What do you want me to say? I know this is terrible. Tony, hey!"

She poured the rest of the whisky into the glass.

"Hey?"

Catell didn't answer.

"There isn't anything you can do. Or anybody, hey? This is terrible, lovin' cup, I really mean it. But you're making it worse. Don't make it worse. Listen to me. Listen to Selma, lovin' cup!"

She drank the last of the whisky. Standing in the middle of the room, she looked around. Her shoe was under the leg of the girl. Selma went over and pulled it out. She put the shoe on and poked Catell with her foot.

"You better get up now, Tony. I said— Hey, Tony, what's the matter with you? Get up now. Hey, Tony, I know exactly what we'll do, listen. First we get outa here and head back for Detroit. I been doing you some good there, Tony, really I have. Listen to this. We go back there, and Paar— you know Paar—he promised—Tony, now cut this out! You don't like what I'm saying? Listen, you, Selma is the little girl what can help you, Tony. You and me got a lot of life left, you know? Tony, get up from there, for chrissakes. You trying to drive me bats? I'm not used to talking to myself. You better buck up now, Tony, up, up, up."

Taking him under the arms, she pulled Catell off the floor. He stood without protest. He turned around, facing her.

"Tony, come on now. Now's the time, Tony. Let's blow outa—"

She stopped, wondering at his eyes. He was looking at her, but not really looking. Fumbling in his pocket, he pulled out a cigarette, stuck it in his mouth, lit it.

"That's it, Tony, the old get-up-and-go. Yessirree."

He was still looking her way, but his face was unnatural. Like dead clay, even his eyes.

She smiled at him, cocking her head. Then she stepped around him with a prance, hands on hips.

"Tony boy, hey, Tony boy. Damnit, Tony, say something when a lady speaks to you. Tony boy, you have to forget all about all this here. You and me gotta start out now. I said let's go, you sonofabitch, hear? Christ, where's that bottle? Empty. Chrisalmighty. The cops'll get you, lovin' cup. The coppers! They'll get you, and dead to rights this time. Answer me, you filthy crud, you! The coppers, I'll call 'em, ya hear? I'm calling them!"

Screaming the words, she ran to the phone and dialed. Catell smoked and watched her. He watched her through the whole conversation.

"So there!" She hissed the words in his face. "So there, I've done it, you no-good sonofabitch. The cops are coming and I don't care! I'm sick of you, sick of you!"

Her voice, shrill and hysterical, sank to a blur. She stepped back under his cold stare, puzzled.

"They're coming," she repeated.

"They're coming," he said.

Didn't he care? Was this the end? She started to laugh.

"Little Selma keeps her word, you bastard, even if you don't. Washed up, Catell, and now you know it. You shoulda known before but now you know it. A no-good, washed-up has-been."

Stepping close to him, she grabbed his lapels and tore at them with each word. "Has-been, has-been—"

Time was running out.

"You rat, you! Trying to ruin everything, aren't you? Catell, listen to me. Where's the gold? Open your mouth just once, before everything's over. Where is it, you rat? The gold, where—"

For a moment Catell came alive.

"Say it, Tony, say it. We can still—"

With a wooden motion he reached out and pushed Selma aside. As she stumbled she saw him move away, like an automaton, his back to her, walking to the door. He wasn't waiting for her, and in her haste to follow him she fell again, her hand touching a cold leg. Hysteria ripped at her throat and her scream was like a knife.

Catell was gone when they got there.

Twelve o'clock.

Chapter Seventeen

"He won't get away, you know that."

Driving with one hand and fiddling with the dials of the short-wave set with the other, the detective gave Herron a short look and then turned his attention back to the traffic.

"I don't know any such thing," Herron said.

"Jackie, a guy like this Catell never gets away with anything. History proves it."

"That's the first I heard of it," Herron said.

"Christ, we got the whole town roped off for that bird."

"Sure. He was gone who knows how long by the time we got to that apartment, and it took another half hour to get an intelligible answer out of that howling dervish."

"Whirling dervish."

"Howling. This one was howling. And then you got to figure another hour, a good hour, before your roadblocks would be anywhere near effective. But here's the clincher, Rosen: It's now twelve hours later and we haven't got him yet. History be damned."

"That's only twelve hours—"

"Which you can add to all the time I've already spent missing that hood. Rosen, I am in fact getting the eerie feeling there is no such guy."

Rosen made a sharp turn to avoid a hot rod coming the other way. Traffic was getting worse as they entered the downtown area of Los Angeles.

"Listen, Jackie, that was no ghost what knocked off that one we found on the floor."

"What makes you think Catell did it? Could have been that howling lush there, that Selma dame."

"I don't think so," Rosen said. "I don't think so at all."

They drove in silence for a while. The air that blew in through the open windows felt gritty and hot.

"I think you're wrong, Rosen. I think it was that Selma dame. That is, not counting the chance it was one of those weird accidents."

"Crap," Rosen said. After a while: "Wanna know why I say it was Catell? Because of his record. He's a longtime heavy, he's ruthless and vicious, he never showed any feeling for anybody yet who got in his way, his whole history proves it."

"You know a hell of a lot for never having run into the guy."

"I know crooks, Jackie. But I shouldn't brag. What makes this so simple is the circumstances of the crime. Here he was, laying this young thing, when in walked his moll. Now this young one was probably just a one-night stand, picked her up at that Pink Shell, but this don't cut no ice with that other dame. They all start screaming, and Catell gets annoyed. I can just see him get mad there. But all this time his real sympathies are, of course, with his old-time sweetheart, see? When the one-night stand gets the drift, she starts getting vicious. You know how those little blonde spitfires can be. And that's when Catell has too much. He grabs this dish, the young one, and throws her back into—onto—anyway, you saw it. Now the other one starts to howl. Catell has enough of her too, it looks like, being a woman hater deep down anyway, and starts slapping her around, right? She won't stop, so he just ups and walks out. He's the real filth, and this proves it."

"Christ," Herron said. "You live too close to Hollywood."

Rosen turned into the police garage. "Anyway, that's how I feel about it. And also it might be true, Jackie, it might be true."

Rosen had parked the car and they went upstairs. The inside of the police station was cool. Herron kept moving his shoulder blades to keep the wet shirt from sticking to his back, but it didn't help. He took off his jacket and pulled at the shirt with his fingers. They went into one of the offices and sat down.

"I'll see what's new," Rosen said, and he called the switchboard.

Herron took his hat off, fanning himself. His moist hair started to itch and he rubbed his head. He knew that when his hair was wet or sticky, the balding scalp showed up more. Self-consciously he put the hat back on.

"Nothing," Rosen said, putting the phone down. "They should have another interview out of that Selma." Herron lit a cigarette.

"Interview! You shoulda been there when we tried to question that dame. Interview!"

The door opened and a policeman with shirt sleeves rolled up came in. He was carrying a folder.

"Infirmary sent this over. For you, Herron." He threw the folder on the desk and went out.

"Infirmary?" Herron started to open the folder.

"Probably another *interview*. That's where we took your friend Selma. The state she was in—"

"She sick or something?"

"All I know is they were sedating her when we left. What's it say?"

Herron leafed through the papers in the folder and pulled out one of the sheets.

"Here's a tentative medical report: '...alcoholic, hallucinatory. Severe hysterical state makes diagnosis difficult at present.' Then something here—hallucinosis."

"That's the d.t.'s, the heeby-jeebies."

"No. Not hallucinosis. It's worse."

"Crap. Probably she just needs a drink."

Without answering, Herron went through the rest of the papers.

"Here it says 'Interview' and today's date. This morning." Herron read on. "What kind of an interview! Listen to this, Rosen: 'Q: Did you push the victim? A: Dash. Q: Did Catell push the girl? A: Dash. Q. Was he trying to assault the girl? A: Dash. Q: Was the girl known to you? A: Dash.' What in hell are all these dashes for? What kind of a—"

"They probably mean: 'She screams.'"

"So at least let 'em put that down instead of those crazy— Wait, here's a note: 'Where answer is followed by dash, witness screamed.'"

Rosen laughed, slapping himself on the thigh. "Witness screamed. Boy, that's hot. She's a witness!"

"So shut up already. She was there, wasn't she?"

"That makes her a witness? Christ. She was probably witnessing bats, snakes, and elephants, all waltzing along the molding on top of the room."

"Wait, here are some answers. She says: 'So he came down the long chimney, all covered with snow and the loveliest kind of horsehair—' What the hell?"

"Go on, Jackie, go on. This is interesting."

"Rosen, will you be serious a minute?"

"So go on. There he was and here she was. What happened next?"

"Nothing. She stops. There's another dash."

"Scream, no doubt."

"Rosen, do you know how important that Selma is in all this? Besides, I don't think it's so funny, all this she's going through. Anyway, here's more: 'I tried to tell him I loved him but the slimy sonofabitch just turned around and out he goes. I love him, I tell ya. Jeesis, I want him around. Come back, Jackie—come back, Otto—come back—' Then she goes on with all kinds of names. Wait. Jackie Herron! She's got my name in here too!"

"I told ya, Jackie. All she needs is a drink."

"Why don't you shut up?"

Herron started to flutter the pages irritably, trying to find one sane clue in that demented interview.

"Here, wait. She gives places: 'Santa Monica, Manitou, Toulouse, Louse, House, Grouse—' Off again, I guess." Herron put the papers down and leaned back. "Guess we gotta do our own figuring."

"Any notion where he's heading?"

"No. South, probably."

"To get his gold or just to get away?"

"Both, I guess. It's probably the same to him."

Southeast of the city a shivering man sat crouched behind the wheel of a big car, roaring over the hot highway, and thinking of nothing. He just drove. With the dull, single-minded determination of an animal he held out against the terrible weakness that liquefied his bones and made his muscles like dead meat. He was thinking of nothing, but he drove toward the desert.

"Anything come in during the last three hours?" Herron stood behind the man at the short-wave set. The monotonous garble of police calls and report messages filled the room, but none of it interested Herron, because none of it told him anything about Tony Catell.

"Hold it, Mr. Herron, here's something now." The man scribbled notes, then took his earphones off. "Man answering description of Catell gassed up at this crossroad here. Take a look at the map. Looks like he's going to Palm Springs, maybe? He had a stained bandage on one hand."

"This sounds like it. Relay that. I'm going to take a cruiser up there."

Rosen drove with Herron. They kept the short-wave on but nothing new came on.

"Bet that murdering bum is plenty scared by now." Rosen turned the siren on to get himself a clear way through the traffic. "If he's really in that neck of the woods, he must have slipped two of our checkpoints. How in hell he did it, I don't know."

"You underestimate those types, Rosen. When they want something, they're driven by furies, and nothing gets in their way."

Catell knew he was close to the place but it meant nothing to him, except that he was close to the place. Not any more. His awareness of things was automatic, and his actions merely coasted on the strength of what had been planned long in the past. So he looked as though he were coming from somewhere and going somewhere, but since he had left the apartment, far back sometime in Santa Monica, there had been no will in him. The wheel had stopped turning.

"You know what's going to happen if that bird ever leaves the highway, don't ya?" Rosen said.

"What? We lose him?"

"That's right. We lose him."

"Catell's a city boy, don't forget. He wouldn't hole up out there someplace. He wouldn't know what to do."

"Where there's a will, there's a way."

"My guess is he isn't going to stop for anything. He needs distance, Rosen. He's trying to get away as fast and as far as possible. And not just from us. From the mess he left, too."

Rosen and Herron were on the highway now, traveling at a good clip toward the darkening east.

"Think they'll snag him before dark, Rosen?"

"Ought to. Look at the map. Blocked here, here, here. Even this burg here, Joiner's Creek, they even got an alert out for him there."

"Not that it matters," Herron said "If I know my city boys, they'll always stick to the highway and rely on a fast car. And Catell's no different."

The rutted side road wound through a landscape of caked dirt and dry sage. Every so often there were rocks. Catell never slowed down. He had started with high speed; he had stayed with it. He did what he was doing because he was doing it.

When the road dipped he saw the green trees for a moment. They were some distance off, but they meant that Joiner's Creek was there. Catell slowed down, looking. With a sudden twist he pulled the car off the road, bumped over the sage that rattled under the car, and stopped beside a gray outcropping of rock.

Catell got out of the car and walked around the rock to a place where the stone sank vertically into the ground. Squinting in the failing light, Catell stooped low, walking, then stopped. He went to his knees.

For a faint moment the old fire tried to leap in him again, but there was no fuel to feed it, and it died.

Catell just dug.

When his nails hit the metal, he reached down, felt the handle, and pulled out the dented cartridge box. He carried it to the car and set it on the floor in the back. Then he drove away.

Herron had slept badly and the morning sun coming up over the flat land felt like a sledgehammer. He left the cabin and walked across the gravel court to the diner. Rosen was already there, working on a cheeseburger and French fries.

"Sit down, Jackie, sit down. Ready for some breakfast?"

"Rosen, please, you trying to make me sick? And keep those potatoes out from under my nose."

"Jeeze, you always like this in the morning?"

"I forgot my toothbrush. I thought this chase would be over before long, so like a fool I took off minus a toothbrush. Coffee, miss. Black."

"Don't bother buying one, Jackie. This caper is almost up. We got the planes out now. Patrol just came by and told me."

"You talked the same way yesterday, Rosen. By now history is beginning to prove you're wrong."

"Crap. How can we miss? You know what this countryside looks like from up there? A pancake. Like a pockmarked pancake."

"For chrissakes, Rosen, let me enjoy my coffee. And put those damn potatoes someplace else."

"Sensitive, ain't ya? Well, Jackie, I can understand that. Some guys, when they don't have their toothbrush in the morning—"

"Aw, shut up."

After they had drunk their coffee, Rosen pulled out a map.

"Take a look here, Jackie. We figure he's in here, and bottled up good. Now the planes are going to spot this area there, other side of Joiner's Creek, and over here, too. I can see that crazy hood right now, shivering behind some rock there and watching the planes overhead."

That same afternoon the big car was racing its sharp shadow down the white highway. Catell handled the car with no wasted motion. He sat stolidly, without blinking, even though he headed south with the sun in his eyes most of the time. Sometimes he switched on the radio and listened to the police calls. But you couldn't tell by looking at him that he knew they were chasing him farther north; he had crashed the dragnet during the night.

During the day he stopped twice. Once he stopped for gas, and the other time for water. He forgot to eat. Toward evening the heat got worse and he passed truck after truck loaded with melons, lettuce, and more melons. The Imperial Valley. The dragnet was far behind. When Catell saw the sign that said Brawley, he took the next road to the right. He avoided big towns and traffic with a sure habit, catching the main highway again on the other side.

That's when he blew the tire. The car took a wild lurch and threw Catell sharply against the side of the door. He grabbed for the wheel, fighting it while the car bumped to a halt on the soft shoulder of the road. He got out and changed the tire. It took him only a short time, but when he straightened up from the wheel, he suddenly felt deathly tired. Waves of fuzzy blackness came and passed; his eyes burned with a purple ache. He had to lean against the car and wait for his strength to come back. Then he went back behind the wheel and started the car. The wheel with the shredded tire was left behind. It lay near the edge of the road, forgotten. Or perhaps Catell just hadn't cared.

He should have.

In the middle of the night, two trucks loaded with produce came barreling down the road. They piled up on top of each other, spraying fruit and leaves, because the lead truck had hit the discarded wheel. From the time that the state troopers checked the scene to the time when they knew that Catell was nearby, only a few hours had passed. They checked the odd-sized tire; they wondered about the wheel; then they took a routine rundown of cars wanted, and they found that a man who had slipped them in Los Angeles was driving a car like the one that had lost the wheel.

"Did you hear that?" Rosen said, turning down the shortwave.

"No, I didn't hear that. I was musing to the soft hum of the tires on the shiny road. I have no other interests in mind, so I don't listen to the radio."

"Now, Jackie, don't act like it was my fault. Didn't we do everything there was to be done?"

"Obviously, no."

"Well, it beats me how he got out. We had every crossing sealed up, the planes—"

"Yeah. And now I'll tell you how he did it. He left the road and went straight across the prairie, as big as life and as long as he pleased."

"But the planes—"

"At night, my friend, they couldn't tell one shadow from another, even if they had been flying. And all Catell needed to get around was a little moonlight. Now, where I come from we got ditches next to the highway. You couldn't just barrel off the road and into the prairie, even if we had prairie."

"Don't think we won't keep that in mind from now on. Besides, there's no prairie in the Imperial Valley. We got him bottled up but good this time. Just let him try hiding in a lettuce field. There's only one way out for him now, Jackie, and that's straight up. Or straight down, maybe."

And Catell began to notice it.

He began to notice how the cars were bunching up in front of him. They were coming fast and at even intervals from the other direction, but his side of the road had become slow and glutted with cars.

Roadblock.

He couldn't see it yet, but that didn't mean a thing; there were twists in the road. Creeping more slowly all the time, Catell edged forward, hoping for a side road before the roadblock came in sight. There weren't any, just fields and fields with plants standing low and in straight rows as far as the horizon. His hands started to sweat. Closer, slowly closer.

He had almost passed it before he saw the dirt lane that angled off through the fields. It was a wide, rutted road, used only by the trucks that picked up the produce from the fields.

With a sharp swing Catell jerked the car out of his line, across the highway, and into the field. Everybody could see him, but he didn't worry about it. In a cloud of dust he raced along the planted rows, which seemed to come at him like a spreading net.

There were no turns, no dips. When the end of the field came in sight, Catell noticed that the next highway was empty. He turned onto the pavement, letting the car leap forward on the smooth cement. A curve, and there they were again. Two cars across the road, two guys putting up a striped wood barrier, a third one hitching at his pants, just looking. When they saw the black car tearing around the bend they straightened up and looked. The one who had been hitching his pants up started to wave at Catell in a halfhearted way before he jumped. The other two men were already in the ditch. When the barriers flew up in splinters and Catell watched his left front fender crumple like a piece of paper, a couple of shots cracked out from behind. They didn't hit a thing, because when the car was clear of the roadblock Catell pushed the gas pedal to the floor and shot off like a rocket.

But now he wasn't just driving anymore. Part of his sharpness had returned, tingling through his body like a charge of electricity. Long before he heard the sirens howling after him he was looking for a way to leave the highway, to ditch the car, even to make a lone stand, no matter what.

Because nobody was going to get Tony Catell.

When the clump of woods showed up on the left, Catell slowed down enough to take a screeching turn off the road. He kept the car on the narrow lane that wound through the trees, but his attention was wandering. Sirens wailed, sometimes loud, sometimes barely audible. He was trying to figure their position, their direction, but the wooded road, winding to avoid a tree, a rock, kept throwing off his judgment. When the sirens got louder Catell had to slow down. The powerful motor was barely growling and the car dipped and swung, edging ahead, nodding its hood.

Catell started to jump at movements in the trees, started to jerk the wheel too hard. His slippery hands itched, and that faint trembling began to shake him again.

Then the sirens stopped.

They must be off the highway. Where were they? The unbearable tension ripped loose in Catell and he jammed his foot down against the floorboard. The car shot ahead with a howl, barely missing a tree. For a few seconds the straining car found its way, and then, just as Catell could see the trees thinning out in the distance, the tons of roaring power shot off the road into the crunching underbrush. For one strangling second the car kept edging along, wheels whining; then the motor choked.

Catell didn't get out right away. He sat limp, smelling the strong odor of gasoline, breathing with a shallow movement. When he got up it was with the same dull automatism that had wrapped him for most of the trip. He got out of the car, listened, and reached into the back for the cartridge case. The weight of the thing made the handle slip out of his fingers and he had to lift it with both hands. Carrying the box in his arms, he started to jog toward the thinning trees.

The light was almost gone. The cloying night air smelled of earth and rotting matter, but Catell didn't notice. The short distance through the woods had drained him of all strength and he could barely get his breath. Through his swimming vision he saw a light in the distance. It was steady and small, looking like all the distant lights that call to children lost in the woods.

Catell started toward the light. He stumbled and lurched across the ruts of a field, his eyes on the light and nothing else. It seemed as if hours had passed when he saw what it was. There was a farmyard and a truck, and two men were standing by the motor, their heads under the hood. Every so often the motor roared, and then they jiggled something under the hood.

Catell crept forward, the box a heavy weight in his arms. No one saw him, heard him. Not many farms in the Imperial Valley have animals. When Catell got to the back of the truck he smelled the load. Stacked high over the panels, lay a soggy mess of wilting lettuce leaves and rotting stalks.

First Catell threw his box up, then he climbed after it. When the truck pulled out of the farmyard, Catell was buried in the soft mush of decaying stuff. It was warm, soft, and vibrating quietly with the motion of the truck. Catell almost went to sleep. Or perhaps he did. What made him jump was the sudden change in speed as the truck slowed down, crawling along the road with gears whining. Catell knew what it was without looking.

Roadblock.

Struggling as if in a morass, he came erect, the box with the gold under his arm. There were lights ahead, and without any thought but to get away, Catell jumped. Dragged down by the weight of the gold, he hit the pavement with a bad jolt, rolling sideways and into the ditch. He lay there feeling nothing but pain and terrible exhaustion. When he looked up, he could see five cars, all in a line, and the checkpoint. He could have yelled at them and they would probably have heard.

With the last twitching of his muscles he clawed himself slowly up the side of the ditch into the meager bushes that marked the end of another field. More lettuce, he thought, and then a thick unconsciousness dropped on him like a weight.

When the sharp sun hit his face he bolted up with a panic that knew no degrees. There was the road, here the field, his hand was on the battered box heavy on the ground. The road was empty and even the checkpoint looked deserted in the sun. The barricades were farther than he had thought. And there was no one in sight.

Hefting his box, Catell got up and turned toward the field.

"Hey!"

They were there, two of them, by the barricade. "Hey, you!"

Catell turned the other way, down the highway.

They were there.

As in a bad dream, they had popped from nowhere, coming toward him. Catell started to run across the field.

"Hey, Mack, stop!"

For a second the old anger rose in him, giving strength to his flight, but then there wasn't enough. All he could do was run, the box dragging on his arms. The box? My gold, he thought. This is my gold.

With a sullen stubbornness he made his feet thump along the narrow rut. They were behind him, yelling sometimes, but he didn't have the strength to turn. Even the fear had left him. In front of Catell the lettuce field stretched to the horizon. The long vanishing lines of the field converged as in a nightmare, gathering him forward as if in a rush of speed, but never changing, never making the horizon come. The sky was wide and naked, the field lay in a shadowless sprawl, there was nothing but the nightmare lines leading nowhere.

Catell's legs pounded the sod with monotony. He didn't know whether they were coming; he didn't consider whether they were coming. Trapped in an expanse of nothingness he went forward, forward, and when the horizon changed it was like a sudden shock to him.

Sloping down the field, he hit a row of trees and bushes that grew along the edge of a creek. On the other side was another thicket and beyond that a field. But Catell didn't look that far. When he plunged into the narrow underbrush they came across the rise behind him, but Catell didn't think about that, either. Gasping painfully, he stumbled on, looking only for the densest, darkest place in the nightmare of his flight.

Where the low creek had broken the soft bank, Catell crawled under an overhang of roots and earth. Dragging the heavy box along the ground, he squeezed and burrowed into the recessed space, like a night animal seeking the shelter of the dark. Then he just lay still. He listened to the roaring in his ears, the hard beat of his straining heart, and he could also hear the soft sifting of the earth that ran down from above, gently. He fingered the box absently while his dull eyes looked along the creek. A little farther down he could see the battered form of an old house, black in the brash sun, and on the side of the house a large old water wheel that had not turned in a long time.

The little stream, the sun filtering through the leaves, the old wheel of the mill in the light—it was a romantic scene that lay before Catell.

Then his ears caught the voices and the rustling. They were here. Catell heard it but didn't move, except to push his heels into the earth to lean closer into the damp, close hole he had found. Catell was tired. He lay there looking, and he never thought that they might get him. When the voices had passed above him he moved once, to shift his weight. After a while his idling fingers touched the box at his side. Turning his eyes to see his gold, Catell undid the latch. The box toppled, lid open.

He looked for his gold but saw nothing. There was no strength in him to turn the box and shake it out. Catell leaned forward, looking, and the sun brought out a quick white gleam deep in the box. It crossed his mind that the gleam should be yellow, a warm gold yellow, but his thought was without interest and he let it pass. Then he pushed the box out of the way to rest himself more closely against the covering earth.

He did not look at the gold again. It sat inside, in the dark hole where it had lived out its rottenness, with only a lost speck of mercury to show what had happened. It was clean gold again.

Once more Catell moved. It was then that the new ache spread through his chest, and he had to raise his head to get breath. It suddenly gripped his chest with a hellish pain, ripping at his heart and freezing the motion of his chest.

That too passed, and Catell sat quietly a while longer.

When they found him the sun was in his open eyes and they were staring at the wheel that had stopped turning a long time ago.

THE END

TOBRUK
·····················
BY PETER RABE

1: The End of the War

The column looked awful when it entered Algiers. As if in shame, the trucks angled off toward the sea just short of the city and down a dirt road which avoided traffic on the way to the port.

The Afrika Korps had pushed within one hundred miles of Suez which meant that some of their prisoners in the convoy had covered as much as nine hundred miles of slow hell.

Everything was covered with dust. The men were red with sand burns, their lips felt like bark to the touch and some had brown skin cancers on their cheeks, gift of the Libyan sun. Life was a jarring truck, sand in the teeth, a shirt stiff with old sweat. But this was Algiers on a warmish night and Algiers meant that the war was over. The thought was there but it stayed a secret, giving no joy. The ride smoothed when the trucks rolled down the paved pier, giving comfort, though that was a secret too. To admit relief was now like committing an act of disloyalty.

The dozen trucks stopped under the lights which angled out from the warehouse wall. The lights were high and seemed alive with an unsteady pulse because of the bats which hunted in and out of the aura.

The prisoners did not pay much attention to the bats but they considered the lights. They were shining in the middle of the night because Algiers, Vichy France, was a neutral port and that meant more or less that the war was over—

The first thing the men saw when they got out of the trucks was the very clean, very shiny black Mercedes Benz.

The men formed a haphazard line along the warehouse wall and hardly looked at their guards. But they now watched the French. Their guards had been Afrika Korps and the enemy, but it had been an enemy to understand, a clean enemy. Now the very neat French took over and they were dirt. They were victors by the grace of their own conquerors and the complexity of this moral dilemma made the French testy. They were curt with the prisoners, and rough. But the tramper was waiting for them, rubbing its side at the pier, and this meant more or less that the war was over. The black Mercedes Benz stood by the gangplank and then its two rear doors swung open.

The prisoners did not know whether the two men in the black and silver uniforms were Gestapo or Waffen-SS. They had not been exposed to the Gestapo nor had Rommel allowed the Waffen-SS in the Afrika Korps. He did not consider them soldiers.

Von Hahn, a small and bland-looking man, wore the important

epaulettes. It was a remarkable rank for a twenty-five-year-old, but he had flattered the right people and had slept with the right people so that his rank and his mission now almost measured up to his own self-esteem. He stood straddle-legged, his hands folded in back of him, which was a conscious reversal of the Führer's hand-folding posture just over the crotch. Von Hahn slightly flexed one knee back and forth, producing an elegant flash of black riding-boot leather. Von Hahn did not wear a monocle. He was aware that neither one of his protuberant eyes looked very good behind glass.

"Kaufer," he said.

"*Zu Befehl.*"

The lesser rank next to Von Hahn stiffened his beefiness and slammed his heels. He wanted the prisoners to hear this triumph of alertness in a man built like a barrel.

"Go to the Frenchman who is sorting the officers. And bring back the right ones."

Kaufer left, affecting the tigerish strides he had copied from Il Duce. He had at one time attempted to copy the Führer's more somber gait but it had been too ludicrous.

When the French officer heard the snap of the footsteps behind him he stiffened a little and started to slap his left boot with the clipboard in his hand.

"Lieutenant Sanft," he said, "Major Craig. *Avancez, s'il vous plaît.*"

A lieutenant and a major stepped out of the group. Their lightweight tunics were equally wrinkled and their motions were equally tired. They were anonymous under the same russet dust which discolored their hair and gave their five-day beards identical color.

Kaufer checked prisoners' roster, prisoners' tags and looked at the officers' pips on the tunics. Then he nodded and looked at the Frenchman.

"I want two guards."

"*Comment?*" The feigned ignorance of German was like a last, poor act of honor to the young Frenchman.

"*Deux soldats,*" said Kaufer. To speak French made him feel cosmopolitan.

While the rest of the prisoners began to file toward the tramper, Sanft and Craig were led to the rear of a truck which was empty except for the familiar, hard benches. They climbed in and sat down and their two French guards sat down too. Nobody looked at anyone else. Then the truck started to move.

It is a warm night, thought Craig, and the smooth pavement is a delight to my rear. I am too tired to worry about anything else. I will worry later—

The trick of his monologue was something acquired since capture: it gave him a sense of completion and in that way stopped worry. The trick usually worked for five minutes.

He ignored the French guards and he ignored Sanft who sat opposite him, but none of the men in the truck was able to ignore the black limousine which was following them.

Sanft put his head down and feathered both hands through his hair. There was a lot of dust. His hair, it turned out, was sandy. Sanft, in spite of his stubble, looked suddenly boyish.

"You must be very important," he said to Craig.

Craig thought the other one's smile looked almost boyish, but then it became a grimace, meaningless except for the effort it showed.

"I thought it was you," said Craig.

Sanft laughed. It was ghastly because this was a happy sound coming out of a very strained face.

"No friends of mine," said Sanft. "Don't understand it." He tried to laugh again but gave it up. "But why would you be here?"

"I was captured," said Craig.

He wished he had not said it because it caused Sanft to laugh again. Then Sanft stopped abruptly, but this time apparently with cause. He made a display of staring at Craig's shoulder patch. "Hadn't noticed before," he said. "You're Long Range Desert Group!"

Craig leaned back and looked up at the tarp overhead as if there were a long, lovely view.

"You seem filled with envy," he said. "Same dirty truck, same mindless mess, and you seem filled with envy."

He kept looking up at the tarp and waited for Sanft to laugh but instead Sanft talked in a voice which sounded shy. "Matter of fact, Major, yes. I do envy you."

Craig looked down but this time Sanft was not looking at him.

"L.R.D.G.," he said at the air, and then he looked at Craig. "They must have got you behind their lines."

"In a sense," said Craig. "Their line extends to wherever they catch you, wouldn't you say?"

Sanft was silent for a moment, while looking at the black limousine.

"Also," he said, "I envy you that remarkable sense of humor." Then he looked back at Craig. "They're Gestapo, you know."

"I didn't know. How did you know?"

Sanft lowered his head so that his face did not show.

"I am afraid," he said quietly. "That's how I know."

And this was the first time, thought Craig, that I have really heard him. And he's more honest than I—

The truck squealed very badly and then came to a stop. The limousine in the rear kept moving and then slid out of view. The two French guards jumped off the end of the truck and stood waiting.

"*Sortez, s'il vous plaît*," said one of them.

Sanft looked quite composed now.

"How eternally polite of them," he mumbled.

"When out of everything else," said Craig, "hang on to good manners," and then he jumped off the end of the truck.

He saw a small airfield. If there were any landing lights, they were all turned off. One strip disappeared into the dark of a flat terrain and another strip, crossing over, ran down a shallow apron which disappeared into the sea. There were soft water sounds from the surfless Mediterranean.

"Gentlemen, at your service."

Von Hahn had walked back from the limousine which was now parked near a cinderblock building. Two windows showed light in the blank façade and nothing else. The town of Algiers lay in the other direction.

"If you will follow me," Von Hahn went on, "I will arrange for your comforts."

Craig and Sanft walked slowly, their guards following. "You were saying something about politeness?" mumbled Sanft.

"No. Good manners."

Von Hahn waited for them at the door of the building. He was smiling, Craig noticed. It's the Sanft-smile, he thought, but without the strain. And *sanft* is a German word, come to think of it, meaning soft and gentle. Don't think of it—

"If you will go with my assistant," said Von Hahn, "he will show you where you might clean up."

Von Hahn smiled, turned in the door and preceded the two prisoners into a corridor. Kaufer was waiting at the other end.

There will be a bath and there will be soap and there will be more water than I care to drink—

"I meant Major Craig," said Von Hahn. He stopped at the first door in the corridor and opened it. "Come with me, Sanft. We shall start with a glass of wine, *nicht wahr?*"

It was no surprise that Von Hahn should finish his sentence with the commonest German phrase. Craig went past Sanft and past the door which Von Hahn was holding open and he thought only of the bath and the soap and the water, more water than he would care to drink

"Von Hahn, *hören Sie mal zu ...*" Sanft started to mumble and then the

German cut him off.

"*Später*," he said and shut the door.

Craig took two more steps before the surprise hit him.

They had not said anything significant. Sanft had started to talk and Von Hahn had told him to wait till later. But Sanft had known the German's name and his own German had been flawless-

2: The Frigate Bird

The building, thought Craig, was mainly a repair shed and the washroom at the end of the corridor was for the maintenance crew. The cinderblock room smelled moist and faintly greasy. There was the kind of French public toilet which is a porcelain slab on the floor with a hole in the middle and two sole-shaped depressions which show where to put the feet for a properly aimed position. The wash basin in the middle of the room was big and round and had faucets for six. Craig got undressed and lay down in the basin.

He turned all the faucets on and stayed there for a while with the cold water soaking his skin. Then he used soap. It was a can of soft soap which felt like jelly and smelled like rancid nuts. When he was done with the soap half the can was gone and he was freezing. He stayed naked for fifteen more minutes which was the time it took him to shave with the same brown soap and with a German straight razor. His face burnt and he shivered but he felt alive and distinguishably himself again. His hair had become black again and his eyes showed their startling blue in the dark tan of his face.

Some of the lines in his face were heavier than normal. They had been building into the long planes of his face for some time.

Craig, for his size, was decidedly underweight. He was long-boned and angular but moved without the deliberate slowness of the undermuscled or the tall. A slight awkwardness came into his gestures only when he put his clothes back on. He felt unreasonably irritated when he had to put his stiff socks and the stained tunic on his skin again.

He looked around the damp room and found it distinctly unattractive. No windows, he mumbled. He looked at the air-duct as if he were still not sure that it would admit nothing larger than a cat. Then he went to the door, opened it and looked at his two guards. They were not the Frenchmen with whom he had come. They were two Wehrmacht men in regular gray of the continental issue. One of them stood back, his machine pistol leveled, and the other one took the straight razor which Craig had hidden in his left boot. Then they took him to the door where

Von Hahn and Sanft had disappeared.

The room was an office. There was a desk and a chair and there was a bank of short-wave equipment. The way in which Von Hahn looked at the mess on the desk made it obvious that this was not his own place of work. There was also a small table with pretty, curved legs, like an afterthought of ornamentation which did not really belong in this place. On the little table was a plate of chicken.

The baked skin was red with saffron and shiny with fat. Next to the chicken sat a bowl with couscous and there was also a carafe half full with thick wine. White steam tendriled up from the cereal and the odor of baked fowl caused a pain in Craig's throat. Von Hahn looked up from the desk which was not his and smiled.

"Please eat," he said.

If I eat this I will love him forever, thought Craig. I will then do anything, everything for him out of that moment of love and he will know— He is keen on knowing just when that love moment occurs.

"I will join you, if you don't mind," said Von Hahn. He smiled, left the desk, bringing a chair with him. Craig noticed that the size of Von Hahn's eyes did not change when he smiled.

And now he is pushing me and doing it well. I feel like a ravening beast next to that food there and he knows that I do not want to share it— He wants me to devour it, now!

It was still night outside. Then Craig heard the moan of wind. They did not call it the gibleh this far west so it must be the sirocco. But this was not sirocco weather. And the far moan sounded human. Then it stopped with mechanical abruptness.

If it had not been for Von Hahn's eyes which now did change in size for no apparent reason—except for that, Craig would not have looked for a reason.

The black Mercedes Benz was visible outside the window and then it was not. Three men walked by, obscuring the view. Three men, though only two of them seemed to be properly walking.

"You may look closer, if you like," said Von Hahn.

Craig went to the window. By leaning his head sideways against the glass he could see two men drag a third between them. The two on the outside wore mufti and the one in the middle wore desert khaki.

"Sanft—" said Craig. "Why, is he dead—"

"He is not dead, Major. He is unwilling."

"But what— I mean, why—"

"Because he was unwilling. Now, tell me, Major Craig— Are you listening, Major Craig?"

Craig turned back to the room. Nothing had changed, including the bland young man in the black uniform with the silver piping. Only Craig had changed. He was no longer empty with hunger; he was now full of fear.

"I was saying, Major, would you like to eat or would you rather we conversed a little? I am perfectly willing to leave the choice up to you."

Bastard—the uncanny bastard and his tricks— I must hide instantly, thought Craig, and he did.

"Donald Craig, Major, 762513, Long Range Desert Group."

Von Hahn sat down by the little table and smiled up at Craig.

"How conventional of you," he said.

"Geneva Convention. Would you like to hear it again?"

Von Hahn was listening, but not to Craig. He was not even looking at his prisoner. He had his hands on his hips which made him look almost coy.

"Don't move for a moment, Major. Just listen."

Von Hahn's holster flap was now open and the Luger butt was right under his fingers. Von Hahn still had his hands on his hips, like a coquette, very sure of results.

The timing of the shot was a masterpiece of terror tactics. Craig leapt with fear and then he trembled with confusion. Von Hahn had not moved and the Luger was where it had always been.

"I did not shoot," said Von Hahn. "Outside. You may look closer, if you like."

When Craig saw them come back there was no question about Sanft this time. The two men in mufti were dragging him close to the ground. The sandy-haired head was hanging down as if there were no bone in the neck.

"The placement of the bullet used to be called *coup de grâce*," said Von Hahn behind Craig. "However, we have used it in concentration camps too. Matter of efficiency."

When Craig turned Von Hahn was nibbling a chicken thigh.

"Sit down, Major."

Craig sat down on the windowsill because he could no longer stand. His stomach was a black hole which was devouring itself and his eyes were mesh-covered holes which admitted nothing that made sense. His ears produced their own din and babble and that kept him safe too.

In a while he could see and hear again. Von Hahn had been talking and it had all been questions. He sat as before, except that he had dropped the piece of chicken on the floor. Von Hahn and his uniform looked now very geometric, the pointed wings of the lapels, the silver accents on neck and shoulders. Craig thought of the Frigate bird.

In the strong blue of the sky far over the summer heat of the Florida

Keys there would hang a bird, a still silhouette of a bird which was like an abstraction, like a cut-out done by a Japanese in black paper, the Frigate bird. It would hang there in the currents rising from the flat Keys and look very beautiful, very distant and immaculate in the pure drift of air. This bird, however, had a disgusting habit—

"Don't worry about Sanft, Major. Your case is not comparable, as I see it at the moment."

—This bird fed by harassing others. It would swoop and dive and jab at a sea bird in flight until the troubled victim, in an access of despair, would vomit up his loaded crop and then the Frigate bird would catch the mess. This was the way the Frigate bird fed.

"You are not listening, Major. Glass of wine?"

"*You shot him!*" screamed Craig.

"Stay where you are, Major."

"You shot a prisoner of war!"

"And a British officer?"

"And a British ..."

"No."

Craig took a deep, purposeful breath. He sat down on the windowsill again and watched Von Hahn. The technique, of course, was still the same and the harassment would not end until the point of vomit. The Frigate bird always won as long as the full bird was determined to give nothing— I will give him nothing, decided Craig.

"Lieutenant Sanft," said Craig, "wore the patch of the Fifty-First Highlanders."

"I know. They were only recently deployed. Cairo based."

"How do you people do it," said Craig.

"You should know, Major."

"I'm Long Range Desert Group. We're not Intelligence. Reconnaissance only."

Von Hahn smiled.

"You play the game well, Major. You blurt spontaneous information which I already know."

"Very resourceful, your Wehrmacht Intelligence. You know how to read shoulder patches."

"I am not with Wehrmacht, or with the Canaris group. Major. I give you this information so you will better appreciate your position." Von Hahn smiled, the coquette very sure of results. "Heydrich has his own and a far more effective Intelligence branch."

Sanft had known that Von Hahn was Gestapo—

"Quite an effect," said Craig, "killing a prisoner of war."

"It upsets you?"

"No. It revolts me."

"In that case," said Von Hahn, "let me relieve you. We did not kill a prisoner of war. Sanft was a German agent."

Craig did not bother to conceal his surprise. But he tried to conceal that he wanted to know more.

"Maybe that's why your novel type service is so effective. You kill your own agents."

"Sanft performed his assigned function well. Beyond that one job he was not reliable. He was a Jew, you know. Even German Jews are capable of just so much loyalty."

Craig touched his breast pocket for a cigarette. It was his gesture of necessary distraction.

"If you think you're reassuring me ..."

"Cigarette?" said Von Hahn.

Craig caught the flat silver case in midair and after he had taken a cigarette Von Hahn threw him a lighter.

"How did you know Sanft's unit—his reputed unit—had just moved up from Cairo?" asked Von Hahn.

"I keep in touch."

"I ask, because you were caught far behind our lines."

"I had just arrived there."

"Apparently. Why the hurry to get to Sollum?"

Craig did not fall for it. Von Hahn had no way of knowing where Craig's unit had been heading and Sollum's importance to an Intelligence man was insignificant. What Von Hahn wanted to know was just exactly where Craig's unit had been going.

"I follow orders," said Craig. "I was not in command of the unit and the C.O. was very secretive about destination. Fanatical, you might say."

"I know. He's dead."

Craig kept silent.

"Apparently you did not know," said Von Hahn. He toyed with the plate of red chicken pieces and in a while, when there was no answer from Craig, he picked up a curled length of neck and held it in a tentative gesture, half question, half offer. He smiled at Craig, but this also was a gesture. It blended hope and resignation in a delicate balance. The coquette, it seemed, was ready to switch tactics.

"No?" said Von Hahn, sad and gentle. Then he shrugged and let the neck drop to the floor. "You did not know your C.O. was dead. But now you do know, Major Craig, and you know why we consider you the only surviving prisoner of any importance to us."

"I don't know why I'm important."

"Because you were eighty miles behind our lines."

"In the previous sortie, when you did not catch us, we were eighty-three miles behind your lines."

"Where were you going?"

"From trackless waste to trackless waste."

"I remind you, Craig, that ..."

"I forgot. Donald Craig, Major, 762513."

"I want more."

"All right. I was born in Montreal, Canada. I was educated in England, after my eighteenth birthday, that is."

He was prepared to fill the time with a much longer recital. He did not think that it would distract Von Hahn for very long but Craig had now a strong, sudden need to distract himself. He was caught in an access of fear and he had to trample it out of sight with a stampede of vital statistics, something dead-meaningless, something safe. This special fear was unique in Craig's experience. The encounter was unique. Von Hahn, of course, was not really human. A Frigate bird was not human. A tank was not human either and an encounter with such a mechanical thing was also very frightening. But not like this. At least a tank did not look like a man—

"We do have a deadline, Major Craig. Are you listening?"

"Donald Craig, Major, 762 ..."

"Stop that. There is no point in trying to go mechanical on me, Major Craig. We have ways of reviving you. We have ways of keeping you alive for some time—"

The plump, elderly man was sweating profusely but Von Hahn was not. Von Hahn walked vigorously around the cinderblock building—four times around, when the exercise was completed—and if the plump man in the rumpled, white ducks wanted talk, he damn well had to keep up. The sun over the airfield came down fierce and straight and the Mediterranean at one side of the field looked shrill with reflections.

"Edmund," said the plump man. "You didn't have to kill him!"

"*Freiherr* von Hahn," said Von Hahn. "Our working relationship, Mister Portman, entails neither familiarity nor liking."

The other one wiped his face with his hand, which produced an even sheen, like pink candy. The cherub cheeks and the baby mouth worked with emotion and the thinning white hair seemed entirely out of place. The head should either have been baby bald or there should have been a Santa Claus beard to cover the face.

"You didn't answer me," he said to Von Hahn.

"I killed Sanft," said Von Hahn, "because he only did the Cairo job for us in the belief that it would save your daughter's life, Portman. Once he found out that her life was in no way endangered by us—in fact, that she was working for us—then he would immediately have turned around and betrayed us."

"But he was my friend, he was my daughter's ..."

"I convinced him myself, Portman. I told him that the threat of your daughter's death in a concentration camp was no more than a ruse, and you should have heard what he said."

"You—you what? You taunted—you told this nice young man—"

"Did it ever occur to you, Portman, that your British tolerance for alien races is actually due to a lack of backbone?"

"Don't try to make enemies," said Portman in a tone of voice which did not fit the innocence of his expression. "You've got enough of them without trying and you're too young to try for more! I was a Mosley disciple before you could spell your name, Freiherr! I'm a believer in the Führer out of conviction, not out of opportunism!"

The implicit comparison was not lost on Von Hahn. He immediately walked faster, knowing how it would distress the elderly man.

"Von Hahn? Listen—" Portman had to raise his voice because Von Hahn was now far ahead of him. When the other did not stop Portman decided to take a rest and wait till Von Hahn came around the building again.

This trivial turn in events made Von Hahn unreasonably angry. He ignored Portman, he continued to walk, and he only paid attention to the way he felt. He needed an instant act, something involving the hands, something violent and totally final. But Von Hahn knew that such a need for immediacy was very childish. He was an adult and he knew how to do all manner of things much more slowly—

Portman walked into the shade of the building where two large sliding doors were standing open. The dim hall beyond was empty but when Portman walked in he saw the German infantry man. He sat on the stoop of a door and his rifle was leaning next to him. On the door it said *W.C.*

"He's in there?" Portman asked in German.

The soldier nodded without much interest.

"But I can't let you in there, Mister Portman."

"I know." Portman smiled, as if it did not matter. It mattered a great deal to him that he should not see the Canadian prisoner. There were aspects to this espionage business which left Portman squeamish, no matter how powerful the ideological foundations. "I mean, he's all right now, isn't he?"

"Sure. He ate good."

"Haha. Have to keep up the strength."

"That's what Freiherr von Hahn says."

"Haha."

"Yes."

The soldier wished that Portman would go away. He had no objections to Portman, even though he knew that the elderly gentleman was not a real German, but he wanted to go back to his alone-thinking again, go over the whole thing again of how he would come home on that day to Waldheim, how he would beat up that man who was surely living with Else, and how he would buy a new cow, open the back pasture, how he would eat *Knödel* at noon and then have Else, and *Knödel* in the evening and then have Else—

"Well now, have a good one yourself," said Portman.

"Haha," said the soldier.

Portman walked away, briefly puzzled by the stupid laugh he had just heard. He waited for Von Hahn by the open door until he decided that his punctual German was not very punctual at all. He had not walked around the building as expected, he had not cracked the prisoner as expected, and of course all this punctuality was simply a national façade. Even Hitler's timetable was off. Rommel was *not* in Cairo yet. Contrariwise he, Portman, would of course do his bit. Which brought him to a consideration of another German myth: that entire, incomprehensible race business and that revolting *Blut und Boden* fabrication. This, after all now, did not prevent the German ideologists from freely utilizing the true talents of the English race, such as himself; of the Jewish race, such as poor Sanft; such as the Polish race for slave labor. After all now, they would soon have to come to the enlightened conclusion that everybody had his place. How else had the British Empire been established? How else was the Thousand Year Reich going to come into existence? By enlightened placement!

Good title for a book. Once this current unpleasantness was done he, Portman, would of course not go back to the import-export business. No need for that. Everybody would be One, under enlightened placement. He would devote his time exclusively to the final compilation of a definitive work, combining geopolitical, colonio-social and enlightened placement theorems under one final solution. In the meantime now, where in hell was that rotten kraut!

3: The Prisoner Had a Good Meal

Edmund Von Hahn sat in the small office which had a view of the landing strip and of the Mediterranean beyond. He sat by the desk which was littered with somebody else's work and he stared at the sea basking and glittering outside the window—and that view was not his either.

He remembered the gray and slate sight of the Baltic from his window in the big *Herrenhaus* where his own family had been forever. That was his, the steel flatness of the sea, the moist green of woods like a deep fur over the Pomeranian countryside— But that was not really his anymore either.

He had come home that day in the winter, frightened and too young for catastrophe. He would never go back to the academy in Berlin and they would lose the *Herrenhaus* too. The stables were no longer for play, the woods were not his anymore, and the long stretch of beach was as alien as the moon. And the servants' quarters were not for snug visits but were rooms cluttered with somebody else's belongings. In those places he had learned the dimensions of his world and all that was over. He was too young for words like "depression" but he quickly found the meaning of loss. And gradually, in the cramped flat in Berlin and in the crowded school where anyone from any station could sit next to him, he learned to ignore loss by feeling less and less.

In time, this development made him very efficient. He had no friends, he had only connections. He was not cruel, he was only inhuman.

The trick gave him safety from loss and caused him to operate somehow like an impersonal force in an indifferent vacuum.

He did not question the price. That would have introduced doubts which once again would have made him human—

The door to the office opened behind him and Portman came in. Von Hahn did not bother to turn around. He could tell who it was by the way the old man was breathing. Kominski used to breathe like that, he thought, the old steward who wheezed so hard while following Edmund's pony—

"I waited for you," said Portman and slammed the door. "And now I see you are sitting here, doing nothing."

Von Hahn did not bother to answer. If Portman wanted to face Von Hahn he had to cross the room and stand at the other end of the desk. Portman did all this, which made him feel peevish.

"And your prisoner, I gather, has had a good meal."

Von Hahn put his booted legs on the desk and studied the polish.

"Von Hahn, are you or are you not aware of the fact that the Cairo group is apparently ready for us, that Cheryl will return from Rome in a matter of ..."

"If—as she has been instructed—she went to see Von Kesselring in Rome then she is now undoubtedly on her way to Berlin, because that's where the general has gone."

"All right," said Portman without bothering to hide his irritation. "Nevertheless, when Cheryl returns with the document we *must* be ready to leave and we *must* be fully apprised of your prisoner's intercepted mission."

"The mission," said Von Hahn with studied boredom, "was stopped. Or we would not have the prisoner."

"And if it was as important as it might have been, then we damn well better know about it because the L.R.D.G. will try again. They don't give up, you know."

Von Hahn leaned forward and spat on his boot. Then he rubbed the slime into the polish.

"You sound positively chauvinistic," said Von Hahn. He looked up to watch Portman's reaction. He gave the older man time, the way a wise mother gives a child time to get over a tantrum. Von Hahn smiled slowly and with savor. He enjoyed the sight of the ridiculous. Portman, short and fat and with the insignificant face of an elderly grocer, had reared himself up as if he were a taller man. His face flushed with theatric fervor, though in the case of Portman it looked more like an apoplectic fit.

"With this mission to the Near East, this mission which has been entrusted to me since its inception, we stand now on the brink of the encompassing move, the realization of what destiny has proscribed—I mean, prescribed—in the annals ..."

"Did you read that somewhere, Portman?"

This interruption was devastating. And then Von Hahn hit his victim with the hard, clanking voice which he reserved for certain stages of a long interrogation.

"Your value, Portman, like the spent value of Sanft, is highly specific. You know the Cairo group because you have bribed and marketeered with them for all the years of corruption which supported your merchant business. Sanft was a messenger boy, you are a trader. That's all. The security of the mission is my business. And the methods are my personal specialty." Von Hahn dropped his feet off the desk and let the heels thunk hard on the floor. Then he got up slowly, as if bored, and when he turned he looked almost languorous. "Would you like me to tell you how I will handle a dull-eyed straggler from the desert who claims to come from nowhere and be going nowhere, and turn him into a fount of military information?"

Portman acted his own size again. He coughed a little and wiped one palm over his forehead.

"The methods are your business."

"You won't have to watch. Besides, I don't have the proper equipment here."

"Equipment—"

"Nothing. Sticks, fists, knives. Ridiculous and primitive. The subject might even die without saying a word."

Portman looked ill and Von Hahn smiled at the other one's weakness.

"I have arranged to take Craig to Grenoble."

"France? But Cheryl will come with the document ..."

"There will be time precisely because I will take the subject to Grenoble." Von Hahn leaned toward Portman and pretended politeness. "You don't know about Grenoble?"

Portman glared as sternly as his Santa Claus expression would permit and then he walked past Von Hahn to the door. All that time the back of his head developed unpleasant sensations, as if he were expecting a blow or a kick as punishment for being a loftier person than this creature from a basement full of iron tools—

It was time for the beating. The regularity of the interrogations had been built into Craig's bones after a very short time. Also the wisdom of the method was soon apparent. After Craig had waited something like fifteen minutes he started to tremble with anxiety. The certainty of pain was better than the uncertainty of no pain. He started to pace back and forth in the washroom, but the aimlessness of his limping walk only added to the waves of mindless fright which came and went inside of him. He started to walk along the four walls of the room. He kept very close to the walls, he turned the corners with a feeling of squeezing himself through a narrow bend in a tube. After a while he organized the number of steps per wall, per turn and for the entire circumference. He wished fervently that nobody would interrupt him before he had totally mastered this system of controlling his universe.

No one interrupted him. In a while he began to stoop while walking which added the comforting quality of hiding out. The illusion blew up when the door creaked and then opened.

It was not the chunky one in the black uniform. More confusion. The infantry man with the bowl of food came into the washroom.

They had a little routine which they observed religiously. The soldier would stay by the door and Craig would stay at the opposite end of the room. In that way Craig bought a few minutes of conversation and avoided getting shot in the abdomen. This had been explained to him. The soldier also bought a few minutes a conversation and avoided having to shoot the prisoner in the abdomen. This shot had been explained to him. He had not wanted to hear the explanation and he did not care to think about it.

"*Wie gehts?*" he said and put the bowl on the floor.

"*Danke gut*, Seppel."

They went on in German. Craig spoke slowly because he did not know the language too well and Seppel talked slowly because he could not manage High-German in any other way.

"And how is the cut on the head?" he asked.

"It does not go boom-boom anymore. It only goes tick-tick."

"It looks better."

"Thank you. Have you heard from home, Seppel?"

"Bah."

"Have you heard about me?"

"What?"

"The *Schweinehund* did not come as usual."

"Oh that. The *Schweinehund* is going to send you away."

"Away," said Craig. "Where?"

"I don't know. It's where he comes from in Vichy France. The headquarters where he works."

Craig said nothing. The sound of the other one's voice had instantly become an impersonal thing, like something printed in two dimensions and when you looked away it was no longer there. The trick worked for only a very short time and then Craig started to tremble. The ghastly thing was that the trembling occurred without any emotion, as if he, Craig, were not really there.

He was already in Grenoble. He could see it the way Ricard had described it, Ricard who had gotten away to join the Free French and who later had died from drinking fighter plane fuel.

"The *mairie* is now their headquarters," he had said, "and the bottom windows are boarded up so that you cannot look in. No need, however. Nobody goes into the square anymore because of the screams you can hear."

And when Ricard had died in a nightmare of his own making and from the poison he had gorged into his own body, he had screamed all night the way he had described the sound—

"When?" Craig said, and then he had to say it again because the first time had been a croak.

"I don't know," said Seppel. "When the plane comes, I think."

Then he closed the door because he did not want to watch what had happened to the prisoner at the other end of the room-

4: An Oasis away from the War

Eight hundred miles south of the Libyan port of Tobruk lies the oasis of Kufra. There are trees, there is water, and since the rest of South Cyrenaica lies dead and dry under a sun which comes down like a weapon, there are at all times about seven thousand people in Kufra. Immediately north of this water-fed isolation lies the Great Sand Sea. In places, this waste is impassable even for a camel. Between this Great Sand Sea and the Mediterranean to the north moved the desert war. It moved east and west and sometimes it bit itself into the ground for a standstill. But then it always found enough desperation for another debauch of strength, for another success on the map.

But no one got pushed into the Mediterranean and no one went into the Sand Sea. Kufra was safe.

The Via Graziani had not changed in a very long time, except for its name. Before the Italians had taken Libya this street in Kufra had not had a name. It took the Italians an additional thirty years to take control of the province of Cyrenaica and then they called the street in Kufra Via Vittorio Emanuele. Nobody else called it that. Ten years later, while Marshal Graziani was losing ten years of control, the Italians changed the street name in honor of their valiant medal bearer. Now that the Italians existed only in the north, and entirely by the grace of the Afrika Korps, the Via Graziani retained its name by way of Arab derision.

It was a street of yellow mud walls, dark door holes and a great deal of traffic. It was wide enough to have cafés on both sides of the street and the amount of camel dung on the ground showed clearly that Graziani was vital to commerce.

The café where most of the traders sat was on the ground floor of an almost European style, two-story building. Most of the ground floor was coffeehouse, blessedly dark, devoid of ornamentation. The second floor was a hotel. An inside balcony gave access to the rooms, and the inner court which this arrangement created was used for nothing. Sometimes dogs slept there.

A few of the rooms were occupied by more or less permanent guests. There was Ibn Kabir, an elderly Senussi, who because of requirements of his trading business spent four months of the year in Kufra. He occupied one large room by himself and he maintained two small rooms for his rotating harem. On the harem side of the inner court was a two-room rental arrangement contracted for by the Inter-Sudanese Liaison Mission which was an organization of various countries who found the location of Kufra a fine gathering point for liaison. Nobody knew what that was. However, Italians had used the company office during their murderous campaign against the Senussi sect. The British had used the unusual radio transmitter as a beacon during Sudanese border action, and at one time a German combine had headquartered operations there, something that had to do with the establishment of an ivory syndicate. The original charter of the company had been taken out by a Dutch archeologist.

Ibn Kabir, who looked big and spongy inside his seersucker suit, sat in the coffeehouse with a Dutch girl named Lotte. As a new member of the Ibn Kabir ménage, she still required a few special attentions. He ordered her a banana.

"Lotte," he said in English. "After the war we will travel, dallink."

"Where?"

"Alexandria."

"But we just came from there."

"Not the cabaret. We go back and you are just for me, eh?"

Ibn Kabir smiled and ran his hand up the girl's thigh. This was publicly plausible because they sat close together and because Kabir had dressed her in a voluminous Tuareg cloak. And it was made possible because Lotte expected this sort of thing. Next, Kabir sipped his arrack.

Lotte said, "When is the war over?"

"Move it this way a little, dallink."

She did and then she asked him again.

"And there are even soldiers here," she said. "Upstairs."

"Inter-Sudanese?" Ibn Kabir laughed. "It means the war is far away. They are like deserters and they like it here."

Ibn Kabir tried to get his hand back between the girl's thighs but she would not let him. She was angry and forgot her station.

"If they are with Inter-Sudanese they are fine. It is a cultural organization founded by a famous Dutchman."

"Come here."

His hand hurt her and she remembered her station. She bit her teeth together and allowed his hand.

"Now, about Inter-Sudanese, my child," said Kabir while looking elsewhere. "That is and always has been a den of Senussi subversion. You don't remember. That was in 1930. And if you ask Joko Three, who runs the hotel, he knows that it is a cell of an international conspiracy to tax hashish and kef out of existence."

"Please, Kabir. It hurts."

"I am sorry, dallink."

He took his thoughtless hand away, put his elbow on the back of the chair, which permitted him to shift for convenient reach with the other hand. He put it through the fold of the drape where it crossed her front and then he held one small breast. He had provided her with a Tuareg cloak but with nothing else.

"Where was I, dallink?"

"I can't remember."

"You don't pay attention. I am telling you about the British. They are here on legitimate leave from Alexandria. They send double-talk telegrams to their headquarters about illness and transportation problems and as long as it works they can stay away from their war. Have they tried you yet?"

"Have they what?"

"This."

The girl yelped but held very still.

"No," she said. "Of course not."

"Tell me when they do," said Kabir. "You are blond and they will."

"They look very strict."

"Ha!" said Ibn Kabir. He took his hand away so that he could pick up his arrack. "This Colonel Harker he looks so much typical—the British career soldier with the flag up his ass—he therefore must be a faker. He looks like a uniform filled with duty and he writes the telegrams to keep him out of the war."

"I understand," said Lotte.

"Dallink, you understand nothing. You have seen his aide-de-camp?"

"His what?"

"His friend, the Lieutenant Boyden." (Ibn Kabir pronounced it "Left-Tenant.")

"The one like a boy. He looks dutiful too."

"Oh, yes, dallink. Those two you don't worry about. They are so full of duty, at night they sleep with the swagger stick, nothing but the swagger stick, between them, you understand, dallink?"

"No."

"Ugh," said Ibn Kabir. "You are very young and have much to learn." He got up. "We go upstairs, dallink."

"You mean now?"

"You have much to learn and I will teach you something," said Kabir and his big egg of a stomach jiggled up and down while he laughed.

She followed him and was glad that she could now lie down. This business in public with him always embarrassed her.

They passed Colonel Harker on the inside balcony but though both of them stared at him, he paid no attention. He turned away and went through the door to Inter-Sudanese. It was the only door in the hotel which was not made of open lattice work. The door was solid wood. However, the loss in air circulation was a gain in privacy and when Harker slammed the door behind him he felt free to look worried.

"Boyden?" he called almost immediately.

There was no answer. The first room was zebra-striped with the sun which came through the shutters. There were meaningless files along one side of the room, a kidney-shaped desk which looked more like a washstand and a tinted photo of King Victor Emmanuel III on the whitewashed wall. That was meaningless too. The next room was something else.

The transmitter was there, and a work desk with a working telephone, a cabinet with one bottle of gin and one siphon of quinine water, and there was the leather pouch whose contents burst into chemical flame if improperly opened. Lieutenant Boyden, prone on a rattan couch, had his head on it.

"Boyden, damn you!"

"*Sah!*"

Young Boyden's transformation from a sleeping youth with an out-of-place mustache into a braced sample of the pride of empire was extremely fast. Harker harrumphed and slapped one hand to his barrel chest as if his cough were real. The worry lines on his leather-skinned face stayed as they were, which meant little. Like a bloodhound, he always looked worried. Like a professional soldier, his personal feelings rarely showed. He threw his swagger stick on the desk, flapped the front of his tunic to get some air and looked at the telephone which had a crank.

"Are they coming?"

"There's been no call, sir." Boyden added without hesitation, "I would have heard, sir."

"I know."

It was true that Everett Boyden reminded him of Eton collars, gray toppers at Ascot, Coldstream parade and Sunday pig-sticking in the Rann of Cutch. Harker also knew that Boyden nevertheless had the stuff. When the boy took on a rank, he took on a job. When he took on a job, he finished it. It was a simple formula. Harker was reminded of how long he had been in the army before he had decided to adopt the formula. Eight years a lance corporal— Shocking, in a way. And young Boyden? Must have something to do with breeding.

Harker had no compunctions about this analysis which, after all, put

him and his aide-de-camp into two categories, two different worlds, with
Harker in the lesser one.

Boyden had a big, dark patch of sweat on his back and he pulled at
the skirt of his tunic to unstick the cloth from his skin. In front he looked
immaculate and his wide-legged shorts showed only the regulation knife
edge, front and aft. This uncluttered appearance of his shorts had to do
with Boyden's anatomy. He had no rear end to speak of. While this was
of no concern to him, he preferred to wear jodhpurs or breeches and
boots because he believed that his legs were too thin.

"May I ask, sir," he said, "whether Kurt Bergman is to be treated as
a military person?"

Harker finished sitting down behind his desk. The swivel chair made
a sound like an old man hawking up something from his bad lung.
Harker crossed his legs while Boyden had a childish twinge of envy at
the sight of all that bunchy musculature.

"I know he wasn't identified in the signal," said Harker. He had a tic
with his upper lip, a movement as if he were bristling a mustache.
Harker had no mustache. This rare tic was a sign of irritation. "Bergman
is a captain in the Palestinian Special Identification Group." He let that
sink in.

S.I.G., at that time, was a fairly awesome organization. It was not
large, and in the minds of most it lacked definition. This impression was
partly intentional and partly due to the group's metamorphoses.

Under the British mandate of Palestine, a very few Jewish settlers had
joined the British in their two-cornered policing action against Jews and
Arabs. At that time the moral dilemma of the Jewish privateer was to
weigh his dislike for the British against his survival instincts in regard
to the Arabs. In a sense, only a fanatic could bridge that dilemma, a man
intent on his kill no matter what the price. In a draw, hard-core S.I.G.
were men who would kill Jew, British and Arabs alike for the sake of
securing their homeland. At that time, the Arabs took most of the
brunt.

The picture changed only slightly with the Second World War. The
intent remained the same, but the victim changed. S.I.G. was still
made up of Jews, they still wore British uniforms most of the time, but
their recruits came from everywhere and the sole enemy was now the
German.

This was Armageddon and the S.I.G. felt uniquely ready for it. Death
was only meaningful when the enemy died. The helpless kibbutzim
whom the marauding Bedouins used to call Children of Death for their
passive dying, they did not exist anymore. Instead, the S.I.G. had
become Children of Death in the manner of children who are strong

because they are loved by their father. Death was not their enemy, which made them death's most effective agents.

Their uniqueness was based on a freedom achieved by very few: the freedom of choice between life or death, and they readily decided on either.

"Captain Bergman will be assigned to your command, sir?"

Harker looked away as if he was thinking of something else. He wished in fact that he was thinking of something else.

"My command?" he said. "Yes," and then he did his tic. "In a manner of speaking."

There was a brief knock on the door. The small sound rather surprised both men because they had not heard anyone coming. The door to the hall always made a distinct, ratchety sound and the floor in the outer office always creaked like old bedsprings. But not this time.

"Come in!" said Colonel Harker as if he were ordering, "Charge!"

The door opened and Bergman came in. He wore regulation khakis with long trousers tucked into his combat boots. The boots were special. They had thick, heelless soles of black rubber and the right boot had a knife scabbard built into the shaft of the shoe. A wooden handle showed, suggesting a kitchen knife.

Boyden caught the small deviation from standard, but the more striking thing to him was that Bergman looked somehow as if he were in disguise. He was a tall man who looked embarrassingly Teutonic. The source of the impression, Boyden felt, was hard to define. The hair was blond and clipped very short. That, in itself, was not a definitive sign, though the head was squarish and the eyes were blue, a stereotype for many people. Neither the eyes nor the mouth showed very much expression. In fact, thought Boyden, he is pinching the mouth as if holding something back. It could be a laugh, though that seemed unlikely. Posture? There is no such thing as a military posture. Body build? It was strictly Bergman's build, with an impression of bull power which seemed to have something to do with the fact that Bergman had no waist. His hips seemed as wide as his shoulders and his legs must be at least as big around— Boyden stopped himself. He was trying of late to overcome his preoccupation with leg musculature.

Bergman was done with his salute and stood at ease without being asked. He looked over at Boyden without turning his head.

"I feel like a specimen," he said. The mouth performed a curling motion. It did not look unpleasant but it was hardly a smile.

Boyden became flustered, something which rarely happened to him. He considered that someone like Bergman had, of course, never happened to him.

"Terribly sorry, suh."

Bergman shrugged. In some strange way the motion of head and shoulder—a rather gentle motion—made his smile more real.

"Quite all right," he said. "By the books, I'm a genetic mistake."

At this point in the exchange Harker stiffened the way anyone might who is meeting the unknown. Partly he did not understand what Bergman had said, partly he did not understand a man like Bergman. To his surprise, Boyden did not seem troubled at all. The young man laughed, as if he had heard a capital joke, something clever, something said at an American cocktail party. Clearly, Harker knew, it was once again a matter of the difference in background. Boyden had never been stationed in Palestine. Harker had—

"We'll get right to it," said Harker without looking at anyone. "Have a seat, Captain Bergman. Gin and tonic?" He did not wait for an answer. "Bring us the gin and tonic, Boyden. And a glass for yourself. And hand me— Never mind, I can reach it."

Harker bent sideways to reach the leather bag which was still on the rattan couch. He was busy with his hands now and did not talk. He had only talked so much before because he had not known what else to do. The situation, after all, was extraordinary and by the portents, so would Bergman be.

Boyden had gin and tonic which was mostly tonic, Bergman had his half and half and Harker had mostly gin. He got busy with the proper procedure of opening the bag, so as not to have it blow up in his face, and then took out a communiqué, datelined Cairo where Harker's HQ had moved. Harker himself had already been in Kufra for more than a week, and within that time he should have been on his way out again. But that had not worked out. If the gods were as willing as HQ was wise, then all well and good and Harker would finally be on his way in short order. If the gods were not willing, or if HQ was not wise— Harker did not want to think of either.

"Do you know a Major Donald Craig?" he asked and handed Bergman a photo.

"No," said Bergman. He looked at the photo. "Is he S.I.G.?"

"Er—no," said Harker. "Desert Group. Like myself. Why do you ask?"

"The clothes," he said. "I thought perhaps he was shown on a mission."

"It's a civilian photo," said Harker. "Like yourself, Craig is not really a military person. Er— What I meant to say was ..."

"Quite clear, Colonel."

Bergman made his unfinished smile. There was no resentment in his remark and no bite whatsoever. The very absence of judgment made Bergman that much more unfathomable.

"Craig was—er, is, I should think—a topologist or geologist, that sort of thing. We're relying on the maps he has made rather heavily— At any rate, that picture was taken near the Qattara Depression. He was doing survey work for Shell Oil."

"I didn't know there was oil in that hell hole."

"I don't think there was. He'd worked his way through this, er— other hell hole here," and Harker grunted slightly while leaning back to the wall behind him where he pointed at a topological map.

The gesture was imprecise but Bergman was sure that Harker meant the dead stretch of terrain north of Kufra, the sea of sand where a mirage, any mirage, was a relief and a diversion.

"He was here," said Harker, "when we went into Libya. Civilian, at the time."

"A most helpful asset," said Bergman. "He must know the terrain like the palm of his hand."

How many men, thought Boyden, really know the palm of their hand? The platitude had disturbed his image of Bergman. He had begun to think of the man as totally original—a genetic mistake? As unpredictable as anything novel. Of course, in a sense that was still true. Boyden had not expected to hear a platitude. Curious thing also, Bergman's English had suddenly shown the touch of an accent, not a purely German accent, but distinctly un-British.

"Here you are, sir." Boyden handed Bergman another ink.

"Thank you," said Bergman and turned back to Harker. "Will he be going with you?"

Harker shook his head absently and kept looking at his communiqué.

"I'll have another one too, Boyden," he mumbled. "Never mind that bubble business."

He drank straight gin which gave his throat a fake sense of aliveness.

"Craig's knowledge of terrain isn't at issue," he said. "He is not assigned to my mission. Matter of fact, Craig is a prisoner of the Germans."

Bergman nodded and sipped. The poise rankled Harker who had hoped for an interruption.

"Subject of this unscheduled meeting," said Harker, and then he stopped as if the sentence were over. Then, "You will have to get him out."

There was a moment's silence while Bergman seemed to be waiting for more. He raised his eyebrows and said, "Or else?"

Thank God he did not smile, thought Harker, and then he felt like stealing a glance at Boyden. It was a lot like an impulse to protect the pure—

"Or else, kill him," said Harker.

Bergman finished his drink without change in pace. Then he put the glass down.

"Where is he?"

Boyden, who had not known about this detail of the order, had barely absorbed the shock when Bergman's lack of any sort of clearly natural reaction struck him. Why? That would have been the natural reaction. Why kill Craig?

"Is he a traitor?" asked Bergman.

"Of course not!"

Bergman shrugged at Harker's tone. Indignation was clearly a waste of energy, of critical energy. Bergman, in spite of his calm appearance, had lived a long time under conditions where energy was always critical.

"The point is," Harker was saying, "that he is being held for interrogation."

"What uniform was he wearing when he was taken?"

"British, of course."

"In that case, I don't understand why, as a regular prisoner of war, he would ..."

"Major Craig," said Harker, "was on the original Tobruk expedition."

"The one that blew."

"Er—correct. I was not there myself, but I understand that the particular vigilance which the Germans exercised was totally unexpected."

"In the Tobruk perimeter?"

"No. Craig's group never got that far. The point I am making, Captain, is the Germans were extremely sensitive about something—we don't know what—enough to question survivors of the debacle minutely."

"How do you know?"

"Because some of the dead which the prisoner convoy in question left behind had not died from exposure. We received reports on two of them, once the convoy reached Algiers. They both had been part of the Tobruk expedition."

"The one that blew."

"Boyden?" said Harker. "Why don't you just put that bottle on the desk here instead of leaving it on the file over there." Without looking at Bergman Harker said, "They died from beatings. One of them was the C.O."

"Most unusual for treatment of prisoners under Rommel's command."

"Precisely."

"Did you say Craig was regularly with the L.R.D.G.?"

"I didn't say, but he was."

"I've been led to believe," said Bergman, "that a man from the Long Range Desert Group wouldn't give under that kind of interrogation."

"The two we found didn't," said Harker. "Or else there would not be the continued interest in Craig."

"What does he know?"

"He knows our means and method of getting into Tobruk—since his survey maps were the basis for the sortie."

"You think he might give?"

"If he tells what he knows, we won't have a second chance."

"You didn't answer me, Colonel."

Harker looked at the bottle of gin and then at Bergman.

"I don't know if there is enough time for you," he said. "But Craig *will* give. They are taking him to Grenoble."

Boyden had the unpleasant surprise of seeing Bergman display emotion. The big man seemed to sink, and then his tight mouth disappeared until there were only teeth.

5: The Dhow and the Focke-Wulf

Von Hahn bit into the chicken leg but ended up by nibbling only a tiny sliver into his mouth. Then he dropped the leg on the floor and forgot about it. Von Hahn's first sign of anxiety was a total loss of appetite. He had not really eaten anything in two days.

Outside the office window the Mediterranean was throwing the sunlight back up into the air, as if nothing mattered but light, as if the dark would never exist again.

They were supposed to come that night. It was vastly important to maintain the schedule. The Cairo matter was easily at stake. The matter of Von Hahn's career acceleration was most certainly at stake.

But it would go well. Craig was in very good physical shape, considering, and he was in very bad psychological shape. The combination was excellent for Von Hahn's business. Von Hahn looked out of the window and contemplated a simile. A fishing boat with lateen sail bobbed about in the sea beyond the landing strip. An agitation of wind now would produce desired motion. The available agitation of wind was like the subject's psychological state. However, none of this would be to much avail if the body of the ship was in very bad shape. The thing might even sink. The thing, such as Craig, might even die from the agitation.

Von Hahn stood very still, thinking about all this, and the loftiness of the simile and the thinness of his subject all served to preserve Von

Hahn's efficient sense of balance. He did not think of Grenoble and of the room he would use there, and the ways he would use there, but he thought clearly of all the desired results. He thought of the removal and replacement of his current insignias—no. He thought of French tailors. He thought at length of their indefinable touch for giving the garment that discrete quality of the ornamental. He thought of French women. Von Hahn thought they too were primarily ornamental. He rocked back and forth on his heels and thought that he might get a monocle after all. Then he stood still again and watched the boat without wind. He wished that he had an appetite—

Craig paced. When he went past the door, he looked at the empty bowl which was there on the floor and gave it a kick. He wished Seppel would come to the door. Craig did not want conversation, he wanted food. One of his first signs of anxiety was an abnormal appetite, as if his chewing would make all problems malleable, because a full stomach cures hollow fear.

And then the Frigate bird, he thought. And then, when I am helplessly full, comes the Frigate bird. But I am empty! I will be empty like a cave with the wind howling through the chambers and that will be all he will hear, the howling, my awful, empty howling when the Frigate bird—

Craig stood still and listened. He thought he was standing still in order to listen because he had heard something outside; though the fact of the matter was that he stopped to listen like that regularly every fifteen minutes, regardless of events. He listened for the sound of the plane-

The Arabs in the dhow pulled their jalabes back over their heads and then reset their caps and their turbans. The evening wind had come. There had been no motion of air all day. It had been like holding one's breath, that still, and that full of tension. But now the wind came as suddenly as the Mediterranean dusk, when the light falls away, a balloon of light collapsing, and there is nothing left but an emptiness into which the wind rushes with the same sense of trembling and shaking as the cold side of malaria fever.

The Arabs looked at their sail which started to snap and pluck and wondered which way they should go. They had no lights for night fishing, which was just as well as the fish in their basket had already started to stink. They did not usually keep their catch in the open boat because the sun steamed all the fresh moisture away. But it had been a bad day for sharks—small, insistent Makos who had torn at their baskets in the water so that the shredded carcasses of the dead fish had floated down into the murk like chum. Then more sharks had come.

They were still wheeling and circling with the mindless patience of their breed.

The Arabs wondered whether they should take the long haul back toward Algiers or whether they should beach near the airstrip and wait there till morning. They were wondering whether it was true that the French no longer ran the installation and whether the new owners who wore tight, angular black were as unfriendly as had been said—

The office was dark so that Von Hahn could look out without having to fight the window reflection. When the door opened he turned and watched Kaufer come toward him. His aide had a pair of night glasses slung around his neck and when he was closer Von Hahn could see Kaufer blinking his eyes.

"This damn sand in the air," said Kaufer. "Like a wind on the beach. Except here there is no beach."

"From the desert," said Von Hahn, and then, "Well?"

"That wasn't one of ours. I thought it was a Focke-Wulf but then it didn't sound like it. Do they have a patrol out of Gibraltar coming this far?"

"The boat," said Von Hahn. "This is a neutral port and that I don't give a damn about their patrols. I want to know about that boat."

"The boat?" said Kaufer. "I didn't see the boat. You mean the fishing boat that was out there all day?"

Von Hahn cursed with considerable heat. He rarely cursed and he rarely felt heat but in this case he felt such an overwhelming concern for every detail of the operation that he did not care how his conduct veered from the proper norm. He was not worried about his prospective success with the subject once they were in Grenoble, but it would truly be the ass end of fate smiling at him if a hand-made fishing scow, designed no doubt one thousand years ago, if such a bagatelle should interfere with the flight pattern of a seven-hundred-and-fifty-thousand-mark Focke-Wulf, and wreck it!

Neither of the two runways was long enough to handle a two-engine plane which could cover the nonstop distance from Grenoble to Algiers. This idiotic French design of an airstrip would not even accommodate a plane capable of landing here from Cannes and then lifting off again for the return trip with five men aboard. It would therefore be the two-engine seaplane which would have all the runway it needed right out there. That is, unless it splintered into that abomination of a prehistoric fishing boat.

"Come along," said Von Hahn.

When he was in the lit corridor he got a good look at Kaufer. In addition to the night glasses hanging over his belly Kaufer was wearing wind goggles over the band of his cap. Von Hahn, sensitive to appearances, felt irritated again.

"Did you know," he said to Kaufer, "that Rommel is not even a party member?" Then he took the glasses and the goggles away from Kaufer.

With that shape and that face, thought Von Hahn, the Bavarian pig should not even be allowed to wear this uniform.

On the other hand, he thought, I really must get that monocle—

Craig had been listening to the wind for over an hour. He had listened to worse winds in the desert—black winds and yellow winds, the kind that bite and scream and the kind which won't let you be with their nervous plucking. You never learned to like them but, as with most natural phenomena, you began to live with them. This was different, thought Craig. This was not natural. This was an exhaust roar three thousand feet up, a prop wash at fifty paces, the whistle of a final approach with props feathered, this was the Frigate bird pouncing—

The Arabs could see the two shapes standing where the runway dipped into the water. The black shapes were outlined against the lights from the building farther back: one of them angular, somehow like a bird with wings folded, hunched on a tree, and the other a black barrel shape propped up by two stumps of legs.

"What are they yelling?" said one of the Arabs.

The one who was holding the tiller shrugged his shoulders. "I don't know."

"Yell something back."

"What?"

"Anything. They don't understand Arabic."

The Arab who was holding the tiller started to scream like a banshee. Abominate in the offal of your own making; choke on the breast of your mother who is a sow; burn yourself impotent inside a very dry woman; eat with your left hand!

From the boat they could see a third figure joining the others. It was also black but looked sloppy.

"Portman," said Von Hahn. "What the devil are they saying?"

"Er—What are they saying?"

"That's what I said. What are they saying."

"They are saying—Arabic, you know. I'm afraid it would get lost in the translation."

"*What?*"

"In brief, they are simply expressing displeasure with—uh, adversity."

"Well, tell them they've got some more adversity coming. Either they get out of there or I'll have them shot out of the water. Kaufer!"

"*Zu Befehl!*"

"Bring the Weatherby from the trunk of the Benz."

"*Zu Befehl!*"

When he heard the rifle shot Craig fell flat down on the floor, hands pressed to the ground, feet splayed sideways so that the heels would not stick up and make a target. He knew that the act was nonsense in an empty washroom but it was better to imagine that this was an ambush in a wadi and any minute now there would be a life-sized, real enemy whom you would have to fight, whom you could fight.

As a game, this was not nonsense. It was a game in which he could act instead of think and any act kept him for that much longer away from the vortex of vague, flitting shapes of his own devising: himself strapped in a chair, things done with needles, low-power things done with electricity to the tune of a humming motor, smell of singe, sound of breath stuck in the throat like a stone, feel of eyeballs pressed out of their sockets—

Then there was a whole series of shots. Craig sat up on the floor and changed his game.

The bastards had come equipped for big game. He had heard the sound of a high-powered rifle, no army equipment that, a .300 Weatherby Magnum perhaps, as if Von Hahn had been toying with the idea of a quick little safari between workaday stints with the wires and the needles.

Of course, there was no big game here. Von Hahn was an idiot of ignorance when it came to the outdoor life.

Then the gun banged again, making its typical high-velocity crack. That thing, thought Craig, was good for one thousand yards. Undoubtedly with scope, four-power at least, six-power much better. You could put Sanft on the steps of St. Joseph's Oratory, walk back down to the bottom of the north slope of Mount Royal, and then execute him.

There were no further shots. This left Craig without impetus to continue his speculations, except that he was stuck with Sanft.

He had been a German agent, he had come from Cairo, and he had served his purpose. His execution, thought Craig, meant either that he was a traitor to the Germans or that he was a prospective risk. If he had been a traitor then Sanft, replete with Divisional markings and British papers, would hardly wend his way back toward his own execution. His plausible exit from Cairo toward prisoner status was undoubtedly stage-set with the help of German Intelligence. His death was just barely expected by him, Craig considered. In the truck to the airstrip, Sanft had been afraid.

Of course! He had done the job under pressure: Either you run this errand for us, or we kill someone you love. That sort of thing. Very clever, like the entire uniform thing. There was no easy way out of Cairo, either by car, plane or boat. Alexandria was worse. If he had been in transit through Alexandria he would have been under scrutiny like a nudist traversing Times Square. Nothing moved in Alexandria. The bulk of the French fleet was interned there, creating a monstrous mess for Security, with a proportional increase in their suspicions. No. He had left the Cairo area with the British unit whose patch he wore. Then he had probably disappeared as early as Sidi Barrani and gone on by sea. It was by far the safest way for an important courier. An inshore craft was the least likely target for the overworked Desert Air Force. They went after desert craft and they went after aircraft. Where did Sanft join the prisoner convoy?

Hard to tell. There he was on the pier, and then there was the transfer to Gestapo custody. Only one explanation for those complicated shenanigans. Rommel knew nothing about this, or he would have been asked to supply much faster transportation. Rommel, who had his own rules of conduct, was not a very good Nazi. He reminded one too much of a gentleman and even insisted on outmoded chivalries in the conduct of war. In brief, there was something disturbingly unchivalrous in the offing under the heading of "Cairo"—

And he, Craig, ranking survivor of a minute infiltration sortie, was possibly so important in this curious scheme of things that it was worth the delay of a trip to Grenoble, seat of the *Dauphiné*, center of tourism for the *départment de Isère*, HQ in Vichy France for the *Geheime Stoats Polizei*.

Craig started to sweat.

The Arab wiped the salt spray off his face and looked carefully over the gunwale. The other two were behind him, also out of view from the shore.

"He is not reloading."

"I don't think he was trying to hit us."

"But he wants us to go away."

"You are very funny this evening."

"True. Nevertheless, here comes something worse!"

"How low he is."

They craned their necks and looked for the plane which was coming. Very suddenly and with a burst of raw sound the craft shot by overhead, no more than eight hundred feet up. The landing lights were on under the wings and the white light whipped over the black water and then raced up the runway.

Having checked the approach, the seaplane went into a turn, banked up to one thousand feet and then doubled back out to sea.

The men on the landing strip watched the dhow sway with activity. The Arabs were trying to work up their sail which had slid down the mast and looked like messy laundry. One of the Arabs was paddling furiously with a pole. So far the boat had not succeeded in getting out of the landing path but it kept going farther out to sea. Von Hahn watched and laughed because the men in the boat looked ridiculous. He picked up the night glasses and watched how the plane came streaking back. The motor sound was now a low burble.

"Kaufer, get the prisoner ready."

The pontoons hissed over the water and then, quite suddenly, the plane mashed down.

"Portman," said Von Hahn, "why don't you come along?"

"I'm leaving. I'll be in ..."

"You will be back from Grenoble before Cheryl can get here. And by then we will know if there was something important about the Major's little invasion, *nicht wahr*, Portman?"

There was no answer and when Von Hahn looked he could see Portman going rapidly toward the building.

The plane swam forward, bobbing in an ungainly way. The dhow moved as if sucked by the plane's propellers. The engines chugged and coughed and then the propellers stopped. The pilot was fearful of his equipment. Then the mast of the boat hit the inboard side of one of the nacelles.

It was unfortunate that they were so far out. Von Hahn could not catch the conversation. He could see the Arabs gesticulating and in the glass he could see that they were yelling and talking continuously. Then the plane's hatch swung open and a crewman leaned out. He was waving a Luger and he was yelling too. Next, there was all kinds of to-do with pole pushing, line throwing, jumping on the pontoon. The soundless conversation between crewman in the hatch and Arab on the pontoon went on vigorously. Then it stopped. The crewman disappeared. When he came back he was holding a submachine gun.

Von Hahn nodded with appreciation. Swashbucklers, he thought. Very good. Very impressive. Except soon the war will be over and then they won't have much to do. But we always will—

All three Arabs were scrambling wildly on the pontoon, giving a distinct list to the plane. Then the crewman fired. This time, Von Hahn could hear it. The fast hammer sound went on without interruption while the tracerless bullets cut the boat in half. The water churned and splashed vigorously and then one half of the boat drifted free and the mast leaned over and smacked flat into the water.

The Arabs were climbing into the plane. The pilot, it seemed, did not like the way the plane was listing. Gallant of him, thought Von Hahn. They're getting their first airplane ride—

In a while the engines turned over with a reluctant whine and then they caught. They revved up rapidly, driving the plane ahead, and each big pontoon had a white bone in its mouth—

He had heard the plane shoot overhead and when that happened nothing else happened, to his own surprise. Craig heard the plane and that was all. He felt nothing else and thought nothing else because in a wonderful way he now seemed armored with a skin of metal. It was true he could hardly move, but he felt nothing.

Also time was no longer a dimension of anything. There was the sound of the plane, there were meaningless shots, there were heels clomping down the corridor on the other side of the door.

"*Kommen Sie.*"

Craig could not move.

Kaufer came over and slammed his open hand across Craig's face. It worked. Craig now moved as directed, with the Luger muzzle in his left kidney.

He had one more moment of life protesting in him when he crossed the bare landing strip and felt the wind run all over him. He felt that and saw all the empty space where even the blackness farther away was not the limit of the space around him but was instead a very deep distance.

Von Hahn was already climbing into the plane. And then Craig ran.

Kaufer, of course, did not kill him. With surprising speed he knifed the Luger muzzle into the softness of one kidney and then, when Craig froze in an access of pain, he swiped the butt end of the gun across the back of Craig's head. Craig collapsed, still thinking that he was running.

6: The Gothic Quality

First he felt the vibration and then he heard the sound, but he did not know where he was until the inside sensations came back. There was now the knot of pain in his back, the wild sting of pain in his skull, and then again the roaring hunger inside his gut.

But he must have waked too soon, he felt, because now a faint nausea crawled up into his throat and the rest of him felt dull and removed. He could see but there was a mustard tinge over everything, or something like dull, wavering gauze.

He lay on the floor and had the cold metal smell of the plane in his nose. He could see the sides and the roof curvature of the fuselage, a view like a vault. In this arch, by the side where the narrow seat plank had been pulled down from the wall, there sat Von Hahn. Seen at some distance and from below, Craig discovered the quality in the man, the very still, erect posture, the motionless face which shone like wax and the distinct symmetry of peaked lapels and sharp shoulders. But the real symmetry was the man's calm. Von Hahn seemed somehow folded inward, with only his posture suggesting that he was here at all.

The Luftwaffe major next to him looked disheveled in contrast. Craig could see him past the figure of Von Hahn, one leg out into the aisle of the plane, one arm propped on the leg, hand dangling idly. The hand looked very large and reminded Craig of some brutish head lolling down while the rest of the monster was asleep.

The major's face looked abstract in the overhead light, with no shadings between highlight and shadow. His leather flying cap was scuffed and very tight on his skull and his blue coveralls were totally wrinkled. He was leaning on his arm and looking at Von Hahn with interest. Nothing moved, only the earphone wires which dangled down from the cap, and the little brass chains which flicked with light where they hung from the coverall zippers.

They were talking in German. It was simple enough for Craig to understand.

"Is he tough?" asked the major.

"Yes. In the ordinary sense."

"Is that why he goes to Grenoble?"

"Yes."

"Then he isn't ordinary."

"He will be. Afterward."

"But why Grenoble?"

"Orders."

"How important is it, Von Hahn?"

Von Hahn did not answer but in a while he moved slightly, getting a little bit taller, and then he sighed, as if he had just stretched.

"Orders," he said again. *"Alles Andere ist mir Schnuppe."*

The major grinned but did not make any sound. Then he put his head down so that his whole face was black shadow.

"Your interest is much too elaborate to be nothing but orders, Von Hahn."

There was no answer again and Von Hahn just sat. Craig's vision wavered with faint mustard tints. Von Hahn's paraffin face stayed immobile.

"Von Hahn," said the major in a low voice, almost gently. "It's a long trip. Talk to me."

Something extraordinary seemed to be happening to Von Hahn. He showed emotion. He showed this rare part of himself with the simple, slow gesture of closing his eyes. He closed them and rested his head against the metal wall behind him.

"Do you know," said Von Hahn, almost in a whisper, "do you know I have really nothing to say?"

The major nodded and listened again.

"Nothing I have not said before," said Von Hahn. "Nothing I have not heard from others." His voice dropped, sounding tired. "Nothing new— Nothing really my own."

The major sighed and for a while kept silent. Then he said with a very dry, a very impersonal voice, "Do you want to jump or do you want to fall?"

Von Hahn opened his eyes and nodded while staring straight ahead. "Let me fall."

The major nodded too.

"Bis bald," and he sat up slightly.

Von Hahn's motion was much more abrupt. He arched, as if wanting to stretch again, and he made a raw sound, as if wanting to cry. The major put his hand on Von Hahn's mouth and Craig could see the black blood run out between the fingers. Von Hahn's eyes, as if under glass, were still open.

It was a very bad dream and Craig fainted.

When Craig woke again it was like after a sleep and he remembered everything instantly. But the light had changed. The mustard tint over everything was no longer there and Craig could see the faint, flour-white light of early morning. The bench where Craig thought he had seen the two Germans was an empty bench now giving no clue to anything.

The plane was in flight. Craig could feel the slight fuselage shiver under his back. And his hands were there too. They were crossed in the small of his back, handcuffed together. "Good morning," said the major in English.

Craig could not see him until the tall man had walked to the end of Craig's legs.

He was not wearing the leather cap anymore and his short, blond hair was standing up like messy feathers. He looked down at Craig without a smile.

There is a look, thought Craig, of inspecting something inanimate, or something to be stained and dissected. This one is not a Frigate bird— I could hate the Frigate bird; but of this one and his look, I am afraid of this one and his look— And without foreknowledge, Craig lashed out with his feet.

His heels clunked back on the floor and Craig felt exhausted.

"I thought you might," said the major.

"I'm going nuts," mumbled Craig.

"You just made that quite obvious. May I help you up?" Without waiting for an answer the major stepped back of Craig and hoisted him up to his feet.

"Are you—uh, oriented?" said his voice close behind Craig.

"I'm here—confused."

"I mean, can I take the handcuffs off without throwing you into another fit?"

"Where's the Frigate bird?"

"I see," said the invisible major. "Sit here. I'll give you a cigarette."

"Unlock me."

"The hell I will. Sit here."

"I saw it. I was right here."

"You don't seem to be."

Craig felt himself being pushed down on the bench and caught the links of the handcuffs on a strut behind him. The German unhooked the link but did not open the cuffs. Then he went through the business of lighting a cigarette. It was very black and smelled like a Gauloise.

"Von Hahn!" Craig yelled at the major. "*I saw him!*"

"Oh," said the German. "Yes. He went down the hatch. In fact, I think it was the draft that woke you. We had to drop the other four too. Take a drag."

"I'm going nuts," said Craig.

The hand with the cigarette was in front of his face and Craig could see the strong wrist of the man where the coveralls did not reach. The skin was brown and the tattoo was blue. It was a five-figure number.

Craig closed his eyes. When he felt the end of the cigarette touch his lips he grabbed at it and took a deep drag. He held that in for a while and then let the smoke out with a grunt.

"I see everything," he said, "and I still don't know."

"The human condition. I think I can take the cuffs off now, Major Craig."

Craig leaned forward in silence while the other unlocked the cuffs.

"Captain Bergman," said the German while he tossed the cuffs down the length of the plane. "S.I.G."

"Gimme that cigarette, would you?"

Craig smoked while Bergman went forward and through the door to the pilot's compartment. Craig looked up at the hole in the roof and the plastic dome over it. There were twin forty-fives sticking through the bubble but they were not Spandaus. Bergman came back with a Thermos bottle.

"Coffee," he said. "Egyptian. Very good."

"You've got that number there," said Craig.

"Belsen," said Bergman.

"You got that number there for all to see and if they should take you—happens, you know. Happened to me. So if they take you ..."

"I told you I'm S.I.G. The Mark of Cain doesn't matter because I don't get taken alive. Will you drink it black?"

"Thank you. This is the seaplane I saw at the runway?"

"Right."

"How—"

"We must have boarded her before you came out. Drink your coffee."

"And the four others you mentioned?" Craig looked at the hatch.

"Three dead Luftwaffe, one heavy Gestapo, and of course Von Hahn."

"The one you killed." Craig looked at the empty bench opposite.

For a moment there was only the sound of Bergman unscrewing the Thermos top.

Then he said, "He died well. I did not expect it." Bergman drank coffee.

"He died well?" said Craig. "You mean he bled in a human fashion and then he turned properly lifeless?"

Bergman's face became stiff. In contrast, his blue eyes seemed to glitter with life. When he talked his voice was sharp and fast.

"I meant," he said, "that he died in the best tradition of the self-possessed human being who finally, in the face of death, handles its coming better than he has done all his life. And I mean that since I detest Von Hahn as a Nazi I am apt to overlook the possibility that he is partly human. And then, when he dies like a human being, I am surprised. I am confused. It is a dilemma with me. Did I answer you?"

"Yes," said Craig.

He did not want any more of this particular Bergman whose sudden intensity leapt at him like a beast. Craig had once again felt the touch of fear with Bergman

"I did *not* answer you," said Bergman. "To your question with the preordained answer the reply should have been: You are right, Don Craig. I am as prejudiced in my way as he is in his. Correct?"

Craig did not answer.

"Correct," said Bergman. "And it is fathered by my hate. Sometimes I get rid of it when it serves me, sometimes when it takes me over. For the rest, it fathers my prejudice."

"You're well matched," said Craig. "You and them."

Bergman laughed. It was a belly laugh and a heart laugh, as uncomplicated in its way as his knowledge of hate.

"I'm better than they," he said. "They are very cold. I match their coldness with my heat."

The door to the pilot's compartment opened. The man who came through was working his arms out of the Luftwaffe coveralls. He closed the door behind him and then finished the job of getting out of the suit. He did not wear any kind of uniform underneath, only a long Arab shirt. He kicked the coveralls to one side and walked over, barefooted and shirted.

"Salaam," he said and touched himself like an Arab in polite greeting. "I am Mohnfeld."

He could have been an Arab, thought Craig. His hair was black and full of lively ringlets. He had berry-black eyes and a distinctly curved nose. It was Arabic, Jewish, Italian, Spanish or like the sharp noses of some of the French in Montreal. He was a short, wiry man who moved like an alert cat.

"Bergman," he said, "I can tell by the sickish look of your victim that you have been talking to him."

"Lieutenant Mohnfeld," Bergman said to Craig, "likes to take advantage of the times when we are not in uniform. Likes to criticize where it helps the least."

"It's the most irritating kind of criticism," said Craig.

Mohnfeld laughed and sat down on the seat opposite. His laugh was not like Bergman's but seemed to be something that caromed noisily around on the inside of his skull, or like a tin can tied to the tail of a cat dashing back and forth in a panic. The quality of panic was unmistakable, thought Craig

"My disguise," said Mohnfeld, "does not include a watch. What time is it, Kurt?"

"Five A.M."

"Bruckner says to start watching after five-fifteen. We'll hit the patrol zone about then."

Craig looked out of the nearest window and saw the sea about six thousand feet down. The sun had by now made the horizon and there was a lot of wild, liquid sliding of light on the waves. He could not see the sun itself. The plane was heading dead into it.

"Due east," said Bergman. "But we'll be turning southerly now and pass the coast going inland."

"Whose patrol zone?" asked Craig.

"Ours."

"Or did you forget," said Mohnfeld, "that we've got the dreaded Maltese cross and the ghastly swastika to identify us?"

Craig nodded and looked up at the gun turret.

"Forget it," said Mohnfeld. "Those two belchers are the only armament we've got. They look just arrogant enough to provoke a Spitfire into a pass. And then what?"

"Is this Bruckner our pilot?" asked Craig.

"He thinks so." Mohnfeld fluffed his shirt and saw to it that it draped just right.

"Not much he can do," said Bergman. "He can't speed up and he can't maneuver."

"I forgot," said Craig. "We got pontoons."

"We are banking on the possibility," said Mohnfeld, "that the Spitfire will take one look and decide that there is no such thing as a pontoon plane over the Libyan Desert."

Mohnfeld laughed again but nobody took it up. Bergman looked at his watch, sighed, and climbed into the bubble.

"And if we get there," said Craig to Mohnfeld, "where are we going?"

"Kufra. You mean he hasn't told you?"

"He told me about himself and the Nazis."

"No he didn't," said Mohnfeld. He smiled, showing very white teeth. If anything, they distracted from the smile. "He told you about himself and the world," said Mohnfeld.

7: The Possibility of Pan in Politics

Berlin in the summer of nineteen forty-two was the capital of a victorious nation. Reversals in the field served to strengthen the muscle, and continental conquests were realistic aims. The Berliners' traditional summer resorts were all changed. Warnemünde, Rügen and the Danish island of Bornholm had no more than prewar standards. Even for a longer vacation the Tegernsee, Garmisch-Partenkirchen and the lovely solitudes of the Schwarzwald were becoming merely middle-class. One planned on Vienna, Paris, Rome, Prague, Budapest, Athens, and if there were still pockets of local difficulties, they would disappear as surely as the present problems with London, Cairo or New York.

In spite of this sunshine of prospects many Berliners went no farther than the crowded Wannsee. They were too busy for extended travel. Berlin hummed. The main nerve trunk of the Thousand Year Reich was rooted here, and its divisions of *Regierung, Partei* and *Wehrmacht* all merged into one source of action, a nodal point as complex as a superbrain.

This electric sense of importance possessed Berlin everywhere; the old man who swept the streets after the recent parade; the Hitler Youth who inspected all the attics in his block for the prescribed presence of sand buckets; the fifteen-year-old BDM girl who lay under a Tiergarten bush with her blouse unbuttoned and her skirt awry, smiling up at the sweaty soldier because she wanted a hero's baby; the young baroness in the same position, but on silk, with that evening's lover a Turkish embassy clerk, and she loving it night after night because *Abwehr* required information; and the champagne salesman turned diplomat, the schoolteacher turned executioner, the Jesuit turned mass molder of minds, the pilot turned airforce marshal, the hysterical corporal turned maniacal Vessel of Providence-

Cheryl Portman stood at the mezzanine railing which made a delicate curve and then an ornamental bulge. It followed the wide stairway down into the gilded gala room. She looked down at the laughter and music, the soft gowns, the stiff uniforms. And her father, of course, was right. These were her peers. She was not the slim baroness, she had never been a bumptious singer and hiker in the young maiden's corps. She had not even been born in Germany. But her father was wise. He was a quiet man and looked insignificant, but he had the vision of a sage. He could see the time when all would be one. She put her gloved hand to her mouth, to cover a champagne giggle. The gesture placed her forearm between her breasts so that the silk of her gown tightened over the curves and cupped them with shiny folds. She glanced down at herself when she felt the silk but could not finish the thought that came because she had to giggle again. She looked down at herself and thought of her escort.

After champagne, she thought, he sounds just like Papa. "Let us be one—" Even the intonation of a higher mystique was there. Her escort had not said, "Listen, I want to go to bed with you. I've *got* to have you, and naked. Listen, I feel like an animal and I love it and you too—"

She turned her back to the hall below and leaned against the banister.

I want to say that, she considered. She was on a tiny, pleasant island of soberness surrounded by the light blond sparkle of a whole sea of champagne. Hers was a lovely little island and anytime she wanted to cavort into that foamy sea she could and she would.

Where was that escort with the dish-plate epaulettes? He took longer on the W.C. than a woman in the powder room.

Ah yes. She put one finger to her mouth which made her look pert and girlish. She squeezed herself with her forearm and giggled again behind her finger.

I don't think I will say this with the escort, she went on to herself, but I will say it some other time. Not with him. With Eric. Eric taught me how to say it and so it's only right that I do—that I say it with Eric.

And there hadn't even been a moon. There was the big shadow of Cheops, black as the inner tomb itself, and making love at the foot of a pyramid might be romantic enough, except that she had felt as if lying in a basement. And all that miserable sand. In her hair, in her shoes, up under the clothes, which, of course, recalled all that awkward business-

She smiled, without the champagne giggle this time, and said, "God, that was beautiful—"

She saw her escort come toward her across the wine-carpet of the mezzanine. He made black flashes with the patent leather of his boots and he seemed to tinkle when he hitched his epaulettes into place. All this time he smiled at Cheryl and looked much too beautiful. She smiled back at him and felt playful. And he, she thought, is the mouse—

"It iss goot?" said her escort and sparkled.

"I don't know. Was it?"

"Vat, vat, darrlink?"

"Let's talk German, shall we?"

"No, no. Vit you I am training it."

"Oh no you won't."

He did not understand her laughter. He knew primarily that she moved freely in some of the trickiest circles and when he had been assigned to escort her he had heard the Voice of Providence inside his own head and it had hollered, This is your break, Franz! But his tool, so to speak, for furthering his providential climb had so far not been allowed to come into operation.

A matter of technique only, of course. She was not German and in that sense constituted, so to speak, virgin territory.

Mal à propos. With those looks she has never been a virgin. Hair black as sin and just as shiny. Long eyes with a slant of acquiescence and a mouth that showed hunger— Yet how cool the posture, as if she did not know what that body could do—

How to proceed. He thought of a film with Jean Gabin in operation. He could not think of a German star.

"Darrlink." Arm on the balustrade in back of her, eyes searching nearer and nearer. Somehow, noses were in the way. "Ve now go aveck from here."

"How nice."

"It is time."

"It's eleven o'clock."

"I do not mean the clock time, Shereel. I mean time for knowletch and confrontayshen. Time for great moofments, vat I mean ..."

"Please speak German, won't you?"

"*Nein!* It is time for the Universal, uh—de globe—vat I mean iss, all for van and van tink for efferbody. You understand?"

"No."

"Loff!"

"Oh. I thought you were talking geopolitics."

On the other side of the Kürfurstendamm there was an upper-story room with the light of only one green-shaded lamp. From this room the gala occasion on the other side was visible but of no importance. Schlemmer sat late at his desk and when he sat up to look out of the window his bald head would turn green from the shade.

"*Panem et circensis,*" he said.

Schlemmer wore moldy tweeds but his lapel was adorned with a party button surrounded by a gold rosette. His membership dated back to the pioneer days when Hitler still carried a whip and when he might have an occasional fit on the floor. All that took loyalty.

The other man in the room stood by a file cabinet and wore Navy uniform. *Abwehr*, at least in inception, was a Naval Intelligence branch.

"If you consider the number of clothes dummies and idiots who are gyrating over there," he said over his back, "you wonder how anything gets done in the capital."

"Dear Von Epp," said Schlemmer, "I don't wonder. It is almost midnight and I am still here. Therefore, I don't have to wonder. The file, please."

Von Epp brought the file to the desk and placed it next to three others. Together, they formed the dossier of Portman, Cheryl, 24, Mischling. Nationality, British. Born, Cairo. Father, Portman, Henry, 60, Aryan. Nationality, British. Occupation, President Euro-Asian Supply & Storage Co., Ltd (assets, £2.6 million), offices London, Berlin, Cairo, Hong Kong. Mother, Sarita, Barily, non-Aryan, deceased. Nationality, Egyptian.

"In one sentence, Von Epp, why is this young person running courier service from here to Cairo?"

"To Algiers, Herr Schlemmer. Her father takes over from there."

"In one sentence, please."

"Because she has the social contact and exposure which makes her high level presence both useful and conspicuously misleading. She is here for the wedding of Von Kesselring's niece, and she is here to see Von Kesselring on the matter ..."

"I know that. Is she a party member?"

"No."

"Any party at all?"

"None."

"I am puzzled, Von Epp."

"She adores her father. That's all."

"That might last for a while. Does she—uh, believe in any of this?"

"Does she have political convictions?"

"Precisely what I asked, Von Epp."

"Well, she believes in pan— I don't quite remember, but there's a letter here under section P.D., Personal Documents, to a girl friend in Hong Kong ..."

"Aryan?"

"Oh yes. She's the daughter of the Hong Kong head of Euro-Asian and has a name like Blitherforth or something like that— Why don't we just look that name up here where it says ..."

"Never mind. Blitherforth sounds Aryan enough. Not really important. Go on, please."

"Of course. In that document she details her pan-something convictions— Why don't we just look ..."

"I will, I will, Von Epp. I am at present asking for briefing only, even cursory briefing. In one sentence, please."

"Yes. I distinctly remember that it has to do with Unification. There is a great emphasis on love, I recall."

"Love? Love of what, for heaven's sake?"

Von Epp reminded himself that, he, not the other one, was wearing a uniform and that this sort of browbeating by a bureaucrat, even an Intelligence bureaucrat, was not really in the necessary order of things among cooperating bureaus.

"Herr Geheimrat," he said, "I am, while limited to documentation, in no position to be specific about the young woman's love-objects. However, I do wish to point out that they—she and her love-objects—have apparently received *carte blanche* clearance by all other departments concerned with her present and past and purely marginal activities in the matter of the Cairo affair."

"Except by my office, Von Epp."

"Precisely why I am here, Herr Schlemmer, at one hour past midnight."

Schlemmer did not answer but looked across the street at the great arched windows where the lights danced and the idiots danced and where undoubtedly spit-and-pomade *Abwehr* liaison officer Von Epp would do a much more creditable job with love-objects than he did here. Nevertheless—

"Question, Von Epp."

"*Jawohl.*"

"Mode of transportation, please."

"Under section MT we have detailed conveyance by common carrier— airplane, I think it was— May I just take a look ..."

"Never mind! How is she transporting the document, I want to know."

"Concealed, Herr Schlemmer."

"Very good. *Where?*"

"That, Herr Geheimrat, is sealed under provisions of the directive covering Documents, transport of, via courier, female, our office. Without specific authorization from the Canaris office ..."

"Canaris is dead."

"His office is not."

Geheimrat Schlemmer leaned back in his chair. The change in position turned his bald head from green to gray. He coughed feebly and then he sighed.

"The idiots are gyrating," he said. "Are you getting the distinct feeling, Von Epp, that they are not the only ones?"

"Yes sir."

"Very well. Go home. One thing only. You are sure she has no contacts between pickup here and delivery in Algiers except with official personnel in this matter?"

"Entirely."

"No assignations, no contact with friends, friends of friends—"

"That, Herr Geheimrat, I cannot guarantee. She is even now at that ball across the street."

"Over there is not important." Schlemmer sighed, wondering how much he should tell.

"Are you suggesting that she might leak some aspect of her assignment?" asked Von Epp.

"It is the other way around. I am a little bit worried what might leak to her."

"Beg pardon?"

"Her father, Von Epp, was not her only love-object—"

8: The Unorthodox Use of Three Types of Planes

When the seaplane was late in Cannes the small Storch which was to provide the commuting service between Cannes and Grenoble was kept in readiness but with nothing to do. After eight hours of this a young Oberleutnant with initiative sent the Storch out as far as the 42nd parallel; and at six thousand feet, with Corsica to the east, the Storch should take a look around in order to discover what might have happened to the seaplane. The Storch met the seaplane. The Storch was promptly shot down by the seaplane which was on patrol out of Gibraltar.

The incident, observed from a German frigate in the Gulf of Ajaccio, produced the execution of the Oberleutnant with initiative and provided an explanation for the absence of Von Hahn and his prisoner.

Four *Mädchen*, two wives and one young man wept over the deaths of the three crewmen. Kaufer's mother got drunk when she heard the news, and Von Hahn's colleagues at HQ in Grenoble reshuffled their pecking order at flank speed.

When Henry Portman heard the news in his hotel suite in Algiers, he tried to calm his nerves for one insomniac night with alternate readings of *The Prophet* by Kahlil Gibran, and *The Decline of the West* by Oswald Spengler.

The men in the missing ship had other problems. They knew where they were, they could even see the five oases of Kufra below them. The problem was how to land a seaplane in the desert. In sight of Kufra, Bruckner the pilot had broken radio silence. He was a Lance Corporal in the S.I.G. but in the seaplane over the desert he was in command. Bruckner flew the ship, nursing his gas supply at very low revs.

Mohnfeld sat next to him, running the radio.

"Mohnfeld," said Bruckner.

The other one did not hear.

"Mohnfeld!" yelled the corporal.

Lieutenant Mohnfeld took the earphones off and looked at his pilot.

"You're talking to a superior officer, Bruckner, and I'll not brook none of that disrespectful yelling."

"All right!" yelled Bruckner, and then, "Get me Bergman in here, *sah!*"

"That's better," mumbled Mohnfeld and scrambled to the cabin aft.

The exchange had been an effort for Bruckner who did not look like the light-hearted joker. It was only the needling presence of Mohnfeld which egged him into an attempt to talk Mohnfeld's double-talk language.

Bruckner had thick hair, a thick neck and he was big in the shoulders. His low forehead bulged down over his eyes, as if its own weight had pushed it there. But his thick frame concealed a delicate nervous system. He had the quickest touch on a sending key, he could sense what was wrong with a troubled machine just by ear or by feeling the vibration, and when it came to the most sensitive of all encounters, with another human, the damage that could be done to bull-necked Bruckner was appalling. He had learned that early, and he had learned to protect himself by keeping away. He no longer broke out in a sweat of embarrassment and he rarely blushed anymore. His gruff look, his sullen stare and his heavy tread when he walked made such a pat impression that it kept others from knowing him. Except with Mohnfeld, Bruckner was monosyllabic. Except for Mohnfeld, no one could joke with him. It is a matter of symbiosis, Mohnfeld had explained.

Bruckner had not understood.

I am weak and nimble, Mohnfeld had said, and you are strong and slow. We need each other to stay sane. You get it, Bruck?

Bruckner got it that he admired Mohnfeld. Anybody who was that slight and who was that fearless deserved admiration. And that's how Bruckner would willingly contort himself in order to imitate his friend.

"What is it, Bruckner?" Bergman leaned into the compartment, looking worried.

"Take the radio, sir. The lieutenant isn't much good at it."

"Ridiculous. I'm having a briefing with Major Craig back there and ..."

"The lieutenant talks too much. And then he forgets to release the button."

"Goddamn it, Bruckner, we're practically on top of ..."

"And we've got twenty minutes airtime left. At near-stalling speed."

Bergman stopped arguing and squeezed into the seat. It would have

been nice to know ahead of time that it was going to be a seaplane they
would pick up from the Germans. It would have been nice to have had
the time to arrange for a transfer en route. It would be nice to know how
in hell they were going to set this thing down—

"Harker to Boogy, Harker to Boogy. Come in."

"You are Boogy, sir," said Bruckner.

"I know that. Where in hell is the sending toggle on this thing?"

"Under the ammeter dial. You're working the old Blaupunkt.
Discontinued."

"I'm glad. Hullo! Requesting landing instructions. Over."

"Is that you, Bergman?"

"Right."

"Thank God for some straight talk. First instructions: Stop passing the
northeast oasis. You are spooking the camel auction ... Do you read me?
Over."

"Is this code? Over."

"You talk like that other idiot! This is straight, Bergman. Over."

"This is straight, Harker. We've got fifteen minutes airtime left.
Request instructions. Urgent. Over."

"What the devil is this, Captain? You've got standing instructions,
south approach this time of year, smoke pot set for you, sand drifts
southwesterly, intermittent ripples toward middle and end of runway.
Over."

"Colonel Harker," said Bergman. "Next pass around, take a look out
your window and check what we're flying."

"Ten minutes," said Bruckner, "and we're dead."

Cheryl Portman, due to recent developments, was diverted for the last
leg of her journey from an approach on Marseilles to a course heading
for Rome. In Rome the preparations indicated the importance of her
mission. They had spared her no inconvenience. They took all her
luggage away, they requested she take off her dress and change into
coveralls and then they stuffed her into the minimal space of a combat-
armed Stuka. Two additional Stukas came along to fly wing. Since the
landing speed of these planes did not permit for a landing at the
seaplane base to the west of Algiers, that city was thrown into a near
panic when three German dive-bombers screamed over the rooftops as
if on a strafing run. It was the necessary and fastest approach to the
commercial field on the other side of the town. Cheryl, in a tight knot
right behind the pilot's seat, could see very little. She could see the pilot's
brown neck and how it suddenly glistened and how the moisture
beaded on his skin. Then a striped pylon flitted by, just past the port

wing. The sudden change in prop pitch made a new sound which convinced her that the engine had died. She clawed her way up so that she could see over the pilot's shoulder. The runway was close under the nose of the plane, so close and expanding that she thought of a giant sheet—a valley, a bowl—rushing to engulf her. The nose leveled up and pointed straight at the scrub and rock farther on. It was not farther on, it was coming, coming fast, and when the wheels hit and screamed she was sure that this plane was caroming into the desert.

When she opened her eyes again it was because the roaring had stopped and the motion was over. The nose of the Stuka was pointing at the blank sky. The pilot exhaled and wiped his neck.

"*Ende gut, alles gut,*" he said without turning. "What are you doing tonight, Fraulein?"

"What did he say?" Bruckner asked.

At that moment the plane started to shiver and there was a distinct feeling of sag in the stomach. Bruckner moved very fast, his right hand jumping about like a flea and coddling each thing he touched with the gentleness of someone who has all the time in the world. He altered flap control, pitch, fuel mixture, and he overthrottled enough, thought Bergman, to cut fuel time by at least three or four minutes. Bergman had not watched the altimeter and therefore did not know that the craft had dropped a full three hundred feet. He had no intimation of it until he saw the palm tree reach up for him like the head of a very large feather duster.

"Christ, Bruckner—"

"All right, sir. Steady at three hundred."

"For how long?"

"What did Colonel Harker say?"

Colonel Harker, at that very moment, was done talking. He left Boyden at the open transmitter and with the telephone at his ear. Boyden had to call the motor pool for an ambulance, the local doctor for his immediate presence, the staff car for the doctor's transportation and the repair shop for the truck with the cutting tools. All this was to rush to the sand-polluted airstrip.

Harker himself ran to the apartment of Ibn Kabir on the other side of the inner court. His dash along the balcony described a letter U and each time Harker came to the angle of the railing, he grabbed the corner post and swung himself through the turn like a monkey. He had not done anything like that, he recalled, since approximately the age of seven. And not at home, either. Mother too strict.

The apartment was open, and empty. Damnation, it's siesta! So why isn't that fat man in his quarters? The café? Or the—what is it, his secretarial pool? Harker sprinted back the same way he had come.

The two rooms had one door each and because of his momentum Harker came to a stop by the door which was closest to Inter-Sudanese. The door was not locked and Ibn Kabir was there. He was not alone.

Closing the door behind him with deliberation gave Colonel Harker the time to reorient himself after his first, stark look at the unknown.

It was not unknown to him that a man and a woman might make love during siesta time, though he, Cyril Harker, had not done anything of the sort since Jaipur. Still a noncom then. What Harker did not know, at first glance, was the manner of love-making which was here to commence, or had just been completed.

He had seen the girl before. She was the blond, rather round-proportioned young thing with whom Kabir was seen on occasion. Harker could see her bare thighs, as round as he had thought they might be, and her legs which were dangling from the edge of the table. The rest of her was covered by the great folds of a Tuareg cloak which had been pushed up on her. She was lying on the table and might have been asleep.

Kabir was standing near her legs. In the cup of one hand he was holding a small mound of salt and with the other hand he was stroking the head of a yellow-eyed goat. The goat jerked his head around and stared at Harker.

"Salaam, Colonel," said Ibn Kabir.

"Yes—er, is anything wrong?"

"No," said Kabir. "Except your manners, Colonel."

Kabir lifted his cupped hands to his mouth and licked the salt. He then offered the hand to the goat who lapped up everything with one drag of the tongue.

Harker tried to collect himself and did the trick with his upper lip.

"Kabir, terrible emergency. I need your fire equipment. You have a lorry of extinguishers going to the Sudan. I must have them—payment no object—immediately, foam all over the airport—"

The goat had gone to the window with slow, mincing steps and was now looking out. Kabir was wiping one hand on the other.

"It is siesta," said Kabir. "But we might discuss it. Won't you sit down?"

The girl dragged in air with a sound as if she were surfacing. She half rose, eyes closed, and the Tuareg robe slid down to cover her belly. It seemed to Harker that she was trying to rise, but she lost her grip on the table and rolled off to the floor. Then she just lay there.

"She is all right," said Kabir. "They pass out, you know."

Harker had the sudden wish that she would never wake up again, that it would be best if she died. The thought shocked him—

The plane rumbled overhead, the sound much too low.

"Please," said Harker, almost in a whisper. "Or they'll never—or they'll die—"

"Look!" yelled Bergman. "Look at the strip!"

Bruckner did not bother to look. He had not said so yet but he had made the decision.

"Ambulance!" said Bergman. "Look at them lining up there with the lorry— What the hell, dozens of fire-extinguishers."

"Steady on, sir. This will be a tight one," and he wheeled into a turn which would point him into the wind but would permit him, at best, to land about one thousand feet beyond the airstrip.

"Bruckner, don't you see the field? They're laying down the foam for us, man, they got the ambulance ready! Where in hell are you ..."

"The foam won't do the job for us. Only the ambulance will."

"This is an order, Bruckner!"

"The foam soaks right into the sand."

"Gimme those controls, you bone-brained bastard!"

Bruckner did not answer, or rather, he did not answer by yelling back. He looked at Bergman for the first time since they had started to circle the five oases of Kufra. Bergman saw the seriousness of the other man, and the sureness which was like an immovable rock and which was also like the only safe thing for anyone in this plane to hold on to.

"I captain this ship, sir. Please join the others."

Bergman stared at his Lance Corporal but then he only saw the man who was surer than any of them.

While Bergman worked himself out of the copilot's seat, Bruckner adjusted the trim.

"Captain Bergman?"

Bergman was now in the open door and everybody from the cabin was standing behind him.

"Only three instructions," said Bruckner without turning around.

"Zu Befehl," said Lieutenant Mohnfeld.

"Shut up!"

They all stared at each other, because Bruckner never talked that way. When he talked again his voice was normal.

"No more jokes now. Right now you have to have serious silence, so you can feel the plane, feel what she is going to do. Three instructions."

"All right," said Bergman.

They were over the main body of the town, losing altitude at an intentional angle. The airstrip was a few miles to the rear.

"One. Close the door tight, so that it stops you and you won't fly into my cockpit."

"Brother—" said Craig.

"Two. I want low center balance, so everybody get together on the floor where the fuselage is the widest. That's midpoint on the pontoons."

"You mean, lie down?"

"No. Sit. Because number three, when I yell loud, everybody gets into the tail, but immediately."

"Where are you landing, Bruckner?"

"If I cannot yell," said Bruckner, "you must feel it when I need all the weight in the back. It is the point when she sags in the back, just ever so slightly even, because right after that she will want to nose over. Clear?"

"Yes."

"Aaron," said Mohnfeld. "When you yell, please yell *mazel*."

It had not sounded like a joke but like a very serious and a helpless wish.

"I will yell *mazel*," said Bruckner.

The northeast oasis had the most trees and the narrowest waterline. It was also the longest. This conformation made more water accessible from the shore than at any of the other watering holes of the Kufra oasis. As a result there were also more buildings, more cattle and more people.

They all saw the monster a long way coming and they all knew that all Europeans were crazy. Perhaps, in their craziness, they had hit upon a new type of machine? A machine which could race like a comet but could also stop dead and at will, like an ass?

At the end of the pond where they were auctioning camels, they were so curious that they even crowded around where camels and water had made nothing but mud.

"*Wallah!* Look at the straw fly off that roof!"

"He is below the trees."

"Look at his turban unwind—and fly up into the air!"

"They will never make the water. Watch."

The plane not only made the water but kept racing across it with the effect of a diamond dashed hard across glass. A sharp, thin spray of water hissed away at both sides of the plane. It was the only sign that the pontoons were touching.

The speed was too great. There were now solid sheets of water like wings on the sides of each pontoon but the monster kept coming, both motors deafening now. They ran as best they could out of the mud. There was no doubt that the plane would keep coming and coming and then would continue away after slicing off several heads.

The plane did not really mush down until it was almost time to climb out of the water again. And then it did.

First the tail sagged, then the knife-edge pontoons sliced into the mud, kept slicing up the bank with the two motors roaring. And then the nose came down.

The nose-dipping and the tail-raising motion seemed as slow and as stately as a genuflection. And then, as if exhausted, the monster abruptly collapsed on itself.

Bruckner hit all the switches blind because he could not see with the blood running into his eyes. But he had to hit the switches. Perhaps she would not explode

Aft, the problem had not been lack of space. Craig, it was true, was still in the tail section, his arm hooked through a strut. Bergman had careened into the forward door at the last minute and then Mohnfeld had followed him.

After the motors, it seemed very silent. But then they could hear the horrible screeching outside.

"What now?" said Mohnfeld.

Bergman picked himself up to go and get Bruckner. "Now," he said, "I will report to Harker that we stampeded the bleeding camel auction."

9: Et Tu, Brute!

Eight hundred miles north of Kufra lay Tobruk which Rommel had taken after months of siege. This reoccupation was Churchill's most critical defeat.

Rommel had originally landed with a small, mobile force whose sole purpose had been to hold Tripoli so the Italians could escape. Two years later the Italians were gone, for all serious purposes, but Rommel was still there. His Fifth Light Panzer Division had mutated into the Deutsches Afrika Korps and had then become the Panzer Armee Afrika.

A fox had turned into a panther and then had become a tiger.

And yet the British Desert Air Force commanded the sky and the British Eighth Army was better equipped than the Afrika Korps. Rommel was outmanned for most of his African stay. But he had pushed the British almost to the Delta.

When Rommel insisted on Tobruk the reason was obvious. He needed that harbor the way a muscle needs a strong source of blood. When he took Tobruk the port became his umbilicus. And then the muscle did not move.

"What we need to know," said Colonel Harker, "is just what the devil is going on there."

Bruckner was getting six stitches put into his scalp, and Mohnfeld was getting out of his Arabian shirt and into proper uniform. Bergman, his job done, was preparing for his unit's departure. Craig was sitting in the second room of Inter-Sudanese.

He had taken his first hot-water shower in over two months and his desert khaki was brand-new too. His shave and haircut made him feel naked and the gin and tonic made him feel rather civilized. The illusion was heightened by the presence of a lady. Everybody was very polite.

The lady was Sergeant Lent, but neither her callous rank nor her mannish Wren uniform could distract from her female presence. When she turned her head her brown hair jumped in a lively fashion. When she smiled her cheeks firmed up to give a sheen like an apple. Her high-button uniform jacket was as nothing when viewing her two prominent attributes, and when she took shorthand she crossed her knees.

Sergeant Lent had come with Captain McGowan whom Colonel Harker had introduced as Intelligence liaison from Cairo HQ.

"Major Craig," said McGowan, "the reason I'm here is because your unsuccessful recon mission which comprised twenty-five men was stopped by a hasty convergence of almost five hundred Germans, one Storch recon, and one dozen half-tracks from garrisons as divergent as Tobruk and Al Jaghbub."

"We were shook up too," said Craig.

"In addition," said McGowan as if he had not heard, "two captured members of your expedition seem to have died during interrogation and you—as you know better than I—were slated for inquiry extraordinary at their specialty house in Grenoble."

Craig sighed, which sounded casual enough, except that his face became very drawn for a moment. Whoever else noticed it, only Harker took it up.

"Craig," he said. "How about another drink?"

It was the warmest gesture, thought Craig, except that the bottle was almost empty.

"Your little trek behind the lines," said McGowan, "was entirely recon, to ascertain what—if anything—is moving in and out of Tobruk."

"Are you asking me?" said Craig.

"Of course not."

McGowan's smile looked like a cheap attempt at therapeutics to Craig, like a pat on the head. And now he, Craig, was to wag his tail and ask for more. Craig's own irritability worried him. He was not overtired, there had been a good stretch of time to be self-indulgent with warm water, soap and very clean clothes; there was no prospect of damp nights on the concrete floor of a washroom; and the Frigate bird was dead. Obviously, he felt rotten for no good reason, but rotten he felt. He felt as hostile toward McGowan as he had felt towards Von Hahn. But he could not possibly show this. He wished Harker would come back with that bottle of gin he'd gone out to get.

"I am suggesting this," said McGowan. "You went behind the lines at a time when Rommel showed little activity. His forward mine-field patterns had been altered to defensive depth, his supply losses due to our activity out of Malta were seventy-five percent! Tobruk depots, we would guess, must be well-nigh empty. Did you know this, Major Craig?"

"So what was he so sensitive about?"

McGowan blinked his eyes a few times which made him look a little as if he wanted to cry.

"We don't know," he said. "Except for this."

McGowan and Craig had to wait while Sergeant Lent flipped to a new page and to a new crossing of legs.

"Where was I?"

"Except for this," said Sergeant Lent.

"Yes. One of our Spitfires lost his head and blew his cannon into a hospital ship. This ship was out of Messina, bound for Tobruk."

"Milk run," said Craig.

"The hospital ship blew up."

"*What?*"

"Blew up. Tremendous billow of black smoke, one single explosion."

Craig frowned and waited for the rest.

"That," said McGowan, "rules out ammunition. Instead, there were flames licking all over—including a broad area of water. Did you know this?"

"No."

"This same hospital ship had been boarded by one of our corvettes while rounding Passero. This ship was clean."

Where's that gin, thought Craig. Also, a rounding passero at the sergeant of the dimpled knees

"Except that her bilges were obviously pumped full of petrol."

"Shocking thought," mumbled Craig who had been thinking of other things.

"Beg your pardon?"

"That can raise hell— I was thinking, that must raise hell with your figure of a seventy-five percent loss in supplies for Rommel."

"Yes, we are as concerned as Rommel must be. And now," said McGowan in his business voice, "we come to you. It is suggestive in itself that they were terribly anxious about questioning you." Then he looked at Craig. "Did they interrogate you at all?"

"Yes."

"How did it go?"

"Without benefit of Queensberry."

"I see. Go on, please. What was the direction of their interest?"

In the belly and in the groin—

"They wanted to know where we had been going."

"What did you tell them?"

"Name, rank and serial number."

"What else, Major?"

Harker came back in. "You're drinking too fast," he said. He took Craig's empty glass and put gin into it and quinine water.

"I don't remember what else. Some chit-chat—diversionary, I thought at the time."

"Did they alter the line of their questioning?"

"No. Always, why were you behind the lines, where were you going, why was your deployment toward the north, why Sollum, why Tobruk, why Bardiyah, why Al Jaghbub."

"That was south, of course."

"To throw me off, I think. Because he was happy when he did throw me off."

"What happened?"

Craig was sweating. He thought that he *had* been drinking too fast and that was the reason why he was sweating. He picked up the glass and held it against his forehead. He wished there were some ice—

"When he asked about Al Jaghbub I got smart with him—it seems to help sometimes, keeps up the spirits—and I said we were heading north to throw them off because we wanted to go south, actually. Of course, he had me there. We had neither the gas nor the provisions to get anywhere south except if we wanted to commit suicide in solitude. Al Jaghbub was way beyond our range."

"He knew this."

"He told me so. But my answer ruled out the possibility that we were heading south to join up with some other party of our own. I wasn't gone enough to suggest links with another unit."

"He knew that."

"He dropped it, the southerly inquiry, and never picked it up again."

"What did he pick up, Major?"

Craig had started to lean his elbows on his legs and nobody had paid much attention. But he had continued to double over and his voice had changed.

"Why Sollum, why Bekh-Bekh, why Tobruk, why Benghazi—"

"Do you have a stomachache, Major Craig?"

Craig straightened up immediately. He put one arm on the desk and folded his legs. He now looked again as if the conversation were normal.

"Go on," he said to McGowan. "I was listening."

To what, thought McGowan, and then he said with surprising softness, "Von Hahn is dead, Major."

Craig nodded his head.

He remembered how Bergman and Von Hahn had sat side by side, and how *intime* they had sounded. And Bergman, with the death camp tattoo on his arm, had said later how well Von Hahn had died. As if talking about a dead comrade, a buddy. There was something distinctly weird about Bergman, something more than a genetic mistake—

"Major, did they ever make Tobruk more plausible as your target than any of the other places which were suggested?"

"I don't think so. I think he kept fishing the same way in the same murk all the time."

"Plausible," said McGowan.

"It hardly matters what Von Hahn learned, seems to me," said Harker. "First of all the man is dead, and secondly his attempt to move Craig to Grenoble shows clearly enough that he didn't learn a damn thing from Craig in Algiers."

McGowan did not resent the comment. He was not really interested in it.

"What I really want to garner," he said, "is what, if anything, Major Craig might have learned from Von Hahn. We need to know why Von Hahn was so interested."

"He wanted to know if we were headed for Tobruk," said Craig.

"Plausible. But you did not learn that from Von Hahn. You assume that because the Germans have tried persistently to regain Tobruk, because they just got it back, because their flak in the Tobruk perimeter is equivalent to the defenses of a much larger city and, of course, because that's where you had been heading. But what did Von Hahn contribute?"

Craig thought about it and then he said, "Nothing."

"Intentionally?"

"What else?"

"How about unintentionally?"

"I don't know, damn it. I don't."

"Anything at all that did not matter."

"Everything mattered, Captain."

"To Von Hahn?"

Craig sipped his drink now, without tasting it.

"It didn't matter to him," he said, "because I was going to be dead anyway."

McGowan did not interrupt.

"Cairo," said Craig.

Craig looked at McGowan and thought that the man was holding his face unusually still.

"He mentioned Cairo because it wasn't important."

"Cairo wasn't?"

The prompting did not help because Craig was not even in the room with McGowan anymore. He was at the window and saw how they dragged Sanft one way, and then he saw how they dragged Sanft the other way and his neck hung differently.

"There was another man whom they had picked out at the dock, him and me, and that other one was a German spy who had just come from Cairo. His name was gentle— I'm sorry. His name was Sanft."

"You have that, Sergeant?"

Craig said without looking around, "He was wearing our khaki and a Fifty-first Highlander patch. Lieutenant's pips. Somewhere along the line he joined the prisoner convoy. I have no idea how he got there."

"We do," said McGowan. "As a matter of fact, we've left it open."

"So why the surprise?" Craig sounded nasty.

McGowan got up, stalked to the window and then back to his chair. He wished that Craig did not persist in his feelings that he was still in Algiers, on his way to Grenoble.

"Professional pride," he said and tried to smile. "We did not know that their underground reached as far as Cairo."

"Might as well," said Harker, who had no appreciation for the ways of Intelligence and who did not intend to learn now. "Might as well be Cairo as Alexandria, if you leave some damn hole open for them."

"We knew they got in and out of Alexandria," said McGowan. "They're keen on the interned French fleet, since they think we're going to change the internment status to an act of requisitioning."

"Well, aren't we, damn well soon?" said Harker.

"Classified," said McGowan, "but, no. The French never throw anything away, it seems."

"What's in Cairo?" asked Craig.

But McGowan would not answer. He looked preoccupied wishing that he could get away. But apparently he did have enough to feel that he was finished.

"Anything else, Major?"

"It seems you got plenty."

"Any other prisoners arriving, any activity at that airport which does not even necessarily relate to your presence there?"

"I don't know," said Craig. "I didn't see anybody else. I saw the noncom who brought me my food, I saw ..."

"Talk to him?"

"Sure. We talked about his— He did say there was somebody else who had come in while I was there. *Verdammter Engländer*, he said."

"What's that?"

"Goddamn Englishman," said Sergeant Lent by way of translation.

"Thank you, Miss—uh, Sergeant," said McGowan. Then he turned back to Craig.

"Did you see the Englishman?"

"No."

"Hear him?"

"Well, once. Out in the corridor."

"And?"

"I don't know what he said. All I know is he talked German with an English accent and then he fell into English. He raised his voice. He was excited."

"What kind of English, Major?"

"What kind?"

"Try to remember the inflection, the general sound, and your association with it. Australian, Canadian, American ..."

"London. I've lived in London and that's what I was reminded of."

"London where? Mayfair, Soho, waterfront cockney—"

"None of those. Just London, I'd say. You want to know what class, is that it?"

"In a manner of speaking."

"No upper-class affectations. Not military, I'd say. No particular school, either. Sorry."

"Quite all right. I'm asking a lot. Was he old or young, would you say?"

"When I heard him," said Craig, "I already thought of him as older. My guard mentioned—let me try and remember. Yes. Always sucking about, with that baby face of his. He said something like that."

McGowan did not think much of that piece of information until Craig went on.

"Which was a point," said Craig, "because he was supposed to have white hair. I don't know how much."

McGowan, as if performing a comedy routine, slapped his thigh with a crack and said, "*Hah!*"

Then he coughed immediately and looked fairly calm.

"You have that, Sergeant Lent?"

She nodded.

"Please warm up the set now."

She got up and went to the short-wave console. Whatever McGowan had learned and whatever was firing him into a rather deceptively smooth series of actions was lost on Craig. He no longer felt irritable but dull. And if I don't watch it, he thought, the dull will turn brown, or blue, and this is no time for depression. I've got free time coming—

"I'm afraid this might somewhat change the complexion of your expedition, Colonel Harker," McGowan was saying.

Craig looked up, toward the bottle, but Harker mistook Craig's interest.

"I'm heading the second recon attempt on Tobruk," he explained.

Craig thought about it and then he started to laugh. The laugh was not appropriate, except that it had to do with Craig's depression.

"Through that?" he said and pointed at the map behind Harker, where Kufra lay at the bottom and Tobruk at the top, with the blank expanse of the Great Sand Sea in the middle. "With a standard recon team you'll need an additional truck of supplies for every two hundred miles. And your nearest watering hole is Jalu, three hundred miles as the crow flies from here."

"As the sand flies," mumbled Harker, which was an unusual remark for him.

Captain McGowan cleared his throat and then caused a silence. In a strange way it suddenly felt as if he were the ranking officer in the room.

"I'm afraid, Colonel, this second recon mission may have a different complexion after this meeting. It may not be recon at all. Sergeant Lent?" He looked at the girl who had sat down at the transmitter and was now ready for him. "Are we ready for the signal?"

"Ready, sir."

"Just a moment," said Harker. "Shouldn't we ask Major Craig to leave? We're actually through with him, I believe."

"Afraid that'll be Cairo's decision," said McGowan. "My guess is, he'll have to go too."

Craig seemed to give no particular reaction. But he reached for the bottle.

10: The Annoyance of a Hair
Under the Roof of the Mouth

"I'm afraid," said the German attaché, "that she cannot come with you, Mister Portman. Under the circumstances, I'm told, it is really out of the question."

Portman looked as if he did not belong in his own skin. He felt harassed and put upon with details. A factual "No" by an embassy underling was truly a minute thing in the scheme of things, but like a hair stuck under the roof of the mouth, it was completely annoying.

The attaché thought that the Englishman did not even belong in his own hotel suite. The white walls with their gilded plaster adornments were reminiscent of Sans Souci; the Moorish arches of the deep windows of the view in the palace of Rabat. No matter the mixture, the setting was rich. On the other hand, Portman looked rumpled and sweaty, an anxious trader waiting for his ship to come in.

The German attaché touched the damask of his chair and waited for a clear-cut reaction from the Englishman. Portman was saved from the chore when Cheryl came in.

She had thrown away the coveralls, she had taken a bath, and the attaché took note of the housecoat she was wearing. It was the sort of garment which said nothing out loud about the woman underneath. But it whispered about it.

Portman was pleased with the sight of his daughter and he was pleased with the attaché's reaction. Such interest produces helplessness

"This is Herr Binzwanger," said Portman to his daughter. "He is involved in our matter of business as a sort of liaison from the local embassy." And after that reduction in Binzwanger's importance, Portman took another step to debilitate the other. "As you can tell by his name," said Portman, "he is a good Bavarian." And with quick solicitude toward the attaché, "Has your family settled there long?"

As a matter of fact, the attaché was not a Bavarian at all. His family was originally Swiss. Binzwanger himself was an Innsbruck Austrian, but Portman's innuendo had been well put. Neither the Bavarians nor the Austrians, and least of all the Swiss, were known for their staunch love of Hitler.

Thus weakened, the attaché was now presumably ready for slaughter. Portman knew how to do this sort of negotiating rather well.

"And just as you came in, daughter," said Portman, "Mister

Binzwanger raised the point that you should not go to Cairo with me at all."

So far, Portman had been too agitated to sit down with the attaché but he now lowered himself on a vast, Algerian hassock which sighed under him with a sound of relief. It was, of course, very important that his daughter stay with him. She would now handle Binzwanger herself.

"When are you leaving?" She looked at her father who did not think that she had managed a very effective opener.

"That is partly the problem," said Binzwanger. "There have been—how to say this—some factors of uncertainty have been introduced." Binzwanger felt pleased with the diplomacy of his answer. He was not certain whether the girl knew such details as Von Hahn's disappearance—

"Nonsense," said Portman. "We would have moved whether a prisoner had been forthcoming with information or not. You know that, Binzwanger. In other words, there are no new factors of uncertainty."

But the German attaché did not like being called by his name without the correct form of address, particularly not by an Englishman whose character was suspect by the very fact of his defection. The encompassing ideals of the Universal were less meaningful to him than the fact that Portman was after all a traitor to his own country. Binzwanger would now give Portman a corrective jolt.

"It has developed," he said, "and you do not seem to have been apprised of the fact so far, that our usual route of entry into Egypt and Cairo has been closed."

"What was that?"

"Very recent development. And totally unexpected."

"What the devil are you saying?"

"Entry, as you know, was through Alexandria."

"Of course. Most difficult place to police."

"And yet, policed it was. Our two agents are dead, their wireless has been destroyed and our undercover arrangements have been rendered ineffective due to the simultaneous arrest of the various legitimate Egyptians in our employ."

"Did you say killed?"

"That has to be our assumption. There is no reason why our agents should have swallowed their own cyanide pills unless they were badly distressed. That places the responsibility for the distress upon the enemy. Therefore, the deaths are tantamount to murder."

It was a fine point but Portman felt ill. Cheryl reacted somewhat as she might to a thriller by Edgar Wallace; it was terribly shocking and thank God I am not really there—

"Rather an un-English way," said the attaché, "of handling the opposition, wouldn't you say?" And while he said it he walked to the tall windows. His manner was a study of underplay. It was obvious that Binzwanger wished to belittle any possible note of importance. Therefore Portman noticed when Binzwanger glanced out of the window.

The attaché saw two Arabs walking by on the street below and he saw a *colon* sitting in the park opposite, reading a paper. Then the attaché turned back to the room and smiled abruptly.

"Nothing to be alarmed about, of course. Even though we are not dealing with the usual methods of British fair play." Binzwanger cleared his throat, looked down at his shoes and folded his hands in front, in the manner of Hitler. Then he looked up. "In other words, Herr Portman, you would hardly wish to subject your young daughter to the—uh, uncertainties of the new route which you will have to take."

Portman looked at his daughter but that was no help. He could not tell whether she looked impatient or whether she was simply thinking of something else. It did not matter. Portman only knew that he would have to take her along—

"What new route?" he said, just to be saying something.

"The original coastal route is now most inefficient," said the attaché. "British patrol action has increased enormously. They are even firing on our hospital ships!" This produced a satisfactory blanching in Portman. "And, of course, entry through Alexandria is suicide."

"Did you say hospital ..."

"You will avoid all that. Your entry into Cairo will proceed—" The attaché hesitated. Though he did not look at Cheryl it was obvious that he did not mean to reveal a secret route in front of someone who was not going to use it.

"It is contingent on my success in this mission," said Portman in tones of a proclamation, "that my daughter accompany me."

"Her function has been adequately fulfilled, most admirably, I might add," said the attaché with a bow at Cheryl. But then he did not get any further.

"I'm not going to Cairo," she said.

She spoke quietly, without special emphasis. She was relating a fact. "I'm not going to Cairo," she said, "until Eric gets back."

"Eric?" said the attaché and turned to Portman.

The older man had to control himself greatly. This was not the time to broach the subject of Eric and the ghastly fear was that Binzwanger did not feel the same way.

"I don't understand," said Binzwanger. "You don't mean Eric Sanft, do you?"

Portman got up, making the hassock hiss air. He was a frightened father, a harassed old man and suddenly a very inept conspirator.

"Cheryl, would you mind waiting in ..."

"I *do* mean Eric Sanft," she said to the attaché.

Binzwanger, who knew nothing of the relationship between the dead Jewish spy and the daughter of Portman, handled the matter like a communiqué on his desk.

"He died. In line of duty, so to speak. Did you know him?"

She stared at Binzwanger for a moment while everything inside her held very still. Then she threw back her head.

"Oh my God!"

When Portman got to her Cheryl had doubled over. He could not hug her, because her arms were in the way. He could not stroke her head, because she had her hands clawed into her hair. He could only pat her back which made him feel terribly helpless, because the curve of her back was hard and she turned away.

It was the nature of Binzwanger's job to take little steps within the scheme of large purposes, to act on orders whose sense was of no concern to him. He had not been told why Cheryl Portman was under no circumstances to leave for Cairo, a city still well within enemy territory. He had no idea that she might become a most unreliable risk.

Portman knew it. He wanted his daughter close by his side because he knew what the Germans would do with a most unreliable risk.

"Darling," he said, trying to reach her, "please, Cheryl darling—"

She moaned and then she uncovered her face. She straightened up and went to the wall, to lean against it. "Darling, I did not want to tell you like this—"

She looked past him. She wanted him near, but she did not want to look at him. She wanted him to hold her, but she did not want him to touch her.

"He is really dead?"

"I'm afraid so," said Portman. He felt badly inadequate. He wanted to touch his daughter, but did not know whether she would permit it. He wanted to shelter her, but he hardly knew how. He wished that her mother were here, that everything would for a while be many years ago—

There was no mother, no wife and no family. There was, of course, an ultimate kind of universal family thing at all times, though at this time that was quite inadequate. There was instead—

Suddenly Portman shouted, "Goddamn you, Binzwanger! Don't you have any sense of human consideration? Goddamn you all to hell!"

Cheryl looked up, very much startled. Her father rarely shouted and he never swore. His wild voice had sounded a lot like a scream for help-

Binzwanger had no sense of human consideration in this case. He did not know these two foreigners and there was of course no time to start joining in their privacies. He was able to assist, on the other hand, along official lines. He was even quite gentle about it.

"*Meine hochachtungsvolle Bedauerung,*" he said, which nobody understood. "Such a fate," he went on, "is always a possibility. You understand."

Cheryl looked at him. While Binzwanger was not sure that she saw him, he felt that she might well hear his helpfulness and that she would then be consoled.

"He died, as it were, in the service of his fatherland." Binzwanger thought that he sounded a little bit like someone by the side of a grave, speechifying, but he felt that it would be quite appropriate. "He did his job well, Fraulein Portman. He did all he was asked to do."

It was a beautiful speech and Fraulein Portman, in spite of her obvious grief, had a beautiful face. The attaché watched her face for some sign of gratefulness, for some recognition.

Her color went the way definition might fade out of a photo which has too much exposure. The exposure was harsh, sudden and terribly painful. But she suddenly saw very clearly.

Her Berlin trip would have turned out a meaningless thing and the final leg of the journey to Cairo would have no point at all—if Eric had not come back to Algiers safe and whole, to deliver the go-ahead word from the people in Egypt!

She screamed.

"That means *you* killed him!"

If Binzwanger were not here, Portman thought, how much I could do for her— If Binzwanger's official ear would not hear what she said, how she felt— Now even Cairo might not be safe for her—

"Why?" she screamed. "*Why?*"

It was out of control. It was beyond Portman's skills of manipulation. His daughter was something else now, a ravening beast, a Medea—

Binzwanger knew that his official presence was for the moment out of place. He walked to the door, his eyes solicitously turned away. And yet, he felt, he might help a little—

"You understand," he said quietly, "that he was not reliable. He was a Jew."

The explanation was given without heat. It was only official.

11: A Gathering of Friends

She stopped suffering almost immediately because on the inside she was dead.

She knew of a theory about Jews and she had heard of practices in regard to Jews, and all of that had the quality of great intellectual distance, spatial distance and a distance in time such as the Middle Ages. None of that had anything to do with Eric who loved her and whom she wanted in return. But then the safe distance of intellect, space and time had shrunk in with the panicky speed of a nightmare and had killed Eric and a good deal of herself. And that death was good too.

She looked at her father who also felt nothing, though he was grateful that she looked so calm.

"Cheryl, where are you going?"

"I feel cold. I'm going to put on a suit."

Portman did not feel cold but went to the window in order to catch some of the tepid breeze. He looked at the park opposite and envied the quiet man who sat there reading his paper.

Cheryl went to the bedroom and changed into a suit. Then she went into her father's room, from there to the foyer and from there out to the street.

She walked in the little park which was manicured in the spirit of Les Tuileries. The plants were desert plants which looked wondrous and large due to an excess of water. She did not notice the heat eating into her or the color of the plants in the park because there really were no colors and no heat but instead there was only a cool, bone-gray evenness to everything. She did not notice the man on the bench though he noticed her. He had the aggressive look of a successful *colon* and though his mustache was artistically trimmed and his clothes were expensive, he had the dark dryness of skin which comes from long hours of work in the open. He watched the girl and folded his paper. Quite naturally, he got up and followed her.

Cheryl crossed the street on the other side of the park and when she came to the café she sat down at a table.

Her chair was a pretty affair of bent wood and her table had a veined marble top and rested on a cast-iron leg with clawed feet. Very green potted trees marked off the sidewalk domain of the café. The blue-and-white awning overhead gave shade with a breeze—

The woven rush awning overhead made speckled light and splotches of heat which Bergman felt on his head and his back with a niggling sense of irritation. He leaned on the wooden table which caused the four legs to clap down on the floor in an odd, alternating succession. Little black flies walked around on the table top. The air bit his nose with the smell of camel's dung and with the sourness of very bad wine. Bergman decided that one smell was enough. He got up and went into the dim coffeehouse.

The rooms of Inter-Sudanese were directly overhead. Bergman glanced up at the low ceiling with distaste. Instead of being gone and two days away from Kufra, he had spent that time upstairs with Harker. They had been plotting and planning insanities—

"Arrack," he said to the boy in the dirty shirt.

"Me too."

Bergman turned and when his eyes could see after the glare of the street he recognized Craig. The Canadian sat humped over his little table. Flies were walking over his hands but, like an Arab, Craig ignored them. A glass carafe sat empty before him and his glass was empty too.

"Sit down," he said and looked slightly past Bergman's head. "They got no beer."

"Ah," said Bergman and sat down.

"Otherwise, wouldn't touch this stuff."

"I can see why," said Bergman.

Craig thought that he detected a note of covert disapproval and decided to let his eyes go very hard. The actual effect was that he suddenly looked dull witted and sleepy. He forgot about the pose when the boy came to the table with two arrack carafes and the glasses. Craig started pouring immediately. He took a pinch of salt from a dish on the table and dropped it into the arrack.

"Salt of the earth," he said. "Have some, you bastard."

"Throw it over your shoulder," said Bergman. "You'll need it."

The remark struck a bad note for Craig.

"Listen, Von Bergman," he said. "All that time on this Mack Sennett trip we took over Death Valley, all that time not a word out of you about this insanity we are going to commit. Such secrecy positively alienates me, you know that, Von Bergman?"

Bergman leaned on his forearms, holding them with his hands. His tunic was short sleeved and his hands bunched very slowly, very hard into his own muscles. One hand dug deliberately into the tattoo over his wrist.

"Don't call me that again," he said quietly.

"And why in hell not?"

I wish he would pass out soon, thought Bergman. It would be best—

"Because," he said, "we've got eight hundred miles coming. That'll be tough enough."

"Don't worry," said Craig. "I'm the scout master. Harker told me. He said, Craig, he said ..."

"I know what he said. You're an expert and you happen to be here. Harker's in a hurry."

Craig drank, as if disgusted with the taste in his mouth. He gave the same impression when he talked.

"And you happened to be here and Harker is in a hurry. You an expert too?"

Bergman drank arrack and did not answer.

"Of course you are," said Craig. "I saw you."

Bergman looked at the next table where the fat Arab and the blond girl were sitting down. Craig, feeling ignored, turned very rapidly. Then he held his head absolutely still while something on the inside of his skull seemed to continue to move with independent momentum. In a moment, he decided to be sociable.

"Haven't I seen you before some place?" he said to the girl. "And him too. I've seen him under a stone some place before and you in a bed some place before."

"That is possible," said Ibn Kabir and smiled like a marriage broker.

The response, Craig felt, was disappointing. Not enough sociability.

"Try some," he said and handed the bowl of salt across. "Very earthy, you know."

"No thank you," said Kabir. "Not at this time. But may I offer you ..."

"Sure. How much?"

"Craig," said Bergman, too quietly for any normal emotion.

"Shut up, Von Bergman. Last fling, don't you know. Fling the salt."

"You are leaving?" asked Kabir. His expression suggested that he was terrified of losing a friend.

"Right," said Craig. "Down to the sea in pontoons, and down with the pantaloons. I'll show you."

And then he tried to get up—a sad sight of a man who did not have the strength for his size, who was taller than he wished to be, and whose eyes were struggling to stay alive while his face was already numb.

"I'll help you," said Bergman. He was really murmuring to himself.

His hand stayed near the spot on Craig's neck where it mattered for the briefest moment, but it was enough. Then Bergman grabbed the sagging body and let it down gently, placing head and arms on the table as is proper for a sleeping drunk.

Bergman went out to the street where his driver was parked. He took his man back into the coffeehouse and told him to put Craig to bed.

"Let him sleep," he told him. "Don't let him talk."

"What a shame," said Kabir at the next table.

Bergman watched the driver carry Craig out to the street. He sat down again. There was still a lot of arrack on the table.

"And so young, really," said Kabir. "Don't you think so, Lotte?"

"Yes," said Lotte. "But he did not seem young."

Bergman looked at the girl and wished that he were drunker. The illusion would then come more easily and the blond girl in the Tuareg cloak would perhaps have less of the look of flotsam, of the awkward ones on display in the cabarets, of the dulled ones who lie in the curtained cubicles along the *corniche* in Alexandria

"She is European," said Kabir. "Like you."

Bergman drank and the illusion took hold—

When the man spoke to Cheryl from the next table the illusion was terribly perfect for that moment. Eric had not said the same thing to her but the surprise had been similar. It was in both cases composed of a sense of relief that it had finally happened and of an exciting sense of being not quite prepared. It worked that way because Cheryl sat in the café with the growing illusion that nothing had really happened to her and that this blankness she felt was really free time and empty time for her, to be filled with whatever might happen next.

"I was trying to decide," he said, "if you are really waiting for someone."

He was French and his gambit caused no offense.

"I am not waiting for anyone," she said.

He did not remind her of Eric at all. Eric had been German and all his affectations had been entirely British. He preferred to speak English and he spent his yearly leave from the Cairo job with Euro-Asian by going to London. He would come back with new clothes which were all very horsy and full of checks.

This man had a mustache and his dark clothes were very bourgeois.

"Is it possible," he said, "that we could spend that empty time together?"

He was very good. He did not change tables, which would have meant he considered her answer redundant, and he did not push her reply with a suggestive smile. He simply waited and watched her with interest.

But there is this fierceness, she thought, which comes to me like a heat. He does not comb his hair to show the nobility of his profile and he does not wear epaulettes to tell me that he has very broad shoulders. He sends me heat because I feel cold.

She nodded at him but stayed with her own thoughts while he came over. There is, she considered, an Italian method to this, a table-

changing advance, designed to push right through to the skin, straight
to the sexual organ, and then two animals look at each other across a
small table pretending that they know how to talk while continuously
wrestling for the quick, prone position.

"My name is René Serrat," he said, and Cheryl forgot about the Italian
method because Serrat, being French, did it differently. Love-making was
now taken for granted and the only thing to distinguish it from anything
else predictable would be the amusement of the delay, the artistry of
unfolding each other, the means, so to speak, instead of the end.

"If I already knew you," he said, "I would decide upon a drink for you.
Pastis, to soothe you if you felt too intense, or a fresh Chablis, if you felt
dull or tired—"

Eric had been more impulsive about it, though he did not lack skill.
He had avoided the cheaper trick of ground-breaking by never stressing
that he worked for her father's firm, that he was—in fact—the old man's
protégé. They had not gone to Cheops until several days later but they
had their first fight before they had ever made love.

"Look," Eric had said, "you're talking geopolitics and I'm talking you
and me. Where's your sense of importance, Cheryl?"

"My father thinks it's important."

"You've got to be an old man to make love to an ideology. Crap on
Unification. Let's unify."

It had turned into a shocking fight, but the shock had been somehow
delicious.

They had started to fight almost as soon as he had picked her up at
the station. Hannover was not his favorite town, Marlies was his wife
but no longer his sole preoccupation. An ideological lie had preempted
all that. Bergman was Jewish and his wife was not.

Bergman swatted a fly off his cheek but he was not really back in the
filthy coffeehouse until Lotte said something and, of course, she was not
Marlies at all.

"Could I have something too?" she asked Kabir.

"Another banana."

She nodded and got her banana. She would have nodded, Bergman
considered, if Kabir had offered her a bottle of vinegar. What accord,
what harmonious Oneness between East and West. Or was it North and
South—

"She speaks English," said Kabir. "I mean, in case you should like to
address her. Where are you from in England, Captain?"

Kabir's smile went with the question. It was equally impolite.
Bergman, a Central European for most of his life, was still offended with

the habits of insinuation of the Levant. He did not even bother to lie.

"I am a German," he said. "I am a clever spy for the Germans. Look at me."

Kabir was familiar with all manner of duplicity. This one, however, was somewhat a stumper. He did not argue about it, not—that is—until the subject would either be much drunker or somewhat softer in spirit due to some other device.

"You are soon to leave," said Kabir.

Bergman did not argue the obvious. Some troops and vehicles had been gathering at the airstrip for days.

"Let me therefore make you a gift," said Kabir, "so that you may take with you a memory of pleasure. When are you leaving?"

"What have you got for me?"

"She speaks English, German, Dutch. She is versed in several cultural things."

"She won't object?"

"She objects to nothing."

Bergman looked at the girl and saw that she was embarrassed. That, he felt, was the only surprise in the three-cornered tête-à-tête at the filthy table.

Strangely enough, it was her embarrassment which excited Bergman. She did not hide her face, though the Tuareg cloak hung large enough around her shoulders to make a cowl which could have hidden all of her. Instead her head and neck remained straight, looking fragile in the midst of the massive folds. The black cloth seemed to give a contrasting life to her skin and even her cow-like eyes came awake.

"She will show you," said Kabir. "The room, I mean." Then he got up and left.

Bergman and the girl looked at each other. She chewed on her banana and he drank arrack.

She had looked desirable and totally distant. He was drinking coffee and she licked the torte on her fork.

"I know you don't like it here," she said. "You've never liked Hannover." She looked down, as if she were shy about licking her torte. "But I like it. My family has lived here a long time."

"I know," he said. "King August once gave your great-uncle a gold watch."

She stabbed at her torte and then swallowed the whole creamy piece which she had hacked off. "I can't help it," she said. "And besides, I don't think there's anything wrong with—with ancestry."

"Oh my God," he mumbled and looked at the heavy head of the tree which spread overhead. The sun-specked leaves almost made him forget where he was, in the middle of a city; in a crowded café, and not alone at all.

"It means something," she went on, "coming from an old family."

He looked at her and was back again.

"Marlies," he said. "I remind you—redundant though it be in my estimation—that my family has lived in Frankfurt-am-Main since the fourteenth century. And Prince George-Eugene once gave my great-great-grand-something or other a vineyard which covered a hill on one side of the Main and another hill on the other side of the Main. That Nacktarsch '34 which the *Oberstaffelführer* is drinking at the next table is from those very slopes where I myself, just two days ago, took a look at this year's crop of ..."

"You never told me you've been in the business that long."

"I haven't been. I'm only in my thirties."

She did not like his humor. She had liked it, not too long ago, but not since the time when Hitler had sent German squadrons to Franco. Marlies disliked politics and she disliked Kurt's preoccupation with it.

"Anyway," she said and glanced at the SS man at the next table. "He likes it."

Kurt put his cup down, which made a brown stain on the tablecloth where the coffee splashed over.

"Do you know what else he likes?" he said in a sharp whisper which reflected no normal emotion whatsoever. Then he roared. "Do you know what else that *Oberschweinehundführer* would like? He would like my hair to be black like yours, he would like my name to be less German than his and he would like you to tell me ..."

"Kurt!"

"Are you screaming at the lady at your table?" said the SS man. He was with a whaleboned, elderly lady who lifted her lorgnette. It was necessary to make an impression.

The tableau was silly, but at that point everything was bound to work against Bergman. He had the satisfaction of breaking the SS man's front teeth. The SS man had the satisfaction of seeing Bergman arrested. Marlies had her family's condolences when one thing led to another and Bergman's misdemeanor was judged a crime against the State.

The causes of the incident were not contained in the events under the tree of the Café Kroepke. The causes of Bergman's punishment and his subsequent flight from his homeland dated back at least to the fourteenth century—

A very long time ago this sort of thing had been very important, Serrat considered. It had been meaningful and very much fun. He looked down at the shut face of the girl, at the strain in her neck, at the moist sheen on her naked breasts.

"Cheryl," he said. "I now want ..."

"No. Not yet! More like this—"

The greed for suspense in this girl, he considered, was unbelievable and there was nothing fake about the violence which she held contained. But of all the awkward situations— He looked at the watch which he had kept on his wrist and noted that he was at least two hours late. This was no *cinq-á-sept* arrangement. This girl and the pickup was strictly a job. Nonetheless, he was in bed with a woman and he was a gentleman. To rush her was unthinkable.

She felt a heat like sunburn all over her skin and wherever his hand touched her or held her or dug into her body, there she squeezed herself into the touch. But it was not good to finish. The rest afterward was defenseless and only safe with a lover. René, of course, was not a lover but only an instrument for exciting a wish. And since there was no lover to answer the wish there was no point in finishing.

"Finish it," Eric had said. "I don't know what your father is up to or why you approve of it and I don't want to know."

"Coward."

"Yes. I have come to the very vulnerable point of living on love, Cheryl. If that dies, I die."

"It's not vulnerable at all, Eric. It's my strength. I can leave you for this little while and know that I can come back."

"From what, geopolitical copulations?"

"You're a bastard, Eric."

"I'm worse. I'm a pure, unmixed enemy alien to the Wave of the Future."

"I don't believe any of that business, don't you know that, Eric?"

"Yes. I also know that you don't understand any of it, Cheryl."

"I don't care."

"My point entirely."

"I want you, Eric. Entirely."

"How long do I wait?"

"As long as a lover, Eric. Promise and wait—"

She screamed the illusion away when Serrat could not wait any longer and she felt his weight on her and his weight filling her so that it seemed to gorge her. But in a moment she took him without protest and stopped screaming. There was even a touch of oneness to the end of the business—

In a moment it no longer disturbed Bergman at all that Inter-Sudanese was only six inches of wall away from his head. And the illusion of Marlies was gone like the rest of that life, because he had now turned all that around.

He took the naked girl by the shoulders and shook her. The bedsprings screeched but she kept silent. The motion made her small breasts bounce like rubber but her eyes remained flat and calm.

"You want me again?" she said.

"Why? You know the difference?"

"Yes, *Effendi.*"

"Goddamn it, don't call me that!"

When he let go of her, she stretched. The fact was, she felt rather good. She had liked the way he had taken all of her and the way he looked at all of her now.

"Is your name really Von Bergman?"

At that point he hit her.

His feeling was more severe than the beating he gave her, and so was his reaction. He did not stop from a sense of remorse but from a feeling of uselessness. He stopped like a stunt man trained to interrupt in the middle of a fake swing. The swing had not been fake, but the interruption was—

When Kabir saw him later he was surprised at Bergman's entirely foreign ability to show no effect after love-making.

"Was I right about her?" he asked. And then, with a touch of desperation he added a little bit of the truth. "Lotte said that she enjoyed you."

"Thank you," said Bergman. "For Lotte, I mean."

"A shame that it takes a war to make such a friendship as ours."

Bergman had a rare and highly nervous attack of the giggles. He disguised it by pretending that the arrack had hurt his throat.

"Excuse me," he said. "I will have to spit on the floor."

After Bergman was done spitting on the floor Kabir tried in various ways to find out where Bergman, who had come to Kufra in a half-track, who had visited Inter-Sudanese, and who had then disappeared to return in a mad-looking plane with Luftwaffe markings—where this British officer who looked as if he were in disguise might be going. Kabir's very lack of success stimulated his imagination.

Kabir was nobody's agent but his own, but he sent a message through improper channels to a real agent in Cairo: A British contingent of highly irregular nature would soon be heading north.

After all, the war was north of Kufra and not south.

Colonel Harker was not a desk man on leave, what with the tan he had. And therefore only a Long Range Desert man would stray this far south of the war, under the pretense of vacation.

Captain Bergman was S.I.G. because his tattoo showed that he had been in a concentration camp. His return in a German plane showed—to say the least—that he had been on a most special assignment.

Major Craig had been an important prisoner of the Germans by the looks of his face and the state of his clothes. And why else would he return in a seaplane whose natural habitat was the coast which was held by the Germans—

This reasoning and the information was duly received and transmitted and when this intelligence reached Algiers it caused a mighty flap of new preparations.

Portman's new egress to Cairo had one vital lay-over point, the oasis of Jalu. The same would be true for anyone crossing the Sand Sea from Kufra going north. It was imperative that Portman should not run into any irregular-looking contingent of British troops—

But when arrangements were complete, Portman would not leave until he had found his daughter.

12: A Gathering of Enemies

It was in the nature of the trip that some trucks left alone, going east, and some others, as if unrelated, went north. There was also some noisy to-do about getting a Bishop started, a high-silhouette armored affair composed of a 15-pounder on top and a Valentine tank chassis below. The self-propelled gun had a motor with a mighty roar and an internal battle injury which caused a lot of black smoke. This small monster went seemingly all alone into the wilderness.

Rendezvous was one day's drive north of Kufra.

A few men and vehicles of the expedition had not left. Craig was still in Kufra, sitting alone in the second room of Inter-Sudanese. He had moved the bottle of gin out of sight because he did not want to look at it. He had covered the desk with large sheets of maps. Since the topological markings depicted the desert, the maps looked fairly blank. Craig worked with protractor and compass and made pencil notes on a pad. One of Bergman's men stood on the other side of the door. His machine pistol held a full clip plus a round in the chamber and the action was set on automatic. Craig knew this, though the fact did not give him a sense of safety. Nothing could really give Craig a sense of peace or safety that day, though he blamed his apprehension entirely on the young guard. He did not know the man, but Craig felt that the man's sense of devotion was totally soulless. There was an unpleasant distance in his eyes and the kind of stillness about him which leads to the suspicion that some great violence lies concealed in the man somewhere. Craig blamed his apprehensions only in part on his vast hangover. When the door made a sound he gave a start. The guard held the door and Bergman walked in. Bergman too, so it seemed to Craig, appeared in need of uninterrupted silence. He sat down at the desk and stared at the opposite wall for a moment. He did not seem to be looking at the map.

Craig decided to take the offensive.

"You look awful," he said to Bergman.

"Yes. It's the heat." Then he turned to the guard who was closing the door. "Leave it open, Zwi."

"But in the event ..."

"Just leave it open!"

"Yes sir."

But Bergman did not seem to like that attitude either. He sighed, as if regretting the day, and changed his tone of voice. "Have you met Sergeant Ben Manta?" he asked Craig.

"No."

Bergman introduced the two men.

"Zwi Ben Manta," he said, "happens to be the only *Sabra* under my command."

"A privilege," said Ben Manta.

"A unique experience," said Bergman while looking for the bottle of gin. "As a Jew raised in the shelter of European civilization, I continuously marvel at the ease with which the jungle mentality is available to my sergeant."

"I was raised in the desert," said Ben Manta. "There was no jungle."

"And that," said Bergman to the wall, "coupled with a positively Teutonic penchant for exactitude, makes my sergeant a friend to cherish and an enemy to be avoided at all cost. Where is that goddamn bottle, Craig?"

"It's here," said Ben Manta and picked it up from under the rattan couch.

"Thank you. Want one?"

"No thank you, sir."

"You, Craig?"

"No sir."

Zwi Ben Manta, thought Craig, reminded him in some curious way of Mohnfeld. One would suspect the same, quick intensity in the man, though here it was hidden under calm. One would expect the same rapid mind in him, though he harnessed it with a seriousness which, at first sight, seemed pedantic.

"In any event," said Bergman who seemed intent on using Ben Manta as a curative for his spleen, "we are safe with Zwi's trigger finger trained the other way. *Shalom*," and he drank warm gin.

"By the way," said Craig. "I want to apologize for that performance in the coffeehouse."

"No harm done."

"Thanks to you."

Bergman seemed unusually pensive. He put his glass down gently and moved it from the Great Sand Sea to the Qattara Depression.

"Any calls while you were here?"

"No. Yes. Bruckner called. He wanted to know if you were here."

"That's all?"

"He said that was all."

In a moment, Bergman said very quietly, "That's also too bad." Then he sat up and sounded quite different. "Sergeant, go downstairs and send my driver to the depot. Message: Tell Bruckner to double up. We're leaving in six hours."

"Yes sir."

"Leave the gun here."

Craig waited till Ben Manta was gone. Then he leaned on his maps and looked at Bergman.

"That's no good, Bergman. We'll get there ahead of rendezvous and what's the point of that?"

Bergman did not look cool and he did not look angry. There was almost a touch of supplication in the worry of his eyes.

"The point is," he said, "I think I mucked this one."

"Bergman," said Craig, "I'm not the enemy. You may talk freely. Like, why didn't you use the phone to reach Bruckner at the depot?"

"Because it would seem," said Bergman who was getting his polite sting back, "that I am not the only one who is using this phone."

"I think," said Craig, "I'll have just a short one now."

Bergman pushed the bottle over and his own glass.

"You remember the blond girl with the fat trader?"

"I'd rather not," said Craig. "Was she any good?"

Bergman did not answer right away. He felt hurt by the memories which had come with the girl and he felt regret that he could not simply have been in bed with her and nothing else interfering with the straight act of the flesh between them.

"You look squeamish," said Craig.

"She was fine," said Bergman. "And Kabir was too."

Craig raised his eyebrows. The unusual rottenness of his spirits since coming to Kufra was waking in him again, the misery of fright and surprise at being really no more than something to be used, both by friend and by enemy—all that came up again underneath the secondary discomforts of a very bad hangover, and he was ready to say something nasty.

"Kabir," Bergman went on without looking at Craig, "was so good with the questions after I came down again, feeling tired, that it didn't occur to me until much later that it was perhaps not just ordinary curiosity which I'd been sidestepping with him, and perhaps I did not sidestep enough."

"Christ—" said Craig. "What did you tell him?"

This time Bergman looked up.

"What did you tell Von Hahn?"

Craig was stung with something, though he only admitted to himself that it was a discomfort of memory, but the unusual rottenness of spirit, all of it, was back now.

"All right," he said, and poured gin without knowing it. "So you don't remember. You do a cheap job of humping, and then have a cheap drink with the pimp, and then it turns out like a cheap novel that that little sinfulness in the sack is now jeopardizing a glorious victory, not to mention my own dreams of a bon voyage, goddamn you."

Bergman did not understand Craig's irritability but he could accept it. Criticism or praise had lost their meaning for him. There was only success or failure.

"I checked him out. Bruckner found the splice in our straight line to the Sudan. It was downstairs in that hole which used to be a basement. The jury rig ran right into Kabir's room. When Bruckner phoned you he said that a call was received at the end of our line in Wadi Haifa. The same man we talk to also talked to Kabir."

"Reliable agents you got there, Bergman."

"He had already sent Kabir's message to Cairo, something about units leaving Kufra."

"And you're just going to sit here and handle the whole thing by leaving six hours earlier?"

"The man in Wadi Haifa is already dead," said Bergman.

"And Kabir? What about that goddamn Kabir?"

Bergman shrugged.

"What's the difference. It's too late."

"Admirable largesse," said Craig and leaned back. He sipped gin which he was beginning to feel. "Then why did you have to have the Wadi Haifa man killed?"

"Necessity. To kill Kabir would be no more than vengeance."

While Craig still tried to sort out that reasoning, Ben Manta came back into the room. He walked quietly and the first thing he did was to pick up his machine pistol. He acted as if he did not feel fully dressed until he had it slung on one shoulder again. Bergman talked to him without looking up.

"Did the Arab leave while you were downstairs?"

"No sir."

"Bring him here, would you?" said Bergman.

This time Ben Manta took his weapon with him.

He was a Sabra who had been born and raised on a kibbutz within sight of the Jordanian border. During the first twenty years of his life he had seen the silicon glitter of the *serir* change to moist earth and he had helped to change the irregular terrain into trained rows of vegetation. He had seen the Jordanian militia, replete with uniforms and German arms, and he had met the ill-kempt bands of Bedouins who rode in out of nowhere. They invariably left charred huts, trampled fields and many corpses. Most of the corpses were their own. Life at an absolute level of survival makes for a great simplicity of ideation. Zwi Ben Manta felt that a dead Arab meant life.

Ben Manta walked into Ibn Kabir's large room without knocking and told the Arab to come along. He nodded his head at the open door and when Kabir smiled instead of getting up from his chair Ben Manta kicked the older man across the room. Then they went to Inter-Sudanese.

Once in the office, Ibn Kabir was not asked to sit down. Ibn Kabir talked rapidly in three languages for a while, hiding his real fear of death under a fake anxiety over not wishing to offend. Bergman did not interrupt the Arab since he considered that useless. When Kabir noticed that he was being ignored he stopped talking. Also his throat had suddenly become as dry as felt.

"This won't take long," Bergman started, but was interrupted by Kabir's sudden screech. The Arab was not talking anymore, he was simply showing his terror with the same naturalness with which a face shows its nose. When the noise became too exhausting for Kabir he let it die down and only rattled his breath. Craig looked at Bergman with a feeling which he could not identify.

"You got some reputation," he said in a low voice.

Bergman ignored all that.

"We traced your call," he said to the Arab. "That part of it ..."

"*Wallah! le vous en prie* ... What I mean is, *Verzeihung* ..."

"Don't interrupt again."

Ibn Kabir covered his mouth.

"Your contact is dead," said Bergman. "So that part of it is over. The only reason you are here is because I want to know for whom you are working."

The question filled Kabir with genuine astonishment. Before he could draw his customary conclusion that he was faced with a trap, the truth was out.

"For myself," he said to his own surprise.

"Who pays you?"

"Who pays me, who pays me? What is this insanity, Effendi? The man who buys from me pays me."

"Who buys from you?"

"Who buys from me? Effendi, what is the meaning of this question which I don't understand? You buy from me, he buys from me, they buy from me. *Wallah—*"

"Shall I hit him?" asked Ben Manta.

"Of course not. Can't you tell it's the truth?" Then Bergman looked at Kabir again.

"To whom did you sell in Cairo?"

"I don't know. Your man—uh, our man in Wadi Haifa knows people in Egypt who want to know about you."

"Me?"

"What you do. You, he, all of you. The British."

"Who are they?"

"I don't know. Perhaps German, perhaps French. I don't know," he said with an obvious inflection which showed that he also did not care.

"What have you sold them before?"

"Effendi, you drive me mad! I don't know who they are!"

"What have you sold to anybody before, anything of military nature?"

"Nothing— That is, once I saw a competitor of mine bring in ten camels with German jerrycans. I told my man—our man, *excusez moi*— about this and he sold the information to a Colonel Whitherford in Wadi Haifa. This colonel of yours considered my competitor's caravan route and where the cans must have been picked up. Then he ambushed a squadron of Germans."

"How did you transmit the information to the colonel?"

"A friend of mine was flying there from here."

"Why not with the cable you used more recently?"

"Because I just put it in."

"When?"

"After I talked to you."

"Are you trying to find out if he's a professional?" Craig interrupted.

"Yes," said Bergman.

"Are you?" said Craig to the Arab.

"Professional what?"

"I think he is," said Craig.

"It is strange," said Bergman, "that you should just happen to have the telephonic equipment to cut into our lines."

"But I have it, Effendi. I have been sending electric things to Chad for months."

"Bullshit," said Craig. He wondered how interrogators kept their patience.

"That happens to be true," said Bergman. "S.I.G. has even helped one of those shipments to get to the border. The French are building a new command post in Fort-Lamy."

"So much for that," said Craig. "What about him after we leave?"

Craig had not specified the matter of leaving early, but Bergman understood that the change in departure time might attract Kabir's attention and stimulate his instinct for a profit. For about two days the information could be highly damaging. After that, the expedition's progress would not be affected by the departure intelligence. Ben Manta, who had a way of merging, as if absent, had been following the problem at hand.

"I will take care of it," he said.

Kabir began to shiver.

"Take him to Montelli's house," said Bergman, "and tell Montelli to keep him locked up for a week. Then he can let him go."

Kabir began to cry.

"Who's Montelli?" Craig wanted to know.

"A friend of ours. Obviously." He turned to Ibn Kabir who seemed ready to kiss Bergman in an excess of love. "Go now," said Bergman. "And forget that we met."

"But we met!" cried Kabir, still loving the Jew in the Teutonic disguise. "And I cannot forget it, I will never forget it! What to do— There is Lotte for you, there is Sarina, and Balou, and if you want ..."

"Who?" said Craig.

"His secretaries," said Bergman and then, with a jerk of the head, he got rid of Ibn Kabir and Zwi Ben Manta.

Ben Manta came back to the office in a very short time. Bergman had just finished cleaning out the office of significant matters and Craig had stopped drinking and had rolled up his charts. Ben Manta was in the room as if he had never left.

"It's all right?" said Bergman.

"Yes sir."

"What did Montelli say?"

"He has to leave tomorrow, but he will take care of the body."

"The *what?*" said Craig.

"As I said," Ben Manta explained, showing that he felt that the explanation was redundant, "Montelli was not able to be there for the next two weeks. I had to improvise."

Craig did not say anything or do anything while he looked at Ben Manta. The Sabra's calm reflected no normal emotion of any sort.

"Zwi," Bergman said very quietly, "I don't think I will give you such freedom of choice in the future."

"I'm sorry," said Ben Manta. "I did not know that there was a choice."

Then Bergman told Ben Manta to get out.

When the sergeant was gone the office was very quiet for a moment and then, very suddenly, Craig grabbed the nearest thing, which was one of his charts, clawed his hands into it and tore it apart.

Bergman watched Craig throw the pieces down and then he watched him sit down. He said nothing because he was sure Craig was not through.

"I used to think," said Craig with a voice as hoarse as if he had been screaming, "I used to think that I could tell a difference between my friends and my enemies."

"I see," said Bergman. "It seems you had a simple way of telling."

"Yes, damn it. Yes. As simple as that black-and-white, right-and-wrong, light-and-dark, life-and-death world of that Manta there."

"Presumptuous of you," said Bergman and picked up the bottle of gin. "Considering that you were not raised in his life-and-death world."

"Stop that double-jointed Jesuit talk with me!"

"I think you mean Talmudic."

"And you! Did you know that I've been afraid of you and never knew why? I can tell why now, because Manta is a simplified version of you. Manta is what you're going to grow up to be, Bergman!"

"It's an ugly chance, yes. I can feel it sometimes, how I'm getting brutalized."

"Wrong word, Bergman. It's mechanized! As complex as a human being, but without any sense of pain."

Bergman drank from the bottle.

"Sometimes," he said. "If I drink enough."

"You and that Manta and Von Hahn!"

"Ben Manta does not drink. Did Von Hahn drink?"

"How in hell do I know? But I know that if that German and that Jew were to change uniforms ..."

"And enemies, Craig. Don't leave that out."

"Gimme that bottle."

"You don't know how to drink, Craig. You seem to think that sucking on that thing is going to make a new person out of you."

"And your boozing, I suppose, is devoid of such illusions."

"Yes. It doesn't make me new. It just puts the old one to sleep for a while."

"Talmudic distinctions. And I'll take the glass too. Makes me feel like a drinker instead of an alcoholic."

Bergman watched Craig with bottle and glass for a while, noting the anger in his gestures and then the deep swallow without conviction.

"Don," said Bergman quietly. "I can tell you the real reason for your hangover."

"Don't bother. I'm an expert myself."

"It's the great end-of-the-world fright which happened to you with Von Hahn. And that fright hasn't ended."

Suddenly, Craig blew up.

"And you know why, Von Bergman?"

"I have my own hangovers," said Bergman without raising his voice. "You call me Von Bergman again and I'll treat you like one."

"Because you remind me of one," Craig went right on. "I look at you and your still-as-glass eyes and your face which says nothing and your majestic calm like an iceberg that's ready to rip a fifty-tonner in half, you goddamn robot programmed for—for fanaticism!"

To his own consternation Craig saw no important change in Bergman. He watched the man turn and walk out of the room.

"Where are you going?"

"Keep your gun on the table," said Bergman over his shoulder. "You've still got those charts lying all over." And then he left through the outer door.

Craig sat for a while without moving. He noticed that the zebra-striped light from the shutters had moved to throw a marvelously straight avenue all the way from Kufra to Athens, Greece. This arrangement left the route to Tobruk in relative darkness. It upset Craig. He did not think that it was the liquor which gave him this insane sensitivity. As a matter of fact he felt suddenly and most unpleasantly sober and awake. But this waking was bad, because everything Bergman had said had been true. Never before Von Hahn had Craig run into such a totally unmalleable quality of disregard for the other person.

Ben Manta reminded him of that and Bergman came into focus, too. They were all unassailable because there was nothing left to assail in their desert of feeling—

No. His desert had not been the same thing. It had been empty but that had meant space to him instead of barrenness—

His childhood landscapes had been busy with detail—grasses, leaves, buds, trees, stones, houses and vistas from upper windows. And when he had grown all of it had been touched with hands, feet and eyes. All detail had been exhausted and used.

He did not know this until he went to work in the desert. This now was an expanse which kept its sweep. Nor did the land feel hostile. It just did not know him. And when he learned to know his desert it became his with every step, every sight, but remaining always unused. In that way it was true that his charts and his maps were only a very limited replica of his knowledge. What this land meant to him could not be charted.

All this was changing now. The Great Sand Sea was a trap charted by everyone but himself, the Von Hahns on one side, the Ben Mantas on the other, the sweep of the eye gone now with the necessity of discovering the trap, the space closing in, hemming him down, the innocence of his land shrinking— And how did a Bergman stand it? Of course. The robot is not programmed for such skinless sensitivities. When Craig heard the sound, he snapped his hand to the gun; but when he saw that Bergman was coming through the door, he shifted his hand to the glass.

One of the Children of Death, thought Craig. Who got the visitation this time?

"Ready to go?" asked Bergman.

"No. I've got to burn these."

He took one small sheet which was covered with figures and put it into his tunic pocket. Then he bundled up the maps. Bergman sat down on the rattan couch and took the bottle of gin. It was almost empty. He drank from the neck and watched Craig burn papers on the stone floor in one corner.

"Would be nice if you could just commit those figures to memory."

Craig looked at Bergman and thought that the big man's relaxation in the rattan couch looked one hell of a lot like a pose. No. It was the absence of the kind of feeling which makes you laugh with joy, cry with pain, shiver with fright, nod with tiredness, bristle with irritability— No pose. Bergman, for example, was simply not afraid to take that insane trek across empty space to a map point called Tobruk.

"I wouldn't commit the coordinates to memory," said Craig with a good deal of venom, "because then you and the rest of the missionaries won't have to worry that the Von Hahns or the Von Mantas—should the latter decide I am not his true friend—could get the information out of me by means of sudden or very slow methods."

Bergman smiled but it looked more resigned than amused. "You are beginning to think like one of us."

"Like how? Like expecting the worst?"

"No," said Bergman. "Like knowing that it is at hand."

Craig kicked the black ashes to pieces and then went back the desk. He sat down and took his glass. He had a slow drink, without the previous haste.

"*Lachaiem*," he said and toasted. "To the Talmudic mind which always knows of a third twist to the spokes of the rack."

"*Hals und Beinbruch*," said Bergman and when he smiled this time it was with amusement. "You know the German expression? It means good luck. And curiously enough it is the German expression which has the truly Talmudic twist of meaning. It actually means that I wish you would break your neck and your leg. You like that?"

"From you?"

"Between friends it means the opposite of the stated wish."

"In that case, Bergman ..."

"Just shut up a minute, Craig. Look here. By rank, you are my superior officer, but till we join up with Harker I'm in command of the contingent. Neither I, your pro tem CO, nor Harker, head of mission, can ever do without you. Because none of us can find the way. Therefore, I listen to you now and will listen to you later. And I will help you survive ..."

"You did once already," said Craig to his own surprise.

"... just as you may wish me and the others to survive. But this working together," said Bergman, "would be easier, would be somehow more human, Craig, if you did not look at everything like an enemy."

"That's how I feel."

"Since Algiers?"

"Gimme the bottle."

"You are no longer a piece of meat to be made to jerk with electrical wires, to be cut up with precision knives, Craig."

Craig drank too much of a swallow and it seemed to go straight into his head.

"How do you manage to talk about it with such detachment, Von Bergman?"

Bergman got up from the rattan couch which made a slow creak. When he stood by the desk his fist lashed out so fast and so hard that Craig did not grasp the sequence of events until he flew off the chair and bounded against the wall behind him. He looked up and when he no longer saw double and when he could identify the taste in his mouth as warm blood, he could focus on Bergman who stood over him. Bergman's face looked wild and strangely attractive with the anger in it.

"So much," he said, "for my detachment."

Bergman stepped back while Craig got off the floor and helped himself along the desk top and in that manner back to his chair. Bergman set the chair up for him.

"No," said Craig and sat down so that it jarred his head. "No mistaking you for the Frigate bird."

"Take the drink. It's the last."

Craig nodded and drank. He noticed to his disgust that his gin had turned pink. He held his head and closed his eyes. Mercifully, nothing revolved around on the inside.

"All right, *Rebbe*," he said. And then the most recent, the interwoven events with Ben Manta floated up again.

"How do you do it, Bergman? What's your first name, Bergman?"

"Kurt."

"How, Kurt? How do you walk away from a thing like Kabir getting killed like a bug that crawls across your hand in his stupidity?"

"I don't always know. And I never know ahead of time."

"Kabir is not ahead of time. He sank like a stone. And there aren't any ripples?"

"Yes."

"Of course," said Craig and smiled. The movement hurt the cut on the inside of his lip. "He left these three women. Is that where you went just now?"

"Two of them are local and have left already."

"But the Dutch girl is all broken up."

"I don't know. But she is alone here." Bergman brushed one hand back and forth over his very short hair. "I have arranged to have her sent back to Alexandria."

And in this way Craig got some small idea of how Bergman was able to take all the things that had happened to him.

13: A Time for Love and a Time for Loving

She did not look at the ceiling over the bed or at herself on the bed but just knew herself by the animal smell on her and the animal comfort in her while she was stretching. She could hear René in the alcove and the water whisper of the bidet.

Why is he washing all of it off? We made this together and we enjoyed this together and now he is washing it off. She turned her head and could see him sitting on the bidet, washing, and his other hand resting on his thigh. He was wearing his wristwatch.

The watch on his wrist jarred her a little in the new world she had found, because it reminded her of the other existence where you coordinate yourself with everyone else in multiple ways. But now there would be no more multiple coordination of private to public, of social to personal, of intellectual to sexual, of spiritual to secular and of all that truly incalculable multiplicity where one step in life always required a thousand preordained cautions.

It had not worked with Eric and now Eric was dead. And now she was here on the rented bed, Cheryl who had been best with Eric, but not needing any other source than herself anymore. She was now best this way. There was only the rhythm of breath now, not the rhythm of waves of the future. There was Cheryl after the break, and still whole.

But he should take his watch off and he should stop washing himself. She would wash him. It would please his misplaced sense of cleanliness and it would please her to touch him. And then he would pay attention to her again.

He got off the bidet and took a towel.

"Bring the towel, René. I'll do it."

He smiled and came over with the towel.

"You are dripping," she said. "You drip limp. You are not built to drip limp."

"Cheryl," he said, "I am rather happy this way at the moment."

"Limp, was the word."

He sat down on the bed and put his hand on her belly. Then he bent down to her face.

"For which I thank you, chérie."

"I am ready, by and by, to make you more thankful." She noticed that he glanced at his watch. "*Cinq á sept?*"

"No *cinq á sept*," he said. "I am not married."

"But you want us to leave."

"It is necessary, Cheryl."

"Why? I have money to pay for the room all night. And more."

"I know."

"You know? How?"

"Because, *ma chère*, I know who you are." And while he said this he moved his hand to her cheek and touched her so lovingly that she was surprised.

Love-making did not surprise her and a loving touch on her was not new. But Serrat was a stranger. She and he knew each other in the palms of the hands, in the skin of the bellies and from there on down.

Nothing else was needed and nothing else would ever again come her way. And now, from a stranger—

"Here," she said and held one breast in her hand so that it reached up at him.

He gentled his hand over her.

"I want to tell you something," he said.

"Yes." She put her hand under his towel.

"And that too," he said with concentration, because he had something to say which only words could say. "I will make love to you again," he said, "and I want you to know why."

"I know why you want to make love to me. I'm delicious and you like it."

"Yes. I am telling you this so that you believe me, even later."

"I know it now."

"But perhaps not later."

"René," she said, paying attention only to the feel in her hand. "You are not answering me."

"I am concentrating on something else."

"How can you?"

"It is, *sans dire*, almost impossible."

"Ah— Do that again."

He did not know what he had done. He talked more quickly.

"I did not introduce myself or come with you in order to make love."

"You are a liar."

"Now, yes. When I picked you up, no."

"And why didn't you pick me up in order to make love to me? Why did I have to do all the work?"

"*Zut alors*," he said with distraction, "what do you mean you did all the work!"

She laughed and pushed down on the hand he had on her breast.

"*Quel dommage*," she said. "Such work."

But then she felt it in his hand—his disinterest—while his hand became merely anatomical. She put her arms to her side and held still, to listen.

"You were my assignment, Cheryl. I was to deliver you for interrogation."

He now felt the change in her, the breast under his palm no more than glandular and adipose tissue.

"It matters to me that you know it, Cheryl. Because I did not make love to you in order to fulfill an assignment. I made love to you because I love making love and you answered. Also," he went on, "it does not matter that I tell you why we met, because you will not be allowed to go away."

He felt her trying to get up, a bad, startled contraction in her, and then he felt her slump almost instantly, and that change felt worse yet.

"First Eric," she said. "Now me."

"You are afraid," he said, sounding helpless. "Please do not be afraid."

Then René Serrat heard the ugliest laugh he had ever heard. It was a clattering of stretched cartilage, like the sound which sometimes comes out of a corpse when it is turned over.

His instincts as a sensitive man, a man who finds no reward in pain and a man who has learned to be protective with women, all this made him turn without design to the naked girl on the bed who was so frightened that something good and alive might now die in her, if he did not give her some shelter. He leaned over her like a father and like a mother and meant to hold her so that nothing would break in her or get lost.

She felt this but then the inner workings of her head gave her clarity and a very great distance.

What she had felt from the man was completely insane. He was neither for her nor was she with him. The only thing real, and therefore not insane, was the feel of the blood inside her, moving secretly. She would never lose her blood sense again, this sense of herself alone, herself separate from all others, this thing she had found and used when she had taken the free step from dead Eric to this live man whose name might be René.

It was nice that it had been this René because his past use entailed no attachment. While René held her in his arms, she now knew that she could also do without him. When there was a knock on the door René jumped up immediately and it did not interrupt anything.

There would now be another man at the door. Cheryl worked her thighs at each other, feeling the moisture there and how it reminded her of sap. I am a tree full of sap. I can be tapped and there will always be more.

"Open the door, René," she said.

He was appalled to see the plain and deliberate nod of her hips.

Portman had never felt cold when excited. Quite the opposite. He would run with sweat, his skin would feel spongy and the color would move over him like a red-tinted shadow. But in this case not. He felt dry like parchment.

The mid-Victorian luxuries of Algeria's German Embassy did not impress him. His own Berlin office was twice as large. His own London office had cost ten times as much. He ignored Binzwanger and looked at Hoelderlin who wore a uniform of immaculate black.

"For the sake of our mission, Herr Portman ..."

"As long as we are speaking English, and as long as I am English, you may call me *Mister* Portman, Mister Hoelderlin."

Hoelderlin had a title both as an officer of the Waffen-SS and as a deputy on the Kesselring staff. Portman ignored all those amenities and Hoelderlin was much too pressed with developments to take offense at Portman's manner. He tried again.

"The mission, Mister Portman, the entire political picture right now and for a long future to come, Mister Portman, requires your immediate embarkation for Cairo. All is in readiness—for these ten hours."

"And my daughter?"

"We will take care of your daughter, Mister Portman. While you complete the mission in the safety for which we have provided, we will attend to the safety of your daughter."

"Where is she?"

"Here in Algiers, of course."

"Then let me see her."

Hoelderlin groaned like a door which is not used to being swung about. In this old man he was of course dealing with an errant child. Hoelderlin did not have any children of his own. He did not know what to do.

"I have explained to you, sir, that I do not know at the present time where your daughter is."

"And Von Hahn explained to me that a former friend of mine, by the name of Sanft, would be perfectly safe and all right also."

"Fine," said Hoelderlin and wiped at himself where his white collar and red neck dented into each other. "Very, very fine." The white collar was getting visibly stained.

"Why do you say fine?" said Portman. "Sanft is dead."

"I know! But your daughter is alive!"

"Aha! You have not found her."

"*Herrgottsakramentkruzifix!*" said Hoelderlin so emphatically that the swear word sounded as if he were rasping his throat.

"I will personally guarantee," said Binzwanger, "all necessary safety and shelter for your daughter in your absence. My villa, since I am permanently stationed here, is not only spacious but well guarded." And then he made the mistake of his argument. "Your daughter, as you know, Mister Portman, is not to accompany you to Cairo anyway."

"I know that, you dolt! And therefore I know that you have abducted her!"

Hoelderlin had now had time to recover from his lengthy curse. He reentered his role of the administrating executive in this matter, the ministrating angel at the portal of the geo-political heaven.

"Your function in the scheme of things," he said, "is important, and your person, Herr Portman, is privileged. Yet all that is contingent upon your execution of at least this one phase of the plan. If you fail, as you propose to do by your refusal to leave as scheduled, you will be replaced."

"When?"

"Now."

"How? You don't have the document, you don't have the time to reestablish Cairo contacts and you don't have the freedom of movement behind the lines," he said with emphasis, "which my residence in Cairo commands." He used the pause which these truths created to add the next thing with such mildness as to insult the gravity of everything. "And you cannot find anyone else trustworthy enough, in time enough, so you might as well spend that time to produce my daughter." He cleared his throat with the sound of a carnivore resting over his kill.

Hoelderlin sat down behind his desk, but once he had managed that he found he could not talk.

"What the *Herr General-Leutnant* means," said Binzwanger who was the only trained diplomat in the room, "is to reiterate the aforementioned fact that at this moment we are not certain of Miss Portman's whereabouts."

"Who is certain?"

"We shall of course ascertain that."

Portman was tired of the contest of wills. He did not believe what the two men said and he did not intend to take off for Cairo without his daughter.

"You do not know where she is," he said quite calmly. "I believe that. Your chain of command in the Wehrmacht is exemplary, but your chain of command in your party branches is really something demented. You don't even know which minion in the chain of command did what to my daughter, or where, correct?"

"We don't. What I mean to say ..."

"I will look for her myself."

"*Mister* Portman," said Hoelderlin, "*dear* Mister Portman, the length of time it will take you as a private citizen of another country in the town of Algiers ..."

"Don't worry. This private citizen is also very rich, very determined and not without connections."

"But you will never ..."

"Unless you have killed her, I will. And even then. Good day, gentlemen."

"*Hals and Beinbruch*," mumbled Binzwanger and watched Portman close the door.

René, saronged with towel, opened the door less than the chain would permit.

"*Vous me dérangez*," he hissed through the crack.

"Send him in," said Cheryl on the bed behind him.

"It's a man," said René over his shoulder.

"I said *him*. Send *him* in."

Merde, if that girl does not talk like a virgin who is trying to learn how to be a whore. And I comforted her, thought René. I talked to her like a man who appreciates this woman and her remarkable *joie*. I talked to her so that she should know my regard and not misunderstand this unforeseen pleasure in bed. *Ta gueule*, if she wants to pretend like a whore. And how sad that she must.

"Very well," he said at the door and then he closed it to get the chain off the hook and opened it to let in Marcel. If he is French, thought Cheryl, then he is half French. And if he is an Egyptian, then he is part *fellah*. His mouth is dull but the eyes are alive and he walks like a boulevardier instead of a man who pulls his own plow.

Marcel looked at the naked girl on the bed only as long as it took René to close the door and to chain it. He looked at her foreshortened face, the moist hair which stuck to her forehead, the breasts which lay on top of her, and for a moment he watched her lift one knee which made one thigh move away from the other. Then he turned to René.

"*Copain*," he said. "You have indeed fouled everything up."

"I had problems."

"The evidence speaks otherwise. Meanwhile, we have missed the connection because of what you care to call a problem."

"I'm telling you ..."

"I am telling you, though I shudder to think of the consequences. She was to be delivered hours ago and instead all hell has now broken loose."

"How?" René dropped his towel and grabbed for his shorts. He put them on and then he worked himself into his pants.

"How! They are looking for her. Instead of being done with this business, we now cannot leave until I don't know when."

"Make sense! When is that?"

"They will come and tell us. The others, in the meantime ..."

"What others?"

"*Sacré côeur*, what others, the other half of the embattled world, *crétin!* Anyway," Marcel fished for a cigarette and put it into his mouth. "Now we wait. It is not safe outside." He started to light the cigarette but stopped halfway. "Would you like one?" he said to Cheryl in English.

"She speaks French," said René. He buttoned up his fly.

Marcel nodded at that. He had a very bony face which was kept from looking brutish only because his facial movements were so agile.

"She speaks," he said, "many languages." Then he smiled at Cheryl without a touch of insinuation.

She sat up slowly while Marcel sat down on the bed. He lit her a cigarette and gave it to her.

"The tobacco, mademoiselle, is from the Canaries. Very black, like your eyes, very mild—surprisingly—like your temper."

She took the cigarette and while she smoked she crossed her arms, which did not so much cover her breasts as give them a hard shape like marble.

"What do you know about my temper?" she said, and then she added, "Marcel."

"Because you look calm and do not fight me."

"Why fight you?"

"I thought perhaps, fear."

"What you want from me does not give me fear. Only pleasure."

"*Crême de la merde*," René mumbled at the ceiling. "Why does she have to act like that?"

"What did you say?" and Marcel looked at the other man. René popped a button on his shirt.

"I said, don't encourage the monster in her."

"She looks lovely to me."

"She was. I mean ..."

"He means," said Cheryl, "that he and I made very good love and he wants me to know that his enjoyment was human, *masculin, c'est á dire*, and not political."

Marcel looked from one to the other.

"What is she talking about?" he asked René.

"*Foom-foom*," said Cheryl. "*Avec toute la mesure*."

"I envy René," said Marcel.

"You don't have to." She moved her leg so that her thigh came to rest on Marcel's thigh. "And afterward, Grenoble."

"*Comment?*"

"Or Buchenwald? Or what is the one in your new Vichy France?"

Marcel filled a short stretch of silence by blinking his eyes and then he made a sound in his throat which was like a quacking duck. He inhaled smoke hastily and started to talk with the smoke coming out. This made him sound angry.

"Mademoiselle, I look at you with admiration and with an onset of lust. But I hear you with bewilderment and a conclusion of insanity. *You* think that we are Gestapo."

"You don't have to try it this way," said Cheryl. "You can have me, with willingness, without the lie. In fact, I want you. I want very much to feel you inside me and out, and even if you were death I would then feel alive. After that, I don't care."

Both men sighed, as if they were respectively uncle and father.

Marcel looked at Cheryl again and touched her cheek so that it reminded her of René not too long ago.

"We received word," he said as if talking to a child, "that your father is doing something for the Germans. The word came from Cairo, via a long chain of events. And since it is very much more difficult to get to your father, we decided to get you."

"Not Von Hahn?"

The two men now thought she was feeble-minded instead of insane.

"He is dead. In the process he lost a British prisoner—et cetera— At any rate, we received the order to fetch you."

"Not her. The father," said René.

"*Pareil.*" Then Marcel shrugged with a smile. "Or rather, there is a considerable difference." He patted her thigh and she could feel the warmth of his palm. The palm was hard but very warm.

"And what will happen?" she asked and gave the stub of her cigarette to Marcel. He dropped it on the floor and stepped on it.

"It depends on the point of view. Politically, our point of view is limited. We do not know what the British want with you. Our personal point of view, *au contraire*, foresees no limits."

Cheryl closed her eyes in order to feel Marcel's hand with more concentration.

"The fabric of your cheap pants feels wrong to me," she said.

"*Tout de suite*," said Marcel. "I have the answer."

She felt him move and then he was back and his hand was waking her. She stretched and waited before moving herself, the way René had taught her. Then she felt her left breast because the hand was feeling it, and then the mouth on her mouth, and the mouth below. She laughed into the warm breath of the man.

"I forgot there were two of you," she said, and wriggled down on the bed.

She was tired and very happy with not wanting when she opened her eyes and saw the door fly in. It had been an awful crash but she had not been startled, only rather surprised. She was in no shape for swiftness and the unexpected, so she did not see what was happening to her two men. She only saw her father and how he looked very hard and so very un-vague, as never before. Then he sat down on her bed. Now she was much more surprised, vastly surprised, when she felt his arms around her and his hand very lovingly on her cheek. It was a strange thing to feel this from her father.

14: A Crowding in the Emptiness

By dint of adroitness and instant decision such as Henry Portman, Esq., had not mustered or utilized since the early times of concocting his mercantile empire, he managed to gain his airplane only six hours after finding his daughter.

He could not use the German Heinkel which was waiting for him because he was supposed to leave without his daughter. His plane was a very old three-engine Ford which he had to purchase outright and that within a matter of hours. The effective range of the plane, as equipped, was less than the 1,700 miles from Algiers to Cairo. That did not matter. They would reach the oasis of Jalu with ease and from there the rest of the infiltration route had at any rate been arranged. In spite of a few days' delay the mission was safe. Because of the delay Portman's daughter was safe.

The Egyptian pilot carried half of his pay as well as a flat Beretta. He had been in the habit of carrying the gun for years. Portman, on the other hand, carried a .9-mm. Luger which was the first gun he had ever carried in his life. But it had been a happy escape, all things considered. It would not be a happy trip, what with so many puzzles and suspicions—

"Cheryl?" he said and looked at her on the next seat. "Are you awake?"

"Yes, Father."

"I just wanted to know if you were asleep."

"No. But I'm tired."

"Yes," said Portman and looked front again. "Too much excitement."

"Quite a bit," she said and shifted in her seat.

He wished she would comb her hair. He wished she would do something to her face, the way she had always done, so that it would not look so naked.

"When we get to Cairo," he said, by way of summarizing a lot, "I am going to send you to Mirabelle's establishment with no delay."

"I don't need a doctor," she said and yawned.

"For heaven's sake, Cheryl!"

"Yes?" She looked at him. The turn of her head placed their faces very close together.

"I mean," said Portman and looked front, "I mean, it should be obvious—hours with those, with those animals—"

"What happened to them?"

"Happened to them. At any rate, that's done."

"Did you know that they had heard from Cairo that you and I were on our way there?"

"It seems," said Portman, "that you already explained that to me when you offered your mysterious—shall we say—explanation why they were not dangerous."

"They were not Gestapo."

"At the moment, Cheryl, and speaking as your father, that is of small consolation to me."

She smiled and reached her hand out to him. She touched his thigh but felt no response.

"I know," she said. "You came in and you held me."

"Nothing else mattered," said Portman, fighting an embarrassing catch in his throat.

He blinked and pretended to look out of the window on his side. It was night and there was nothing to see. He wished that he felt it again, that rich moment in the strange room, that great sense of completion, the truly simple fact of having found and therefore saved his child.

"In any event," he said. "You will see Doctor Mirabelle." He chewed on his lip, wishing that he had a cigar.

"I want to tell you something," said Cheryl in a voice much more reasonable than her father's. "It is a medically established fact that the mixture from two or more men at the same time hinders and or prevents conception."

Portman gagged, though he was careful not to make a sound.

"Two or more—" he managed to say.

"I'm just being scientific about it. Covering all possible cases, so to speak. Actually, there were only two."

"Two—"

"You promise it's true that you left instructions they shouldn't be hurt?"

"Cheryl!" said Portman, and once again it sounded to her as if he were crying for help. "They raped you!"

She sighed, like someone patient with the very old. "They did not rape me. I told you. I told you exactly how the situation ..."

"One of them," said Portman as if from a great distance, "was an Arab."

"You deal with Arabs all the time, Father."

Portman found a cigar in his pocket. He immediately stuck it in his mouth and held onto it with his teeth.

The Mirabelle Clinic in Cairo would not do. The man for her—God in Heaven, that is to say, the *doctor* for her—would have to be Eisenstein. And if this beastly war had not been prolonged beyond all reasonable expectations, then of course one would send her to that really reliable place in Zurich, Switzerland—

For the time being there was no further communication between Cheryl and her father. She slept and he smoked. Then he slept and she went to the pilot's compartment. She talked to the pilot in an Egyptian dialect, which he liked. She squeezed herself into the seat next to him and he liked that too. But he could not leave his panels and controls and she, for her part, could not get any closer.

"I concede," she said. "Due to your incapacity and due to my ignorance of acrobatics, I concede defeat."

The pilot felt strangled in his harness. Also her words strangled him.

"What do you mean, incapacity! *Zut*," he said, because with impressionable females he liked to use the French words he knew. He said "*Zut*" because the other word was not in order. "*Zut*, incapacity!" he said once again.

Cheryl listened for her father's snore and then she smiled like a Botticelli. She smiled like that for some time while she improvised test and proof that her Egyptian was not in fact cursed with incapacity.

"Tell me what you want to do later—"

As they talked about it, the thought of over one thousand miles like this before they would reach Cairo was sweetly unbearable. Another hundred miles like this, and it became plain unbearable. However, they soon had an engine failure.

Cheryl felt, on the basis of her newly discovered identity, that nothing important could interfere with her for very long. She was content with the engine failure and accepted the emergency landing at Touggourt as her due.

Only Portman was worried, especially since the repairs would take three days. He spent most of that time hovering in and about the hangar where they were fixing the plane. Cheryl spent most of that time in a number of places; on two different beds, on a pile of goat skins, in a ditch, on a field and a few times in a secret place which even the Egyptian did not know about. She did not tell him about it because she knew how the Egyptian disliked the Bedouins and his feelings would surely be hurt if he were to know that one of them was only eleven years old.

Portman's trip by private plane in wartime Algiers could of course not remain hidden. He might manage a six-hour jump on the bureaucrats at the embassy, but a three-day delay in Touggourt would be enough for them to catch up. And then there was the matter of missing his Jalu contact. To forestall bad blood and other forms of unpleasantness Portman called the embassy in Algiers to explain his moves, motives and rate of progress. At this point of developments he had them by the short of the hair. They asked only that he progress with all possible speed and that he not neglect to keep a protective eye on Miss Cheryl. They also told him, by way of adding some urgency, that word had been received from Cairo—through a circuitous route which had started in Kufra—how a hostile contingent of British soldiers seemed to be moving toward Jalu. However, motorized *Stosstruppen* were already on an intercept course. Contact should occur at about this time and the enemy would certainly be rendered ineffective—

They did not doubt for a moment that contact would be made. But they also had only the vaguest notion how this could be done in a sandbox terrain which shifted contours every time there was a wind. It was entirely a matter of trusting the leader.

When they found the Long Range Desert Group it was not because they could see the column. All the vehicles were moving below the bank of a wadi which cut through the terrain like a wide river of sand. They spotted the column because it included the Bishop. Before there was a sound from the self-propelled gun there was a long view of its motor exhaust, a black plume of smoke which hung in the heated air, rose with it and then wafted about like dirty feathers.

"Catch up with them by following the lip of the wadi."

"We could close on them faster at the bottom."

"That would be the unfriendliest move. You keep forgetting, we are not expected."

There was not much more talk than that. Afterward, contact was established and the event was over in a very short time. It was as simple as a maneuver on paper and the efficiency of the moves looked as effortless as something rehearsed. And then there were no longer two columns but only one.

As seen from the air the sight was well regimented. Leading the line was the troop carrier. The emblem in white paint, visible in three places, showed the palm tree with overlaid swastika. The truck was Afrika Korps. The four trucks which followed were three-ton and snub-nosed. From any angle they were plainly what the British 8th Army drove. These were followed by a half-track—Afrika Korps once again—and the column was closed by the tell-tale Bishop. Its bulky 25-pounder barrel looked off-balance on top of the tank carriage for which it had not been designed. The Bishop hung about in the rear because nobody wanted to breathe its black exhalations.

The British vehicles were plainly brushed with a wide, heavy booty stripe and the front and rear Afrika Korps kept its catch in exemplary order. The view from above told of contact concluded with the usual victory. *Natürilch*. The German fighter plane was faster than the British. The German Panther tank was lower and no target till it was too late. Their half-tracks could maneuver better and their gasoline cans never leaked. The view from above showed legend and fact. Two German vehicles herding five British vehicles. The view from farther down was more messy.

The German guards on the tail gates were as dusty as their British prisoners. The victorious German who was allowed to drive the Bishop was coughing soot out of his throat. The British prisoner who had a bloody bandage on his skull cursed the sand itch in his hair and scratched the wound as if he had no feeling. The German Kapitän who rode in the lead swatted a sand fly swarm ineffectually and cursed in fluent Yiddish.

In connection with these various events, Colonel Harker suddenly had enough. He took his arm out of its sling and pounded it three times on the roof of the driver's cab in front of him. Then he stuck two fingers in his mouth and whistled like a hoodlum.

The view from above showed how the prisoner column stopped in unison. Only the Bishop overtrundled its mark a little way. Its muffling device had in the meantime dropped away entirely and the resulting engine roar did not allow the German driver to hear his English Colonel's whistle. Then all the engines stopped and the desert had its silence again. In a little while the Bishop's flag of fume disappeared too.

"All right!" roared Colonel Harker. "Prisoners form over there, the Germans opposite, if you please!"

Lieutenant Boyden, as the aide-de-camp, repeated the same thing in a more military manner. He lifted the bloody bandage off his skull, jumped down from the truck and organized the prisoner assembly to his left and all the German captors to his right. When separated according to their function and their uniforms the left comprised 62 officers and men of the Long Range Desert Group, in their own uniforms, and on the right 21 officers and men of the Palestinian Special Identification Group, in German uniforms. There was no alteration in the rank, except for Sergeant Zwi Ben Manta who had somehow become an *Oberleutnant*.

A further and obvious difference between the groups was the respective weapons distribution. The S.I.G.'s were fully armed, with German weapons. The L.R.D.G., with the exception of six men who had scrambled to the lip of the wadi and stood watch, were weaponless. Their standard weapons plus a few special ones were out of sight in the false bottoms of the trucks.

Colonel Harker wore a dirty sling and had a torn pocket but did not look slovenly. He walked through the empty space between the enemies, stopped with his eyes examining his shoes and started to talk without looking up. The introverted pose did not make him sound any less commanding.

"Briefing," he said so that it sounded to each man as if Harker were addressing him point-blank. It went on in the same way while Harker rarely looked at anyone.

"Object: Tobruk. In general, you all know the plan. Your unit commanders will drill you on details." He paused and did the trick with his upper lip. Sometimes his men would snicker about it. This time, they thought, it made him look like a beast. "We are no longer a recon mission," he said. "This time, under recent revision of plan, we are combat. We are assault!" If they had heard it before, it now sounded terribly final. "Tobruk pumps the lifeblood into every leap of the Fox! We don't know if there will be a next leap, we don't know how well Tobruk is pumping. We are charged with finding out." He suddenly lowered his voice to a pitch like murmurings in a drawing room. The contrast was startling. "We enter Tobruk as prisoners of war under the guard of the men of S.I.G. If caught, we will still be prisoners of war. If they are caught, in those uniforms—"

Everyone knew what the fate would be of a captured British soldier in a Wehrmacht uniform, not to mention the added fact that these were all members of a Jewish outfit.

"They will therefore fight in a manner you may never have seen before. And I want everyone who gets into Tobruk to live up to that example."

There was one man in the third rank of the L.R.D.G. who fainted and fell down in the shape of a bundle. The heat was heavy in the wadi.

"We go in," said Harker in a tone which he meant to be conversational, "and seek targets. Details later. For that matter, I'll be perfectly frank, we are not sure about targets. Petrol tanks for sure. Ammo dumps possibly. Vehicle pools. What map and intelligence entries are available you will be shown. I might frankly add this," he said with a failing attempt at levity, "which is that the pump might be quite empty. There are even intelligence reports to support that possibility." Then he bellowed, sounding like a different person. "But this is nevertheless big enough for the combined effort! Air, sea, diversionary amphibious feints to the north." Then he added, "We are the ground forces."

He seemed exhausted by the image of the enormous, coordinated effort. What exhausted him in point of fact was the bizarre possibility that Tobruk might indeed be pumped out—

"Conduct en route," he said next. "In order to stress the reality of our performance there will henceforth be minimal contact between prisoners and guards. S.I.G.s are autonomous and will keep to themselves. Desert Group personnel ditto."

The fainted man was still lying in the sand as before. Harker looked at the man for a moment and then he looked at Boyden.

"Permission granted," said Harker and then watched while two men dragged the limp one toward the shade of a truck. There was another man now who double-timed over with a canteen of water.

"Lieutenant Boyden!" Harker gave it the parade ground shrill, a sound which always has an edge of the frantic.

"Suh!" said Boyden. He snapped to and did all of that in the manner of a barely controlled explosion.

"I want that man on report."

"Suh?"

"That one, Lieutenant. *The enemy!*"

The order had two mechanical effects. The man Kuntze, who was wearing a German *Feldwebel's* uniform, would after surviving Tobruk lose his stripes. In addition, the man who had fainted for unclear reasons did not get any water.

"To finish," said Harker. "Chain of command: Myself, Colonel Harker, overall. Lieutenant Boyden, all of Desert Group. Captain Bergman, all of Special Identification. Major Craig, in charge of all movement, excluding only those which fall entirely under combat. Any conflict of command is of course referred to me."

For a moment they all thought he was through. "Major Craig?" said Harker.

"Suh!"

"I want to see you at the map table. The map table, Lieutenant Boyden, will be placed here. Corporal Bruckner!"

"Suh!"

"You are to say, *zu Befehl.*"

Bruckner did and then waited.

"Fix that damn Bishop."

There was a pause while Harker did not look at anyone gain.

"Sergeant Ben Manta!"

This time there was no "Suh," no "*zu Befehl.*" There was silence.

It lasted almost long enough to change the hot wadi from an assembly area back to its true desolation in the middle of emptiness.

Harker addressed Ben Manta once more and after that attempt he simply said, "You!" and pointed at him. Harker's finger was shaking.

"English or German?" said Ben Manta.

Harker did not react like the English colonel who is identified in a shorthand manner by the port-wine nose, the consternation sputter and the apoplectic fit under stress.

Harker was capable of a very personal kind of rage. The back of his neck would turn livid. His ears seemed to flatten and he was a carnivorous cat ready to spring. From the front view it was clear that he was going to tear out somebody's gullet. From any angle it was clear that this man was prepared to commit rapid murder and furthermore that he would get away with it.

"You did not respond," he said to Ben Manta.

"No applicable address or command was issued," said Ben Manta. Nobody believed their ears but they kept listening. "In compliance with the intent of your ruling on troop separation I cannot be responsive to British rank designation. I am not a sergeant. I am Oberleutnant Ben Manta, *gehorsamst*."

And then he clicked his heels.

Perhaps Ben Manta was a novel mutation, comparable to nothing that existed, and therefore nothing happened. Or the sound he produced was of a range which would not cause an echo, and that was the reason why nothing seemed to happen. Or, Colonel Harker was an unusually strong man in some secret way and therefore his response did not fit the expected.

"Lieutenant," he said to Boyden. "Give the order for vehicle deployment in camping pattern. And camouflage well—"

The development, thought the man, was in the nature of a stand-still.

That evening something in Cheryl came to a halt.

When she went to the room of her Egyptian she found him asleep. When she woke him, she found that he did not want to wake up for her. She nevertheless tried with a will but he kicked her out.

She left in a state of profound confusion, as if halted on a perfectly open road because the road was suddenly no longer there. Whatever was feeding her sense of being seemed to have dried up. She had clearly offered her presence and he had not wanted it. He could not have known she was there! Therefore, it was possible that she did not exist—

When she got to the Bedouin tents she was winded with the breath raw in her throat and her skin prickled, very hot with moisture, and she was unable to talk. There was really no need to talk. She went into the tent which she knew and immediately kicked off her shoes. That was really all she had to say in order to tell them what she wanted next. She turned to the side where they had spread the pelts but the bed was no longer there.

The boy in the tent was rolling the pelts into a bundle and tying them up with a raffia rope. His sister, whom Cheryl knew less than the boy, whom she only knew by her large, watching eyes under the Bedouin cloak, was putting the clay crocks and the wooden bowls into a goat-skin bag. The two mothers—Cheryl had never determined which was whose—were tying the bag of grain and the several legs of their chickens. They did not say anything but it was obvious that everyone was leaving. Then the old man of the tent came in and the younger one. Cheryl knew these two best.

"I'm here," she said in Arabic.

"We are leaving."

"But *I'm here!*"

They were not too familiar with her kind of Arabic and her past behavior had always been incomprehensible. They had ignored the incomprehensible and had taken what was obvious, but they had no time to take anything now and the note of weird insistence in her voice had escaped them completely. The younger man started to push her out of the tent when the older one proved the wiser. He talked to his son in their own dialect which Cheryl did not understand.

"We'll take her," said the old one.

"I don't want her anymore."

"Dung brain," said father to son. "We take her to Waddan and sell her."

"She's too thin for that."

"Worm head, we travel three weeks. For three weeks she eats nothing, but mutton fat and we keep her hung in the sling."

The son sniffed his nose a few times. It had nothing to do with the chronic dryness from the sand but was his sign of thinking.

"She is not the kind who'll just stay as ordered. She is different. Therefore the great expense of all the mutton fat is a very risky investment."

"Cloaca," said father to son. "To begin with, you will naturally fix her."

"Of course," said the son. Now that he knew what was needed he did not sniff again, because there was no need for thought. And he did not resent the various forms of address, because his new knowledge made them no longer applicable. He beckoned to Cheryl who immediately smiled at him and then he pulled her closer by taking her wrist.

"Lie down on your stomach."

"Open the skins first. The sand gets into everything."

"On the stomach."

"I don't like it on the stomach."

He felled her the way he would toss a goat. It was a new manner for Cheryl, which made her feel curious, but she landed on her stomach though she had just said she did not like that very much. Also, she still had all her clothes on and she had never liked that at any time. The more clothes, the less she felt. To feel was tantamount and it required repeated demonstration. Not to feel meant not to exist and there was nothing worse, it was the ultimate loss. There were going to be no more losses in her life.

All this was on the order of a natural law built into one's body and therefore she commenced to answer all metaphysical and all physical demands by a simple turn of head and body. Which is how she happened to see the knife in his hand.

She felt one of his knees on her shoulder and the other one was leaning into her buttock. In that way her near arm was lying between his spread legs. He was looking toward her legs, though this observation was merely incidental. Her activating knowledge was something else. She was going to live without any knife in her.

The near hand reached up under him and found his scrotum with sufficient skill. She grabbed and pulled. She had no tricky training in commando tactics but simply knew what she knew. This man would pass out on the spot, which he did.

Only after that act did the beginning tendrils of panic grow in her and as this happened she jumped up and ran into the night possessed with great strength.

In part she got away because such behavior was entirely unheard of in the case of a prospective sale. Besides, there had been no intention of killing her. One cuts the heel tendons so that the sale cannot walk. The mutilation is unimportant since the ability to walk or to stand does not affect the function which determines the merchandise's value.

But Cheryl spent the night trembling in her locked room. She knew that the value of her body had changed. She therefore knew that she was losing her knowledge of being.

She was strong and bore the panic all night. She learned that all the others had been wrong and that she was after all right. The Egyptian thought she did not exist because he was blind and the Bedouin had been blind enough to mistake her for something else. A goat. He had been hungry and therefore had hallucinated her into edible meat.

None of them had her inside knowledge. And no panic of loss would splinter that knowledge now. She hardened a capsule and would live in its protection. On the outside she would pretend that she looked as she did but on the inside, in the capsule, she would hide and hoard everything really vital.

The Egyptian woke from a dream before dawn and thought immediately of Cheryl in her room down the hall. He went there and knocked and was not surprised that she opened in very short order.

There was enough light from the bathroom for him to note her appearance. Her face was bathed in sweat and there were dark patches on the blouse she was wearing.

"Fell asleep in your clothes?" he asked her.

"I woke up."

"Had a bad dream?"

"No."

"Me neither." He reached for her. "I had a good one." He smiled at her but she did not smile back. When he entered the room she did not close the door.

"Look," he said, "I was tired before. All right? I mean, after all, enough is enough."

"I don't think you're enough."

"Huh?" But then he shrugged and smiled and leaned against her. "Huh?" he said again, with a sound as if he were licking at her. "I'm not tired, huh? Notice that?"

"I notice. But it can no longer reach me."

"Reach you? *Salope!*" which was the other French word he knew.

"You would not understand," she said. "I am now much too deep for you," and then she pushed him out of the door.

He had of course not understood what she meant. At least, he had misunderstood her. Only Cheryl knew that she had now safely crowded herself into a deep center place in the middle of her emptiness.

15: First Stop, Second Impressions

There was no definitive safety in staying beneath the horizon inside a wadi. Seeing nothing, the enemy would look there first. But to camp there for the half-day would do and then they would move by dark.

Bruckner would have to make do. The minimum tools which the Bishop carried were not enough for the trouble which Bruckner found.

And the baked wadi floor would have to do for the maps because Harker's request for a map table had overlooked the fact that there had been no room to carry a map table. Harker had been too preoccupied with other details to remember this. But he now remembered with a very private sense of gratitude that Boyden had not said at the time and in front of the rest of the troops that there was no map table on this particular mission. In the middle of his tightly controlled turmoil over that Ben Manta person, Harker insisted on thinking of Boyden, of the good grace shown by the young man's sensitivity. That was the importance of something as mundane as the forgotten absence of a map table. It showed whom one could depend upon. No Boyden would compromise his superior officer by broadcasting that he, Harker, had forgotten his own order about no map tables on this unprecedented mission. On the other hand, there were the Ben Mantas—

"Major Craig reporting, suh."

Harker returned Craig's salute and asked him to step into the shade of the canvas square which had been staked overhead. Craig bent over the map which was held down with four rocks. In the Tobruk area a waft of sand had obliterated the objective. That, thought Craig, would be nice— He shortly noticed that Harker was looking elsewhere. The colonel was staring in a direction where there was really nothing to see. Cracked sand, naturally, but so was all of the wadi floor. Nothing to contemplate there. Until, that is, when there would no longer be the wadi floor and heaven help us when we get to the drifts—

Craig looked down at the map again and at the straightest line of progress which he had been able to work out. The route was fairly crooked. And an anxious guessing game at that. The routing was based on recon reports from others, on his own survey maps which had been made without military considerations, and on his notations since his last passage through the Zighen area. He knew that in that sector alone three giblehs had blown across since then, driving the tops off the dunes and hiding the tell-tale colors which showed where the terrain was safe for driving. Naturally, the horizon would look all different too—

"Any difference in your outlook, Major?"

"The winds were bad," said Craig and kept pondering the contour lines on the map.

He did not notice the silence but then he heard what Harker said.

"How poetic of you, Major."

Craig straightened up rather abruptly. The quick motion changed a sweat line near his lid and he blinked his eye as if he had a tic.

"You were saying, sir?"

"I've noticed," said Harker, "that there is a sort of relationship between you and Captain Bergman."

Craig was still not sure that he understood.

"Friendly, I'd call it," Harker went on. "I wondered if this incident with that Palestinian native in Wehrmacht clothing had altered your outlook on the—er, type of men in S.I.G. in any way."

"All of them?" said Craig.

"You think there's only one Zwi Ben Manta?"

Why, thought Craig, doesn't he grow one of those mustaches that always bristle. Might make the tic redundant—

"I don't know, sir. But there's Captain Bergman. Behind you, that is."

Harker turned in time to see Bergman step under the shade of the tarp. Harker's return salute looked like a gesture of rejection.

"As C.O. of my special branch," said Bergman, "I came for instructions concerning Sergeant Ben Manta's misconduct. For myself, sir, I came to apologize."

"You've got your foot on the map, *Kapitän*."

Craig had seen that expression on Bergman's face before. The last time he had caught it he had also caught a sharp hook to the jaw.

"Why are you here?" asked Harker.

"For any orders which you ..."

"I wouldn't give that order to you, Captain. But I meant something else with my question. Why are you here, in this war?"

"To win it."

"Indeed. To win Palestine, would that be more specific?"

"To be specific, Colonel, no. Palestine is a British mandate. To win Israel."

"I'm informed on that," said Harker. "First-hand."

"Your advantage," said Bergman. "I've never been in Palestine."

"Full advantage of first-hand encounter, Captain, with your Haganah. You know them, Captain?"

"Jewish defense force of Palestinians, yes."

"Which was declared an illegal organization! Gutter tactics, sir! I've fought them!"

"I understand," said Bergman who had no wish to fight past battles.

Bergman of course had his unfinished battles too. But he could take care of a great number of defeats which had occurred in the past by the fight he had entered in the desert. Bergman had a goal on the other side of the battle while Harker did not. Harker's fight was a performance in craft; and an inadequacy in that performance, such as a defeat, was a black mark on the merit sheet. A victory elsewhere did not alter that.

"Those so-called Sabras," said Harker, "they were worse than the Arabs in Palestine."

Bergman nodded, to allow Harker the last word, but Craig was something else again. He was neither a fighter with an ideal nor a professional with a reputation. His acts came chiefly from the personal encounter. And Harker was being an idiot.

"Of course they were worse," said Craig. "You had to fight them. You had no quarrel with the Arabs."

Harker was out of his depth. As a professional soldier, the issue, of whom to fight and for what reason was purely academic for him and not part of his job. He therefore could regard Craig as an incompetent and the only issue at hand was why the man was not reading his maps. Of course, they were waiting for Boyden. Harker ignored Craig and turned back to Bergman.

"No action concerning Ben Manta," he said.

"The men are talking, sir. I felt that the cohesion of our force ..."

"Precisely my point, Captain. I cannot treat Ben Manta as an insubordinate soldier. First of all he is not a soldier, secondly he is only insubordinate when it serves to defeat the enemy."

"But what enemy ..."

"Me. In return, dealing with my enemy, I would kill him. You follow my figurative example?"

"Figuratively yes," said Bergman. The other man's calm worried him.

"But since Ben Manta and I still have a few aims in common, we are not going to kill each other. His problem of finding enemies everywhere is his own. I am only concerned with his efficiency as a soldier."

Bergman was sure that Harker's concern went further than that. He followed Harker's glance across the wadi and saw Ben Manta supervising the placement of four machine guns.

"Very efficient," said Harker and then he got down on his knees next to Craig in order to work on the map.

Bergman left the tent with other worries. The quarantine of his men would henceforth be less for show and much more real. As Harker had said, there were still a few aims in common, and Bergman meant to make sure that his men remembered that. He saw Bruckner taking his shirt off next to the Bishop and he saw Mohnfeld standing nearby. Then Ben Manta walked toward the Bishop. If that one, thought Bergman, had some sudden parade ground notions about improper uniform, then Bergman would not have to worry. Mohnfeld was right there.

As a person, thought Bergman, that Mohnfeld had something of the false, or rather of the cheap, about him. The manner was too facile for Bergman's taste, so much sparkle—in a manner of speaking—that Mohnfeld himself could hardly be seen. Excellent performer though. Accurate in a fight, quick with decisions when there was need for tactical switches. That patrol action at Siwa. Bergman himself had not been there but Mohnfeld's sketchy account of the action had been borne out by the results. There had been an unexpected encounter with a double-strength German combat patrol. Mohnfeld had lost every man. But Mohnfeld had come back with the German lieutenant's map satchel after garroting the man while he had hunkered down after the fight behind a dark rock for privacy and with his pants all the way down.

Then Mohnfeld had disappeared in the dark and reappeared the next morning where Bergman's group had been waiting—

"Leftenant Mohnfeld?" said Ben Manta.

"*Zu Befehl, Herr Oberleutnant.*"

But Ben Manta had no sense of humor. He did not smile back when Mohnfeld smiled and he suddenly did not like the way Mohnfeld was leaning on the tracks of the Bishop. He could lean, if he wished. He was really a lieutenant and Ben Manta was really a sergeant. Besides, S.I.G. in the field had never bothered with rank preoccupations. However, what was the point of these German uniforms, what was the effectiveness of their value as a trap, if one did not force oneself into the proper identity which went with the disguise?

"That *Feldwebel* tunic there," said Ben Manta and pointed to it where the shirt hung from the snout of the Bishop, "is that Bruckner's?"

"I'm afraid he's out of uniform, *Oberleutnant* Zwi."

The insult of combining the German rank with the Jewish name had no effect. Ben Manta was not sensitive to condescending treatment or to any other type of needling. A matter of proper values. Such talk was surreptitious fighting not worthy of the name. It was really playing. There were no games for Ben Manta.

"Are you under there, Bruckner?" and Ben Manta leaned over the track.

"Goddamn it!"

Bruckner rarely swore but that voice from a space narrow with sand and steel and also foul with caked grease and black oil was Bruckner's in a rare temper. Only stupidity which interfered with his professional excellence would sometimes produce this reaction.

"This is your sergeant," said Ben Manta with a quiet voice.

"Zwi," said Mohnfeld. "Tell him it's his *Oberleutnant* speaking."

"Lieutenant," said Ben Manta, "I am Bruckner's immediate superior and I'm executing ..."

"Move your feet!" yelled Bruckner. "I'm coming out!"

"You better," whispered Mohnfeld. "He's coming out. Did you ever see a Panther tank execute a break-through maneuver?"

Ben Manta was not even listening. He stepped back because he wanted Bruckner to come out and as far as Mohnfeld was concerned he could ignore the man because it is easy to ignore the inferior. The man's constant levity at a time of critical change in the order of everything was as foolish and detestable as standing at the Wailing Wall in Jerusalem and laughing out loud.

Bruckner was the black-haired type who has a body color like a maggot. But there were all those muscles. While Bruckner pushed his naked torso out from under the carriage, the muscles moved like thick snakes and made sliding highlights of sweat on the skin. Patches of gray and brown sand had stuck to him, looking like emery paper. There were also black streaks of grease, wicked like warpaint patterns. He stood up and blinked as if he had just come out of a cellar.

"The sergeant wants you to put your tunic on," said Mohnfeld.

Bruckner ignored the remark and acted his usual self. "What is it, Zwi?"

"I want you to move the Bishop. It interferes with our line of fire that way down the wadi."

Bruckner breathed as if he had just reached a mountain top.

"The pan is off."

"What's that?"

"Pan is a German euphemism for *Panne*," said Mohnfeld. "It derives from the French word *panne*, which refers to a mechanical breakdown. Translated into Hebrew it means Sabbath: Nothing moves and everything is *verboten*. Even Bishops stand still."

"Mohnfeld," said Bruckner. "Stop talking." Then he looked at Ben Manta. "I can't move it. The pan is off and the guts are hanging out."

"Why is the pan off? Why isn't the exhaust thing off?"

"The exhaust thing is off too."

"Put it back on so the thing stops smoking this way."

"I can't put it on because it isn't here. I don't know where it is. Also, we don't need it."

"But that black smoke ..."

"Has nothing to do with the stack. And if you want to know what it's got to do with I'll explain it to you when we get to Tobruk a month from now."

"Bruckner," said Ben Manta. "You're interfering with my forty-fives."

"Whereas," Mohnfeld put in, "Bruckner here has a twenty-five pounder. It is bigger than both of us, Zwi."

Ben Manta had no particular feeling for rank in others but he had some very clear-cut and simple criteria of value. If it interferes, it is bad. If it assists, it is good. This particular "it," namely Mohnfeld, was bad. Worse than Harker, as a matter of fact. Harker, at least, retained his British pretensions of impersonality. Mohnfeld, on the other hand, was the worst type of European Jew. A threatening influx of that element had been reaching Palestine, for that matter. They were like an intestinal worm, highly personal but inaccessible in themselves; deeply involved with you but giving you nothing; their effect was impressive but you could not impress them.

Ben Manta decided to treat Mohnfeld like an intestinal worm. He would ignore him as best he could but feed him a little something.

"The lieutenant," he said to Bruckner, "understands the importance of moving the Bishop. He'll make you see it," and turning to Mohnfeld, "if you will, sir. I've got pressing business at the other end." Then Ben Manta left.

"What end?" Mohnfeld called after him, though he did not expect an answer.

Mohnfeld watched him go while Bruckner looked at the sun. He was worried about time. Mohnfeld was worried about something else.

"What?" said Bruckner when he saw the expression.

"Hard to tell," said Mohnfeld and looked as if he were thinking.

"Yes," said Bruckner. "Something there I don't get." He reached for the rag which hung out of his rear pocket. He wiped his hands and felt both the slip of the grease and the grit of the sand which was everywhere. "Of course, he's not a German," said Bruckner.

Mohnfeld turned with more surprise than he cared to show.

"German?" he said. "Who are you, the prize bull of Aryan propagation?"

Bruckner was now as surprised as his friend had been but in his case the mood made him turn very slowly. His face looked lumpish and worn, but his eyes looked up with something like very young innocence.

"I'm a German," he said.

The look made Mohnfeld touchy.

"I know," he said. "*Kleider machen Leute.* That damn uniform will do it to you every time." Mohnfeld spat with distraction. The act was mostly the sound of a spit because there was not enough spit for the real thing. "Anyway," he said. "Sounds to me like you're fighting on the wrong side."

Bruckner dropped the rag to the ground where he could grab it once he crawled under the iron belly.

"Sometimes I don't understand you at all, you know that, Mohnfeld? I'm a native of Germany, I learned my trade in my home town, I got friends there."

"Traitor," said Mohnfeld. "Shooting at your own friends."

"I was talking about the Germans," said Bruckner. "What I'm shooting at here are the Nazis."

He got down on his hands and knees and then Mohnfeld watched the big butt and next the legs disappear. Bruckner had told his view very simply. It was this very simplicity which gave Mohnfeld pause. He had the sort of finely tuned mind which hungered for nuances, and when there were none the result was bafflement. There was no such simplicity, Mohnfeld considered. The impression given must therefore be artful and deliberate. A remarkable veneer of unmarred evenness which could only be achieved by deliberate craft. Mohnfeld had befriended Bruckner as soon as he had joined Bergman's unit. And since that time Bruckner had never altered the impression which he had made during the first five minutes. If that was not subhuman, then it could only be suprahuman—

To Portman's consternation his daughter spent the entire day in bed. Though it might be for the best, he thought. She had looked rather worn lately and in remarkably rapid progression she had developed a curious soddenness which did not seem properly human. He spent most of the day in arrangements with the people in Algiers. The trimotor had developed additional ailments as if the very repairs brought them forth. Algiers would send, it was now decided, the Heinkel which had originally been prepared for the trip. It had gone to Marseille in the meantime but would be made available to him in a matter of days.

Though that would be all right too. Hitler caused other delays elsewhere, when it came to that, and the delay in the timetable here might even be good for Cheryl. When Portman said good night to her in the evening, she did not seem to have moved. A fine moonlight mood hung in the dark room. Not a touch of that worn, coarse quality about her anymore. Instead, she seemed frail, somehow suprahuman—

16: The Bishop Is Like a Fifth Column (from a Book on Chess)

The desert under the moon, thought Craig, is a place where you forget everything else. That is the reason why the desert at night can make you feel clean.

He was on the lead truck, half straddling the fender, half leaning on the hood. If the truck had not been German he would have been less comfortable. The British counterpart had a steep-sloping, sharp-angled snout which was not very good for riding a fender. He leaned his body on the hood as much as he could because the warmth was delicious. When he looked at the night desert the way he liked to look at it, then nothing interfered with the stillness in the view and the stillness in him, which came from the viewing of this. He did not hear the laboring of the motors or the agonizing of the springs. Even the trailing Bishop did not matter, though its periodic convulsions were an embarrassment to the ear.

But when Craig looked at the night view because it was his job and the purpose was war, then all the qualities changed. Every vehicle sound became a threat to the nerves because something happened at night which increased the listening range to a frightful distance.

It has to do with the sky, Craig decided. It curves more and there is none of the velvet depth which the sky has when seen from the edge of the water, but there is a black-polish hardness to the immense arch which bounds sight and sound back at you with unbearable clarity.

The air was cold. The sun smell of the desert was not there but only the smell of cold stone. It is a smell, Craig knew, which had none of the qualities derived from an object. Nothing smelled like a plant or a fruit or a body. Instead, it is the smell of coldness in everything. They don't smell it on the Bishop, he considered, when the black beast at the end of the line suddenly made its sound of obscenity.

Sometimes the Kamansho Flats glittered like a sharp miniature of the skyscape full of stars. And then the glitter went dead.

The sand had moved. Craig motioned at Bruckner who was driving and hoped that the new direction would not be worse than the old one. Night in the desert, of course, was not for moving but only for viewing. Harker had no such convictions. At night you cannot be seen, ergo, you travel at night. Harker had never learned that you do not navigate on the desert by contour but only by color. It was the shading of color which told you that the ground was hard, that it was mush, where it was bottomless and where it would break your spine. Harker, of course, could not even see the color. When asked by his grandchildren in the calm years of retirement what the desert had looked like, Harker would probably say that it had the color of sand.

The view ahead flattened out like an invitation. Craig could feel how it was drawing Bruckner because the motor went up. Craig slammed the flat of his hand on the hood abruptly. Then he jumped to the ground. The lead truck gave a respectful jolt and stopped immediately while the rest of the line did the same, domino fashion. The Bishop, by the sound of it, took a little longer. Also, it ended up to one side of the line.

Craig hunched inside his clothes and grinned. Ben Manta was driving that thing now. It would be a case of an irresistible force driving an immovable object.

Then there was silence except for the low, idling sound of the motors. All the look-outs, two on each truck, sat up very alert now in the cold air. Craig walked a little way to the front of the lead truck and stood there for a while.

Now, he thought, it feels again as if there were no men with me and no machines. The desert looks itself again, neither good nor evil, just a still, big view which asks nothing of me; an attitude which is beautiful in its uselessness. Of no military value, this good feeling. Harker would be appalled to know that there could be such a thing and Bergman could not bear the feeling. He would instantly feel the loss of his past and the worry over his unfinished future—

The first one to reach Craig was Boyden. He had draped himself in an army blanket which in his case made him look particularly unmilitary. He looked very much like a young man who was sleeping over on the downstairs couch.

"Trouble, Craig?"

"I don't know yet. Where's Harker?"

"Rear lorry. He'll be along." Boyden shivered and held the blanket around him. "If they knew about the desert," he said, "they'd issue daytime uniforms and nighttime uniforms."

"They" always meant HQ, Staff, London, Churchill, et cetera, and all such distant forces that be.

"This desert," Boyden said, "is really two countries."

"Yes," said Craig. "Though the map doesn't show it."

Boyden dropped the blanket off his shoulders because Harker was coming up.

"Never mind that," said Harker and ignored Boyden. "What's the trouble, Craig?"

"I think," said Craig, "we're looking at a mine field."

In Touggourt, in the middle of the night, Cheryl got up from her bed and got dressed for a walk along the inside balcony of the hotel. There was light in the foyer downstairs but no direct light where she was walking. She noticed on her walk that all the paddle fans which were spaced overhead were standing still. It was cool at night. Nobody noticed the paddle fans unless they were standing still. She was aware of the fact. At the bend of the balcony she did not follow it but went into her father's room. He was up too.

He sat by his desk with the yellow lamp light on his head. His white hair stood up in frizzles, the way it always does when a man has tried to sleep and found that he could not. Aside from that, he was a round ball of comfort inside his quilted housecoat. Beyond him the French doors stood open. This was all right because it was cold enough so that the flies were quite dormant. The French doors were open to admit the view. There was a white minaret standing all alone with the black sky about it. Portman, at his desk, was reading a pamphlet.

Cheryl looked at the view again, which was really bigger than the slice which the French doors admitted, and felt once more that she had her first really clear view of anything. Her father was a fool.

He looked up and was pleased to see that she was so calm and sane.
"Are you all right, darling?"

"Yes," she said. "I don't think we are going to make it."

Portman knew better. What this situation needed was the chortle of a fatherly laugh.

"Don't worry," he said. "You just don't know how extensive all the preparations really are."

Cheryl just nodded. You don't want to hurt someone who is only safe in his little delusions and you certainly don't bother to argue with a fool—

"Unheard of!" said Harker. "Nothing on the charts! And with that snail's pace you've been setting us, Craig, how could we be anywhere near a zone they would bother to mine!"

"If you're worried about the snail's pace," said Craig, "I advised against night travel."

"Clearly my responsibility," said Harker whose big asset and point of honor was never to insist on a mistake which he recognized. "I won't insist on night movements again."

"As for the presence of a mine field," Boyden put in, "I am put in mind of Captain Bergman's report ..."

"So am I," said Harker. "That messy business with Ibn Kabir." He turned to Craig. "In terms of terrain," he said, "is it possible for them to get a crew here this fast, even if that Kabir report reached destination within a day?"

"I don't know how they did it," said Craig. "But here it is."

"As you say," mumbled Harker and peered at the flats in the moonlight which looked entirely like flats in the moonlight to him. "How the devil did you see it?" And for that matter, he thought, what did you see?

Craig walked ahead and the two officers followed. The moonlight, Boyden said to himself, illuminates primarily the imagination. Therefore, it is no good for war. Much better for something else— Must tell that to Isabel sometime. On the other hand, better not. Might ruin the tactical advantage—

"That's it," said Craig up front and spread his arms.

They stopped next to him.

"See the humps?" he said.

They saw the humps. They saw humps all over and had been seeing humps for some time.

"No," said Craig. "I mean this. Southerly wind this time of year, Colonel Harker, which will make a drift pillow against anything that stands up. You put a mine down and pack it over, you'll leave a raised area more likely than not."

Harker knew that and Boyden knew that. They saw what Craig meant but they had seen the same thing all along.

"And here," said Craig, "is one of those drift pillows that's built up. Young sand. Maybe a day or so."

"Craig," said Harker, "I believe you, simply out of a sense of caution. Though I confess I don't see a thing. Get us a bayonet, Boyden."

The deformity in question was smaller than a plate. The sandy hump at the southerly side looked like the sandy hump at the northerly side. They waited for the bayonet.

The situation, Harker considered, was unmanageable. They had no detection equipment and they had no time. They had no time to dig up the Sahara with a bayonet every time there was a hump.

"They're undoubtedly tremor types," he said. "I'd suggest we snake along the incline to the left over there. Stands to reason that the drift topography which you describe has made a good, soft pillow there. We'll unload and send the heaviest vehicle ..."

At that moment the Bishop gave a loud bark. It made Harker jump. The sound was like a signal in the night. "Who the devil is on that thing?"

"Ben Manta," said Craig.

After that sound from the Bishop it now seemed especially quiet.

"Has it occurred to you," said Harker, "that if this is a fresh field, and if it is for us, that they'll still be in the vicinity?"

"And waiting for us? Yes sir," said Craig.

Bergman, with his startling habit of walking up silently, finished the thought for them.

"And the first mine we blow," he said, "will tell them where we are. While we don't know where they are." Then he talked directly to Harker. "With your permission, I've given orders to arm your men."

The order was totally sound. The manner in which it had been given was highly intolerable. But Harker, in his conduct, remained completely professional.

"Thank you," he said. "Whom did you leave in charge?"

"Lieutenant Mohnfeld."

"I see," said Harker, and only a nuance in tone gave some faint sign that his reaction covered more than the purely military.

When Boyden brought the bayonet, Bergman took it. "Show me where," he said to Craig.

"You're volunteering?"

"Or I wouldn't be here," said Bergman without any humor.

Craig shrugged and showed Bergman the patch of ground and then he stepped away. He wanted to step back and lie down in the proper fashion because he did not have the ideals which give comfort to heroes, dead or alive. But he went and stood where Boyden and Harker were standing. He hated himself for that.

Bergman kneeled down and then he looked over his shoulder.

"You may commence," said Harker, "when I wave at you. All right, gentlemen," and then he went to stand behind the hood of the truck.

Boyden followed suit and Craig followed, feeling like an ass.

After Harker had raised his hand they watched Bergman's bent back and his small movements of digging. Craig could see the back. It was solid enough. But then his vision would flicker and swim as if it were best not to see this at all, not to remember that it had been there after the sudden blossom of light and the shattering of this view which looked so solid

Then Bergman stood up.

"Nothing," he said.

Craig's reaction was silent and awful. He saw Harker and Boyden walk away, he saw Bergman stand as before, but he himself was still hung on the point of waiting for the explosion, and to finish the suspense it was necessary that Bergman be ripped into shreds

Whatever he was holding in came through in a small way with the sweat that squeezed out of his skin.

"Take a deep breath," said Bruckner from the truck cab above him.

Craig grunted and then he nodded his head. He hoped that nothing else would show. Oh where, Sainted Donald, he said to himself, is your sainted sense of proportion— You did not scream before to stay alive and you want to scream now to turn X dead—and where in hell is there anything like a useful proportion—

"... made a useful mistake," Harker was saying. "What do you say, Craig?"

Then Craig took the deep breath Bruckner had mentioned. He walked to the group. Then, for a while, he simply looked at the flats under the moon again.

He saw his desert again, the one he could see without touch of war, and when he looked at it in that way he knew now that his desert was spoiled. He knew what he knew but he did not know how.

"If they're here," Bergman said to Harker, "they didn't have much time. The fastest way is to lay them in tandem."

"Right there!" said Craig when the pattern jumped at him.

It was true that his desert had been spoiled. Its wholeness, for an eye like Craig's, was the desert's natural growing and changing and that happened without repetitions and without regularities. Whether he had seen it with the head or the gut was unimportant.

"Gimme that," he said and took the bayonet from Bergman.

They watched him from a distance and a little bit later, when they watched him come back with the German *Teller* mine in his hands, they were not really surprised.

"Just antipersonnel," said Boyden while they watched Craig lock the trigger.

"Or anti-tire," said Harker. "Boyden?"

"Suh."

"Tell that Lance Corporal in the first lorry to go to the rear and get the Bishop up here." He touched the flat, circular mine with the tip of his boot. "Should be good for something, all that weight—"

They stood for a while and looked at the metal dish on the ground, an unpleasant sight like a symmetrical beetle.

"I think," said Bergman in a moment, "that Bruckner will tell you that one of these will be enough to finish the Bishop's steering linkage."

"The hydraulics?" Harker turned briefly when the Bishop's gearing made a penetrating thunk in the distance. "It's encased."

"Not anymore. Has something to do with the way he had to doctor the transmission. That's where the oil smoke came from."

Harker looked to the east. The horizon there had the same color as the rest of the sky.

"Two hours till dawn," said Craig.

As once before, the Bishop gave a mighty bark. It made no other sound and did not seem to be coming closer.

"Regular clarion call," Craig said to no one in particular. "Maybe we won't have to wait till daytime—"

Harker said nothing for a moment and then he sent Lieutenant Boyden once more to detail the next change in plan.

"While we wait," said Harker, "I want to ask you, Captain Bergman— I want to ask you a number of questions. Please stay, Major Craig."

The three men walked a way toward the rise of the flats where the sand, as Craig had explained, would be deep and soft. They left the trucks below them and when Harker sat down in the drift they watched the deployment of guard positions for a while. As the truck motors stopped one by one there was a progressive growth of silence.

"They wouldn't be behind us," Harker said without transition.

"In terms of terrain," said Craig, "quite impossible. We traversed what's passable."

Their view was wide. It seemed as if one could not look farther. The sense of being alone was very real, and possibly very deceptive. But it was very still. All near sounds were subdued and there were no far sounds at all.

"Even assuming," said Harker, "that the Kabir Intelligence was transmitted with no interruption and a search party was formed and sent into action with providential speed, how—I would damn well like to know—how would they know to mine us right here?"

He did not get an answer.

"We have three transmitters," said Harker.

Craig frowned. "I've got one of them in the lead truck."

"I know," said Harker. "Do you also know how often you left the cab to walk ahead, while your driver remained alone?"

"Bruckner?" said Bergman. He sounded as if he meant to explode. "I've known Bruckner since my unit was formed!"

"I'm sure," said Harker. He allowed a pause, deriving a peculiar pleasure from the sound of Bergman's arrhythmic breathing. "But let's consider the performance of that Bishop for a moment," said Harker.

"You recall, Colonel," said Bergman with considerable ice in his voice, "that I advised against taking that shot-up piece of equipment on a mission such as ..."

"That Bishop," interrupted Harker without any heat, "has been with my unit for some time."

"I hardly think this is the time to discuss company mascots," said Craig who felt much too irritated for the niceties of etiquette. "What about that damn thing?"

"Bruckner repaired—" Harker interrupted himself, "Bruckner worked on it. That is my point."

Craig laughed. It was an unpleasant sound. It was even worse than the very spiky and unpleasant mood which hung over the three men who made their own ugly crowd in the empty desert.

"And so," said Craig, "we have Indian smoke signals by day and secret clarion calls by night."

But the absurdity of the joke did not take the suspicion away.

"And I have one of the transmitters," said Bergman.

"And the third transmitter is on the Bishop," said Harker.

"*So what?*" Bergman let the words out like throwing two stones.

"This Ben Manta," said Harker as if he were impervious to any emotion, "is *not* known to you since formation of your unit. Correct, Captain?"

"He joined in Kufra," said Bergman.

"And it was he, wasn't it, who with most peculiar dispatch killed Ibn Kabir after the latter had completed his job of Intelligence."

Bergman, for all his composure, felt totally rattled. He had no agility with the kind of guesses which go into the invention of possible reasons for probable facts. Nor did he understand the sort of mind which had that kind of speculative ability. He thought Harker had a spot in him which was mad.

Craig's reaction was simpler because hearing of Ben Manta he saw again another picture and heard a sound. "He did his job well," Von Hahn had said. Sound of shot, picture of Sanft hanging down—

Craig heard Harker's voice again. It was unusually sharp.

"And if you will abandon your almost national prejudice for a moment, Captain Bergman, you will agree that the possibility of clandestine allegiances does exist both for Ben Manta and Bruckner."

Craig had not seen Bergman speechless before and it was a bad sight. It was worse that Harker should get up at that moment and dust his breeches with his swagger stick.

"Takes a certain type of mind," he was saying. "The kind of mind, I might point out, which can even now tolerate to wear the uniform of its executioners."

And at that point Bergman got up and Craig knew that the whole fluid motion was totally dangerous. Bergman had not gotten up just to stand on his feet in a drift of sand to better see his superior officer. And he would not have the control of a Harker who could hold his rage at an affront in full view of his troops. Bergman was not looking at his superior officer. He was looking at his kill—

"*Insanities!*" Craig burst out.

He said it as much to clear his own head as to interrupt other two.

He got up all in a scramble which kicked sand in his face made him blow through his lips. Then Bergman put his hand on Craig's chest, ever so lightly.

"Go away, Craig," he said without ever looking away from Harker.

"What's this?" said Harker.

Craig had seen the look on Bergman before.

"Kurt," he said very fast, "are you going to prove him right?" and then, to give Bergman time to recover, he fairly shouted at Harker. "There is one simple explanation for that mine-field placement and I'll be damned if I buy a more complicated one just because it takes more brains!" He pointed violently. "That flat is one passage out of three choices. It looks best and it is best and anyone high-tailing hell-bent-for-leather from Kufra to Jalu would go there as long as he knew about it! I knew about it. I also know that there's dune drift to the west and that we'll hit salt marsh farther on if we move east of these flats. Now," and he swung around to Harker as if he meant to bite his nose. "Where would you put the mines if *you* knew all that?"

"We could have ..."

"*No!* We could not have taken any other way unless we had enough time for a few hundred miles detour around the whole goddamn Sand Sea! And you," he swung on Bergman. "Now you know where they must be waiting!"

It gave Bergman a better enemy. He looked past Harker as if the man were not there. He looked at the lay of the land under the black sky and how it crouched there waiting for the light, and Harker became insignificant—

It stood to reason. The Germans were waiting among the dunes to the west. They would guard its passes, they would have enough time to reach the flats once the mines blew. They would certainly have enough time to catch anyone who decided to get bogged in the groundless mire of the salt marshes—

They waited till daylight came. Craig had made a great deal of sense. He lay shivering under the lead truck, wrapped in a tarp. He shivered and could not sleep because he was torturing himself very much as he had done on the floor of the washroom. There was no way of deciding anything ahead of time.

How plausible were the facts which he had offered for his possible explanations?

17: The Bishop May Move in a Diagonal Line (from a Book on Chess)

The final plan was entirely Bergman's invention and it was not bad. The strategy relied rather heavily on the fact that the S.I.G. men were in German uniforms and that the convoy looked like a load of British prisoners. The plan also involved a shift in personnel. Bergman would be in the lead truck but Bruckner—Harker decided that—was not its driver. The Bishop got the rear spot again but the driver was not Ben Manta—Harker's decision again—but Mohnfeld. Ben Manta was in the gun crew compartment with two other S.I.G. men. In that way there were no British uniforms on the gun and Ben Manta was not left alone there.

The light came to the top of a gentle rise shortly after five o'clock in the morning. Craig was up there. He lay under his sand cape and could hardly be seen. He watched the light grow in the mine field below him and waited about ten minutes more. Then he raised his hand. One after the other, as planned, the motors started up and turned over. Some of them idled well. Some had to be gunned to get the night cold out of their metal. Nothing would start to roll until Craig was done. And if he could not do it, there would be hell to pay—

Now the light was high enough to take the gloom off the slanting flat and it was still low enough to throw sharp, long shadows. Craig could see the tandem arrangement well enough.

He blew on his hands. They were sand dry and cold on the outside and clammy wet in the palms. He put his hands on the rifle again and leaned to his sights.

"I love you, baby," he whispered. "I'm going to squeeze you, baby, and you just answer right back. Don't kick me too hard, baby, because I'm on your side. Give it to the other side, baby. Find 'em and give 'em love like they've never known until their cup runneth over, sky-high that is, baby. Are you with me?"

Baby was with him. She reached out and kissed the mine where she lay shy under her pillow and there was a big lick of flame. The flame and sand and iron scraps banged sky-high with an angry temper and then five more blew in hasty succession. That was the first tandem.

Craig was not sweating anymore but he was hot. He reached for the next tandem and missed. He squeezed again and baby made the death geyser gush up again and then, one after the other, all its little brethren. He did this twice more and watched the tandems void themselves with nothing more serious than a bang.

It was the bang, of course, which everybody was interested in.

Boyden joined Craig with the glasses. They watched the cool skyline to the north and saw nothing. To their right, sloping down, lay the churned ground of the mine field which had died there. To their left and below was the draw which would lead the convoy into the drifts and the dunes.

"You think they could possibly be somewhere else?"

"Give them time, Boyden."

"Of course."

Boyden was so tense that he kept licking his dry lower lip but did not notice the spittle running out of the side of his mouth.

"By God—you see it? They must have their headlights—"

"Settle down, Boyden. You know better than that."

Of course Boyden knew better than that. It was the wish to see something that had made him stupid. There were no headlights, but when the sun comes up from very low to one side of the desert it will sometimes leap its light very rapidly across successive hillocks. The flanks of dunes then jump from dark to light. He saw that and there was nothing else.

"But I can hear them!"

"Yes," said Craig.

As if the leaping light came with a low thunder now. "They must have cleared a barrier between us. Can you make a guess— Hah!" said Boyden and punched himself in the nose with an eye piece out of sheer excitement.

And then Craig saw it too.

"Thar she blows," he said with slow satisfaction.

They saw no vehicles but they could see the dust rise like a lazy spray and then like standing billows which kept bulging along in a steady direction. This was the undulant back of an animal rolling slowly above the wave line of a sea.

"Ten thousand yards, wouldn't you say?"

"Can't tell in this light," said Craig. "But I want their direction."

They waited until it came clear. Whatever threw up that billow was going left to right, which was from the west to the east, and it clearly meandered in a southerly direction.

"Predictable like a dung beetle," said Craig. "Right up the drain."

"Capital! Shall we go?"

They went. They jumped and caromed down the rise and away from the mine field. Their convoy, like something that woke up very slowly, started to roll ahead. They jumped on the back of their vehicle and hid the rifle away. Very soon they went faster.

Craig got to the front of the truck bed where Harker was sitting.

"About eight thousand yards north," said Craig, "well to the other side of the rise."

Harker bent down to the right window of the cab and told Bergman.

"I hope they stay there for a while," said Bergman.

"If that rise doesn't break," said Craig, "we'll make it to the dunes before they see us."

Bergman also knew this. It would be the best place to make a stand. The Germans would turn around and then there would have to be the stand—

There could not be a rout, a dispersal or even a punishing victory. In any such action there was always at least one man who got away to carry the tale. A very strange tale in this case, a bizarre story about a British 8th Afrika Korps— Therefore, that last man would have to be dead too.

The drifts started while the trucks were still making good time. Bergman opened the door on his side and stepped out on the running board. Because of the punishing speed there was an unusual amount of thick dust. When Bergman looked back he could not see too well. As a matter of fact, he could not see the Bishop at all—

He got back into the cab and looked front. Bergman felt nothing for the country he saw. The sun meant heat and the ground meant a footing of sorts. And the rises could be useful for a better view or they were a thing behind which to hide. The hills where he had been born— That had been something different. But he allowed no feeling for that anymore either. And the land which he wanted, for which he would do great, unfeeling things, he had never seen it—

Every *Saukerl* in my outfit is a Moses, he thought. Except Ben Manta. He was born there. Bergman did not want to think this way any longer but he did not know how to stop. But then his view through the dusty windshield showed him how.

The dunes were not far but reached down to make a bowl like an amphitheater, and when the truck entered there Bergman saw the break on his right. The rise to the right stopped abruptly and the open draw which led to the slant of the flats still showed the dust standing high in the air—

"*Gun it!*" he yelled at his driver. "Got to get out of this parking lot!"

Somebody was pounding on the roof of the cab, just in case Bergman had not noticed that they seemed to be within yards of the Germans.

"Gun it!"

"I'm spinning—"

If he knew the signs of the ground the way Craig could see them—

"Try for the dip between the two big ones on the left," he yelled and pushed open his door. "Go on!" And then, holding his machine pistol high, he jumped off the running board.

"… too fast!" he could hear Craig's voice as the truck bounced by, but the advice, which was soon self-explanatory, had come too late.

While the vehicles churned by and slid out of line, Bergman dog-trotted back to the break in the rise where he had seen the dust. Harker would stage-set the rest. Kurt Bergman had one job only now, and that was to become just about the most alert Afrika Korps Kapitän in this part of the Sahara—

There was another Afrika Korps Kapitän who was convinced, *ohne Zweifel*, that he was the trickiest thing on two tracks.

"*Zurück!*" he yelled. "*Stafleln!*" and he swung his arms at the other four half-tracks so that they should know how he meant them to stagger out in a perimeter so they would control the break in the rise.

First, of course, they had to turn around and go back.

There was an unusual amount of sand churned up into the air on the other side. A monster column?

Bergman cursed through his teeth because he had left his sand goggles on the seat of the cab. He felt sand gritting between his teeth and when he tried to swallow he gagged. It did not even feel like glue back there, but like cement. The tears in his eyes felt like boiling water.

Then he could see again. Five half-tracks. That's all? But five half-tracks drawn up in a staggered formation and ready to fight.

But it is to be hoped that they can see as little as I can of what is going on behind me near the slope of those dunes. And it is devoutly to be hoped that they can see well enough not to mistake me for an abominable sandman—

"*Donnerwetter!*" said the young captain. "Afrika Korps?"

The figure in the bowl of dust on the other side of the break had stopped and the silhouette was unmistakable.

"I'm going to meet him. Cover me," said the young captain.

When Bergman saw him clearly, he was almost too close for caution and it would have to be a grandstand play.

"*Halt!*" he yelled.

The other one, armed only with a Luger, saw the machine pistol come up.

"*Wer sind Sie?*" yelled Bergman.

He sounds like a Rhinelander, thought the young captain.

"*Brandenburger Abteilung, Kapitän Liederlein hier!*"

Crack outfit, thought Bergman. They sent the best— Then he laughed uproariously to make the next part good. Liederlein's intonation had been unmistakable.

"*Brandenburg?*" he called and laughed again. "*Aber kein Saupreiss, du da!*" and with that key word of dislike for the Prussians of the north, the Rhinelander who was S.I.G. and the Bavarian who was Afrika Korps had become brothers.

Harker, who sat stock-still and ostensibly weaponless in the lead truck which had slewed around to end up third in line, could not believe his eyes. Those two Krauts were actually hugging each other!

Then they pounded each other's backs and talked in the middle of the desert as if they were meeting in the local *Gasthaus*. Peasant pride thickened their dialect until the Rhinelander and the Bavarian could hardly understand each other. But that was not important. It was tantamount that there should be no problems more serious than the difference between the Bavarian glottals and the sweet diminutives of the Rhinelander's language.

"But did you get lost here, or is it a mission?"

"Lost," said Bergman. "Looking for Scheherazade we got lost."

"We haven't found that one either. But we—"

Until then Liederlein had not been able to see the vehicles in the dust bowl too clearly. It had not been important. He had met a friend. But now he interrupted and stared.

"*Kinder—*" he said. "*Engländer!*" and instantly the war was back.

"*Freilich,*" said Bergman and grinned. The slap-dash and devil-may-care act put a strain on him. "We ran into them at a mine field. We heard the Teller go off ..."

"So did we! We just put them there!"

"... and caught them flying all over the place. The ones that came down in one piece we took along."

"*Kruzi,*" said Liederlein who could hardly believe it even though he was seeing it. He glanced back at the cut and was gratified that all his half-tracks were looking at all the British.

The next problem was, who would get the prisoners and all those lovely, striped trucks.

"You have far to go, Kurt?"

"No. Just to Jalu."

"I was going to take them to Awjilha. We've got gasoline there, so we can go straight on and deliver them at the Sidra Gulf."

"Too far," said Bergman. "You're angling northwest and I'm taking the short, straight run due north."

"Tobruk?"

"Sure," said Bergman, because soon it would not matter.

"I don't approve," said Liederlein. "I'm going much farther behind the lines with them."

"Liederlein," said Bergman and put his arm around the young captain, "would you approve if I split them with you?"

They grinned at each other without saying another word and then Bergman turned Kapitän again and yelled at his drivers.

As a result, his six vehicles began to churn and move into a new line of distribution. It was the first time that Bergman realized that the Bishop was not there.

Harker, who felt as gritty as the sand under his shirt, had been disturbed by the absence for much longer. He would have been less concerned if Ben Manta had not been on the gun. And Harker was turning paranoid for all practical purposes while he had to sit still and watch Bergman make friends with that young killer-corps German.

The command to move the vehicles had been the last straw. Their position for combat purposes had been deplorable enough but now Bergman was splitting them up!

"Craig, when I give the command ..."

"You *must* trust him!" Craig hissed.

"He's cutting off our line of fire on those halfs!"

"*And* they can't see *us* either!"

"Let me through— Boyden—"

Craig did the only thing he could think of. He put his arm around Harker, somewhat the way Bergman had done it to Liederlein. But then he pressed. When Harker said "Boyden" the sound was all choked.

The way they were sitting the two men were literally eyeball to eyeball. When the truck bumped and lurched, their stubbles ground into each other's cheeks. They breathed each other's sweat and they felt each other's muscles shift and strain into each other.

Boyden glared with indecision. It somehow made him look as if he had just waked up.

"Hold it," said Craig. "Or I'll break his back, Boyden."

"He was right—"

"He'll be dead right. Harker? Listen to me."

Harker, who could hardly breathe, got his teeth into Craig's jaw.

If I scream, thought Craig, I'll blow it. If I blow it, I'll die. Better kill him, and quietly—

But he did not know some of the tricks which Bergman had learned. He knew how to hurt, but he did not know how to silence.

But then something worked, something ugly he had seen in a film, a finger pressing up and into the socket of the eye— Harker let go with his teeth.

It changed the distribution of strain in their weird, silent embrace, but it did not change Harker's will. Craig could feel that through the intimacy of their bodies. Before Harker's muscles would turn soft and passive the man meant to die in the completion of some kind of duty. The first duty, the muscles said, was to kill Craig—

The deployment of vehicles was complete, Kapitän Liederlein noted, and the booty had now been divided in half.

Bergman considered the maneuver completed when all the trucks were out of sight of the German guns. And once the half-tracks advanced through the cut, they would pass through a concentrated line of cross fire.

"He *did* it!" Craig hissed into the ear next to him. "You see it now?"

Harker felt a warm spray of spit in his ear. He hated spit.

"*Also*," said Liederlein, "*sagen wir mal Grüss Gott?*"

"Yes," said Bergman. "Good luck and good-bye. Bring your half-tracks in now."

Liederlein turned to give the command which would finish the business and which would also finish him. At that moment he heard the loud bark.

"*Himmels Willen!*" he said. "What was that?"

That, Bergman considered, was a fart straight out of hell and delivered by the Bishop. He grabbed for Liederlein's arm and held on.

"Don't run," he said. "It's ours."

"*Ours?*"

"I forgot to mention it. They had that gun along at the mine field."

They watched it throw up pretty veils of dust, the massive body rearing and nodding, making foundry sounds.

Liederlein thought it was an entirely wrong note that Bergman had not mentioned the gun before. Underhanded, in fact. There had furthermore been no mention of it in the Intelligence signal from Cairo.

"They brought *that* from Kufra?" asked Liederlein.

"Well, it keeps following them—" and goddamn that Kabir, thought Bergman, for handing in an incomplete Intelligence report and the creeping crud on Harker for wanting his mascot along—

Harker's steel of resolve almost turned to mush when he saw the Bishop move up. The entire column was now under its muzzle.

Craig felt the mush come into Harker's muscles and thought that Harker had given up. He did not know what Harker had given up and he did not know that the man had jumped from one kind of sense to another. What now made sense to Harker could be easily misunderstood. Therefore Harker decided to leave it that way. He stayed where he was when Craig let go and he nodded his head when Craig grunted something about being sorry.

"Tell it to stop," Liederlein said to Bergman.

"Tell your men to advance," said Bergman.

Then he raised his hand at the Bishop to reestablish good faith with Liederlein. The Bishop would not stop.

It made a confusion of sounds and Liederlein made confusion of decisions: Advance his men to take his booty, hold his men while the prisoners filed off the trucks, let Bergman have the vehicles and just take the big gun— Something stank here!

The Bishop had veered off on a diagonal course and was now out of sight behind a high dune!

"Is your driver mad?"

"No. The Bishop."

"Order it back!"

"I don't even see it! But get your vehicles in here—"

"*Himmel!* It's back!"

Like a rogue elephant the big gun was snouting its way along an unpredictable path. It was indeed back but there was no telling why, where or what for. It came down an incline which anything that heavy would have avoided like quicksand and then came sliding like a kid toward the bottom of the bowl. Just as unpredictably, it stopped. It was now above the line of the trucks Bergman had deployed and right in the middle of the two flanks he had formed.

The muzzle now took a blind bead on the other side the bowl where the cut showed the Germans.

"Does it go off the same way it drives?" asked Liederlein.

"You better move your halfs," said Bergman.

Liederlein walked very slowly back to the draw. He took the time to look very carefully up at the Bishop and at all the men in the machine.

There were two *Gefreite* in the back. Common soldiers, which was to be expected. Also an *Oberleutnant*. Pretty high for such a limited command. And the driver? *Kruzi!* That driver was an officer too!

Liederlein had a very quick brain. He stopped all alone in the middle of the bowl and looked around as if he had a great deal of time. He took enough time to estimate the German troop strength at no more than twenty men. This small number was big enough anytime to herd five trucks of prisoners. It was most emphatically not big enough to warrant a command of one second lieutenant, one first lieutenant, and on top of that a captain too—

If he had known they were S.I.D. or a crazy outfit like the Desert Group he would not have wondered. They tended to give rank not in terms of troop strength under command but as often as not according to the man's capability.

"*Herr Oberleutnant!*" he called up to Ben Manta. "*Bringen Sie Ihre Mannschaft hier!*"

It took nerve and it worked. He disarmed the Bishop by calling the crew to come down.

Harker knew, of course, that this would happen. He turned, as everyone else was doing, to watch what would happen next. Only Harker knew what came next because only he understood the iron necessity. His submachine gun cut loose with an intended bead on no one but Ben Manta.

Aside from the fact that he missed, he also prevented anyone from getting back on the gun. Which is how the half-tracks got away.

The pandemonium which followed did not include any further firing. Vehicles wheeled to give chase and the only effective kill of the moment transpired silently, with a knife.

"*Bis bald*," said Bergman, and let the young captain slide to the ground.

Harker was instantly back in command. Craig was baffled, but had no time to arrive at a superior understanding. Harker's commands made sense—in sharp contrast to his previous behavior. When Craig yelled at him to attempt a direction to the salt marsh he picked that up instantly. He also ordered the Bishop abandoned and let the Ben Manta matter rest for the moment. The spy's effectiveness as a spy would for the present be nil.

Harker's trucks were much faster than the half-tracks on the hard, pebbly flats; but the enemy was well dispersed and with a constant will sought out the softer ground. Their attempt to delay an encounter till their terrain was more favorable was not only obvious but it started to work.

"They're making the draw," said Craig.

"We got the mobility and we got all day," said Boyden with the hopefulness of one day out of Sandhurst.

Harker knew that it was true. With the salt marsh ahead of the enemy there would eventually be no live Germans left. But he also knew that he did not have all day. The Tobruk infiltration was governed by a land-sea-air timetable which allowed for only minimal leeway—

Boyden watched the enemy's cavalry tactics. They knew their Clausewitz and the maneuver they were attempting had been adapted from Genghis Khan—

"Sainted Heart!" somebody yelled over the roar and through the slip streams of sand. "Who's driving that Bishop?"

Bergman saw Mohnfeld in his truck and Harker saw Ben Manta in the one next to his own. And Ben Manta looked at his two privates and knew that the Bishop was empty.

The rogue was roaring its way across an impossible course.

"I'm going to rewrite the book," Boyden whispered to Craig. "You know what the French call that terrain over there?"

"*Terrain chaotique*," said Craig. "It'll splinter your spine and snap your head off at that speed."

When the Germans churned into the draw, Harker's group commanded the mouth but hesitated to enter for fear of getting swallowed up. The Germans on the inside could climb toward the lip on each side and command the inlet, or they could crest and double back for an enveloping maneuver. Genghis Khan would have loved them for it—

"Boyden, take those two and circle to the left! Bergman— Never mind that for the moment," said Harker and watched the Bishop's erratic approach from the right. The monster was making warfare a disruptive joke. "Except for the Bren teams, everybody out!"

They left the trucks and spread out like ants. They lugged Stens and mortars and brought their flamethrowers along. Harker felt active and fresh and saw everything. The scatter pattern was running well. And Ben Manta was running like a traitor— Later about that. What else to expect from a Nazi in disguise—

Harker could no longer see the Bishop because he had moved his men close to the draw. No matter about that rogue. Couldn't count on it.

After some excellent penetration into the draw, Harker suddenly learned that he had also not counted on anything suicidal in the Germans. They were expected to climb on the inside or they were expected to crest and double back. Instead, within three thousand yards, Harker's effective mortar range, the five half-tracks became erratic. Some wheeled up a slope which they could not possibly make and some simply turned back toward Harker's fire. They maintained no effective firing formation of their own nor did they seem to be seeking one. Gears and tracks screamed as if haunted.

What haunted them bulged up and dipped over an impossible rise. "Sainted Heart—"

And Boyden had another quick thought about rewriting the book, until the black hulk of the Bishop hit the down grade in a way which did not permit further thought.

At one thousand yards the 25-pounder lurched its big eye straight at Harker's troops while its motorized direction cut diagonally down into the draw.

Not much mass damage the way we are scattered, thought Craig, though whoever gets hit by that shell is no more. And that might just be me— Craig was not the only one with that thought.

Harker sensed the disorganization instantly and so, apparently, ran the guess of the enemy. The half-tracks grouped and slowed down to let the Bishop precede them— Then the machine's gears made the unmistakable sound of having crashed into each other and broken their teeth. Stripped, fused and mangled beyond hope of motion, the heavy gun slewed to a tilting stop. Bruckner's repair also had gone completely to pieces. There was a lot of black smoke.

There was a hole of silence now, but not long enough to take a deep breath. Not even the slow and inexplicable swing of the fat barrel interrupted the illusion of calm. Until it roared and spat.

One half-track disintegrated entirely and another one was suddenly missing its nose.

"Holy Bishop—" said somebody and then Harker yelled for the trucks to charge.

The 25-pounder delivered one more shell which dug a hole for one of the half-tracks. The burst did minimal damage to materiel but it tore the heads off the crew.

The rest was machine-gun engagement and after that came five minutes of hand-to-hand. Harker lost six of his men and Bergman lost five. It was an uneven, though predictable and no one complained about it. All the Germans were dead.

Harker counted his own and collected the British tags. He folded them slowly into his handkerchief, his face quiet and showing regard. He did the same thing, in the same way, when he took the German tag off Ben Manta who hung out of the Bishop with a German slug in his chest.

18: Terrain Chaotique

Cheryl Portman folded her things away and had a new regard for their meaning. This suit smelled of goat and this gown looked gala. She did not need either of those anymore. She folded them up and then threw them away. She looked at the minaret from her window, not from her father's window, and let the sunlit view come to her. At night, she considered, the minaret stands out white before a dark sky. The sky at night is possessively deep but it does not absorb the minaret, which remains as its own. And in the day the minaret stands out stark and white before a shrill sky. The sky in the daytime is aggressive and bites with heat but it cannot diminish the minaret, which stands inviolate.

I am not a minaret, she thought, and I do not look like a minaret. But I am as strong in my sameness no matter what changes behind me. And, of course, there is nothing in front of me. Seen from the other side, that is behind me too. Therefore, I am safe in my sameness while things around me might even change. She smiled and felt very calm. Nothing tugged at her. The last terror in the tent, some pain before that, some vain effort and also the boredom, or the satedness and the pleasure she had felt during the fast microcosm of her short, recent life—none of those happenings were effective memories now. Nothing tugged at her.

Since most of the clothes in her bags reminded her of some place or other, she threw most of them away. She kept a few which reminded her of nothing, even though the choices were made without real thought. Her need to think was marginal. It concerned itself with a hole in the sky. Directly behind that minaret—she moved her head back and forth, viewing it—if directly behind and out of view there were a hole, only then could the minaret possibly fall away. Nonsense, of course. In this concrete way she deftly manipulated the fact of a hole in her memory. It was nonsense to assume that there was anything behind what she saw.

Her father came in with an Arab porter and smiled at hopefully.

"You are ready?"

"Ready," she said. "Just these two bags."

"What about all that?"

"Just these two bags."

"I see. All right. I'll be in the lobby."

The Heinkel had arrived for Portman and no new effort had been made to separate him from his daughter. They worried about his reaction.

Portman knew this and was gratified with his effect. They knew this and would decide about the girl later. Portman even had a notion about that. Therefore, the Arab who had come to fetch Cheryl's bags was getting paid vastly more than a porter. The name of his clandestine though very professional guild was the source of the word "assassin." He was also a habitué of the coffeehouses which meant that he knew about Cheryl in detail.

He closed the door and saw that it was true. She had a face for calm rest, a body for frantic excitement. And she never looked away. Before taking the bags he commenced to take her.

She looked down at herself for a moment and at his hands and then she stepped back just enough to hit him severely. The clout to the side of the face loosened a bad tooth he was nursing there. The assassin squeezed a pain tear out of one eye and picked up the bags. In accordance with the oath of his guild, he did not lay another finger on his charge.

The oasis of Jalu is a dry-looking clutter of a few flat stone houses. There are no trees and the water hole is only a hole. All this sits on the bottom of a wide, blank depression which has the geometric barrenness of a strip mine. To find Jalu means that one is there. Before that, Jalu is invisible. It takes the nose of a camel, the memory of a Tuareg or the mechanics of an azimuth reading to get near it at all, that is to say, when hunting for it from the south.

To the north of Jalu there is a manner of road. It is no longer *terrain chaotique* but it is not very visible either. It is more visible from the air than from the eye-and-brain jarring level of a five-ton truck. Nevertheless, having overshot the oasis which was always below the horizon, Craig reoriented when the lead truck came to the road.

After the checkmate affair with the Bishop, every analogy to a game had disappeared. They tried to make up for lost time by taking to the hard bed of a wadi. The speed was good but there was no exit. Even a berserk Valentine chassis *without* the 25-pounder on top could not have scaled those escarpments. The cul-de-sac forced them to progress by going away from Tobruk. This knowledge jarred their backbones as much as the banging they got from the trucks. When they found a possible exit from the bottom to the top, the sky was still blue over the lip of the wadi. But they could already hear the hiss and the sharp whispering sound of the gibleh.

They stayed in the wadi until the sand storm blew by. It traveled like buckshot overhead and it came down like a blizzard. It was a short blow of fifteen minutes. Digging out took another three hours and once back on the desert floor with the rocks, the most absorbing activity was to get rid of the sand under the clothes. Craig had a belt of raw skin where the top of his trousers hugged his waist. Boyden was convinced that he had a petrified forest inside his nose. Bruckner's pedal foot was swollen and his black hair was gray, and everyone on the backs of the trucks shook his clothes out and put them back on with the other man's dirt.

The delay caused them to run critically short of water. A motor idling in a wadi can lose more in steam than the same truck howling away at a breakneck speed of forty miles, hour after hour.

They gave up most of their drinking water. Had they passed Girabub they would have defied its reputation and would have drunk their fill and to hell with the aftermath; even though the waters of Girabub were as predictable as Epsom salts.

When Craig turned the column back toward Jalu it was early dusk. It was cooler and the night's rest was near. They felt almost gay. Bruckner slowed the column. He could suddenly afford to worry about all those hot motors. But then Craig stopped the column altogether. Had the speed not been slow, he would never have seen it—

Bruckner's sand-dry curses got him no more than, "I don't know why. I got to check it first." Then Craig got out of the cab.

He had spotted the signs no more than ten yards ahead and even that distance would not have been enough if the sun had not been low enough to exaggerate the small shadows.

"Don't tell me!" yelled Boyden from the truck. "Don't tell me at this goddamn hour of five o'clock in the afternoon and after working hours, goddamn you all to hell, that every one of those frigging stonsies and rocksies is a goddamn booby trap!" Boyden was running short of the military manner.

"Boyden," said Harker.

"Yeah."

"Watch your form."

"Sorry. Frightfully sorry, suh."

"All right. Go up there and ask him if he thinks that everyone of those goddamn— Go up there and ask him why we are standing still, Boyden."

He was a lithe young man with a lot of endurance but he walked the ten yards like a crab on stilts. He stopped and hung on to Craig's shoulder.

"Please don't move," he said. "Or I'll fall over."

"Right."

"Also, Colonel Harker would like to know—in fact, we would all like to know ..."

"I could hear you before."

"I see. Very well. You moved, Craig. I specifically asked you ..."

"Sorry."

"I notice you are sweating, Craig. Have you been hoarding water?"

"No. I've been drinking hot motor oil."

"I say, Craig. You make me quite ill—"

"There we go," said Craig.

He could feel the shaking in Boyden's long-cramped legs all the way up in the hand which was hanging on to his shoulder. He helped the lieutenant to sit down on the ground.

"You look like hell, Boyden."

"A species of car sickness—in a manner of speaking."

"*Well?*" Harker bellowed from the truck.

"Bend your head down." Craig pushed Boyden over. "Between the legs."

"I haven't fainted."

"You will."

"Are you," bellowed Harker, "testing out every goddamn booby trap in the most primitive manner possible?"

"Lieutenant Boyden is inspecting the treads, sir!"

Harker looked at the man next to him.

"Did he say heads?"

"I think he said wrecks, sir."

Boyden was having the dry heaves, which tortured his stomach. After a moment he was very much weaker and that stopped the spasms.

"Here comes the C.O.," said Craig. "I'm going to tell him you're sick."

"He'll bump me!" said Boyden.

He'll bump me and I won't get bumped. Won't have it. The very thought—Pater will turn over in his retirement—and Elizabeth, damn it, *Isabel*—

He almost burst out in tears when he realized that he had misnamed his fiancée. The rapid succession of humiliations took the bone out of him—

And this is the worst I can take, a cross-country ride in the sun, a bivouac in the sand, a sleep with my boots on, to die with my boots on while throwing up, and nothing but a little foam on the ground—

"Is he sick?" he heard Harker's voice.

It was a dream voice in a very anxious dream and the only one who was not anxious in it was Harker, he of the stiff upper lip which reached from his head to his toes, which was the veneer to hide the real Harker—voice like a bull whip, temper like a self-propelled gun on the loose—

"Of course not," Craig was saying. "Step over here, won't you, Colonel?"

"This way—er, of course, Major."

Boyden could not hear what they were saying but in a while he could see them against the light. He could see more than a sick heaving of brown light and brown shadow again, and he saw Harker and Craig, backs turned, looking along the ground.

You can stop spinning, Pater, he said to himself. Damn it all, Pater, the most precious thing has come back to me! By God, Pater, I've actually got spit in my mouth!

When they came back his way, Boyden was up on his feet, breathing deeply. He was weaving a little but he did not know it.

"Well," said Harker, "I think I agree with you, Boyden."

"Or did you change your mind?" asked Craig. "Those tracks are airplane tires, right?"

"Right," said Harker before Boyden could answer. "Lieutenant?"

"Suh."

"A detail of two men in each direction. I want impact area and length of run. Never mind about the take-off. It would have been into the wind. And Boyden."

"Suh."

"Just send the men. I want you in charge of the column."

While Boyden walked back to the trucks, he saw in his mind that his father was no longer spinning and that Colonel Harker's stiff upper lip did not cover all of him. And one striking difference, he thought. Pater is always the same, constant gloom of stone, like those carved things he had brought back from Malaya, which now sat forever in the garden. But Harker, so help me, he can change from a parade-ground fixture in Kufra, a psychotic schemer under stress, a solid pivot in a fight, to this. Like a human being—

19: Where the Men Wear Veils but the Women Do Not

Before they knew what they would find, they arranged themselves in defensive positions while the armed half-track searched a wider perimeter. They seemed to be alone in the desert.

They did not go into Jalu. The view on the oasis was barren and the very few usable houses could not contain much of a threat. While all this safety of empty space was checked out they also checked out the tracks of the plane.

Tire size and lack of treads ruled out a ground vehicle. Tire size also ruled out a fighter, while length of ground path suggested a heavy plane.

"Short-range fueling stop is out, cargo is out, bomber is quite out of the question. No signs of an emergency landing. Whatever that was, it just came and went."

Concise report, thought Harker. Boyden's in good shape again.

And if I weren't cracking for want of water, thought Craig, and if I weren't hollow with hunger and in a hot sweat over getting lickety spit to Tobruk for some reason, why then I could sit around the camp fire in that emerald oasis all night and spin fine possibles about the plane that ought not to have been but which came and went.

He compressed all that as best he could and said as mildly as he could, "It's getting dark, Colonel Harker."

"Yes, so it is." Harker got up from the running board. "We'll head down and make camp. Getting late."

They heard the call from one of the men posted in the perimeter. They looked his way but he was down flat and invisible. But they could see why he had been alarmed.

The rider sat tall on his horse, on a ridge, with the deep sky behind him. His robe billowed now and then. The silhouette showed no weapon. In a moment he came down the incline, letting the horse feel its own way. The low light from the west was full on him. It seemed to blacken his robe and it glistened on the thick bulge of his forehead.

"But we *searched* this area!" said Harker.

"When you can find a Tuareg in the desert, you can find anything. Ancient Montreal proverb," said Craig.

"Tuareg?"

"Black robe, black face cloth. Among Tuaregs the men wear the veils and the women don't."

"Question him," said Harker. "You do speak whatever they speak, don't you?"

"I think he wants to question *us.*"

"Just a minute now," said Bergman. "He is looking at a German column and he's going to meet a British emissary?"

Harker closed his eyes for a moment and just waved his hand.

"Of course," he said. "I am tired—"

It struck Boyden that the oldest man in the unit was still twenty years younger than the C.O.

"If you will sit in the cab, sir, I will reform the column."

Harker nodded and climbed into the cab. Then he just sat there. He did not even turn to watch Craig and Bergman walk away.

They stopped where their man was posted and told him to move to the back. Now the Tuareg stopped too. He got off the horse with a fine swirl of the robe and then they could see his weapon. It was a bolt-action rifle and there was nothing ornamental about it. He laid it down on the ground.

"He wants you to put your chopper down, Bergman."

"I know. And on the other side of the ridge is a fast mobile unit, marked the same way as ours, but for real. I've seen them do it before."

"I'm glad you're not Manta. Put the chopper down."

"Listen, Craig—"

"And on the other side of the hill he has maybe twenty riders, that's all. If there had been anything motorized we would have found it."

But Bergman did not move. Every so often the Tuareg flicked a highlight of sweat at them from his dark skin over the veil. Bergman touched his lower lip with his tongue. Shark-skin scraping rock, he thought.

"Tell the bastard you're my prisoner and if he doesn't speak up he'll be next. Come on, Craig. I'm nervous."

Craig was nervous too. He had, for a fact, never seen a solitary Tuareg before. However, he had seen as few as ten of them wheeling all around on their horses. They had harassed his column of three armed vehicles into a drift and, after killing two of his men, they had made off with a dozen ammo boxes. They had left six dead Tuaregs behind and had only stopped, beyond range, to call to the riderless horses. When the horses were following, the Tuaregs had galloped away.

Bergman did not understand a word when Craig and the Tuareg were conversing. It sounded entirely like a lot of coughing and squealing.

"Well?"

"He says he's alone."

"*Quatsch.*"

"That's what I told him. So he said that I wasn't alone either."

"You call that a conference?"

"No. It's Tuareg, and unusually short, for that matter. He came right to the point."

"Goddamn it, Craig, enough of the dramatic *pauses*."

"It relaxes me after a hard day against the grain. And besides ..."

"*Will* you ..."

Craig pulled his arm out of Bergman's grip.

"Shut up a minute, will you? I'm trying to tell you. Our talk has to sound long and complicated to him or he'll think I left most of it out."

"All right. What is it he doesn't want you to leave out?"

"His point," said Craig. "He wants to make a trade for weapons. Fifty rifles with two hundred rounds each."

"Right through the head," said Bergman without moving s teeth. And then his machine pistol came up.

Craig, given a weapon, might well have done the same thing. Like a giant sleight of hand there appeared a long string of mounted Tuaregs over the skyline of the ridge. The heads moved slowly and did not make a very good target.

"Put—that—thing away!" said Craig, sounding a lot like Bergman himself.

"I'm going to cover their leader and if they move an inch, tell 'em I'll cut ..."

"Kurt Bergman," said Craig with emphasis, "*they don't care!*"

"They don't care," repeated Bergman and sounded very tired. "I know. They'll just send another one down. Then what?"

"We'll get off-geschleppt to the harem. Now *steady on*. This is Harker's play."

"Don't talk to me about that son of a bitch ..."

"He's there, in a pinch."

"I'm not reassured. Just resigned."

Bergman was no sooner done when the quads cut loose on the half-track five hundred yards to the rear. The guns made a frightening racket and they splattered an impressive claw-mark of flying stone, crud, dirt and dust just below the line of the ridge.

"They understood us," said Craig.

The ridge line was barren of heads.

After that argument the Tuareg picked up the thread again. His voice rattled and whined up and down interminably. Bergman got the kind of shiver which he always had when someone squeaked a fork on a plate. Then it was over.

"He said something or other?" asked Bergman.

"He'll take twenty rifles and one hundred bullets each."

"Let's cut that down with another argument like before."

"No. This time they'll kill the prisoners."

"Of course. The prisoners," said Bergman. "How could I forget about this mysterious bargaining point which you failed to mention. Am I talking too much?"

"He thinks you're charming. Two Germans were dropped off in that plane for some kind of pickup tomorrow. The plane took off, the Tuaregs killed five uniformed escorts and the assassin ..."

"The what?"

"How in hell do I know? And held the very important Germans as prisoners, in order to barter them off once the pickup party came along tomorrow."

"And we are tomorrow's pickup party."

"Right."

"Let's go."

"Wait."

There was more irritating sound of bargaining, name-calling, love-making, door-banging and hinge-squeaking as far Bergman was concerned, but then it was finally settled in mutual friendship and enduring suspicion.

The transaction took place in front of a stone house with one door and no windows which faced the Jalu water hole and the open ground beyond. Harker's men ringed the oasis depression to one side and the Tuaregs had lined up at the other side. When two of the Tuaregs had put the prisoners into the stone house, they were allowed to take their payment from the truck which Craig and Bergman had brought. They slung rifle boxes and ammo tins on their extra horses and rode away. Bergman was inside the stone hut taking the rawhide thongs off his prizes. Then he stepped out into the open and talked to Craig.

"You're out of your mind!" said Craig.

"No. They are *not* German. Signal the column down and explain that we have to keep up the act."

Craig blinked after Bergman who was going back into the hut.

"Did you say one of them is a girl?"

There was no answer from Bergman and Craig started to yell up at the ridge.

"All right! And one of them is—" He stopped and shook his head violently.

"I see Scheherazade," he mumbled. "I'm going nuts. I don't need sex. I need peace and quiet—"

Though he had not finished his ill-advised sentence, he thought that the column came snaking down especially fast.

Bergman unwrapped the cloaks that were covering them. In one of them was an old man, dressed but wrinkled, who seemed to be suffering from exhaustion. He unwrapped the other one and found that she was naked. The Tuaregs had taken away her clothes. She sat up and said, no, that was all they had taken.

"There's nothing else to take anymore, don't you understand?"

"No."

"So I wasn't even there when they had sex."

She looked at Bergman so directly that he got confused. "They kept their veils on, you know?" she said.

"I didn't," he said.

"And I didn't," she said. "Anyway. I would like to wash."

Bergman nodded and went out through the door.

I can give her water, he thought. I don't know how many other things she really needs—

20: An Oasis away from the Oasis

The worst place to hide was Jalu. They rested one hour and took on water and then they left again. They went one quarter mile back into the *terrain chaotique* and camouflaged near the walls of a broken caravansary. Except for two sepulchral chambers, the place was only open walls. There was also a Roman cistern which was as old as the death of Christ. Since that time the water level had wandered to the depression of Jalu and the old caravansary had not been used in years.

The stopover would cost them at least twelve hours, cutting their timetable to the quick. But an exhausted Englishman and his improbable daughter were expecting traveling companions. The sanest guess was that the visitors would arrive from Tobruk. They had to be Germans, because Mister Portman had made one significant statement to Bergman: He, Portman, was also a soldier in the service of the Third Reich. Nothing quite as coherent had been obtained from his daughter.

"Do you believe him?" Craig had asked.

"I believe," Bergman said, "that you can't believe a Nazi, and you certainly can't believe someone who isn't but says he's a Nazi."

"Which means, Talmudically speaking, that you don't know."

"Correct."

They had put it up to Harker, of course, who had decided they should not risk a night encounter with an unknown strength. The two captives and several S.I.G. were left at the caravansary with most of the camouflaged equipment. The rest watched the road to Tobruk and the single descent into Jalu. For the sake of realism and for the benefit of Portman's illusions all British uniforms were kept out of sight. As far as Colonel Harker was concerned, the very thought of a putative Englishman on the side of the Germans was revolting. As for the presence of the girl, that fact was clearly beyond reason.

Bergman and Mohnfeld sat in the dark on a rock and watched the uneven cracks of light which came past the blankets in front of the chamber entrances. When the medical officer came through one of the blankets, he nodded his head at them and then went into the other chamber.

"Go at her," said Bergman. "Maybe charm will open her up."

"After a dozen Tuaregs?"

Our warmest night so far, thought Bergman on his rock. And if I close my eyes and imagine the smell of leaf mold, the smell of the river, the smell of the hillsides giving the warmth of day back to the night, then I could imagine that I am still back— He interrupted himself with a fluent curse.

I want a hole in my memory, he counseled himself. A black hole of nothing, and I would sit here a happy man. The sudden scream was terrifying and the more unsettling because it came from a woman. When Bergman flung the blanket to one side and looked into the dusty lantern light of the chamber he saw Mohnfeld sitting on a box, looking baffled, and the girl, sitting straight up on a cot, both hands in her lap and the fingers knit hard into each other.

"What did you do to her?"

"I don't know," said Mohnfeld. "All I did was ask her why she, as a foreigner, was friendly to the Germans."

"I don't want him to ask me that," she said.

She now wore field gray coveralls which looked ludicrous on her kind of body. But none of that mattered. Bergman thought he had never seen such a harassed face before.

"Go easy on her," he said to Mohnfeld and dropped the blanket.

Maybe she, he thought, could use a hole in her memory too—

"Something wrong?"

Bruckner walked up from his post in the dark. Bergman thought that the man looked like a mother bear.

"Who's on your post?"

"Kuntze is second relief."

Bergman nodded.

"Go to sleep," he said.

"Is she all right?"

"Don't worry. Your friend Mohnfeld is with her."

"Why shouldn't I worry?" said Bruckner. He now looked like a mother bear trying not to worry.

The M.O. came through the curtain of the chamber where Portman was lying and hefted his medicine bag at the door. Then he left.

"All right," said Bergman to Bruckner. "Sit out here if you want." Then he went to see Portman.

The old man looked composed, if not recovered. In any event, he was controlled enough to give Bergman no satisfactory answers.

"I will speak to the commandant of the party assigned to my further transport," said Portman in his bookish German.

"When do you expect him?"

"I told you, Kapitän Bergman. It is Bergman, isn't it?"

"I told you that too. Can't you be more specific than 'between now and tomorrow morning'?"

"No. Why?"

"Because you're holding me up!" This was no lie and Bergman's anger was genuine. "Where are they coming from?"

"I'm not familiar with movements in the war zone."

A Talmudic scholar yet— Bergman got up and felt like kicking the kerosene lamp over.

"If you want them to get here in one piece, Mister Portman, if you don't want my men to shoot them up in the dark as an enemy movement, then you better tell me with more frankness than you've mustered so far where they are coming from, how they are traveling and how large a party it is."

This was the only information relevant to the movement. It was all Harker wanted to know and it was all Bergman was listening for.

"I was not in charge of the details for my safe ..."

"*All right!*" Bergman paced and then he tried once more. "We're packing up. I don't know who the hell you are and I'm on a scheduled mission. You're coming along to Tobruk."

"But I'm not going to Tobruk!"

"*Where to*, damn you? There *is* only Tobruk!"

"Dear Captain," said Portman with genuine weariness. "My mission is extremely secret and of tantamount importance. I am grateful that you rescued me, I am sorry to inconvenience you. But the answers you seek are for other ears, though I will see to it, Captain, I will most certainly make it my business that you and your men are rewarded in accordance with the value of the high mission on which I, through your, though accidental as it may be, assistance for—" Portman lost his way.

He cleared his throat for a moment, as if nothing had happened and then he said, "Incidentally, that scream before, was that my daughter?"

"Sorry. Classified." Bergman started to leave.

"Captain! I insist—"

"She's all right. We got jackals around here," and then he left in disgust.

Bruckner sat by the wall near the other door.

"Is he doing any better than I did?" said Bergman.

"I guess. Mohnfeld finished and left."

"Finished? What did they talk about? Where is he?"

"He went to sleep. They talked about, well, chit-chat. How hot it is in the summertime in Cairo."

"That's an interrogation? Never mind. Didn't mean you, Bruckner. You were here all the time?"

"Sure. Except when I took a leak over there."

"And how long, if you don't mind, does it take you to ..."

"Mohnfeld came out just when I started. He didn't see me so I kept right on and it must have taken me ..."

"Thank you, Bruckner. Maybe some other time—" and Bergman left.

He found Mohnfeld under the camouflage netting and the story was very much the same.

"I left early because there wasn't anything in that girl. She's off," said Mohnfeld.

"Nothing?"

"Just chit-chat, like the weather in Berlin. I thought it might lead up to something, but nothing."

"Berlin? What else?"

"I think just Berlin."

"Sounds to me as if you didn't try very hard to get anything out of her, Mohnfeld."

"That's true. I didn't feel there was any point to it in her case."

It sounded reasonable and Bergman left. He took a half-hour trip. He had a talk with Craig who was stationed on the rim of Jalu, and then he got permission from Harker, who was near the road, to perform a different kind of assault on Fortress Portman.

When Portman looked up from his cot he saw Kapitän Bergman, streaked with dust, and a British officer, streaked with blood. Behind them was a Feldwebel with a submachine gun at port arms.

"*Draussen warten,*" said Bergman and the Feldwebel left.

Both men in uniform were breathing harshly. Bergman gave the British officer a push, making him tumble against the stone wall. The impact was awkward because the man's wrists were tied at his back.

"This," said Bergman, "is an enemy prisoner who, in view of his proverbial British fortitude, is willing to tell considerably more than his name, rank and serial number."

"Good heavens," said Portman. "The man is bleeding from the head and the mouth!"

"They are *not, mein lieber Portman*, combat wounds."

"But, then how ..."

"Would you like me to demonstrate?"

There was no need for an answer. Portman gagged and looked sick.

"Tell him, Major," said Bergman.

Craig was frowning at Portman. It took a thoroughly Prussian salvo from the *Herr Kapitän* to bring Craig around.

"Yes— We spotted the contingent just outside of Jalu ..."

"*What* contingent?"

"Afrika Korps, sir. One staff car, one weapons carrier. So we jumped them."

"So you jumped them. You battled fifteen men with your thirty."

"Yes sir. When we were finished ..."

"Finished. Did you hear that, Mister Portman? Unlike us, the heroic British do *not* take prisoners. Go on, Major."

"Then you came," and in a moment Craig added "sir" again.

Portman was beginning to feel as cowed as the British prisoner. He groaned with relief when Bergman removed the depressing sight of gore and spinelessness by catapulting the prisoner through the flap which covered the door. But Portman's ordeal was not over.

"Which brings us to the fact," said Bergman, as if he were still talking to the major, "that your safety from now on depends upon me."

"I am terrifi— I am terribly grateful to you, Captain. My gratitude will astound and ..."

"Never mind." Bergman turned. "We are leaving for Tobruk within moments."

"Wait!"

Bergman paused at the door and smiled like a snake. It looked perfectly proper on him.

"Of course, Mister Portman. You are not going to Tobruk. You prefer to remain behind and hail a taxi."

"I must get to Cairo immediately!"

Bergman had lifted the blanket on the door and now he let it drop again. Craig, who stood outside in the dark, stopped wiping the animal gore from his face. He was tense with half-formed doubts and when Bergman dropped the flap and did not come out, Craig was badly disappointed. It took another fifteen minutes before Bergman reappeared. He had one hand in his pocket and ordered two guards to flank that door, machine pistols cocked and no nonsense about it.

21: View from an Empty Watering Hole

The night was too cloying. It was good not to be cold but it was bad to be reminded. The summer nights in Munich had always been the worst for Bruckner because a summer night is for two and Bruckner was solitary. And he lived too close to Schwabing. He had a room on the fourth floor and the sounds of the quarter where the students and artists would sing and brawl came in through the open window. The Schwabing sounds were like a taunt to Bruckner and his seriousness. His texts on mechanical engineering were then no refuge for him and the tiredness in his bones was not enough. On such nights there would then come all the dreams. In a way it was good they were over, the dreams about building a marvelous car, the other one about the marvelous girl, the two of them down in the happy streets of Schwabing. Instead he had gone to France in order to work for Renault. Very soon, *fertig* or *fini* with the dreams, and he was here. But it was not pleasant to remember.

He crossed the area, skirted the cistern and looked for his friend.

"Mohnfeld," he said under the netting. "You awake, pal?"

"I'm awake. Are you awake, Aaron?"

"I'm awake."

"How do you know? Maybe you're dreaming."

"Don't say that. Listen, Mohnfeld. You remember that girl in there?"

"Not too well, no."

"I just went in and saw her. She doesn't look good to me."

"Don't let the coveralls fool you, *Kindchen*."

"Come on now. You know I don't mean that." Bruckner, who truly did not quite know what was bothering him, chewed a fingernail and looked around.

"Who's that by the cistern?"

"Looks like Kuntze from here."

"I don't like Kuntze," said Bruckner.

"Me neither. I've never liked a Jew who's changed his name."

"He did? I didn't know that. Anyway, she said she didn't like you."

"Brucknik," said Mohnfeld, "I notice you are thinking again. On account you are not making sense."

"Cheryl Portman."

"Really?" said Mohnfeld.

"Yes. Then she told me she didn't like me either."

Mohnfeld laughed. He lay back on the blanket he had rolled up for a pillow and looked up at Bruckner squatting next to him. It was a massive sight.

"You ever been to Cairo?" asked Bruckner.

"No. Why?"

"I have. Then how come you asked her about Cairo?"

"I don't remember. Did you?"

"I don't remember," said Bruckner. Then he sighed. He rubbed his hand back and forth over his hair. "I don't know what it is, friend, but I feel nervous and rotten."

It seemed an improbable mood for Bruckner, but it was true. Mohnfeld patted his friend on the leg.

"It's the night. It feels warm like peace. But we know that there is no such thing. And that's the contradiction which makes you feel rotten."

Bruckner looked down at Mohnfeld and wanted to know more good things which explained everything.

"You too?"

Mohnfeld smiled up at the untidy netting as if he saw a beautiful thing and it gave him peace.

"No," he said. "I haven't got that problem anymore. I'm through, Brooky."

Mohnfeld's peace disturbed Bruckner even more and then he remembered how Bergman had come slamming out of the old Englishman's hut and that sight had not given any comfort either—

When Colonel Harker saw Bergman cross from the dark to his tent, he had to remind himself forcefully that he was dealing with an ally. Bergman walked with long, hard steps which made his Luger bounce on his side. His face was as hard as any enemy's and there was something inhumanly single-minded about the way he moved. Bergman ignored his trailing guards—since when did Bergman walk around with armed escorts?—and he ignored Craig who was following him and who did not seem to care what he looked like. That Canadian, Harker thought, does look emphatically like a prisoner—

"Throw that tent flap back, Boyden—"

Boyden stepped out of the tiny, lit space of the tent and threw the flap back. If he did not do so, he thought, then Bergman and entourage might march straight through the canvas.

Harker sat behind the box which was his desk and then Bergman and Craig crowded in and also the two S.I.G. guards. Boyden stood squeezed against the canvas, making it bulge. There was hardly enough room in the shelter to throw a salute. Bergman snapped at his S.I.G. men in

German and watched them scramble out of the tent again. Harker had the distinct impression that they were stationing themselves outside in order to guard in earnest. The question was, whom were they guarding from what—

"I will come to the point, Colonel Harker," said Bergman. There was no taunt in his manner, just complete insistence on no interruptions. "Craig is convinced, sir, that this man Portman is the same one he heard in the corridor outside the room where he was interrogated in Algiers."

"The devil you say—"

"The same man whose description alerted McGowan when he questioned Craig in Kufra."

"Get to it," said Craig. "The paper."

"The paper," said Bergman. He pulled it out of his pocket and put it on the box in front of Harker.

It was of the thin, slippery consistency which made folding into a tiny, inconspicuous size possible without undue damage. When Harker started to open it up, it had not been folded to its smallest dimensions. Nevertheless, Harker started out with a square which was no larger than four postage stamps.

The interval of unfolding the paper gave him time to get back into the proper order of things.

"The point, Bergman. You must think it's significant."

"It concerns the silence around Tobruk. It concerns ..."

"You've read this?"

"No sir. I got a verbal résumé from the prisoner. It concerns an extensive line of action, Colonel Harker, which—as would happen—can be cut by us."

"In Tobruk?"

"The pump," said Craig, "doesn't seem to be dry. The pump is gorged, ready to spew."

Harker needed a pause. He looked past the men in front of him and out of the open flap of the tent. He saw Sergeant Tyne come toward the tent and he saw how the S.I.G. guards turned him away. This unprecedented occurrence must have something to do with the document, with the unprecedented importance of this sheet of paper on top of the box

"It's in German," said Harker and looked at the closely written page. Then he turned it over. "And Arabic on the other side?"

"The signature and title at the bottom," said Craig, "identifies the Grand Mufti of Jerusalem."

"*That* politician?"

It was a likely designation, considering that a professional soldier had made it. The Mufti had worked with the British in Palestine while Harker had been there, and now the Mufti was siding with the Germans. Harker's professional interest did not extend to the fact that the Grand Mufti had empire designs to dwarf those of a Queen Victoria.

"And the German text," Bergman said, "is signed—with Supreme Headquarters' seal affixed—by General Feldmarschall von Kesselring, acting as sole representative of the Supreme Commander etc., etc., Adolf Hitler."

A dirty little tent in the Sahara. And the world—so went Harker's unaccustomed train of thought—was ponderously revolving around nothing but this tent.

For a moment he breathed without getting any air. Then he found his true bearings again.

"Well, to say the least, we can progress without that unpleasant sensation of doubt. Tobruk is an absolutely worthwhile target."

"We haven't read the document yet," said Boyden.

Bergman translated the German on the document and Craig managed the gist of the Arabic side of the agreement. The statements complemented each other and gave the ground plan—hereby confirmed and held to be mutually binding—for one gigantic coordinated effort. The common negotiators were a group of Egyptian officers, gathered in Cairo. They were the road-runners between the eastern and the western forces.

The German troops from the west would plunge out of the desert toward Egypt, an undertaking which might look like an intentional *Götterdämmerung*. Except that the assaulted British at the entrance slot to the Nile—El Alamein was mentioned as a possible point of concentration—would have their rearward lifelines and their retreat obliterated by the timed effort of the Mufti's Arabs. They would rise simultaneously from Turkey to Gaza. A minimum of six armed Arab territories, kingdoms, nations, would spring into action to complete an Islamic half moon which would gird all the southern and the eastern coastal lands of the Mediterranean basin.

It was a *jiddah*. It was a geopolitical envelopment. It was to be the first nexus for a grand, Eurasian take-over.

Harker's expression did not make clear whether he was moved with shock or with admiration.

"The military conception," he said slowly, "is grandiose."

"So is the genocide," said Craig, "even though it's just a sub-paragraph here." He read, "'—part of the military action in Palestine will be the programmed extinction of Jewish residents—' The Arab wording," said Craig, "doesn't make clear if the Mufti means 'programmed' or 'preordained,' but anyway, this extermination is offered as their step in the final solution of the Jewish problem."

"I don't believe it!" said Boyden. "The Germans will never be party to such a—such a—" He did not know how to finish.

Bergman laughed. It was an unfunny sound. There were two thousand years of information on this subject, tiresome in its repetitiveness. The ennui in Bergman's attitude rankled.

"There is one German," Harker said, "who would not be part of such a plan. Just as Rommel was patently unaware of the treatment to which some of his POW's were subjected," and he looked at Craig with a hint of a bow, "in that same manner has Rommel been kept totally unaware of the essential purpose and scope of his coming military move. The chain of command through which this document has traveled completely leaves him out. What do you think, Bergman?"

"I think," said Bergman, "that as long as that pump is going up there in Tobruk, as long as we don't move, sir, we are dead." And then, as often, his own, unwanted rancor, "Regardless of our admiration for an enemy general."

There came a silence of waiting. The tent, in spite of the open flap, had become very hot. This heat did not move and nothing else seemed to move either. It grew to become as unbearable as holding one's breath.

"We wait," said Harker.

Boyden could not control a nervous rasping in his throat which he covered with a cough. Craig's impatience, Harker could see, was patent. It would easily burst out by way of some sort of unmilitary anger. Bergman's mood was much more self-contained and possibly much more dangerous.

"With due respect," he started to say. His voice was as deceptively even as the calm view of a bog.

"So far," said Harker as if he had not heard, "we had no way of measuring the importance of our prisoner. After this," and he slapped at the document, "I would not be surprised if they are sending an armored column after him. We wait for daylight. That is all, gentlemen."

Portman, who had found that he was not permitted to leave his chamber, was waiting too. Kapitän Bergman's high-handed manner had been completely unpleasant but his desire for speed would be a positive asset. That had been almost an hour ago. Portman, unreasonably confined and made inactive, lapsed into a sickish sleep. He sat on his cot while supporting himself in the angle of the stone wall. The tilt and twist of his body caused a pinching pressure on the bulge of his stomach. He knew this was the worst thing for his composure but he felt too sluggish to shift. Sometimes his eyes were open without seeing anything. Sometimes his eyes were closed but seeing a lot. His tiredness was the drug which kept a great deal of excitement in check. There were also side effects to the drug. The design of the mud bricks in the wall suffered astigmatic shifts. Once the wall melted away and revealed a sunlit palace. Its Grecian façade bore the legend "Portman's Pawnshop." Then the sun melted and the palace melted and the wall was back.

Such lunacies, Portman knew, were due to the pinching of the stomach. He moved enough to give himself a sensation of health again, and now the angle of his head was toward the floor. He saw the geometry of the slabs and then he saw the same thing as a series of angular waves. Beneath, abysmal depths; above, a hollow wind.

When the abysmal depth peeked at him in the form of a slit in the floor and when the hollow wind began to whisper to him, Portman yanked himself resolutely back to sanity.

But the sane view was not encouraging either. The floor had split open. Near the opposite wall a floor slab had been shifted and from that black space rose a hand, a Luger and a voice.

"You will keep very still."

Portman had not moved.

"I am a friend."

Portman did not believe it.

"You are in real danger."

Portman believed that implicitly.

"And so is your mission."

Somehow it was this more impersonal part of the news which made Portman react.

"*Langsam*," said the hole in the ground. "And don't raise your voice."

"What—"

"You are not under the protection of the Afrika Korps. Kapitän Bergman is a fake."

The implications were too threatening. There was only one way out.

"I don't believe it," said Portman. He sat back on his cot as if he never meant to move again.

"He and his men are S.I.G."

"They are what?"

"Jews in the employ of the British."

"Ridiculous combination. You will please put that gun away and come out."

"I want you to come with me."

"Ridiculous. My guards, placed there for my protection by Captain Bergman ..."

"Old fool, listen to me. Bergman is against us. He has you and your document and he will deliver both—to the enemy."

The proposition was incredible—

"The British prisoner," said the voice, "was Bergman's superior. You did not recognize the major?"

"Recognize?"

"You don't know his name?"

"No. Never met ..."

"Did you ever hear of a Major Donald Craig?"

"My God!" said Portman, and a few disturbing things fell into disturbing places: The seaplane disappearance with the prisoner Craig, the relayed word of seaplane landing in Kufra, the disturbing Intelligence that a British column seemed to be heading north through the Sand Sea toward Jalu—

"What— I must get that document back— I myself must—"

"I will take care of the document. You listen."

Portman listened and then he went like a sleepwalker to the black hole in the ground. When Portman had disappeared from his chamber the slab moved back into place.

It was a smooth-stoned, musty passage, not high enough for upright walk. It was a left-over conduit which led to the dry Roman cistern.

"And my daughter!" said Portman on his hands and knees.

"I will take care of her too," said the lump of shadow in front of him.

They crawled through the fine dust which had grown in the passage for a long time. Portman was wheezing with it and his eyes stung with water. When he could distinguish the arched hole which led into the cistern, the man in front of him stopped and patted his hand along the side of the wall. Most of his arm disappeared inside the joining conduit.

"All right," he said. "Here they are."

"Why don't you— I mean, my lack of experience—"

"I cannot leave. Once they miss me, it's over."

"You could be there and back before the unit moves out."

"I'm not high command here. I don't know when we move out. You'll have to do the job."

Portman groaned in the dark. The stooped posture was pinching his stomach again. Then he felt something in his hand.

"This is the sand cape. Once you're out, open it up and tie it on. For camouflage."

"But it's nighttime. I don't see ..."

"You will have to hide out in the desert for at least part of the day, I explained to you! This unit has to move out before you can go back to Jalu, and in Jalu you may have to wait several days before I can get a rescue party to you."

"Yes, yes, yes," said Portman as if his voice were shivering with cold.

"Next, this is the field phone. Give me your hand. Here. These are the clips. You'll be able to see them once you're out in the open. Remember how they go?"

"I remember."

"Put the strap over your shoulder. And now this."

"What is it?"

"The gun, Portman. *Not* that way."

Portman stuck the Luger under his belt, adding one further pressure.

"Now stay put till I drop a pebble down the cistern. I'm going up to check."

Portman sat in the hole which led into the cistern and felt cramped, bloated and ill-prepared. None of this had been part of the plan. The plan had not even included this possibility, nor should this possibility even exist!

A conduit and a basement view of the sky were not his domain. He belonged in something quilted with leather, behind a desk full of unique notes, besides the shelves filled with his unique books and with a wide view in front of him. He was worth several million pounds sterling, but he had not been able to change his underwear in three days. He had conceptions with a sweep sufficient to unite the world, but he sat at the bottom of a dry watering hole.

Something fell but it was not the stone. There were more subdued sounds from above while Portman shrank into himself until he felt like nothing but a tight ball of wrinkles. Then the small stone plunked down, raising a little dust.

Portman's circular ascent by the stone steps in the wall of the cistern seemed as long to him and as tortured as mankind's rise from the stone ages. And once over the rim he felt so strengthless that the night air did not refresh him and the space gave him no sense of freedom.

"Squat down," said his liberator. Then he pointed. "You see them over there? When Bergman comes out of your chamber again—any second now—you run."

Portman stared at the distant spectacle near the walls of the caravansary. That Jew in disguise, that Bergman, was marching straight for the hole in the wall which led to Portman's chamber. The guards practically flew aside as Bergman entered. The blanket closed again. Then there was a great animal roar from behind that curtain.

"Not yet—" hissed the man next to Portman. "You remember the way?"

"Yes—"

"The instructions?"

"Yes—"

And then the blanket was torn aside and Bergman erupted.

"Now!" said the voice. "*Hals and Beinbruch*—"

Portman stumbled off. "Yes," he stuttered. "Oh God, I hope so—"

With the aid of the angry confusion in camp he made the open desert.

He had expert help. Bergman, in his rage, ringed the caravansary tight as a vise. He squandered useless time with a composed, fairly haughty Cheryl. And then one of his men yelled for him to come back to the empty chamber.

The blanket over the door hole was down and the dim lantern flickered inside. The room was empty, but there was a stealthy scrape which came from nowhere. Then the floor moved.

The stone moved like the flat shell of an unsure, cautious animal. Bergman, without knowing it, slipped his Luger away and pulled the knife from his boot. And then it seemed only one movement when he leapt across the small room and yanked the stone plate away.

He could have killed the man below with one hard drive into the skull. Bergman knew this about himself and waited with that sureness in him, waited to see whom he would kill.

The hands groped up and there was blood on the knuckles.

"Don't," it said, "I'm coming out—"

Bergman watched as if hexed. He stepped back and then he listened.

"I heard them—by the cistern. I went down and there was the hole, the passage going there. I don't know—it was dark—I don't know who it was but I killed him with his own knife—"

Then Mohnfeld keeled over.

Blood ran out of his sleeve and a cut on his cheek looked black and ugly.

They called the M.O. for him and carried him outside, for the air. He sat there, leaning against the wall, and watched them busy themselves at the cistern at the far end of the camp. When the M.O. was done with the cuts on the cheek and the gash on the arm, they were done at the cistern too. Bergman came back and stood over Mohnfeld.

"We found him, like you said."

"Who was it?" said Mohnfeld.

"I'm sorry to tell you, Mohnfeld," said Bergman. "Your friend Bruckner."

Mohnfeld lowered his head until it looked as if he were asleep. Bergman saw how pale Mohnfeld had become.

"I liked him," said Mohnfeld, very low. "God knows, I really liked him—"

They did not get much else out of him. Mohnfeld's personal grief made him monosyllabic and, besides, he had not seen Portman disappear into the night.

They had no idea where the old man might want to go. They did not know that the Germans had maintained the original telephone cable from Jalu to Tobruk, since the small Jalu exchange had been destroyed several times and since the Libyan operators had left some time ago. Jalu kept changing hands as often as the next patrol came through. They would stop, water up and leave again without need for telephone service. The casual possession of Jalu was a mere side issue to the fluid warfare in the north. But ever since Rommel's reoccupation of Tobruk, the Jalu cable had again been maintained. Portman found it one hour later.

The directions had been precise and simple and the baffled search which Bergman directed was still looking in all the wrong places. If it had been daytime and if the nearest watch post which Harker maintained had been standing up, he and Portman could have waved at each other. But the watch was looking for motorized movement and Portman was on foot, looking for a two-foot-high road marker which gave the mileage to Tobruk.

He found the marker stone which was a left-over colonization attempt by the Italians. The stone was in better shape than the Jalu road next to it. Portman paced off six yards due east. There he sat down on the ground.

If it had been daytime and if he had stood up, he could have waved at Harker's nearest watch post on the rise to the south. But Portman sat huddled under his sand cape and his exhaustion made him feel all alone. He looked at the dark barrenness as far as he could see and he saw nothing which was not supplied by his fantasy. The shale looked like flagstone on his Cairo terrace, the ground hump was a fellah hut near the cotton fields out of town. But on the whole this very still view of nothingness could really not be compared to anything. It looked as if someone had started to create something and then had left it unfinished out of sheer despair. Portman felt similarly. There was grit under his fingernails and he had sand in his shoes. His scalp itched from sweat and dust and the air he was breathing gave him nothing. It gave him a sensation of temperature which was the same on his inside as on the surface of his skin. This strange sameness produced the impression that he did not exist and that leads to panic. But the moment passed with a redoubled feeling for all his itchy discomforts.

And now I dig. Use a flat stone, use the gun. The fingers feel useless with that unbearable pressure of dirt under the nails. But dig! Find the cable by a simple act of grubbing down here like a caveman, then the simple use of the machine, the telephone clamped into split innards of that snake down here somewhere— My God, no knife to split the casing— Why didn't that sullen looking functionary back by that unspeakable water tank think— But he did, of course, that deceptively ignorant-looking person had provided! The sharp little tools are in the telephone case. Let me— No. First dig.

First he dug with inspiration because this caveman activity had purpose, mission and a scope of the universal— Never mind that now— Dig.

When he did not find the cable one foot down as promised, Portman felt that he had been deceived. He felt hurt and then indignant. This did not help his digging activity. The sand cape got in his way, the telephone case swung forward to hang between his knees, and when he took the gun out of his belt because of the pressure he kneeled on it by mistake and hurt himself. A thought, which was not ridiculous to him at all, maintained him: I am a caveman working my way toward a better world.

He took the sand cape off, put the field telephone on the ground and pushed the Luger out of the way. Then he dug with desperation. And then he dug with dullness. If he did not dig and find, he was meaningless.

When he found the cable he was so enmeshed in the dullness of digging that the simple sight and feel of a lead-sheathed cable had no real impact on him. For the moment the exposed cable simply meant that he could get off his knees, sit on his rear and rest.

He sat up with a sigh and rested his feet in the wide hole he had opened. For the moment the sand in his shoes did not bother him or the itch on his scalp or the grit under his fingernails. But he started to worry now about all the dirt he would have to push back into the hole. Insufferable not to have the right tools. And then he saw the fellow with the tool.

The Tuareg was standing in front of his horse, watching Portman. He had one hand over the nose of the horse and the other hand was hanging down, swinging the tool back and forth gently. Then Portman recognized the thing. It was a very old, very efficient weapon of brutality, that throwing iron. It was as long as an arm and it curved at one end to an evil point. A partial cross bar gave it spinning balance when in flight and a scissor leverage upon impact.

An enemy? Portman's hand, as if asking a question, tapped for the Luger which lay in the dirt. The Tuareg's iron came up.

Make him an ally! Apprise this primitive of the nature of the mission, offer him money by way of proof of brotherhood, get his assistance on the telephonic job to HQ in Tobruk by explaining the nature of everything

The pink man, decided the Tuareg, was not dangerous. He talked. The gun was in the dirt and the man was standing up. The Tuareg could hardly understand the pink man's choice of Arabic but it did not matter. When waving the iron, the man would move back. He nods, he chatters and he points— He is offering the gun!

Portman, due to his knowledge of the primitive mind, performed a master stroke. He let the Tuareg have the Luger. Aside from getting the gun, this simple tribesman would not want anything else, would not care about the telephonic job that had to be done. While the Tuareg picked up the Luger, Portman—with appropriate smiles and explanations—went back to his hole and the unfinished job.

It worked. Portman began to cut the sheathing and smiled up at the Tuareg now and then. The tribesman paid little attention. He was examining the gun. Portman, exhilarated by his master stroke of dealing with the primitive mind, worked furiously. One clamp was on! And what now?

The Tuareg was garbling in an agitated way and waved the gun around. He slapped it with his other hand and looked as annoyed as a dog who cannot get his nose into the burrow of a mouse. Portman grasped the dilemma instantly. The gun did not work! It was probably full of dirt.

He knew enough about the Luger to decide that he must first free the slide. The Tuareg gave him the gun and watched how Portman tried to jackknife the mechanism back and forth. It made a gritty sound and it did not move too well. After this demonstration and some talk which the Tuareg did not understand, Portman returned the gun and went back to his clamping job. Another minute, and then just one more minute—

The instrument hummed!

The shell of the receiver was on Portman's ear and produced a lovely sound inside his head-

Ah life, thought Portman, and felt a shiver of excitement.

Now the button, then the crank— A moment now! I am indomitable!

He flicked a glance and a smile at the Tuareg but did not reach the man. The tribesman looked churlish and irritated. The slide would not work. And then, in an access of frustration, he heaved the gun into the desert.

"Never mind, never mind," said Portman. "I'll fix it for you. Just a minute now while I first—"

He dropped the receiver in sheer astonishment. The Tuareg stepped back and took a posture.

"Now just a minute," said Portman with sudden haste. "You don't understand!" and then Portman jumped up and ran.

There was no thought in this, just action. When the iron hissed behind him he knew what it was and when he fell with the iron jammed between his legs, he knew what it had done to him. He felt no pain yet, but knew that the tendons were cut.

He rolled over while the Tuareg picked up his old weapon and then Portman was permitted to say one more thing. Portman, as never before, meant every word with heartfelt innocence.

"I don't understand—" he said and then the disappointed Tuareg cut off the pink-and-white head.

22: The End of a Battle

They did not find him until there was enough light for the look-out to spot the wheeling birds in the sky. They found the two dead parts of Portman and they kicked shut the cable hole. There was no time to bury him. From the place of his death they could now also spot the dust column of those who were coming for him. By the time they spotted the column and saw that there were only three vehicles, Harker had completed a troop emplacement whose cross fire could have handled an enemy five times stronger. He naturally assumed that they would continue to Jalu on the road—

"All accounted for?" asked Harker when Boyden crawled up the ridge and lay down next to him.

"Yes sir. Except for the handful that's still at the caravansary. The runner said they'll be in position shortly but seem to have a minor problem—"

Cheryl Portman was the problem. She did not like Mohnfeld and refused to get in the truck with him.

"Miss," he said with obvious exasperation. "It's a five-minute ride to Jalu and that's all. When I drop you there you won't have to see me again."

She stayed by the wall and would not move.

"Come on!" yelled Bergman from the other side of the broken building. "There's no time!"

He could not see Mohnfeld and the girl but he could hear that Mohnfeld had not started the truck.

"She's coming!" they heard him yell. Bergman's truck shifted into gear. Mohnfeld could hear it.

"I'll take a look," said Craig and jumped off the truck.

When he made the turn around the wall he saw that the girl had not moved. He saw Mohnfeld raising his pistol, straight-armed like target practice.

"*Hey!*"

Mohnfeld looked and lowered the pistol slowly.

"She was just going to move," he said. "Nothing else got through to her."

"Well, get her in there!" said Craig. He felt badly agitated.

"I'll go with you," said Cheryl and when he looked at her she was running to the truck. Then she stopped. "Not you," she said. "I mean you," and she pointed at Craig.

"Goddamn it, you're not picking a dance partner. Now let's ..."

"No."

She tore her arm out of Mohnfeld's hand and Craig thought for a moment that Mohnfeld was going to put the pistol to her again. There was a ludicrous struggle and then they could hear Bergman yelling again.

"... *right now!*" was the part they understood.

"All right," said Craig. "I'll take her. You run."

"I'll take her."

"You've got the squad on the south ridge, damn it! There's no time. Put that damn gun away."

"Is that woman running this war?" Mohnfeld's agitation had a weird touch. He seemed altogether not quite the same since he had lost Bruckner.

"Not the first time it's happened," said Craig and pushed Cheryl into the cab. Then he climbed after her. He kicked the motor over and slammed the gear. Mohnfeld, he noticed, was still standing there. He did not turn to Bergman's truck until Craig was turning past the other end of the building.

He went fast, picking a way over broken rocks. It was late in the game and he did not want to raise any dust.

"Won't be long," he said. "See those buildings down there?"

She nodded. The seat under her was shaking her hard and she was holding her breasts.

"You didn't bring my father," she said.

"I'll tell you later."

He wheeled the truck around the rim of Jalu and watched the way with intent. Before he hit the down grade he heard the first shot.

"Goddamn them—" he muttered.

"What was that?"

He wheeled into the down grade and the new angle showed him how the dust of the column had shifted. They had apparently left the road.

"That," he said, "was a shot."

"I'm confused."

"Ditto."

Then he careened down to the level of Jalu and did not care how much dirt he was raising now. They had made premature contact and the fusillade which was following the shot came all from the far end of Harker's deployment. They were trying to scare the enemy off and back to the road so that he would drive into the trap. And if he didn't, they would increase their fire and add mortars to it. Then the Germans would know the enemy's strength and would charge off into the desert. And if they hid their strength on the ridge and just gave the Germans that rifle fire, then the enemy party might feel safe to make a straight run for their Jalu destination and to hell with an enemy who could muster just six rifles.

Craig hoped that Mohnfeld reached his post on the south ridge. If the Germans chose to run for Jalu, that south ridge would have its hands full—

The truck ran straight now, over very hard ground which was covered with powder. Just short of the windowless buildings he slewed the wheel over hard so that the truck spun through its axis. Then it stopped, as intended, facing toward the exit again.

"Were you ever a race driver?"

"Don't talk crap now," he said and pushed her door open. "Hurry up!"

He jumped out on his side and reached her when she just stepped to the ground. Craig stopped and looked up as if studying the weather. The sounds were not good and the rim of the Jalu depression interfered with his judgment.

They had stopped firing to deceive the Germans about their strength. All Craig could hear were motor sounds, both hunted and hunter. And then he heard the mortar. He distinctly heard the accelerating swish of the thing in the air—

Mohnfeld did not have any mortars. He had the quads and machine guns to close off their approach. And if he had mortars he would not be lobbing them to the south of his line, toward Jalu.

"*Run!*" He grabbed the girl and dragged her into the nearest house. Outside, the mortar shell made a respectable bang and raised a respectable billow of debris.

No easy trick aiming a mortar from a running vehicle. The Germans had missed the south ridge position far and wide. Mohnfeld must have gotten there late, or else they would never have spotted his dust—

It was unlikely that there would be another errant shell. But why in hell was there no fire from the south ridge to keep the Germans back?

The house, like the chamber in the caravansary, was a low, squarish affair without windows. It was totally empty, except for an iron pot which somebody had left behind. It was not a good house, thought Craig, if they kept shelling. And the truck was not in a good place either.

He took Cheryl with him and backed the truck along the row of houses which seemed to follow no pattern at all except to make a pebbly ghost-town street running toward one steep side of the Jalu depression. Craig backed the truck until it touched the rise of the escarpment. When he cut the motor he could hear the sounds from above again. It was now like the probings of a careful battle. Mohnfeld's quads still had not said a thing.

The near house they took this time seemed to have been deserted in haste. The chamber contained one balding pelt, for resting, a blackened hole in the ground with the remains of a charcoal fire and a very low table with a rusty knife on it.

"They left," said Cheryl.

"Yuh," said Craig. He stood in the open doorway and looked out.

"Everybody left," she said.

This was not true. The opposite stone hut showed its empty mouth and then there was somebody in it. She was Tuareg and very old. Her face was without veil and her skin was heavily creased, like an old shoe.

"We come in peace!" said Craig and felt like a fool immediately. There was the brief swoosh of a mortar shell and then the sudden blast of impact. After that, debris came jumping down the side of the escarpment. The sound of the little stones was innocent in the silence after the explosion.

"Were you left behind?"

The old woman disappeared and would not answer, but a goat showed in the doorway to her hut. It had a rope around its neck and then the goat fell down on its knees. The old woman was there again, pulling the other end of the rope until the goat made it to its feet and was dragged out of sight again.

Then the quads started barking. The guess was of limited value but they seemed to be looking for their target in an uncomfortable direction. It was possible that the Germans had made it past the main body of Harker's men. And now, they might make it into Jalu—

They might want to hole up in the oasis, holding the jumble of stone huts longer than Harker's timetable permitted.

Above and out of sight, the sound of many calibers cracking at each other— The mortar missed again, bouncing an avalanche of dirt down the side of the escarpment— Unless it was one of Harker's, trying to reach the Germans near the rim, or trying to keep them from getting there with an overshot— A rock came hopping down the dirt street and then lay still.

"Are you scared?" asked Craig. He looked at the girl who sat on the low table.

"No," she said.

He went to the corner of the room from which he could see toward the other end of the depression, where the access road came down.

"You're nuts," he said. "I'm scared." Then he sat down on the floor with his back against the wall.

The next explosion above had a much more penetrating after effect. Somebody screamed and would not stop. It screamed and something wrestled in that voice, something that did not want to go under and then lost.

Suddenly Cheryl was next to Craig and sat down close to him. He could feel her arm against his arm and her thigh leaning against his.

"You think I'm mad," she said.

"Not now. Now you're scared."

"Yes."

"It's better—than nuts," he said.

She sat very still, leaning against him.

"But when you're alone—then what do you do when you scared—very, very scared?"

"I try—I just try not to go nuts."

He had no idea if that made sense to her and at any rate, he thought, it was probably much too primitive for her kind of troubles.

She nodded her head and said, "Yes. It helps when you are not alone." This seemed to have settled something and she looked at him. "You are not German."

"No."

"That's why I was confused. You and that German together."

He did not want to add to the confusion by explaining who Mohnfeld really was and he hoped she would not ask why the S.I.D. Germans were with the L.R.D.G. British prisoners in such a cooperative togetherness.

"When you leave," she said, "I want to go with you."

The point, thought Craig, would not be easy to make, even if the girl were more with it—

"Look," he said, "I understand that something like a dozen Tuaregs can unhinge any woman, but you've got to understand something in your turn. You are an enemy under arrest. And whatever the C.O. decides to do with you, girl, he's most certainly not going to take you along."

"Oh," she said. "You are thinking about my father. But we're no longer together. That's dead."

Craig looked at her but she did not look back. Her profile held quite still.

"How did you know he's dead?" Craig asked her.

She turned her head and Craig could see clearly that she had not known about Portman's death.

"How did I know," she said, "how did I know. I haven't seen him. How *could* I know he's dead. I'm not so mad to imagine it."

Craig stared at her and her eyes, large and shiny, the sheen still and dry, somehow inanimate.

"Honey," he said. "You *are* mad."

She folded her hands around her knees and looked down into her lap. In this quiet Craig listened to the sounds from above. No one seemed to have moved, as if they were pinning each other down from entrenchments.

"I lost him some time ago," she said. "And now that he's dead, it seems like nothing new. You understand that?"

Craig looked at her and then back toward the end of the depression where the road came down.

"A little bit," he said. "I can see it a little."

"Your name is Craig?"

"Yes."

"You never use my name. As if I weren't here. The Tuaregs never used my name, but there of course it was different."

"I imagine. Your name is Cheryl?"

"Yes, Craig."

"Craig is the last name. I'm Don." He felt awkward. "Look," he said. "You don't know me any better than you knew Mohnfeld. That's the one you didn't like."

"I don't know you better but I feel you better. I did not feel anything from him at all. Does that ever happen to you?"

"You should like it. There's less bother."

"No. It's like a hole. Does that ever happen to you?"

He felt the discomfort of the truth but then he told her anyway.

"Yes," he said. "With you."

To his great consternation he now saw how she started to cry. She did not move her face at all but her eyes were full of tears and then they just ran over and the tears slid down her cheeks.

"I'm sorry—Cheryl," he said.

"It's all right. I'm really here, you know, but sometimes it isn't enough that only I know it. I've tried to learn," she said and looked away. "I have really tried to learn—"

Suddenly Craig felt very upset. He wished he were not here but above, where they were fighting. Harker, he thought, might get terribly nasty about the whole thing. Craig had no gun other than his service revolver and the nearby Germans might easily shoot the indispensable truck out from under him, but nevertheless— He got up and went to the door to look to the rim of the escarpment. There was smoke close to the edge. If he were to move the truck they could pulverize it. Then he felt her next to him, and her hand on his arm. Her hand there was so light, it was more as if the hand asked him if she might touch him.

"I'm more frightened now than before," she said. "I just want to stand here."

He turned to look at her and gave a brief smile. It was not enough for warmth or for friendliness, but it showed how he might feel that way at some other time, or how he used to be able to feel that way but not now.

"It's all right," he said without looking at her. "I get that way too."

"Whom did you lose?"

"What?"

"What," she repeated after him. "Did I say what? Yes. Just now. I don't know what." She let go of his arm and her hand fell away. It felt as if she had gone to sleep and had rolled over.

In a moment Craig sighed. He took her by the shoulders and turned her around to lead her back to the place by the wall. On the way he picked up the old pelt and dragged it over.

"No," she said. "I don't want to lie on that."

He dropped the skin as if the touch bothered him. He wished he knew ahead of time what would bring out this disconnection in her, this strange business of her being here, and somewhere else, like someone seen in a forest, someone walking among the trees. In that view the person was there, then disappeared, then showed again elsewhere—

They sat down and Craig stared out at the road again.

"Listen, Cheryl," he said. She sat next to him but this time she did not try to touch him and he could barely feel her near him. "Let me explain a few things to you. What's going to happen here. I don't know why in hell you're here but ..."

"Because my father took me."

"Yuh. That's one solid explanation. Of sorts. Anyway ..."

"It's true, Don."

"All right."

"No," she said. "Something is wrong." She put her hand on his arm next to her but looked down at her lap. "I feel like an *attrape*, sometimes. I mean, I only *look* like I'm here."

Touch of death, he thought. And the worst. To be dead and know it—

Somebody's mortar had found somebody's gas tank. The report was violent and welcome. Real sound of a real event. Then he felt her hand.

"Easy," he said and patted her. "That was one of theirs."

"Somebody's dead," she said evenly.

The very absence of feeling upset Craig and he almost shouted.

"So what! So's your father!"

In terms of effect, he thought, he might have been talking to himself. And perhaps I am, he continued the thought. I have two parents, both alive, and I've never cried or anything like that when somebody died. I have had a very ordinary life which included the right home, the right games, the right schools, the right choice of a job— Bull! Or I wouldn't be here. Anyway, and at least one very right and memorable woman that time, no problems whatsoever, no hangover type gnawing around on the inside for reasons of incompletion. Such an ordinary life that I can hear death blow up in somebody else's face and not one sick chance in a lifetime of faultily imagining that somebody's death over there was for me.

"Didn't you ever see somebody—go?" she asked.

This absence of feeling, he thought now, is something else. It is not absence in her, really, but monumental control—

"I mean," she went on, a little hoarse suddenly, "one moment he—they, or something—are there and then they are not?"

Craig put his hand on his mouth and then he rubbed. Something felt stiff. Something went bang up above and debris jumped in the street. There was also a small impact on the roof of the house, nothing that drew much attention, nothing that held attention when the sound stopped. Craig was still rubbing his mouth and he talked through his fingers.

"Yes," he said. "Once."

He took the hand away from his mouth. He put his arm on his knee and the hand hung down.

"Will you tell me?" she said.

"Why?"

"I want—I thought, perhaps I could see how you did it. How you saw it and then it was—still all right with you."

The gun talk above had been louder than her voice, but he had heard her.

"I was in Algiers," he said. "I saw a young man through the window and he walked one way and was alive. Then he came the other way and he was dead."

She waited for him to say more but he was silent.

"And then you were all right," she prompted.

She could feel him shrug. She prompted again.

"Perhaps he had been bad. That helps."

"No," said Craig. "He wasn't bad." He saw the view and felt lost in it. "He had a very gentle name," he said. "Sanft. You know what that means in German?"

When she did not answer he turned to look at her and for one ghastly moment he thought that all of her face was gone and there were only two eyes. Then the whole face was back and the mouth torn wide open, head back now, and the scream pouring out.

After the staff car with the three axles had blown up, the men in the two escort trucks really had nothing to guard. Since the British who had ambushed them could not have done so except with foreknowledge, the belated conclusion was that the British had found the important Englishman and had gotten all they needed to know out of him. The truck with the antiaircraft turret had five men left in it and the other one still had ten. Harker could see them near the rim of Jalu, at bay, as he saw it, but once again there was something he had not counted on.

In that other case it had been the Bishop that had thrown them. The apparently suicidal maneuver, in that case, had been entirely understandable. But here, at the drop down to Jalu, there was no sudden Bishop to rattle them into a self-defeating maneuver.

The trucks split—that still made sense—but then they each went separately for Harker's heaviest fire concentration. They left the effective range of the men on the south ridge and barreled straight down a suicide alley of Harker's forty-fives, Stens and mortars.

"Sir," said Boyden, "I think the one with the ack-ack is looking for us."

"Damn if you aren't right. He's trailing. The one ahead is running as decoy!"

"Bergman's signal, sir."

"What?"

"Ready for the lead truck."

"Signal now. We'll get him. Let him nail the big one that's trailing."

Bergman got the signal and let go with his three mortars in classic fashion, one shell leading the truck—a wait for the burst and the truck slowing—and then the second shell short of the first and for good measure the third farther back.

If done with good timing, it is a sight of spectacular destruction and everybody who knew about it ahead of time was apt to hold and watch.

And that was how the lead truck, the one without anything heavier than a mounted forty-five, got its free run—perhaps not as far as they had hoped, but while the truck which was trailing got ripped apart, the one in the front lurched up the incline where Harker's heavy concentration was laid out.

Then the men started yelling. The truck was crazy, of course, but he was also too close for mortar fire. Bergman's mortars in good range to the rear of the truck could not see well enough through the smoke of the other one to be sure to avoid hitting Harker's men. Mohnfeld's quads to the rear were too far to be useful.

"Rake, Boyden, rake!"

"We'll hit our own—"

"Damn the angle, *fire!*"

They gave it to the truck from so many sides that they were never sure afterward who had stopped it. And nobody expected that kind of an end.

The truck blew up with such violence that it looked like the impact of an eighty-eight. There was enough bang and updraft to scatter the vulture formation which was wheeling overhead.

Craig had his arms around her and he could feel how her breathing slowed and got deeper.

"Is it over?"

"I don't know," she said into his tunic. "But there isn't any hole back there anymore. Just knowing that he's dead and it hurts."

He stroked her back, feeling shy about it, wishing he knew how to do more.

"I'm here," she said. "Do you feel it?"

"Yes," he said. "No *attrape*."

"But it's hard. Now I want to run."

"It'll take time, Cheryl. And help, perhaps."

He could feel her nod against him and how her arms tightened on him. Then she took a breath and let go. She sat by herself now and leaned against the wall.

"Yes," she said. "I'll be patient." She rubbed her face and looked up. "Even with the pain. No more minarets."

"What?"

"I'm not stone," she said.

He did not understand all she said but she did not sound mad because of it.

The mortar blasts were distant, three in a row. Craig recognized the series— It was time to leave—

"Don?"

"Yes."

"When you saw it, the way they made him die, what did you do afterward?"

He shrugged and did not know how to answer.

"I wasn't over it," he said. "But then it wasn't the same for me as for you." He shrugged again, but it did not do much for him. "Maybe I had to wait for your scream. That helped."

"And now you can forget it?"

"Cheryl," he said and about this there was no doubt in him. "We have different ways, Cheryl, but I can't forget what I cannot finish. I could, if my life were a good life, but it is not. It's abnormal and if I live this way long enough then I become that way too."

"Don't," she said.

"Yes. I want to stay whole, and you must want that too. And when you want that then you cannot ignore the pain of life any more than you would want to ignore the pleasure. That way you stay whole."

"Eric told me that once."

"Don't forget it."

"And then you can forget how he died?"

"No. Because I can't do anything about him, or about Von Hahn who made him die. I can't even hate Von Hahn, who is dead. And perhaps," he said with a heaviness in him, "if I must live this bad life much longer, I might start to look for somebody else to hate."

She touched him but then took her hand away. "Perhaps," she said, "I will try to find somebody else love."

There was a blast like an eighty-eight impacting. It was hard to understand. Craig jumped up and ran out to look at the skyline. It did not tell him anything. It was quiet now, as if everything were over. Then he heard the half-track. That made sense. Mohnfeld had the half-track with the mounted quads and his group was the closest. It was over up there and they were coming for him. Then he felt Cheryl next to him.

"Don?"

He knew what was coming. He looked across the way and saw the old woman who had been left behind.

"Please," said Cheryl. "Will you take me with you?"

23: Harker's Choice

As a matter of strategy after a small-force desert encounter, and as a matter of personal choice, Harker regrouped immediately and left the battleground behind. He traveled up the Jalu road at considerable speed with the convoy played out at careful distances. He did not order a halt until he had gone four hours due north. Then he pulled off the road and into the protection of the open wastes. His men could see very far but the convoy was out of view from the ground, behind the swells of the uneven landscape.

There had been no loss of materiel in the Jalu encounter. The L.R.D.G. had lost eight men and the S.I.G. had lost five. Harker himself had come away with a nasty cut on his face, due to the impact of a flying canteen. Once healed, the cut would be prominent, resembling the barbaric elegance of a German *Mensur*.

While the men tried to find shade under the trucks, the officers grouped around a bare rock in the sun. Harker had not yet arrived to take his seat.

"There's this story," said Mohnfeld to Craig next to him, "about Wellington just before the Waterloo incident. It seems he was sitting on the portable toilet ..."

"Why don't you shut up, you son of a bitch," said Craig. He did not care whether anyone else had heard it. Then Harker came.

He sat down on his rock in the sun. He touched his upper lip briefly but paid no attention to the gauze on the side of his face. With one shoe he worked a pebble around on the ground and Harker seemed to be watching only that.

"The German weapons carrier which blew up," he said, "was apparently rigged for precisely that. The crew—that is to say, the crew of the entire escort party, gentlemen—was made up of an enemy which we have never encountered before."

The M.O. of all people had spotted the tipoff. He had found a naked arm on the ground and the skin, high up on the inside, had borne a tattoo.

"They were Waffen-SS," said Harker. He looked up for the first time. "As the document of that putative Britisher implied," with a brief glance at Craig who was looking elsewhere, "as well as other circumstances, we are indeed dealing with forces not confined to Rommel's command."

Harker sighed. It was a substitute for a curse over the malevolent pain in his cheek. And if his brief explanation was designed to introduce something else, none of the men who had to stand there in the sun paid sufficient attention.

Bergman thought of the tattoo on the arm and absently rubbed his bare wrist against his belt. Craig thought compulsively of the sound the explosion had made and when it had happened—a moment of true change—and then what? And Mohnfeld, who rarely sweated, wiped his face. Boyden paid attention to his C.O. and was the only one who caught the look. He nodded imperceptibly and then looked slowly at the sun-dry stretch of empty ground behind the group and behind Harker. From the ridge behind Harker to the trucks at the other side the dead nakedness under the sun had not changed. But Sergeant-Major Tyne's men—only five of them were visible—had taken position.

"Captain Bergman," said Harker.

"Yes," said Bergman and looked up. It struck him that Harker's tone of voice almost demanded a brace and salute.

"You are satisfied concerning the fact that you had been harboring a spy under your command?"

When it came to the hard, official tone, but brilliant with innuendo, Bergman was second to none.

"No argument, sir. Unlike the presumptive nature of the Ben Manta affair."

"Very well," said Harker. He would bulldoze any innuendo simply by his status of superior command.

"Just one goddamn minute!" said Craig.

It was unmistakably clear that this was not an officer speaking. Since the Jalu events, Harker considered, it was altogether not clear who this Craig was and why he was speaking.

"Were you about to address me, Major Craig?"

Craig could bulldoze an innuendo simply by not caring to pick it up. The driven quality of his voice and the unpredictable changes in his face continued.

"No argument," he said, aping Bergman with a vengeance. "Except that we don't know who the bastard was."

"I did not know Bruckner personally," said Harker. "Did you know him, Major Craig?"

"No. We weren't buddies." Craig turned to Mohnfeld and said, "You were buddies."

It was not a question and Mohnfeld did not answer. He thought about Bruckner and felt weak.

"Did Brooky do it, Mohnfeld? How's it look from the inside view? I mean, straight from your insides, Mohnfeld."

He now has, thought Bergman, the fabulous hostility of someone who has survived the worst without having caused his freedom himself— The Jew who escapes the concentration camp not because he murders every guard but because the guards are having fun with a new carload for the ovens—

"I don't know how to answer," said Mohnfeld with surprising simplicity. The glitter had gone out of the man. The cleverness was no longer fun. "The Bruckner we knew nothing about was a traitor. The Bruckner who is dead was my friend." He turned to Craig and bore the look he got back. "You asked for it from the inside," he added.

"What," Harker cut in, "are you trying to contribute, Major Craig?"

"To what?" said Craig, full of hate. "The war?"

Harker considered that if he were to court-martial everyone who had offended the purity of military procedure on this expedition—a venture which was in itself less military than desperate at this point—then he might end up by walking into Tobruk by himself. And not himself pure in heart either. The Bruckner affair stunk like gangrene and the proper cure for that ailment was a very lengthy regime of regeneration. But Harker knew that he had time and skill only for swift amputations.

"I don't care what you're fighting for," said Harker, "as long as you perform under my command. Understood?"

"Clear."

"Back to Bruckner. He's dead and for me the matter is settled. Supporting the picture of guilt is the matter of that mine field we encountered. Then as now, I have never understood how there could have been enough time to place that field. The time between Ibn Kabir's transmission of his message to Cairo and our arrival at the field was too short. The message to Cairo was sent prior to Ibn Kabir's transmission. And who found the cable tap with such promptness, Captain Bergman?"

"Bruckner did."

"And who had the skill to look for one in the likeliest place and therefore to place one himself any time prior to that inept attempt by Kabir? Rhetorical question," Harker concluded. "The matter is closed."

"And who," said Craig, "allowed a mere three-vehicle enemy unit to parade right past his guns to the brink of shelter in Jalu?"

"I remind you, they are dead," said Mohnfeld.

"It wasn't your goddamn mortar that blew them up into a reversal because you didn't have any goddamn mortar!"

"Enough!" Harker's roar was substantially more commanding than Craig's personal anger. Harker got up and looked at his watch. "We proceed toward Tobruk in twenty minutes. I will conclude the remaining business without further interference. Mister Boyden?"

"Suh."

"Now, please."

They did not understand what all this meant until Boyden had dropped his arm again and they could see Tyne's men moving up with rifles on their arms. So far, no British uniform had carried arms on this trip, except while in combat.

Tyne's men formed an armed ring around the group of officers in the middle of the quiet bivouac area.

"I am not satisfied with Lieutenant Mohnfeld's performance either," said Harker.

"I got to my position late," said Mohnfeld.

"So I noticed."

"Under my direct command at the time," said Bergman.

"And I am mindful of that, and of your delay due to some incomprehensible—or shall I say, unexplained—dealings with the remaining member of a team of spies. No more interruptions," said Harker and waved his hand as if swatting a fly away. "And to the extent that the Bruckner guilt has not been totally established, I am mindful and remind you, Captain Bergman, that the escape of the imprisoned spy occurred at the caravansary. *Nobody* was stationed there, Captain Bergman, except *your* S.I.D. men!"

Harker spread his legs slightly and folded his hands on his back. The stance gave prominence to his chest when he raised his head. He gave a squaring tug to his cap and then folded his hands again as before. His visor now made a black shadow across the top of his face so that his eyes were quite invisible.

"Ten-shun!" said Boyden. He had said it softly, with an intimacy reserved for this group. It had also been very sharp.

When the officers in front of Harker were at attention, he let them stand for a moment because he felt clear and sure and without need for rush.

"Major Craig, you may step aside."

Craig fell out. After a few steps he stopped and turned back to watch.

"Someone among you and your men," said Harker to Bergman and Mohnfeld, "is or has been a traitor. I am not your prosecutor. I am not your judge. I am your commanding officer." He made no pause but joined up the rest like a natural conclusion. "You will surrender your weapons to Lieutenant Boyden."

Craig could only see their backs and he wondered how long they could hold still. He wondered whether Tyne's men would actually shoot and how long it would take the combat-diminished S.I.D.s in the shade to leap out and kill what they could before the Harker men could disarm their dead bodies.

Boyden stepped in front of Bergman and did not look up at him.

"Sorry, sir," he said very low.

Bergman pulled his pistol out and laid it into Boyden's hand. Then he pulled the spare clip from the holster and laid that into Boyden's hand too.

The same thing happened between Boyden and Mohnfeld. Harker, all this time, was holding his lip in his teeth.

"Colonel Harker," said Bergman.

Harker nodded.

"We *are* going to Tobruk." It did not sound like a question.

Harker nodded again.

"You will now accompany Lieutenant Boyden," he said, "to lend your weight to the disarming of the rest of the S.I.D. men."

The execution of Harker's command went so smoothly, so quietly, that the sight was either unbelievable or possibly ominous. At the end Boyden and Bergman stood like strangers next to each other.

"I trust," Bergman said, "that the colonel in his unfathomable ways has arranged some solution for the problem we might encounter once everybody in his personal army enters Tobruk unarmed."

"Yes sir," said Boyden. "Some of your men and a sufficient number of L.R.D.G. will switch uniforms."

Bergman, vastly astonished, displayed no reaction except to tighten his mouth. That decision on Harker's part involved such a breach in rules for the military that Harker had either lost all sense of proportion or was capable of unbending as not suspected before.

"In the event of capture," Bergman pointed out, "there'll be no POW status for his men in German uniforms. Shot as spies."

"Even as your men, and you, sir."

"There's a difference," said Bergman. He slapped his empty holster absently, making a hollow sound. "In this context, Lieutenant—if in no other respect—we are Chosen People."

"I understand," said Boyden.

"With a history of two thousand years of sacrificial experience," added Bergman. "Compared to your fifteen minutes."

The quality of young Boyden was clearly displayed when he addressed Bergman as "sir" again, but also talked to the man.

"While I cannot compare in quality of suffering," he said, "I do feel, sir, that you are rather maintaining an underdog point of view. Wouldn't you say?"

Bergman did not say anything for a moment and then he smiled for the first time in a long while.

"Thank you, Boyden. And join me in the hope that it will not take another two thousand years to drop that Chosen quality."

While the irascible choice for Craig lay elsewhere—

He found Mohnfeld sitting on the running board of the half-track, staring with no interest at the men who were exchanging uniforms. But he jumped up as if he had been expecting Craig. A touch of his flippancy came back.

"How many paces, Major?"

"I'll kill you by any rules, you son of a bitch."

"Well timed, Craig. I have no weapon."

"And I won't need one."

"Don't you think we better step to the side? Unless you can manage to lower your voice."

Mohnfeld walked away from the half-track without waiting for an answer and without looking back.

Craig would follow. He would follow now and he would follow later and for very much longer. Or, thought Mohnfeld, he might jump me now. Though that would be as unexpected as the death of Bruckner—

When he stopped walking and turned, Craig was close behind him.

"It was you, right?" said Craig.

"Why bother to answer," said Mohnfeld. "You've decided."

"Because once you had helped Portman to get away and had killed the hapless witness who just incidentally also happened to be your friend …"

"You," said Mohnfeld, "don't know anything about that death." The very calm of his voice showed how much feeling he was keeping out of sight.

Craig caught some of that but did not care. He put his hands in his pockets, the casualness of his pose an insult to everything serious that went on between him and Mohnfeld.

"And then the girl was left behind, unpredictable enough to be a menace to Portman's precarious trek into the desert, unpredictable enough to spill the beans as long as she was alive."

"I think," said Mohnfeld, "you might possibly know her better than I do."

"Ah? Yes. I noticed you were disappointed when you couldn't take her to Jalu. That is to say, after I interrupted your move to murder her."

"You're obsessed, Craig."

"Right. So watch out."

Mohnfeld looked away and shrugged, the gesture belittling all the intensity that was pushing at Craig.

"Then how, *Leutnant*, did it happen that you jumped me in Jalu all alone and as soon as the shooting match upstairs was over?"

"Need I remind you," said Mohnfeld, "that you were the one who jumped *me?*"

Craig did not need to be reminded. The half-track had come to a very fast halt where the houses began and when the dust settled Craig could see Mohnfeld standing near the hood. The man's machine pistol was slung so that his right hand could guide the short barrel in an easy arc. With his left hand he was pulling his grimy sand goggles down to his neck.

"Craig? Where are you?"

Mohnfeld looked at the debris on the road between the stone huts and wondered if there had been a hit down here.

"Why is he here?" asked Cheryl behind Craig in the doorway.

"The war's over. Spoils of the victor."

"What?"

"Never mind. I'll find out."

He stepped into the road as Mohnfeld walked into one of the deserted houses. When Mohnfeld stepped out again, the gun muzzle preceding him, Craig said, "Here I am."

The distance between the two men was so short that Mohnfeld's startled turn caused the barrel to slap into Craig's side.

"You startled me," said Mohnfeld.

"I have noticed."

They looked at each other. The sand goggles had left large rings on Mohnfeld's grimed-up face, making him look a lot like an owl.

Perhaps this owl was blind in the daylight or perhaps it was thinking, but there was a look of distance coming from Mohnfeld and Craig did not really matter. Then the girl stepped out of the house on the other side of the road and Mohnfeld's look changed. And Craig had one hand on the barrel of Mohnfeld's gun. His hand touched it only lightly but he could feel the gun move. He could feel Mohnfeld's hand in that very small motion. It was as if the two hands recognized each other, which then made them wary.

"She's alive," said Mohnfeld.

"Yes."

"I see. We can't take her along, you know."

At that point Craig could not bear the hesitation in everything anymore, or the pressure of his suspicion, and with a draw as fast as holster flap and gun lanyard permitted, he had the pistol looking at Mohnfeld in a steady way.

Mohnfeld's owl eyes looked down at the gun and then at Craig.

"Are you quite mad?"

"That I grant you," said Craig.

Mohnfeld, who was not calm by nature, suddenly started to shout.

"Aside from the standard procedure regarding spies caught in the field, what—precisely—is the improvement in her fate by mercifully leaving her here?"

As an argument in regard to spies the case was shut and over. As a question in regard to Cheryl, the lack of a bearable answer became a confusion of pain in Craig.

"You tried to shoot her once before," was the only lame thing Craig could say.

"No. I tried to threaten her into moving."

There would have been no end to the possibilities of a see-saw argument, because Mohnfeld did not know how serious Craig was with his gun and because Craig did not really know whether Mohnfeld had come to finish Cheryl. Except for one thing which did not add itself to all the rest until Craig thought of it later. Only when the next truck came bounding down into the oasis did Mohnfeld click his safety on—

Craig looked at the trucks and the men to see if he and Mohnfeld were still alone. There may not be enough time or intent to do anything now, but there had to be time to say more.

"I don't know what makes you tick, Mohnfeld, any more than I know what makes a creature like Von Hahn tick. But I'm going to use a lesson I learned from both of you."

"The comparison is ludicrous, Craig. I could never be Gestapo."

"The attitude has no national limits. And now I'm learning your patience. No more impulse to any of this, Mohnfeld. I'm going to watch you with my ever-waking brain because I know you aren't finished. Neither Portman got through, nor his paper."

"You reason after the fact, Craig. You tell me your intent and then you make up the reasons. Instead," said Mohnfeld, "I think it is simply this: You have found yourself someone to hate."

Craig's hands started to shake. This would go on and they would start fluttering if he did not give them something very steadying to do.

When Mohnfeld's face was very close because of the way Craig was suddenly holding the man, the lines looked remarkably tired in his face and then the eyes closed slowly.

"Better let go of my lapels, Craig, or Harker will do worse to you than simply disarm you."

"I'll trade you off to him."

"No. You've got nothing."

"You."

Mohnfeld opened his eyes and went on as if Craig had made no point at all.

"And that's the why of all this, Craig. You've got nothing. I've known about that state for much longer, and it's awful." He paused and then, "You just left Jalu, and you left with nothing."

Then Craig swung.

Bergman stopped it with very painful efficiency so that the two men were apart in an instant. Only Bergman had stopped it, Craig realized, because Mohnfeld, for that short moment, had not fought at all.

Mohnfeld walked away with a steady pace while stroking the front of his tunic. He stretched his neck by raising his chin a few times, as if he were wearing a tight collar.

"Are you cracking too?" said Bergman with a lot of anger held in. His hand was around one of Craig's wrists, to remind him that Bergman might just decide to flip that arm out of its shoulder joint.

"You can let go."

"I'm reminded of somebody else who cracked when the going ..."

"Shut up."

"All right," said Bergman and at the same time his touch on the wrist changed to something more gentle and then it withdrew.

"You know something," said Bergman, "this is the third time you've put me in this advisory sort of position. The first time when you kicked me on the plane, the next time at the office in Kufra when you kept putting that Germanized name on me and now when you're rocking everybody's boat."

Craig felt like shouting but instead he just breathed very hard a few times.

"Mohnfeld is *the* bastard, Bergman! I can show you!" He was hoarse now, as if he had actually been shouting.

"I'm sure," said Bergman. "And do you know that Mohnfeld was the only one who had ever bivouacked at that caravansary—that's what he told us—and that's how we happened to camp where that tunnel was?"

"Christ—" said Craig. "And you just *stand* there?"

"Yes."

"What do you want, a tribunal with witnesses pro and con and judicial procedure?"

"If we did, we wouldn't have a case."

"While he does the damage."

"What damage? He can't get the paper and he can't throw his cover unless he wants to get killed by either side. Meanwhile, the pressure builds. We would like him to decide to come over. We would like him to tell us who he is and who sent him and how his network works its net, and all that because he wants us to recognize that he exists instead of having us ignore him. Meanwhile, he knows there's a gun on him."

"What gun, may I ask?" and Craig looked down at Bergman's belt.

"Harker knows."

"Isn't that nice. You know something? I don't understand that bastard either."

"Let's walk back," said Bergman. When they started he said, "You have an expression in English, called Hobson's choice. Harker made one. He cannot shoot everybody he suspects because he cannot abandon the mission. He cannot leave those he suspects under arms or it will again invite failure of the mission. There was no choice."

When they got to the half-track Craig stopped.

"Go away," he said. "I don't want to hear any more."

"We're leaving."

"Yes. Can't forget that mission."

Bergman frowned at Craig and started to go.

"As a matter of fact," he said, "you look like you forgot something and can't remember what."

"Bullshit," said Craig and turned away.

He looked at the horizon which sat too close. If it were twenty miles farther it would still be an end to his vision, a stop which made him blind. But as for forgetting, he only wished that were true—

I'll remember forever how she stood there, the life in her eyes again, and then it went when I went.

Harker made the decision but he did not leave her. I did. Though I did not decide. I am blind with horizons of expediency and I don't have the good answers, the ones that finish a question forever.

She was willing to live again and I left her with an old woman who is ready to die—

It had been his Hobson's choice. It had been the most awful step of all, because it had been a choice without any conviction.

24: Götterdämmerung of a Jew

On the stretch between Kufra and the mine field they had known how tough and grave the trip was, but the hardship had not started. They had been tense with the energy which they did not use and they had laughed irritably and made forceful jokes.

Through the Kamansho Flats and up to Jalu they had fought the land which was set against them. The struggle had been simple and without jokes. Die or survive.

After Jalu the trip took on more clearly the quality of a superior mission. Their effort was no longer their own and effects would be long-range instead of direct. Survival was a matter of the smoothness of road and depended upon the quality of their machines. They were more like attendants and less like participants. The very certain nature of their danger was gone and the danger now was its uncertainty. There was unpleasant time to think.

The S.I.G. were under the guns of the troopers. Men who had known each other pretended they did not, and men who were strangers discovered each other with suspicion.

They had swung onto the coastal road, black and shiny in the late light, and could see the blank steel face of the Mediterranean. Tobruk was still out of view.

It had been easier, it had been more fulfilling, to overcome rocks on the ground and sand in the air, to survive the indifferent opposition of the desert. But now the issue at hand was a mission. What was a mission? An order. How to know your enemy? By an order. The decision of what was important lay with someone else.

Mohnfeld, who was past preoccupations over basic issues, could nevertheless avoid them only by going back to the past. It helped to imagine that there were meaningful roots. It helped when there really was no sense of mission, no true loyalty, and when there was really not much sense of self.

Childhood was a solid town and he knew all the streets. They lay there under the childhood glow in which everything was always all right. This was Frankfurt-am-Main where the Jews were not a curio or a problem but an institution for hundreds of years. The Jews were solid, self-assured and safe with tradition.

Mohnfeld came from a more tenuous background, because he and his parents were immigrants to the town. Though his father seemed solid enough. He was a small tailor and he also sold old clothes. He observed the Sabbath because all his customers did. This typed life and its pervasive regularity could have been enough, except that Mohnfeld, in Frankfurt-am-Main, did not happen to be a Jew.

He looked up at the new sound and saw that they were joining the access traffic to Tobruk. Flak carriers, eighty-eights mounted on tracks, troop trucks and Field Police like hornets dashing around on their rackety bikes.

"Mohnfeld," said Craig next to him. "What's your real name?"

"Mohnfeld."

"Consistent of you. Naturally, you play the game as long we play the game."

"A very unfunny game," said Mohnfeld, "since I don't know the rules."

Craig had found that he could now sit next to Mohnfeld and let the man be. He did not know how it had happened but the knot of hate had started to loosen after the near-fight. He had thought of the lost girl in the dry oasis. Leaving her had tightened the knot, remembering her made Craig start to loosen. He did not yet know why. But he could talk to Mohnfeld simply because he felt curious about him.

"The rules of the game are," he said, "that you are not going to rock the boat—which is why you are permitted this trip—until you can get hold of that paper. That's why you're holding still, right?"

Mohnfeld shrugged and watched a half-track snake by the column. It mounted 20-mm. rapid-fires, two barrels. The gunner had strung his undershirts from snout to snout. In the fifty mph wind his laundry was drying.

"What if you don't get it?" asked Craig.

"Look," said Mohnfeld. "I'm a failure even now. In more ways than might show. And what am I doing now?"

"I don't know. Nothing shows very sharp."

"Following orders."

"But whose?"

"Craig," said Mohnfeld. "When you ask that you begin to care. When you begin to care you must make personal choices. You might even care enough to wonder about the orders."

Craig looked away. He looked at the other men in the carrier, the troopers with guns, the S.I.D. bare-handed. That insane order was in effect until the convoy had made the inner ring of Tobruk. He turned back to Mohnfeld.

"Sometimes," he said, feeling the words come out of nowhere, "you don't sound like an enemy."

"I don't have any," said Mohnfeld. "Does the desert have enemies?"

Ahead of the convoy the traffic started to slow. The first checkpoint came up.

There was no special reaction from Mohnfeld. Craig did not know whose gun was looking but he knew that Mohnfeld sat there with a bullet ready for him. And if it came to a kill in full view of the Field Police, that would be all right too. Mohnfeld was now wearing Ben Manta's old British uniform. He sat quietly, not looking at anyone, and the beaten prisoner pose, thought Craig, was perhaps no pose at all.

The striped plank of the checkpoint stayed up in the air and traffic kept rolling. No one talked. There were two machine gun emplacements by the barricade. The two men at one of the guns were playing skat and the other gun was not manned at the moment. The *Feld Polizei* at the barrier kept waving his arm like a pendulum.

It was so easy that the tension in the trucks stayed the same—

Three checkpoints later they had been stopped only once. Bergman, in the lead truck, had presented the proper papers. It seemed, thought Craig, that Harker's Heroes were doomed to success. Entry into Tobruk was inevitable. Craig avoided thinking about how they would get out.

And then, suddenly very close, they saw Tobruk. The city had the low skyline of any coastal town in North Africa. It sat on very flat land and the sprawl of it suggested a haphazard and casual growth. The newest installations in the city were not visible. There would be nothing haphazard about their growth—

There were no suburbs in the Western sense of the word. The convoy was in the city. The façades on their entry route were neo-Roman à la Mussolini and Toothpaste Baroque à la turn of the century. Arab characteristics were confined to the crowds in the street. At that moment started the quick, Mediterranean dusk.

For Craig it was always a moment which reminded him, with its pause, of the top of a breath. One motion was finished, but before its counterpart happened there was the moment, a still and suspended time which did not last very long but was very much there. In a garden, Craig had noticed, the birds stopped their chatter and the cicadas seemed to hesitate. If there had been a wind, there would have been less wind at that moment.

In the street the precipitous change in the light slowed the welter of motion. And then, in a moment, like the exhale side of the breath, there would come the renewed rush of everything which had stopped before.

Bergman, as commandant of his prisoner convoy, sat in the cab of the lead truck. The vehicle racket and the disorganized buzz of the pedestrian crowd pounded at him again. There were Arabs with bundles, looking as if they meant to emigrate. There were Europeans and Indians in mufti who looked as if business was as usual. And there were Field Police everywhere, darting by on their motorcycles, escorting staff cars or directing convoy traffic at an intersection while the teammate sat in the gondola of the machine, watching everything which the other one did not see.

Colonel Harker, as the ranking prisoner, sat between Bergman and the driver who wore Afrika Korps khaki. Harker heard the brawl of civilian noises and saw how rapidly the light was fading. He looked at his watch.

"We'll make it," said Bergman.

Harker nodded. They would just make it if their incredible ease of progress held up and if the British bombers—coordinated by plan—would not hit in the wrong place.

"You tore up the maps?" he asked Bergman.

Harker knew that the maps of Tobruk objectives had been torn up but he was nervous. If he did not say something unimportant, he might say something foolish, such as, do you think we'll make it—

"Fork right," he said to the driver.

"It's the next intersection," said Bergman. "Not this one."

"Of course. Carry on, driver."

Leaving the heart of town and angling toward the harbor area, they followed a land mark which they had seen for some time, the immense finger of the German transmitter antenna which reared up over the headquarters building. Taking the proper turn now, the convoy rolled down a tree-lined street which looked as peacefully civilian as any residential street in a European city. Traffic in the access lanes toward the headquarters building was severely restricted.

The square opened in front of them, showing the disused little park to one side and the high stone façade, Headquarters, Italo-German High Command, North African Theater. There were eight field-painted staff cars in front of the main steps, aligned and with drivers in attendance. Two tanks flanked the building. It was quiet in the square and the tank turrets turned slowly and quietly. The long guns homed on Harker's column and followed its progress with a steady, slow sweep of each gun's iron eye.

Harker performed his tic with the mouth. "Well," he muttered. "That was easy. So damnably easy, everything—"

Bergman only nodded. Once through the square they were now looking for their assigned objectives.

"Do you think Craig is getting anywhere with that Mohnfeld person?" asked Harker.

"I don't know, sir. I can't judge either of them anymore." And then he added what preoccupied him much more. "If you would give the order to rearm my men, Colonel Harker, I think we would gain ..."

"We'll do it as planned, Captain. No change. We pass the depot in a recon sweep, our ostensible destination the prisoner compound. In the bomb-damage area this side of the compound we will halt for rearming. Then we split as planned."

The split had been one of Harker's afterthoughts, based on his conviction that only his own troopers were reliable. He would search out the fuel bunkers in order to do the assigned damage. Bergman would deploy between the bunkers and the bluffs which ran the length of the beach. At best, Bergman's men would assist in Harker's escape toward the beach and away from Tobruk. They had to make Sollum to the east. At worst, Bergman's men would have no chance to interfere with Harker's mission to destroy what he could.

The street became a macadam road which swung down to the harbor area. They could see the port installations first and Rommel's reserve depots only later, but the view was already bad enough. Harker took a careful breath.

"If I were Desert Air Force," he said reverently, "I would hide in shame."

Either their reconnaissance or their bombing runs should have made the sight impossible. There were three tankers unloading under the long arm of cranes which held the thick hoses that pumped into the quayside collection tanks. Unbelievably, the same operation was being performed with three hospital ships. And one hospital ship was disgorging a steady line of armed men.

"Rommel," said Harker, "must be getting desperate."

"So am I," said Bergman.

And then, for a while, they said nothing at all. The descending view toward the harbor area opened up.

By the map, this part of Tobruk had been leveled by previous battle damage. The Germans, with the aid of a few bulldozers, had taken efficient advantage. There were acres and acres of open ground and this ground was packed tight with a view to exhaust the valiant heart: Panther tanks, flak carriers, self-propelled eighty-eights. There were blocks and blocks of them. There were blocks of personnel carriers and long streets of maintenance vehicles. Here, bunched under camouflage, lay the Afrika Corps' unexpected muscle—

"Two full armored divisions!" said Harker.

The other men in the convoy did not say anything.

Then Harker recovered.

"Half an hour till the combined assault," he said, his voice as carefully controlled as if he were bringing death news of a fallen son to a mother.

Bergman behaved as carefully and stuck to the program which would now have to be revised in a hurry.

"It'll be dark in fifteen minutes. Shall we skip the run with the flares?"

"We place the flares," said Harker, sticking to the schedule. "Especially after—er, this," and he nodded at the growing panorama of German reserves. "Make your swing, driver."

They were ready in the half-track which was last in the column. They would not have enough flares, in view of that monster discovery ahead of the column, but as they started to pass the dumps and the depots Sergeant Tyne at the tail of the vehicle started to drop inane-looking things overboard: a worn boot, a dented canteen, a German gas mask canister which seemed empty, and also, in spaced order, some torn packets of desert rations.

The fuses inside were timed. The flares would not ignite until the air strike was coming—

For a prisoner convoy the route was somewhat erratic but such confusion might be expected from a unit that had just driven in from the field. Before reaching the harbor installations proper, they swung away from their northerly progress and headed east. There had been a Stalag sign which pointed the way but they had overshot it, intentionally.

"With all that stuff on wheels," said Harker, "they must have fuel bunkers which we know nothing about."

"We'll have to ask Craig," said Bergman. "He knows what kind of ground they got along this coastline."

Harker looked at the failing light and worried. Topographic information would be no help in the dark when looking for unknown fuel bunkers.

The macadam was new and the open terrain between the bluffs toward the sea and the bombed warehouses toward the land was not a safe hiding place for reorganizing the column's make-up. Nevertheless, they stopped sooner than planned.

The *Feld Polizei* two-ton roared out of the warehouse district and swung after Harker's column. It pulled up to the lead truck and the lieutenant waved the driver down. The two-ton stopped at an angle in front of the column and the six-man crew jumped off with their guns at the ready. They spread down the length of the line of trucks and then the lieutenant came over.

"*Sagen Sie mal, sind Sie verrückt?*" he barked at Harker's driver.

The driver, sweating in his Feldwebel uniform, did not open his mouth and pointed at Bergman. Kapitän Bergman was already jumping out of the cab.

There were proper salutes and there was a staccato exchange in German.

"You passed the sign," said the lieutenant. "May I see your papers, Captain."

Bergman handed over what he had.

"Lost our way," he said. "We haven't been here since that equipment got spread all over."

"Nevertheless, there was a sign."

"My man's half blind with fatigue."

"Three Hundred and Seventy-second Infantry Battalion," said the lieutenant and peered at the markings on the dirty truck door. "Aren't you supposed to be near Derna?"

"Specially detached for this duty, Lieutenant. Now, if I may ..."

"When were you here last, Captain?"

"When we took the city the second time." That, Bergman hoped, would cover his ignorance about the new reserve strength they had passed.

"And you weren't aware that the prisoner compound you're approaching is a dummy?"

Bergman did not know what to make of it, except that he knew that a dummy was meant to be seen. A depot of tanks, made of wood and canvas, was meant to be bombed. A prisoner compound, when seen from the air, was meant to be avoided. There was something in the vicinity ahead which was very valuable—

There was a touch of exhaustion in the failing light. Bergman looked at the lieutenant's men along the road. They too looked peaceful. And he heard the diesel sounds.

There must be a road farther inland, hidden behind the bombed warehouse area. The diesels made a low power sound, something not fit for desert use. They moved east, in the same direction as this prominent macadam road which was straight and shiny and in the open. And it looked hardly used.

"No," said Bergman. "I don't know where this road leads. Where am I heading?"

"It leads to the dummy compound, as the sign would have it. And if you had been here when we took the city and you were with the 372nd before moving to Derna ..."

"Lieutenant," said Bergman with a fine mixture of weariness and irritation. "Why don't you call HQ and satisfy yourself? You have a radio."

"No offense meant," said the lieutenant.

"I'll tell my men to stretch their legs," and then Bergman yelled a command.

The lieutenant did not like that. Only a few soldiers got off the trucks and they were not even carrying weapons but the lieutenant, used to the more exact forms of discipline which existed in the rearward commands, felt sufficiently upset to look for support. He wished to make a friendly gesture, an invitation to be forgiven, an act to assure himself that there was no cause for worry.

"You understand," he said to Bergman. "And I understand that your men must be tired." And then he commenced to display his good will.

He walked up to Harker's driver.

"*Sie können auch rauskommen,*" he said.

The driver nodded but did not move. He did not understand German. Bergman got very close to the lieutenant.

"*Warum antworten Sie nicht?*" said the lieutenant.

"*Ja,*" said the driver.

"What?"

"I mean, *jawohl,*" said the driver, confused with pressure.

The lieutenant was no less confused and turned back to Bergman. The captain, he noticed, was very close. The captain, he realized, had a look on his face which was a bizarre mixture of fright, hate and intent-

"*Bis bald,*" he heard the captain say, very low, and then there was the shock of the knife in him, an incomprehensible feeling, something totally new. Nothing else occupied, only the newness, and then the lieutenant was dead.

Harker looked at his watch. It would be a tight squeeze—

Craig heard the clatter of diesels to landward. They did not sound fit for desert use. To the other side, at the edge of the road looking seaward, he saw the shadow movement of the S.I.G. One of them was getting a light for his cigarette from the F.P. soldier and the lit match fell to the ground. Another one seemed to be laughing and then there was the sound of a grunt. It was dark now. But the ones he could see would be dead now. The quiet of everything was unbearable.

"Mohnfeld," he said. "I think it's time."

"Yes."

"He's going to distribute the weapons. And he'll have to decide about you."

"Yes."

It was now almost as quiet as before, except for the whisper of cloth and the soft thump of boots. The men were getting out of the carriers.

Craig still had no notion about the way Mohnfeld would react, once he saw there was no winning. They walked to the end of the truck bed and jumped off. Harker was waiting there.

"Mohnfeld," said Craig. "Colonel Harker burned the document over two days ago."

It was dark and then perhaps some senses get sharper and perhaps they all work mostly to round out the unseen by an act of the imagination. What Craig thought he knew about Mohnfeld then was a change in the man which left the shadow form next to him truly empty.

"If you will furnish proof ..." Harker said.

"There is no such thing," said Mohnfeld.

"As an enemy agent," said Craig, "we can't just ..."

"Craig," said Mohnfeld, "why don't you kill me?"

The question was really a wish. It was perhaps the only wish Mohnfeld had ever admitted. But Craig did not have the hate anymore and did not know what to say. Mohnfeld brushed his mouth with one hand and made a small sound which might have been a laugh.

"What I want to know," said Harker with impatience, but Mohnfeld interrupted him once more.

"Like the war, Colonel, I will leave you without any answer."

When the poison pill collapsed him, Mohnfeld lay on the ground but did not look changed very much. As if there were no transition for him between being dead or alive—

25: *"Bis Bald—"*

And then hell broke loose.

The high altitude rumble of the bomber formation was so distant that it did not command the attention, but the dive-bombers were suddenly there with their screech.

The perimeter searchlights were just starting to stagger back and forth on the sky. Three of the planes in the diver attack laid their flares to illuminate the second wave's pinpoint attack. For the time being the flares made the biggest impression. Tobruk was a black silhouette. Tobruk was a relief of shadowless light. And then the panorama came alive with explosions.

"Boyden!"

The answer came distinctly.

"All armed, sir."

"Change in orders. We stay together. Relay!"

Bergman came running to the rear, looking for Craig.

"Did you hear those diesels before?"

"Several. I think they were tank trucks, heading easterly, toward the open."

"The fuel dump we don't know about?" said Harker.

He stepped aside while four men opened the bottom compartments of the truck and hauled out the flamethrowers.

"There's a depression that way," said Craig, "and the rock shelf shows broken. They must have sunk them there."

"Ready?"

"Ready over there."

"Tyne?"

"Ready, suh."

"Back on the trucks and as far as she'll go!"

They howled off, skirting the F.P. carrier which sat empty on the road and with its radio open—

When the macadam ended they faced a barbed wire enclosure which held a compound of geometrical huts. The huts were roofs on stilts and the guard towers stood there without ladders. The terrain had no roads.

They abandoned their vehicles and skirted the barbed wire fence going double time and toward the sea. The bluffs made a cove whose land line would pull them around to the mainland again where the hidden fuel bunkers might be. In back of them, Tobruk was crackling with fire and steel. It was silent where they ran through the dark.

There was an unexpected dip which ran to the sea and made a gouge in the bluff. In the dip they could hear the sea clearly, and the other sound.

"That," said Harker, "sounds distinctly like an electric motor."

They did not have to discuss it further because now they could look down the cut in the bluff.

"Christ Almighty— They've sunk a naval gun into the cliff!"

It was an imposing sight and an awful discovery. The coastal defense installation was half a mile farther from Tobruk than the British had known. In one lazy turn to the east it would command the escape beach which the Harker group was to use, and with just a few degrees of a sweep to the sea it would pound the landing-craft route which had been planned.

"We cross their access road from the land side," said Craig, "and they'll see us."

"Down the bluff and along the beach?"

"We're not equipped for mountain climbing, and once down there on the beach we'll never be able to reach the fuel dump area and stay within scheduled time."

"If it's there."

"It's *got* to be there!" said Harker. "Bergman, you know how these installations are built?"

"No sir."

"I do," said Craig. "Catwalks to the front, connecting machine-gun installations. Access road from landward, usually guarded similarly. Pillboxes sometimes. Steel gate is electric, view ports are manual."

"You know what their conduit looks like?"

"We'll find it," said Bergman.

"You'll have to work around the front," said Harker. "Take five men, in Korps uniform. You work around to the far side of the road, we'll stop on the near side. Get them to open up."

"Understood."

"Then continue to the fuel area. We'll clean up here and follow."

"If we stayed together ..."

"You have your orders," said Harker.

Bergman picked his five men and turned down into the cut in the bluff.

"Captain Bergman."

Bergman stopped and when he turned Harker was close behind him.

"Once you're done," said Harker, "I want you to leave for the beach no matter what. Don't look back, Captain Bergman."

"An order?"

"And good luck," said Colonel Harker.

The voice was as always but then Bergman felt Harker's hand. The grip of the handshake said more than Bergman had ever suspected in Harker.

There was one more lone explosion in Tobruk and then only the receding hum of the bombers which nobody saw. It was unfortunate timing. They would have to wait out the silence until the start of the naval assault.

Once through the breach they could feel the wind from the beach and they could see the awesome face of the gun emplacement which looked over the water. The blasted cliff face had been closed with smooth concrete, covering the installation behind, open only where the giant arm of the naval gun reached out toward the sea. The spidery catwalks on the face of the bunker connected minor gun emplacements. The open steel work made a whistling sound in the wind.

"If we work down this way," said Craig, "we'll make the first catwalk and they'll sure as hell hear it if we even drop a stone on the way."

"Over the sound of the barrage from out there?"

"Sure. That's a different sound from a sharp impact on one of those girders— That is, unless they open up themselves."

"God forbid. I understand the blast ..."

Bergman did not get any further because the battleship which they could not see sparked rapidly in the distance. The crash came later, and then the rumble in the air, like the rush of a train, when the shells came landward.

They were lower than the gun in the cliff next to them. They could see the monster arm move against the deep sky. "What's that sound?"

"Feet. Feet on the catwalks—"

"They're leaving those gun emplacements— They're getting out of the way!" And then Craig lay down flat against the incline of the bluff. "Mouths open wide," he said. "Everybody. And hang on, for God's sake—"

He could see the long arm against the sky and how it stopped now and held still. Everything held still. And then the long mouth screamed out its violent fire tongue—

The backlash of the gust hit them in less than a second. The man in front of Craig flailed grotesquely and then fell away, down the bluff.

"*Now!*"

They scrambled like lizards and when they bounced with a crash on the catwalk they did not care about the racket.

"Hold it!" yelled Craig. "Hang on! Don't run!"

When the mouth overhead bellowed again and when the fist of wind slammed into them, they hung on to the railing until it felt as if their wrist bones would part.

And then they ran across the face of the bunker and made it to the other side before the anger of the wind slammed into them again.

The next blast boomed out when they had made it landward and the wind missed them, making them feel as if they had reached eternal peace—

The dark access road on the rear side of the bunker lay before them. It ended where the steel door closed off the interior and the door, on one side, was flanked by a shape like half an egg.

"Pillbox," said Craig and pointed along the bunker. "Harker will have to take that one."

"In this uniform I might make it to the view port of the big door and ..."

"And be shot for looking like a hostile from Mars in this light," said Craig.

They waited for Harker's move on the opposite side. They even hesitated moments longer when they heard the sudden fusillade up the road. They could hear the dominant cackle of the Sten.

And then came the rapid clatter of tank diesels from the direction where Harker should have been—

"They've engaged him up the road, for chrissake," said Craig. "How in hell did anybody know—"

"And those Panthers opposite? They must have followed us right through that phony compound!"

"Let's move up. They've got Harker in a pincer!" They ran up the side of the road and saw that it was true. Harker had moved away from the bunker position to stop two German carriers which had come nosing down the road. And he had the tanks behind him—

There was a hand-grenade flash up ahead and then a gas tank exploded. It showed the ugly scene very well. It showed Boyden at the end of his throw and then the way he came apart when the German machine gun found him.

"If they get Harker—" said Craig close to Bergman's ear. He was thinking of the document which Harker was carrying. Bergman understood.

"He'll blow himself up before they get to him."

"He would— Bergman!"

Craig jumped after Bergman like a tackle and held on to one leg until Bergman held still.

"We've got to get to that fuel dump," Craig panted. "He's got his job. We've got ours!"

Bergman let his head drop and lay like that for a moment, as if he had all the time in the world. I'm Moses, he thought. I've got this route through hell to get to the Promised Land which I've never seen—

There came the blast of a tank gun and the violent impact raised hell with Harker's men. Bergman did not look at the burning light up ahead where the men were dying. He looked toward the dark where their objective might be. With a raw sound in his throat, he jumped up and his men jumped up and they started to run. They did not know what they would find in the dark, but they ran as if they knew that the fuel bunkers were there and then they would all die for something. Craig ran last. Therefore he heard the tank first.

There was a broken rise in front and on its other side would be the depression. It was all right as long as they were below the rise. The tank could not see them against the sky—

"Low now— Over the lip—"

"Maybe he isn't following us. Maybe he's ..."

"You know why he's following us?" said Craig. "Because there are only two ways to the dump, the truck road which we haven't seen and this open country. Finding Harker they figured where we're going and that Panther is coming to make sure."

Bergman had four men left and when the tank's machine gun cut loose it cut up one of them while he was cresting the rise.

They rolled over and down and there was no question that the tank would find them. The bowl of land before them was bare. Low mushroom tops of concrete dotted the bottom and the rest of the fuel reservoirs sat underground in solid rock.

They lay still and could hear the tank groaning up to the crest in the rear. One of Bergman's men unhooked his German hand grenade.

"Hold it," said Craig. "Gimme that potato masher."

"Kuntze is like a cat," said Bergman. "Let him."

"We want that tank operational."

On the other side of the rise the tank cranked closer.

Craig used his bayonet point and worked the lead plug out of the bottom of the grenade. He shook the charge out, feeling it run over his fingers. Bergman watched.

"He must have seen enough of us to know we're no major engagement."

"Yuh— When he crests he'll turn on the lights."

"Give me that thing," said Bergman. "Everybody behind the debris over there," and then he grabbed the grenade and ran for the crest.

They could see him lie down near the top and then they saw the long barrel of the tank poke over the rise. The rest of the monster bulged up and up like something breaking surface in the sea. Then it suddenly nodded itself over the lip and stopped. Bergman could be next to it, under it or in line with a tread. They could not tell because the tank's two headlights came on.

"*Bring mir mal den Scheinwerfer*," said the man in the turret.

The diesels kept ticking over and the stationary lights glared at them. In a while they could make out the silhouette of the commandant again. He straightened up and held a portable power light in his hand. But he did not light it. He seemed to be getting out of the turret. It seemed he was moving without any muscular effort of his own.

"*Bis Bald—*"

"What?" said Craig.

"That was Bergman," said Kuntze next to him. "It means, I'll be seeing you. He always says that."

"Here we go!" said Craig and jumped up when he saw Bergman drop the empty grenade into the turret.

They were ready for them.

They could hear the clattering inside the tank when the crew saw the grenade clanking down with the fuse hissing. They saw the gunner catapult himself out of the hole, going head first. The loader, wearing nothing but shorts, came flying out as if leaping for a dive into water. The driver came out when the other two were already dead and then someone slit his throat too.

"Everybody?" said Craig.

"All done."

"Sound off."

"Kuntze."

"Goldman."

"Domier."

"Richter."

There was a bad moment of nothing while the distant naval bombardment kept booming monotonously.

"*Answer* me, Bergman!"

Craig found him instead.

He was still breathing and where the tank tread had ground off his arm on the rocks the blood ran full and slow, like a lazy river.

"No," said Bergman when Craig started lifting him. "Moses never— made it," and his eyes closed.

"*Bis bald*," said Craig very softly and then he left Bergman's head hang away, very sad, very tired.

After that Craig did not feel very much. He did not want to know why he did anything or how much it was worth. But he took the tank within range of the long tanker trucks which sat near the mushrooms of concrete in order to wait out the bombardment of Tobruk. He stopped the tank in the dark and aimed the cannon carefully. The first round missed, but it showed how well the fuel tanks were protected. The closed steel door which admitted the tanker trucks took the shell impact with nothing to show for it but a fusion stain on the steel and a buckle crack where the steel met the concrete apron. Also the yellow lights over the truck yard went out. Then Craig lit it up again.

The shell found the tanker which was parked on the near apron. The bang of the shell and the roar of the gasoline made the lesser impression, but the big sight was the truck lifting up in many parts and the wild blossom of flame spreading everywhere. Two more tankers blew up, but Craig was not watching for that.

They watched the river of fire run down the incline of the apron which led into the underground chambers. It ran like solid lava and seemed to move just as little.

"Will it work?"

"Question is, how will we know if it worked," said Craig. "The way they built those domes ..."

He stopped speculating.

There was a monster sound of underground rumbling which they could not compare to anything else they had known before. And the longer it takes before the roof lifts off, Craig was hoping, the surer the chance that the interconnections of the giant tank installations would feed the fire to each other.

And then the first dome disintegrated, releasing a ball of flame. Then the gut of the earth split open—

It was more than the eye could tolerate or the brain could hold. It was all the force and all the big dying of war made concrete and instantaneous. This was why they had come, for this giant destruction—

The air grew hot. A fire storm sucked everything movable to its roaring center and threw it into the sky. The tank felt hot. Kuntze started driving away.

"That," he said, "dries the pump."

"Maybe they can still drive as far as El Alamein," said Richter. "But no farther now."

Perhaps, thought Craig, the man knows. Perhaps the man cares and perhaps now begins the end of the war, which is a beginning—

They abandoned the tank where its position would not lead anyone too quickly to the route they took next. It meant they had to walk farther. It meant that they missed the first rendezvous and that they lost Kuntze on the beach, dead with exhaustion. They made the beaches near Sollum at a point when they no longer hoped.

Craig watched the morning steam on the water and when the submarine rose for them he tried to get up. He made it, slowly.

He had made it with two men whom he did not even know. Boyden had gone in a burst, and Bergman had gone, as if dreaming. And perhaps Harker had found the most famous death of all, that of the unknown soldier.

And someone had been left in a dry oasis while he had gone away to find something to hate.

"I will have to try," she had said, "to find something new to love." And he had left her in the dry oasis.

And if she is right—

He thought no more but concentrated on staying alive with each painful step. Then he went into the water and swam out to sea.

THE END